This Family of Things

Also by Alison Jameson

This Man and Me
Under My Skin
Little Beauty

This Family of Things

Alison Jameson

BLACK SWAN IRELAND

TRANSWORLD IRELAND PUBLISHERS
Penguin Random House Ireland,
Morrison Chambers,
32 Nassau Street, Dublin 2, Ireland
www.transworldireland.ie

Transworld Ireland is part of the Penguin Random House group of companies
whose addresses can be found at global.penguinrandomhouse.com

First published in the UK and Ireland in 2017
by Doubleday Ireland
an imprint of Transworld Publishers
Black Swan Ireland edition published 2018

A CIP catalogue record for this book
is available from the British Library.

ISBN
9781784163266

Typeset in 11/14.5pt Electra by Falcon Oast Graphic Art Ltd.
Printed and bound by Clays Ltd, Bungay, Suffolk.

Penguin Random House is committed to a sustainable
future for our business, our readers and our planet. This book
is made from Forest Stewardship Council® certified paper.

MIX
Paper from
responsible sources
FSC® C018179

1 3 5 7 9 10 8 6 4 2

For Irving

Prologue
Gearhart, Oregon, July 2016

Chinook Lane was twenty minutes from the beach but Margaret liked it there. She liked the quiet-back-road feel of it and the cool interior made dim by evergreens. She did not like the white picket fence or the child's shoe on the front step, preserved under a kind of glaze and holding a geranium. When she arrived she delayed going inside and instead sat with her back to the gable, her rucksack beside her, looking through the trees and listening for sounds of the ocean. A fawn came across the lawn in silence then, as if to talk to her. His hooves made no sound at all – he seemed to be floating. He dabbed his nose towards her outstretched hand and was not threatened in any way by this gentle grey-haired woman. The fawn was curious but not expecting anything from her. The cats on the other side of the door, however, were crying in a way that was demanding. When Margaret finally stepped inside, she found a small kitchen painted yellow with large red and cream tiles on the floor. The cats sat watching her – and as she began to move through the house, their eyes followed her everywhere. The house was exactly as the owner had described. A cream bed under a canopy, a ladder leading to the loft – the second bedroom beside the kitchen, with the Union Jack on the wall and below this, red and blue bedcovers.

'We'll call this one "England",' she told the cats and they both stared up at her from the shiny kitchen floor. She wondered why they were looking at her. The cats she had known in Ireland would not have bothered. In Tullyvin the cats were usually left outdoors. But the rent was reasonable here for high season and cat-sitting was part of the deal. 'The cats are not a problem,' she had told the owner, 'no problem at all.' Now she was not so sure.

She fed them and sought out the litter tray reluctantly – it was in England, with rubber gloves and a small trowel at the ready – whenever the urge to go digging for cat shit overwhelmed her.

Later, when it was getting dark, the cats began to run through the house, one of them jumping up on the kitchen counter and knocking a butter dish onto the floor. Margaret wanted to put them out, to release them into the wild – to see what they were made of. Red and Mojo – they had nice enough names but she would refuse to use them. Over the next week both parties would spend as little time as possible together. And yet they were the reason she could rent this house and be near the sea and near other people and also at a safe distance from them. The neighbour's yard was in full bloom. She could see it through her windows, a blaze of sunflowers leaning towards her. A light went on and she saw someone move through a kitchen. Now when she looked in a window at night she wondered about the life of the person who lived there. If that person was lonely at all and if, like her, they had made the decision not to care about this any more.

In the morning, she woke needing to see the ocean. She needed the first blue of it and this seemed vital and more important to her than eating. In the past the wide sweep of sand had been too vast a space for her, it had made her feel lost, abandoned, but today she would endure it and come home refreshed, touched here and there with windburn and feeling like she had achieved something.

'A day at the beach can do a lot for a person,' Olive had told her once. The people of her past swept through her then – Bird, Olive, Midge and Tom – they were like hills behind her, a kind of protection, but she was still not ready to miss any of them.

Travelling alone had a pleasure that was both frightening and exhilarating – she had moved freely across America for almost two years before returning to Portland and Oregon. And there had been new love, friendships – people who had softened her. She had managed to shed some of the hard scales that had grown on her. Margaret had made mistakes and she had enjoyed herself. The pastor from Wyoming was a mistake – the soft lines of the prairies, his large farmhouse built of wood had proved to be very limiting. She had missed her freedom and the sea, the sound of water near her.

'Just see,' she had told herself and she had left him then and continued travelling.

Now the last sound she heard before falling asleep at night in Portland was often the far-off whistle of a freight train. If lonesome had a sound it would be this one, she often thought. It was only then that she might recall with some slight sadness the warmth of a man sleeping next to her.

In the kitchen the soft footfall of a cat slipped past her.

She knew she needed to clean out the litter tray but decided she could leave it until later. 'It needs to be done every morning,' the owner had told her. 'That and watering the plants.' But the sea was inviting her. That was, after all, what she had come here for – the smell of salt, the warm grit of sand under her feet, and that sudden first view of the ocean. To see the chop of waves in the distance, when she had not witnessed it for such a long time, would be a moment when all parts of her life, all the versions of herself, would come together.

The walk was longer than she expected. She stopped at Pops and ate a small ice cream sitting on a bench near there. Apart from this place with its candy stripes and hot waffle smell, there were no landmarks, no way for her to get her bearings. On the footpath opposite there was a real estate office, a post office, a small law firm. A man rode his horse on the street. It was a giant chestnut mare who was holding the man up into the sky. The mare cocked her tail and five round balls landed on the street, steaming – and Margaret glared at them. Even now, she could feel the prickle of some ancient anger. She got up and went quickly to the end of the street and had to walk a long distance in soft sand then. She took her sandals off and seemed to sink further. She went down a slope and into a small hollow filled with seagrass and she put her head back and let the wind blow inside her. She began walking again. There was a hill to climb now, a tall elegant dune with tufts of blue and yellow flowers on it like a crown, and she knew that the sea was beyond this and that it would be a great reward for her. From the top she saw the final blue – a ribbon that glittered from a great distance as the tide was out – and Margaret believed she was at the highest point of the universe. Seeing all of this beauty from the top of the dune, the blue ribbon, the sand, vast in its expanse, the tidal pools left behind in swirls and circles of silver, the wind strong but warm – she believed that there was hope everywhere, that her life was only beginning, that she had been forgiven for everything. It was just a moment but it was like a medal handed to her and placed on her chest, something she could wear for ever, proof.

I
The Whistling Girl

Tullyvin, Co. Wicklow,
9 November 2013

1

On that Saturday Midge and her father were fighting. At times she allowed this to happen, knowing that when he got her home he would drag her from the car and out into the bushes and beat her with anything he could put his hands on. Once when she was a child he used an iron and another time the wheel of an old pram. And all this with her mother, Bridget, watching and not really seeing, a helpless sort of woman, soft and faded like a cushion. The youngest child, a boy, would stand, frozen and staring, and two of the older ones would try to catch her and hold her down for their father. And Midge did not blame them at all for this. She too might have chosen desperate means to stay on his good side – but she had learned a long time ago that there was only one side to her father, the man who had made her and wanted to kill her. So far he had shown her no love at all and instead spent his time trying to plough through her.

This fight was about the money she had made from singing at the Beacon Hotel in Tullyvin. The manager, a man who was known around the town as Rocky, said she could come into the bar that afternoon and sing and then pass a small bread basket around and keep the takings. And she had done well that day too because there was a wedding and a christening. Midge had stood there on the spongy carpet that was damp with stale beer and sung her heart out for them. In truth Rocky only felt sorry for her and he knew all about her excuse for a father. And now because she owed him something she worried that she would have to let him do things to her in the dark car park where all the empty bottles were. She had a tambourine – more of a toy really – a guitar and a small keyboard given to her by her mother.

'The girl hasn't a note in her head,' some old one said and there was a fair bit of laughing.

But because they were getting drunk and stupid they dropped a few notes into her basket and Midge had plans for them. She was going to save enough money to make a new life for herself and her mother. But Bridget had told her not to do that. Her mother who washed dishes at the Italian chipper and whose body was loose and worn out from having too many children.

'Don't plan,' she told her daughter. 'Don't plan because your heart will be broken.'

But Midge was making money to steal away with. Midge was making money to travel to America with her mother – and if it wasn't for these plans in her head, this idea she had of living on the other side of the world with the possibility of something good happening, Midge would have walked out into Lough Rinn and let the whirlpool suck her down to the very bottom. And people said there was no bottom.

Then her father had slipped through the door of the bar with that blonde tramp Imelda Conroy. He was in his black 'leather' jacket, the dirty grey tracksuit bottoms hanging off him, and he took all the money off her. He did it right there in front of everyone and then sat up at the bar with Imelda and filled her up with brandy. Rocky had tipped her a few euros too and that went into their glasses with the rest of it.

To Midge who stood silently by, drowning in this new humiliation, he said, 'Wait in the car.' She was starving and had planned on treating herself to a Snickers bar and a magazine. Instead she cried a bit in the car but stopped as soon as she saw him coming.

14

There was no point in crying. It only showed him that he was winning at something. The car was an old Toyota with daylight showing through the floor and he only had it because it had been left in a ditch to rot by someone. He turned the key in the ignition with a fresh cigarette hanging out of his mouth and the smell of smoke and drink was sickening her. It was after six o'clock and she hadn't eaten anything for hours. Her whole house, the world that she lived in, was beginning to fall in on her. She was twenty years old and as she sat there in the car she began to wonder if she could just stop her own life – and do it in a way that he would be locked up for.

Midge waited until the car was on the lake road, out past the town hall, and he was putting his foot to the floor as she knew he would. Here with the November sky thick and starless all around them, he spoke to his daughter and said, 'Aren't you a great little songbird, pet, making a few bob for your poor old father?'

He leaned back in his seat on the long straight stretch with the Toyota bouncing and swaying, the whole thing making her seasick, her head like a barrel full of venom that she was ready to spit at him. If he crashed the car he might kill her and that would be the end of the two of them. She didn't care that much about herself now and it would be worth it if it also finished him. The Guards would know that he had been drinking again and that he had taken her out the lake road and hit a bump and then a lorry might come and down they would all go into the dark, brown water.

'A little canary,' he whispered, and so then she began at him, pecking gently at the start, not wanting too much to happen – but in her mind she was going to peck the skin clean off him. He was so drunk that he was in a cloud of clown's humour and finding himself very funny. But for Midge it would be the Saturday when she fought with her father and changed her life for ever. So she began quietly and slowly at first – knowing that towards the end

15

it would be as if two mongrel dogs had been let loose in the car with a blood-red steak between them.

'You're a rotten bastard,' she told him in a low, steady voice.

'Shush outta that.'

'You're a lousy excuse for a father.'

'That's enough out of you now, me girl.'

'You're a thief and a beggar . . . What sort of man goes about stealing money from his own daughter?'

'The same man that has to feed her.'

'You give us nothing. Everything we get is charity or Tostetti's or the Welfare.'

They passed through the bog then and moved over the low humpback bridge and by the Protestant church tower. Here the headstones were old and covered in ivy, some leaning in different directions as if they were dancing. She could see Maggie's Mountain in the distance, named for Margaret Keegan by her late father.

Further on, she could see Lough Rinn again, the road pulling back once more to the great circle of it. They would round a bend and suddenly be high over it. She liked this view of the water, that feeling of flying, of escaping.

'You're an alcoholic and you're a bollox.'

'Shut your mouth or I'll shut it for you.'

'You're a wife-beater.'

'And I'll beat the head off you too in a minute.'

Next he was telling her that she was a little tramp like her mother. The car swerved when he changed gears and she banged her small head on the passenger window. She had nothing to hold on to. There was very little that could protect a small woman from this kind of father. He knew her. He had built her. Twenty-one years ago he had climbed on top of her mother and together in a sea of Guinness and whiskey they had sparked her. And then the hard drinking and the fighting started, her father's fists going

16

deep into her mother's big tight belly as he tried to reach their unborn daughter. And she should have been invisible then – tucked away and safe from everything. But Midge was never safe. Her whole life would be about ducking and swerving.

Now she waited in the passenger seat of a speeding car with one small white fist held up to her temple.

'You think you're so lovely, swanning into the hotel,' she said, 'in your shitty coat made from plastic . . . Sure they're all laughing at you so they are.'

'You won't be laughing when I knock the head off you.'

'Do you know that they're all laughing at you? You auld eejit.'

'I'll beat the shit out of you when I stop this car.'

'That's all you're good for . . . beating women. I'm surprised you haven't started thumping Imelda Conroy.'

'Imelda is a fine woman.'

'Will she be fine when you swing a kick at her?'

Midge took a breath then and waited a moment.

'The whole town is laughing at you . . . and why should I care? Sure you're probably not even my father.'

And she paused again and allowed her words to sink into him.

'I'm telling you the truth. Do you not believe me?'

And here her father stopped watching the road and turned and faced her.

'If that's the truth, Midge, I'll go home and kill her.'

And he changed down a gear quickly then which gave the car a sudden burst of power and Midge was aware of a thick vein in his neck that was pulsing and his eyes, bloodshot, in the mirror, the whites tinged with yellow.

But Midge was determined to bait him.

'Sure half the town is ridin' Mammy . . . and you think she's off washing dishes in Tostetti's. Did you not know that Mario was pimping for her?'

17

And here her daddy lunged, the car skidding as it travelled around a soft corner. Midge was aware that gravel was spraying from under the tyres and then there was fresh air, cool in her face and she was finally, thanks be to God for it, free from him and flying. So that's what those long thin arms were for, she thought. He had lunged at the passenger door and opened it and then with the same hand pushed her out of the car so that she tumbled, skidded on the road and started rolling. She knew enough to pull her knees up to her chest and make a ball of herself. She was not like a hedgehog – a hedgehog would not have survived it. She was the shining conker inside the chestnut. Her head hit the ground hard, bouncing off it but she felt nothing, saw the stars falling down on her and rolled on, praying now that her neck, her spine were not broken. Of course, he was far too smart for her. Of course, he would find a good way to move on with his life and still harm her. He had been driving over her since the day she was born.

Midge sat up slowly and looked around her. Her elbows and knees were torn but there were no broken bones and so she sat there humming. She knew that her head was all right if she could remember some bit of a song but for now she could remember nothing. She lifted her hand and felt a small grid of pebbles and stones stuck into her forehead. They reminded her of an abacus with the same bump and feel from them. She had rolled into someone's lane and could see a smooth gravel driveway lined with cut stone walls and trees in perfect symmetry. There was the oblong shape of a house in the darkness, but with no lights on she didn't know it. She got up on her hands and knees and crawled towards the garden. She was aware of hedges and tall grass there, shrubs and old rose bushes ringed with briars, strangled. She crept under a wire fence so that she was off the driveway and in the field closest to the garden. A light came on in a downstairs window and she wondered who might be in there. She hummed the air to 'Waltzing Matilda', some of the words beginning to surface from a kind of third ear hidden inside her. A wave of despair came suddenly then and almost flattened her and she wanted to give in to it. And yet if she could string these words together she would know that her head was not broken, that the two sides of her brain were still attached to each other. When she turned her head a pain at the back of her skull stabbed at her. She could feel something warm and wet sliding through her hair and could smell blood on herself. It was a strange creeping feeling, not unpleasant and not welcome either.

As her eyes became used to the dark she knew that the big whitewashed house in front of her belonged to a farmer called Bird Keegan. She had seen him around the town, a long, thin fellow about thirty or so, who spoke to no one – and the country was full of young men like him – single farmers who ate out of tins and whose voices were not heard by anyone. But the Keegans were well-off people coming from this big place with its own name instead of a number. Red Hill – that's what it was called – whereas Midge lived in a council house on the other side of Tullyvin, 'a real shit-box' she called it. Bird Keegan owned Maggie's Mountain as well as Lough Rinn itself and all the land around it. He had two sisters much older than him called Margaret and Olive. Margaret, the eldest, had been Midge's teacher at school and had now gone into farming like her brother. The sisters lived together in the white lodge just across the water – visible from Red Hill. Both of them were single and well into their forties and too old, that was what people said anyway, for having children, or even marrying.

And now Midge had crawled over their cattle grid without even knowing it, stopping under a big bear of a cypress tree whose branches seemed to reach down for her, a tree that wanted to pick her up and give her shelter. She tried in that moment to remember her father's name. She looked up into those long wet

19

branches and wondered, was it Paddy, Mickey or Joseph? She saw her mam's face, her faded red hair, her skin puffed up from drinking and crying, her nose flat because it had been broken – and she loved all of her.

What was her mother's name? Bridget Carney, of course. She was a Carney from Kilkenny before she was a Connors and the Carneys were decent people. Just pure stupid when it came to marrying.

Her father, whatever he was called, had pushed her out of a speeding car – but her life, as pathetic as it was, still continued to rise up inside her.

What was the bastard's name? Did he even have one?

She could see letters then, stamped out in a row, like stars along the horizon. She had never called him Dad or Daddy or Da. He was Charlie. That was his name. Charlie Connors. She wished with all her heart that she had never known him.

2

Much earlier on the same Saturday, Bird Keegan had been called to a hay shed where he saw a young boy hanging. The barn belonged to his neighbours and they had called before daylight to ask if he would help them.

'Will you come down?' Joe O'Neill said and in the secret language of farmers it meant that they were in a crisis that was bigger than them. The O'Neills, as it happened, were in a new black mist that was bleak and suffocating. This call was not for the loan of a trailer or about a young vet struggling to complete a Caesarean. Cows lived, cows died, sheep wandered into soft-bottomed rivers – but his neighbours did not call him. The O'Neills and everyone around Tullyvin knew that Bird Keegan did not mix with other people and, apart from occasional meetings with his own sisters, he did not share himself with anyone. Now through a galvanized wall in the O'Neills' yard a mother and a sister could be heard weeping. The father, a small warrior of a man, now broken, found a ladder and cut his son down and Bird and the other son, the younger of the two boys, 'received' him. That was the only word Bird could think of to describe what they did, and the full weight of death almost knocked the two of them. The father and son stood back then, unable to move or touch the boy who was suddenly a stranger to them. It was Bird himself who went down on one knee, closing the boy's eyes and

21

checking the smooth line of his neck even though he was clearly cold and not breathing. The mother and sister crept through the door then, their heads low, their instincts drawing them nearer. And Bird had no idea what to do for them, these faces that seemed to plead with him. They were Catholics like himself, he knew that much – but he could not remember the Act of Contrition or even the Lord's Prayer and so instead he used his coat to cover the boy and then stood up straight again.

The boy was called William and there was no life at all in him. He had been hanging there all night when his parents thought he was at his girlfriend's twenty-first birthday party at the Beacon. But the girlfriend had broken it off with him a week earlier and had found someone she liked better and he had been too embarrassed and hurt to tell anyone. William had bought the girlfriend a ring but it turned out that she didn't love him and his own twenty-one-year-old heart wasn't able for the rejection. Now his face was a sheen of blue and white, his hands the same mottled grey of the moon and he was unaware of the sound of his mother and sister crying. He was unaware of his father who was shrunken – and their neighbour who remained calm even though he felt as if there were pieces of his brain flying everywhere. William O'Neill was unaware of everything.

Bird went into the O'Neills' kitchen then and drank tea with the parents, and that was worse than anything. He was thirty-one years old and, apart from the hardship that he had just witnessed and the sight of the bare hedgerows already drenched with rain, the ground soaking under him, the sudden tiredness and the sadness he felt was overpowering. He had been up most of the night himself with a calving. The new mother was a narrow-arsed heifer who was good for nothing and that included suckling.

The ambulance was taking its time getting to them and with no one capable of speaking and the clock over his head rapping out a steady rhythm, Bird's head dipped and he fell asleep at their table. He would never tell this to his sisters and the O'Neills didn't say anything. They allowed their odd neighbour this strange slip-up as they, the boy's family, had been spun around and were still spinning. They no longer knew who they were or where they were going. So what if a man fell asleep in their kitchen? The people who were left behind after a hanging didn't care much about anything. Bird woke to find the O'Neills sitting looking at him. He was unusually shy for a man of his age and he felt himself expand now in front of them, his feet and hands feeling big and awkward but he stayed on, knowing, at the very least, that while he could not think of a single word to say that might be a comfort, he would not leave them. He heard car tyres on the gravel of the yard some time after six and he knew it would be the priest and the doctor and he stood up, nodding once at Mr and Mrs O'Neill, glad to release the empty chair to them.

3

Bird returned home as the grey light of dawn was breaking. He parked the jeep at the front of his house and sat there looking up at it. It was at best a big barn of a place with high-ceilinged rooms and no central heating. There were days when he would walk through its dark landings, finding damp beds and old dressing rooms and deep copper baths full of dirt and cinders. The furniture was uncomfortable and worn. The only warm room was the kitchen. There were people who said Red Hill was haunted and Bird would laugh at them – for him, ghosts were less frightening than the people who were talking. Now he could see that it was too big a place for a man on his own, that the house he owned was shrinking him. The front door was red but the hedge had grown up wild and covered it. The fanlight, a smooth arch of stained glass, came up over the laurel leaves, the branches brushing against it. There were days when he looked out the downstairs windows and hardly saw light through the briars and nettles – and yet a part of him felt protected. The hedge was a moat, as he saw it – the front door a drawbridge that rarely opened. If his lair had a tower then that would be his bedroom, a vast space, where the walls were a deep burgundy colour, the bed high under its own velvet canopy. There were other rooms too of course – his parents' old bedroom, the long narrow pink room shared by his two sisters when they were children, the loft bedroom over the kitchen which had been his as a boy. And it was his father who had positioned him there, knowing he could call him at any time of day or night without disturbing the women. Three stern raps of a cattle stick on the kitchen ceiling would bring the small boy running, his eyes thick with sleep and his legs skidding under him.

He stayed in the jeep and looked up at the black windows. It was not even seven o'clock in the morning and still too early for Sean Weldon, the man he paid to help him. And Bird was afraid to go inside, afraid that his own home – with all its cold rooms and corridors – would somehow consume him.

The suicide, the loss of this boy – William – had put a strange shadow over everything. It seemed to change the colour of Red Hill, even the sky behind it – the clouds like shrouds rising to meet him. Bird's bones felt hollow, his stomach weak and empty. There were people who believed that the ghost of a person who had taken their own life was left wandering until the Lord was ready to call him. Bird worried now that William O'Neill might single him out for a haunting. He had seen the boy's eyes and even now in daylight he could not stop seeing them. Those eyes had looked at *him* – those eyes – without a person or any life at all behind them. William O'Neill was like an empty husk, the kind of thing you would find on a windowsill on a summer evening.

Until this Saturday Bird's life had been Red Hill and the land. For more than thirty years, the seasons, the crops, the animals and their needs were laid out like stepping-stones for him. He had always been a quiet man – a person who wanted to go through life without being noticed, who slipped around and between other people – rarely coming face to face with anyone. He was deaf in one ear – the result of a diving accident, he said – which gave him another excuse to be unsociable. He often missed – and sometimes just ignored – what people were saying. Even his

25

name seemed to allow a kind of freedom. As a teenager he had grown up tall and thin and one of the local girls at the lake had said he was like a crane stepping into the water. From then on he was always Bird, so that if anyone asked his real name he had some trouble remembering. He was, of course, called John, the same name as his father, but he was happy enough to answer to Bird and to relinquish that connection.

Now as he watched a seagull cross the sky he made an effort to reel his thoughts back in – but he still couldn't settle them. He thought about his mother, who had died when he was six, and how his father had gone on then to make a slave out of him. The age gap between himself and his sisters was such that either one could have become a kind of mother to him – but he had not wanted them. Instead he had sunk down under the work his father expected – and tried to silence the quiet calling of a mother who had died on him. Even now he had a sudden memory of her out in the yard – putting a sheet on the line, the wind causing it to wrap around her, the sharp blue of the sky – and him as a boy standing in the empty yard, waiting.

John Keegan Senior had seemed destined to live for ever but in the end the bull, a big lug of a fellow, had caught him in the shed and squeezed him. He had died there and then and after the shed had been whitewashed and the bull sold, Bird had inherited everything. Margaret had taken an interest in farming by then too and he was glad to divide the big Friesian herd with her. And he had heard this week that one of her best cows had been sick since Thursday morning. He imagined calling her and asking if he could help her – but there was a real awkwardness there, a shyness that would prevent this kind of talking. He was not too concerned about the cow because Margaret had a great way with Friesians. He did worry a bit about her though – she had never been the same since Tom Geoghan broke it off with her. The sick cow would be all right. Now that Margaret had retired from teaching, it was well

26

known that she was better at minding animals than children.

It was Bird himself who had dug the grave for their father.

'There now,' he had said, 'this is the last thing I will do for you,' and his sisters had watched and no one was crying because not one of them was able. And yet there would be many nights after that when Bird would cover his good ear with the flat of his hand to stop the sound of his own grief reaching him.

Bird had presumed that he would get married and have a family – but there were no girls in the town that appealed to him. He had grown up handsome enough with his pale blue eyes and shoulders that were broad and very straight like a kind of shelving. He still had the long lean legs of a teenager but when he spoke now his words came out deep and clear with a good deal of thought behind them. His most defining feature was his hair, fair and full of curls, with a thick beard covering his mouth and chin. He had gone to the discos in the local rugby club and kissed a few girls but when they began talking it was always some form of nonsense. There were times now in the milking parlour – surrounded by the dense warm smell of the cows – that he would find himself thinking about women, a wild wasp of feeling suddenly blowing through him. But in truth, he had no one.

Three grey crows watched him when he finally left the jeep and walked down to the yard, feeling some light rain beginning to coat him. William O'Neill might haunt him but the cows needed to be milked and the new calf checked on. The small calving shed was attached to the back of the house, a square shuttered window between it and a small downstairs bedroom. He found the new black calf in the shed, cold and shivering. He hadn't suckled and the heifer, who did not know how to care for her own offspring, was busy swinging kicks at him.

And Bird watched this for a moment without doing anything. There was a fine line for this calf between death and survival.

27

The line lay somewhere between the heifer's stupidity and the calf's determination – and how much punishment he was capable of taking in order to get some beestings. He watched the calf curl up in a ball and knew that if left for much longer the heifer would kill him. He opened the gate and released her back to her life of freedom, her own calf already a distant memory. The calf would have to be fed with a bottle, which was hard work and trouble, but it was this which propelled Bird back inside the house finally. As he stood waiting for the kettle to boil he resisted the urge to turn around and see if there was someone standing behind him. He knew there was no one. In the frigid aftermath of a boy's suicide Bird thought seriously – for the first time – about his own life and his future. As he saw himself now he was like a single star outside the earth's orbit with no connection to anyone. He had read about the distance between stars somewhere, 'about five light years' – and that was how he felt on this dark Saturday morning in November. 'Five light years' – which was around six trillion miles – away from everyone.

28

4

It was still dark when Margaret Keegan crossed her yard, bringing the smell of sickness and manure with her. She had a cow down, one of her best Friesians, and she was afraid she would not get up again. The cow had given birth to a dead calf two days earlier and she was still down on Saturday morning. The men had made a kind of winch the night before, putting wide canvas bands under her, and a long row of them, pulling and shouting, hoisted the cow into the air to give her the feeling of standing. And Margaret had watched this from the narrow doorway, thinking she was at the circus.

'A flying cow,' she said. 'I've seen everything.'

Now as she crossed the yard there was light bursting from the new glass-roofed extension. 'We need more light,' Olive had said and because of her sister's illness Margaret had not wanted to refuse her. Now there were days when she would watch the rain run in rivers over her head; at night the moon seemed to reach in and touch her.

The dead calf was already covered in diesel and buried deep in the slurry pit.

'Think about that,' Margaret had wanted to say to the men, 'think about the womb empty with nothing to show for it.' But she didn't. She could understand why the cow might not feel like getting up, why she might take to her bed and turn her back on all of them.

She put the kettle on in the kitchen, lifted a single egg from the bowl and reached for a small saucepan. She was afraid that the cow would die on her now and the new vet could not do anything. She worried about the loss of the milk production – and the calf – as she watched the egg doing a little jig in the boiling water. She missed Olive and wished she was back from Medjugorje to talk to her. Margaret had already put fresh sheets on her sister's bed and had her breakfast tray ready. Her flight was in at ten and then it would be at least a couple of hours before the bus dropped her at the Beacon. She would arrive then tanned and full of energy. Margaret herself had been up most of the night, directing these men, who were – as she told them herself – 'clueless'.

She carried her cup and plate into the breakfast room where the windows facing her were still black – and she watched herself top the egg in them.

A sorry-looking sight, she decided.

She could see the round caps of her shoulders, the baggy Fair Isle jumper, her hair, wiry now, more grey than brown. She looked unkempt, like a woman who had forgotten about herself, like a woman who had been generally forgotten. A sudden thought moved through her then – which was that she had been loved once, and that she had been beautiful. Even now, she could open up the same well of sadness if she wanted to. She had loved one man more than anyone and he had left her. Margaret stood up quickly and pulled the heavy curtains over. She did not need these thoughts now or to see any more of this particular performance. The man's name was Tom Geoghan and he had almost finished her.

Margaret lifted the empty eggshell and went back to the kitchen to find the biscuits. Here new granite worktops and cabinets in the 'Shaker style' surrounded her. Everything was newly cream and white, the walls painted 'pistachio' – and there was a 'sliding pantry' that annoyed her. She could find nothing in it – tins of soup falling over, a packet of spaghetti spilling itself. And a workstation had been built into 'the island', with a place for files, a computer. Olive had set her email up, giving her an account and a new email address. The oven was still like new. She was a bit afraid of it.

Margaret tried to concentrate on Sky news but the memory of the cow loomed at her. She closed her eyes and lifted her feet onto the low coffee table. She was wearing nylons and a woollen skirt and on her feet a thick pair of men's socks. She was forty-nine years old and her face had begun to show it. Too much wind and sun and almost overnight she had begun to look like she was melting. Below her knees varicose veins had appeared in hard bubbles and she had never had a child or spent an inordinate amount of time on her feet – even as a teacher. It was close to 7am when she used the front stairs to reach her bedroom – and she climbed slowly, the tiredness weighing on her, the rest of the world getting up as she plugged in her electric blanket.

When Margaret woke, it was close to lunchtime and the phone was ringing.

Olive, she thought to herself.

She answered it in her bare feet, the ringing pulling her downstairs and across the red carpet in the hallway.

'Hello . . . is that you, Margaret?'

And she held the phone to her ear, a pulse in her neck beating out a steady rhythm.

'Margaret?'

'Bird,' she answered sharply, 'of course it's me – who were you expecting?'

She thought of the cow and wondered what she would find when she went to check on her.

'How are things?' he asked.

'Things are fine, thanks . . . and yourself?'

'Hanging in there . . .'

Whatever that meant.

'I have a cow down, Bird,' she said, suddenly cutting in.

'I know and I'm sorry to hear it.'

'Down nearly three days and I'm awful upset about it.'

There were tears filling her head now, running into the dam of her throat. Those stupid men, the bloody cow, it would break her heart to lose her.

She could see some cold-looking pine trees in a row outside the hall window, the sky, a navy blue and yellow, down low where the sun had come up behind them.

'And you called the vet, I suppose?'

'I did of course. He could do nothing for her . . . he was useless.'

'I'm sorry, what was that?'

'USELESS,' Margaret shouted. 'A young eejit straight out of the vet college.'

'That's young Geoghan,' Bird said very quietly.

'Young who?'

'He wouldn't have much experience – especially with Friesians.'

'Well, he was no use to me – with his shot of calcium and his bill for eighty euros at the end of it.'

'Give her time,' Bird said and there was a pause then when neither of them said anything.

'Well, I'll see you tomorrow for Sunday lunch, I suppose,' Margaret said finally.

'I suppose you will.'

'Don't forget to buy the roast, Bird.'

And he hung up then without saying goodbye to her.

Through the new kitchen skylights the winter sun was high and fierce over her. There was no heat at all from it and with the wind from the north Margaret was worried that the cow would be frozen. There was a text from Olive saying that she would be at the Beacon closer to two and she followed this with a ridiculous stream of hugs and kisses. Margaret had time now to search out the portable radio and an old wool coat that had belonged to their mother. Outside, the wind lifted her scarf and a cat wrapped itself around her ankles and almost tripped her. The door to the shed creaked when she opened it and the sun bounced off the walls, showing them up, white and dazzling. The cow looked alarmed then. She was awake of course, a sloppy tear running from an eye down her cheek as if she was crying. She hadn't moved an inch since early morning. Margaret turned on the radio and left it playing and the cow watched all of this with some interest. She opened up the wool coat then and draped it over the cow's back and when Margaret offered her the bucket she sucked all the water out of it.

'My girl, my poor old girl,' she said and she turned off the light and closed the door behind her.

5

Midge closed her eyes on the darkness, the cold resting on her. She could feel the damp beginning to sit on her eyelids and on her body, her mind and thoughts drifting. There was no pain at all, no feeling in any part of her. She believed that she was happy now, that this, in fact, might be dying. And who would miss her? Her mother, Bridget, would start drinking as soon as she finished at Tostetti's – and her father had hated her from the first moment he saw her. Midge had been born on the bathroom floor, a premature baby with big dark eyes and long thin legs made for running. Even now Bridget would talk about the silence of her arrival, how there was no cry at life and its newness – just a baby landing quietly on the lino. Midge knew now that her mother had not loved her at all then but she had not hated her either – she had just not needed her. And she was born with a caul, which Charlie said was a disgust to him and everyone else said was very lucky. Afterwards Bridget had found it on the floor near the toilet, drying out like paper and still holding the shape of her head, like a little helmet. And she had hidden the caul in a drawer where Charlie would not find it, knowing that her daughter would need whatever small glitters of luck it brought her.

'Sure, it's like laying an egg for you, Bridget,' Doctor Coffey had said to her.

'I thought I was finished laying eggs like these,' she had answered.

There was nothing special about another red-haired baby in that house. Including Midge there were five children in total – all of them falling out of that small pebble-dash place with wrecks of cars all around it and a meadow to the back which Midge would pretend was the ocean. And in no time at all it would become a place for her to run to. Later, when Midge climbed onto the school bus, her heart sank low when she saw how the other children looked at her and the broken-down house she came from. Even now she could remember their silent knowing. She had hoped that children would not be aware of the differences between them. But they knew – and they made a point of telling her on a daily basis – that they were better than her. Even there in the middle of the thistles and weeds and the smell of elder-berry blossom – even there in those damp bogs and hedgerows – everyone needed to be 'someone'.

But Midge did well at school and she grew taller in spite of the poundings her father gave her. At seventeen she had stopped growing at five feet three and in a certain kind of light, with the red of her hair and the white of her skin, she could still look weak and malnourished. Bridget was drunk as often as Charlie by then, and he continued to beat her, and because of this – and a blur of other hurts inflicted by him, not least his 'taking-up' with Imelda Conroy – Midge had stayed because she could not abandon her mother. Her brothers and sister had left years ago and the few friends she had from school had emigrated or moved to Dublin. She had tried to keep in touch with them on Facebook but they were always showing off with pictures of their new cars or boyfriends and they only sickened her.

Now she put her head down on the grass in one of Bird Keegan's fields, her hair becoming wet from it, the rest of her draining downwards, falling away, melting into the grass and the small stones of gravel. She did not know where she was any more and there was not a sound around her. An animal shuffled suddenly in the hedgerow and she could smell a fox somewhere. She imagined that wild animals, foxes, badgers, wolves even, would come out in the true blue of night and eat her. And she would be ingested by them, become a part of their grey and yellow intestines, the red flow of their blood and be absorbed back into the earth where she would grow up again in summer. The sun would shine and no one would ever touch or harm her. And Midge would become an ear of corn, golden and useful and singing.

6

Bird took the jeep into town and bought his groceries early, on Saturday afternoon. He did this once a week, always on a Monday, and now that he was two days early he felt conspicuous. He could hear music coming from the Beacon and remembered that it was the day of the travellers' wedding. When the door opened to release someone reeling with drink, he saw a red-haired girl with a guitar and she was singing. Outside, people hurried past him in the cold, their heads down, and it seemed that he loomed over them. A sudden dash of rain came down and felt like pebbles hitting his shoulders. The rain stopped for a minute and then started again with a new ferocity but Bird did not hurry through it. His skin was used to the weather and he wore a red wool hat pulled down over his ears and moved with strides that were wide and looping. The cows had been milked later than usual and he had stood watching them file out into the field again. His breakfast of tea and porridge had made no impression on him. The food was of no comfort in a room and on a table that struck him as bare and unwelcoming. The mad heifer had waited at the gate, bawling for the calf that she had not been able to mother. Despite her inability to care for him, she had returned, disconnected and lonesome.

'You wouldn't mind him when you had him,' Bird said to her.

37

He leaned on the gate and she rolled her eyes at him, a hoarse roar sent in his direction.

Bird saw broken glass outside the hotel, empty chip bags and burger cartons outside Tostetti's – the remnants of the previous night's partying. These people did not seem to care much about anything and yet the news would hit them hard, these youngsters who had partied as one of their own was dying.

It was in the small supermarket while lifting some cauliflower that had been grown in Spain that he heard the first whisper of it as the girls behind the counter began talking quietly to each other.

'In the hay shed,' one of them said, her arms folded across her breasts as if to protect them.

'Ah no,' the other one answered and they turned and saw Bird looking at them. He put the cauliflower down and walked towards the counter.

'Well, Bird,' one of them said. He saw now that he was in his own way notorious. People he did not recognize – women in shop uniforms who merged into each other – all knew him. He opened his mouth to say something about William O'Neill, but what would he say to these women who were strangers? How would he begin to discuss the thing that was like a dog eating the insides out of him?

'Have you buttermilk?' he asked.

The two women looked at each other and he saw the look, a kind of smug knowledge – they both thought he was as cracked as a cat standing there in front of them.

'With the milk in the big fridge . . .' was the answer and they did not see his face as he opened the tall glass doors to the buttermilk, which he had no earthly use for. They did not see the awkwardness of his expression, the deliberate lowering of his face and eyes, the shyness like a new heat radiating from him. There was no one here who could help him. A bulb overhead flickered and its yellow light sickened him. It was still raining. He found a sliced pan and some tea, a half-dozen eggs and some rashers. He needed shampoo but found the choices available dazzling, their promises mind-boggling. He did not have dandruff and his hair was not 'fly-away' or greasy. It was simply hair, a thick golden thatch of it, and there seemed to be no suitable shampoo for that.

'Is there anything else you need?' one of the girls called to him. He turned and looked at her. She was someone's wife, someone's mother. She would know all about shampoo for a man with hair but he would not ask her. He could not ask her.

Bird put the groceries into the jeep and drove to the lodge to see his sisters. He could not remember the last time he had called to the lodge to pay them a visit. But today, given how he was feeling, he had a need to place himself safely between them. They still came to him on a Sunday – Margaret often ringing up beforehand and telling him to get a roast of beef in. And Olive following her then with a small bucket of peeled potatoes, flour and eggs for making the Yorkshire pudding – the two of them a bit uncomfortable in the house where they had all been children. Bird thought it strange now, that these children – who had been like all children, wondering and innocent – had slipped away to become an oddball farmer and two spinster sisters, without anyone ever noticing or trying to stop them.

The lodge was built on a ledge overlooking the lake, a low two-storey house with two vast bay windows. Bird could see one white gable from Hope's Hill on his farm, and at night a single light from Olive's bedroom window. The house had been their grandmother's and shortly after their father died the two girls, as Bird still called them, moved in. The drawing room ran the full length of the house with both bay windows looking down over the water. And he had heard about their new extension. Bird could not remember when he had decided to stop going there – or if it had even been an actual decision. The girls moved away from the memory of their father and at the same time their brother seemed to retreat from them. Margaret and Olive did not need to take any furniture from him – there were chintz sofas and curtains in the lodge already and two good wooden beds with carved headboards and ends. Their grandmother had decorated the house after the war and her good taste showed in everything. There was a small library off the drawing room and a neat little sewing room with Chinese wallpaper. It was in every way feminine and seemed to flinch at the shadow of Bird Keegan.

He parked the jeep and walked around the house so that he could see the lake, which always pleased him. The wind was strong when he turned the corner and the water looked rough, its colour the same purple as the sky over him. There could be thunder and hail, it had the look of it all around him. He knocked on the front door. It did not occur to him to turn the handle and call out 'hello' as he let himself in.

Margaret and Olive were in the hall itself, crossing from the kitchen to the drawing room. Margaret was carrying a tray with tea and toast on it and Olive was carrying what looked like a small gift wrapped in gold paper. She was back from a pilgrimage to Medjugorje and looked tanned and was wearing a soft velour trouser suit with two parts to it. Her backside was big and round in the trousers but she was bustling around, all business, the soft look of her in itself suddenly comforting. Her hair, which was blonde, was cropped short to her head like a little hat and she had small blue eyes that were full of mischief.

'Bird!' she exclaimed. 'Is there anything wrong?'

Margaret stopped with the tray and stared at him.

'Are you coming in . . . or what are you doing?' she asked.

'Is there anything wrong?' Olive asked again.

'Nothing at all,' Bird answered. He straightened up in the hall and glanced around him. A wall of central heating seemed to hit him so that his coat was already feeling like a blanket smothering him.

'I was passing.'

He knew they would not believe this lie, of course – Bird was not a man to 'pass' anywhere. He was a man who went on journeys that had a specific end to them. He was not one to make random visits, 'dropping in' and 'stopping by' were not in his nature. There was a dinner gong in the hall, its small mallet hanging beside it – and next to that a long-case clock whose steely ding was familiar to him. Margaret had put letters that had arrived in Olive's absence into a neat bundle on the hall table. The air smelled of toast and through an open door he could see a log fire blazing.

This, he thought to himself, is a home made by women, all comfort and warmth and welcome.

'Come in and have some tea and toast with us, Bird,' Olive said before he could say anything. 'My flight got in late and Margaret had the fire lit and the tea made for me – and everything.'

And everything. Bird turned these words over in his head. 'And everything' meaning that the house was cleaned to a shine and the dishes were dried and put away, fresh flowers cut and filling vases of Waterford crystal. Olive's bed was no doubt covered in fresh sheets so that she could peel off her clothes and climb straight in. He understood now why his sisters had been so quick to move out and away from the draught of him.

'Aren't you good to yourselves,' he said and he gave a sad smile and put his hands deep into his pockets, his feet apart, the red hat at an angle.

The three siblings paused for a moment, each one letting his words sink in. The words had no real significance and yet they had managed to carry a small barb of tension. The long-case clock in the hall gave a sudden grinding sound as if getting ready to chime, but then thought better of it and fell silent.

Olive gave a little laugh and kept walking.

'Come on, will you?' she said and she turned away and went into the drawing room.

'Did you come all the way over here to say that to us?' Margaret asked, staring at him, her voice as dry as a biscuit. She did not have the softness that Olive had but she was, as her brother knew, very perceptive and capable of reading some kind of trouble in his face when she looked at him.

Through the doorway he saw Olive sink down into a low chair near the fire, shaking her feet a little in sheepskin slippers and pulling a soft blue shawl around her shoulders.

Margaret glanced down at his wellingtons.

'You better leave those outside the door,' she said and he nodded and pulled his feet from them. He remembered then that in his hurry to get to the O'Neills earlier he had forgotten to put socks on. His feet were dirty from the boots and his toenails feral.

He followed the girls into the room, cheerful with its cream carpet and the fire hissing and cracking. He sat back on the couch with his sisters in the armchairs and Olive began pouring tea and offering milk and sugar to him. He reached for it with both hands and took the toast as well, savouring this humble meal and the feeling of carpet under his feet. There was an arrangement of small paintings on the walls around him, some silver on display, a writing desk near the side window so that a lady could see the roses when she was composing a letter. The room was a kind of heaven, lovely, and yet to Bird, who seemed to live in a henhouse by comparison, almost unbearable in all its femininity. He saw then that Margaret was sitting in silence and that her eyes had settled on his feet and the yellow toenails. Olive looked across at her sister and then followed her gaze until she too had the pleasure of seeing them.

'Jesus, Mary and Joseph, Bird,' Olive said in a little whisper, 'when did you last wash those feet?'

Bird did not speak but took a bite of the toast and looked around him, taking in every detail.

'Not to mention the toenails.' Margaret spoke in a low voice that was barely audible. 'You could plough a field with them,' she added and this had the effect of sending Olive off into a fit of laughter.

'Ah leave him, Margaret . . . leave him, leave him.' She whispered the last words out as if he was a mad creature that lived in the mountains and they risked vexing him.

The sisters helped themselves to tea and toast and the fire spat and rattled.

'Those logs are wet,' Bird remarked and they looked into the fire and nodded. His presence had brought a strange veil down over everything and the conversation was stilted and formal. He knew that Olive was full of news from her holiday and that she was dying to talk to Margaret. They were always at him to come and visit – although it was not that they especially liked his company. It was that they were concerned about other people saying how odd Bird Keegan could be. The fire warmed his face and his hands so that he reached up and pulled his red hat off backwards.

'We were just saying wasn't it awful about that poor O'Neill boy?' Margaret said.

'God help his poor parents,' Olive added. She was leaning sideways, away from the fire, the heat becoming a bit too much for her. Margaret had already parked her own chair at a safer distance.

Bird did not answer them because he couldn't.

'Did you hear what happened?' Olive asked. 'When the bus left me at the hotel they were already talking about it.'

She leaned over the arm of the chair towards her brother and whispered, 'They found him dead this morning. That young William boy. The eldest.'

43

'And did they say what exactly happened?' Margaret asked quietly.

'Oh, I don't know . . . someone said that he drank weedkiller and someone else said he put his father's shotgun to his head – bang.'

'He hanged himself,' Bird said. 'The O'Neills called me this morning, before it was light.'

His first real words were like a fur of frost over everything. Both sisters were silenced instantly and looked at him then with some kind of admiration.

'And what happened?' Olive asked.

'The poor boy,' Margaret said.

'What do you think happened?' Bird answered and he didn't say anything else about it. What was there to tell them anyway? What detail could he add? The length of rope, the beam that surprised everyone with its immense strength, the father with the very life shaken out of him – worse off even than the mother – the father who was dead himself now, scraped out and empty.

Olive and Margaret sat back and looked at their brother. Olive reached for his cup and refilled it, handing it back without saying anything. He met her eyes then.

'Olive,' he wanted to tell her, 'I saw something this morning that made my heart swell inside my chest, something that stretched me out and then left me loose and ragged. Olive,' he wanted to ask, 'what is the point of anyone carrying on? When a boy who was young and beautiful ends everything, when *a boy* does such a thing?'

Instead Bird took the cup from her and sat back into the cushions of the couch and crossed his legs.

'How was your holiday, Olive?' he asked.

Olive gave a big sigh and said, 'It was grand. We were roasted. I haven't seen a drop of rain since I left here last week.'

From where Bird was sitting he could see rain beginning to

make circles on the lake, small and tight at first and then wider ones that overlapped with others. The mountain looked black as if you could mine coal from it. Seeing this made him think about Red Hill and the kitchen range, which he had still not lit, so the place would be freezing. Here in the heat he could feel his head nodding with sleep again and he needed to rouse himself. He opened his eyes and saw that Margaret was looking at him and that Olive was already dozing in her chair.

'I better be going,' he said and he stood up, his knees giving off a few small cracks and the cup and saucer returned to the low table with a clatter.

'Will you not stay for a bit, Bird?' Margaret said. 'You're looking shook . . . Have some soup maybe or at least take something back to the house with you.'

Bird knew then that they were sorry for him because he had come from a farm where he had seen death and he was marked by it and now, because of the news he had carried in, he had cast a slight shadow on the lodge and on these two women. No one would mention it again, but it was there between the brother and his two older sisters, a feeling of sadness for a boy who would remain forever unknown to them.

'How is the cow?' Bird asked her.

'Not a stir out of her . . . and she'll be on her way to the factory if things don't improve.'

'Give her time,' Bird answered. 'She might surprise you.'

He stood looking down on them, his thick hair falling forward so that he had to push it away from his eyes to see them. Olive stirred in her chair and when she opened her eyes she smiled over at him. At four o'clock it was beginning to get dark already and he knew that they were both imagining the evening he had planned out for himself, a man on his own, his hands and arms and legs kept busy with farm work, his mind, his thoughts wrapping themselves around and around him in the same

45

way that a sparrow would build a tight little nest in springtime.

'I can't imagine what those poor O'Neills are going through,' Olive said.

And for a moment all three were silent.

'It makes you think, doesn't it?' Bird said and he looked through one of the bay windows as if he was talking to himself.

'That it does,' said Margaret.

7

Margaret and Olive stayed on at the fire as if waiting for the damp air to leave with their brother. The latch on the front door was lifted gently and then closed quietly behind him. From where Margaret sat, she could see him following the narrow gravel path that went around the house and then pass the narrow side windows.

'Since when did he start using the front door?' Olive asked and her eyes were mischievous.

'He doesn't want to be too familiar with us. You know . . . his sisters,' Margaret answered, rolling her eyes.

'My God,' Olive said. 'He's getting odder by the minute.'

She reached for the teapot and then stopped.

'Or is it us that's odd?' she asked suddenly.

Here Margaret gave a little snort of laughter.

'It might be genetic,' she said and she held her cup out for Olive to refill it. 'Well, the whole town thinks we're peculiar . . . and no one ever formed a queue to marry any of us either.'

'Never say never,' Olive answered and she sat back in her chair looking very pleased with herself.

'So how was the holiday . . . ?' Margaret asked.

'Ah, it was great, we had the best of weather. I enjoyed every minute of it.'

'Every minute . . . Well, you can't do better than that.'

47

'And here I've a present for you,' and she handed her sister the little gold-paper package. Inside there was a small leather purse and a rosary.

'That's lovely,' Margaret said and she barely looked at them. 'And what were the other people on the tour like?'

'Mostly people from the parish . . . you know, funny types,' and here they looked at each other and laughed a bit. 'Jim Lennon brought his own Maxwell House coffee to drink, can you believe that? The coffee at the hotel was the best part of the breakfast and he wouldn't drink it.'

'What about Paul Gibbons, was he on the trip?'

'He was – and his wife. And her brother – he's a bit simple or something . . . you'd feel sorry for him. I shared a table with them at dinner a few nights . . . and well, you can imagine what that was like.'

Margaret took a sip of hot tea and waited.

'Sure, a few of Bird's calves would have better table manners . . . There was no conversation whatsoever. They just pulled their chairs up to the table and ate with their elbows sticking into my ribs.'

'Who else was on it?'

'Hmmm . . . let's see now, who would you know? Pat Noonan . . . do you know him?'

'The horse trainer? Of course I know him. Sure, doesn't he exercise his horses on a stretch of our land every day of the week.'

'Oh yes, I forgot about that. Well, he was there and we were in the same hotel. He was quite nice . . . actually.'

The sisters looked up from their tea simultaneously. Olive's face became redder and Margaret's eyes narrowed very slightly.

'What do you mean, *nice*? Are we talking about the same fellow? Like a little jockey . . . you'd fit him into your handbag.'

'Yes, that's him . . . a little treasure.'

There was something about her own words then that made Olive want to laugh. She was about to say something about 'goods in small parcels' but could feel a fit of giggles building up and her shoulders gave a little involuntary shake. Margaret was looking very serious, which made it worse.

'I'm tired,' Olive said by way of an apology and as soon as she said it she began to shake with laughter again.

'What on earth is wrong with you, Olive? Were you drinking on the flight?'

Olive took a deep breath. She sighed some of her happiness out and felt a small wad of pain in her chest replace it.

Margaret meant well but she sometimes caused that.

'No. I just had a good time on my trip . . . I had a good laugh, Margaret.'

'And now you're sitting here laughing at nothing,' Margaret answered and gave her eyes another roll upwards.

Olive was suddenly very tired, weary. She didn't really want to provoke her sister now. She could see she was in no mood for it.

Margaret put her cup down on the arm of the chair.

'So you underwent some kind of transformation in Medjugorje.'

Her voice was dry; her mouth seemed to have dust in it.

'I had a bit of fun, that was all.'

Olive looked down into the fire, passing her cup onto a side table without looking at it, suddenly deflated.

Margaret looked at her steadily.

'Don't tell me it was with that Pat Noonan squirt.'

'It was fun.' Olive's voice had lost all of its strength.

'But for what?'

'What is fun for? Is that what you're asking me?'

And here both women were suddenly quiet, Margaret embarrassed by her own question and feeling exposed by it.

49

Her face was red. She got up and lifted the tray and the dirty cups and began to walk to the door. She opened it quietly, changed her mind and came back. She didn't seem to know what to do with herself.

Olive put her head back into the cushions and closed her eyes.

'I only asked if you had a nice holiday.' Margaret was speaking very quietly. 'And instead I find I am trying to have a conversation with a . . . with a laughing eejit.'

She looked around the room seeing ornaments that had belonged to their mother, sheet music, a stack of new books, a tunnel of grey smoke coming up from the fire.

Olive turned her head slowly on the cushions and opened her eyes to look at her sister.

'That's right, Margaret . . . I'm a laughing eejit.'

The words hung in the air and when she turned around again she saw that Margaret was at the door, and their eyes met, their lips giving an involuntary twitch and then there was a snort of laughter from Olive first and then Margaret. Olive laughed hard then and Margaret looked away, struggling with it.

'Things are not so bad when you can have a laugh,' Margaret replied, sighing heavily and coming back to the armchair again.

'Come on now, tell me what Bird has been up to?' Olive asked. 'He sounds like he's in a kind of trance.'

She rose and lifted the tea tray herself and Margaret followed her into the kitchen.

'Oh, indeed he is in a trance. I don't know what's going to become of him.'

'Oh dear God,' Olive said then. 'And when I walked through our yard I saw a cow wearing a pink coat.'

'Lying down?' Margaret asked quickly.

'Not at all – walking around and looking very stylish.'

Olive opened the back door and a cold wind came at them suddenly, hitting them in the face and lifting their hair with it. The sisters glanced once at each other and stepped out in their wellingtons then, their arms linked, braving it together.

8

Midge was lifted by new arms, her head rolling sideways. She could smell wax from a coat and feel some corduroy trim somewhere on it. A single button pressed itself to her cheek. He was a tall man and a strong one, who could lift her up so easily, in a smooth sweeping movement. She could rise as high as the moon and the stars, she thought – but out of the cold wet grass and away from the roaring cattle was enough. For that she was thankful. For that she was very grateful. Her head was a blur of information now, her own life feeling like a carousel. She pulled her knees into herself, her hands joined tightly down near her breasts, and allowed herself to be carried. It was not her father, she was sure of that much – Charlie was not capable of carrying anything unless it was a drink and sometimes he wasn't even fit to carry that.

The heifers came back up the field again, moving in a sudden thumping cloud behind them. The worst part for Midge was that she had not been able to see them. She had been curled up in a ball for hours in the dark – waiting for them to plough into her, to toss her like a doll over their heads and then tear her apart with their thick grass-stained teeth. She could not remember if they were carnivores or herbivores and she had been lying there shaking with the cold and fear and listening for the sound of them, imagining the very worst, their hooves coming closer and closer as they turned up clods of grass and muck and snorted at her with their hot wet breath.

Then they had circled the field in a stampede before returning to the thing in the grass, the white ball of humanity that had sent them into such a frenzy. They had put steam up into the night sky and Midge had remembered the song that she had been trying to think of. She had been humming it and then whistling softly to give herself some kind of courage. But the man who lifted her was not frightened of them. He walked in long smooth strides away from the cattle and they stared at his back and then took off running again. Once he stopped and turned and shouted, 'Whoosh!' to them and another time, 'Go back, you band of eejits' – as if he was talking to a crowd of people or a protest march that had got out of hand.

A small dog was yapping and he seemed to be miles below Midge – like there was a mountain between them. She closed her eyes and made no effort to speak to the man. She felt him climb some steps and then cross a low wall easily without even disturbing her, swinging one leg over and then the other. She had never been lifted like this before, not since she was a baby, and she did not want to break the spell of it. Whoever this was, he was not going to harm her and she felt sure of this. There were no more thoughts left inside her head now. She had never felt so cold and so exhausted. She didn't care to ask where he might be taking her. She closed her eyes tighter as he pushed himself through what seemed to be an overgrown garden, turning around finally and going backwards through a laurel hedge so the branches would not slap her. He came to a tall wooden door with a crescent of stained glass over it. Midge listened as he turned a handle and then stepped into a cold dark place that smelled of damp and dust and echoed around them like a church.

9

Bird carried Midge up the front stairs to the landing with three bedrooms off it. He had considered bringing her into the smaller sitting room and putting her on the couch but the bulb was missing from the main light and it would mean fumbling around in the dark, him and this person who was a stranger to him. On the other hand the bed in the guest room was probably damp as it had not been slept in for months, but when he stood for a moment in the hall and considered his options he decided he could bring her upstairs and put her *on* the bed instead of in it.

On his way back up from the yard he had noticed a commotion in the front paddock. The heifers were running and then stopping and forming a circle around something. He had shone the flashlight into the field and then climbed over the low stone wall and jumped down into a trench. The terrier that had accompanied him started barking, a volley of sounds that was unstoppable, each bark causing its tiny chest to expand. And Bird had seen something white and round then – it was a girl who had curled herself into a ball and she was crying. The dog continued to bark until he shouted at it, 'Shut up, dog,' – and the heifers, on hearing this, took off in a stampede and he hoped they would not run blindly through the fence at the far end taking wire and poles with them. He went down on one knee and lifted the girl up without any real effort. He was used to the brutish weight and strength of his cattle

54

and could hardly feel her in his arms when he began to walk back towards the house again. Lifting her was like retrieving a ball of newspaper from out of the grass or an empty crisp bag that some-one had flung over the ditch. She seemed to lack the bones and meat and muscle of real people. She felt as if she was filled with feathers.

He could sense that she was injured, that something serious had happened. He worried that she had taken a bang to the head. He found a light switch for the landing at the foot of the stairs and began what felt like a long steep climb upwards. He stopped to catch his breath in the return and here the girl opened her eyes and looked up at him. In the half-light cast downwards from the landing, he could only see two dark eyes watching him out of a face caked with muck. He took a small tight breath inwards, suddenly aware of her weight, the warmth of her across his fore-arms and ribs, her small round head nestled into his chest. He had not expected to go out into the field in the dark and to find a young girl lying half dead in it. He had not expected to be called to the O'Neills' house that morning to become a part of a tragedy he would never be able to forget. He had not expected to feel overwhelmed by the life his two sisters led, the comfort and the company they shared. Margaret, who was all dried up somehow – and Olive, who had been so sick, glistening now, like a young one.

He walked the length of the first landing, following a strip of worn red carpet, the dark varnished floorboards on either side of it. He had left the light on in a shed to keep a cow that was calving company – he could see it from the first narrow window. The ceiling was lower in this part of the house and slanted. He had grown up trying to touch different parts of it. He opened a heavy door and laid the girl down on the bed and found the light switch. The shade on the bedside light was pink; a feminine-looking object and it made the room a blush colour, which seemed racy and inappropriate. The girl lay perfectly still with her arms by her sides, not moving and not talking. She only stared up at him, her eyes black and wondering – and he did not say anything but simply stood and looked down at her. The girl began to tremble very slightly then, her thin arms and legs quivering and jumping, her chin moving in small jerking movements, her head beginning to wobble slightly.

Shock, Bird thought, and he covered her up with a blanket. He pulled the heavy shutters over and turned on a big electric heater. He touched a switch on the side of it and three bars began to glow at the foot of the bed. The room was immediately filled with the smell of burning dust. The girl looked up at him again and now she was crying, small panting sounds that didn't seem quite human. He took a deep breath and through the wall of his own exhaustion the sound softened him slightly and he stepped closer to her, wondering what he should do next. She was not much more than a child, he thought.

'You're all right,' he said, but she went on crying, unable to stop herself. He stepped back again and said, 'You're all right . . . Don't be crying . . . No one is going to hurt you . . . You're all right.'

He went downstairs and left the small dog sitting on a chair looking at her. He boiled up the kettle and made tea and added a few spoons of sugar. That would be good for her.

Would she eat a bit of toast with jam? he wondered.

A girl had landed in his field. He had read about such things in books involving spaceships and aliens.

In the bedroom she took the tea, slugging it down and not knowing to put the cup back on the saucer. She ate every crumb of toast too, gobbled it, and her cheeks began to give off some colour.

Bird lifted his hand suddenly and she flinched. It was the slightest of movements but he noticed. He had seen something similar when dealing with nervous animals.

'What happened to you, girl?' he asked finally and he did not really mean that night but in her life up until the moment he had found her. 'What happened to you?' he asked again and no real answer was expected.

The actual happenings in her life were something even he dreaded. He was looking at her now as if she was an object of wonder. And she in her own way understood that his question was rhetorical. He was asking about the runway of her life, the stretch of blue and grey that she had tumbled and bumped and crash-landed on as a baby and as a girl and lately as a young woman.

Bird had asked this question because when he had raised his hand to lift a strand of blood-soaked hair that had become glued down over her eye, she had flinched, because where she came from a raised hand was for hitting someone.

'My father threw me out of the car for fighting with him . . . and it a Sunday,' she said finally and she sounded defiant as if she was expecting her story to be questioned. Her voice was light and girlish but there was a hoarseness to it, which Bird took to be from lying in the wet grass.

'And it a Sunday,' Bird repeated quietly.

The girl looked back at him, her eyes bog-brown now and enormous.

'Is it worse for a father to throw his daughter out of the car on a Sunday? As opposed to on another day?' he asked her then.

His arms were folded across his chest and his blue eyes fixed on her face as if this was a serious question.

'It's not right on any day,' she answered and she seemed confused by the question.

'Did you bang your head when you fell out?'

'I did, of course.'

'I thought as much. Because today is Saturday.'

She stared back at him and then narrowed her eyes slightly.

'What is the point of you sitting there talking about the days of the week and me lying here in this state telling you what happened to me?' she said quickly, and here she stopped abruptly as if she had embarrassed herself.

'Do you know your name?'

'I'm Midge Connors,' and then under her breath, 'as if you didn't know it.'

'I'm Bird Keegan,' he answered. 'And you're like a fighting cock. I'm beginning to see why your father put you out of the car . . . on a *Saturday*.'

That was all he said.

'So you're a brother of Margaret Keegan's?'

Bird looked around the room briefly as if considering his answer.

'What makes you think that? Aren't there Keegans falling out of the trees around here?'

'I'd like to see her falling out of a tree.'

'Do you mean Margaret Keegan the school teacher?

'I do . . . That cow made my life a misery.'

'That sounds like herself – and tell me, do you have any brothers or sisters?'

'I have one sister – who is the oldest – and three brothers, although it doesn't seem like it.'

'And where are they?'

'All over – I haven't seen them in ages. My sister lives in London . . . and one of my brothers – the youngest – is in Manchester, I think. The other two lads are in Australia . . . at least I think they are. They haven't been back to Tullyvin for years.'

Bird took a deep breath, pulling all of this information inside him. He did not want to know about her family at all, he was trying to see if her head was affected by the fall and if he needed to take her to a hospital. He did not ask her any more questions

58

but had offered her his name, plain and ordinary, as some sort of guarantee of safety.

He left the room for a few minutes and then appeared again like a completely different person – without his hat and with a shock of blond hair. He was carrying a small yellow basin and he began to bathe her head with warm water. Midge lay rigid on the bed and wondered why he was being kind to her. She had heard about Bird Keegan, who everyone in the town said was a bit peculiar but he had money and came from 'good stock' – yes, that was what they called it. She, on the other hand, was one of the Connors, which was 'bad stock', and anyone would say, 'She'd steal all 'round her.'

In truth Midge was not beyond lifting something if there was an opportunity and she did not see anything wrong with it.

'What sort of a name is Midge?' he asked her.

'The same sort of name as Bird.'

'And what sort of name is that?'

'A name that's pure stupid – given by people who couldn't care less.'

'Midge Connors.' Bird spoke her name out into the room again and put the bowl of water on the bedside table.

'I was born prematurely – my father said I was like a midget.'

Bird was patting her forehead dry with a towel and unrolling a long wad of white bandage.

'Midge Connors,' she repeated as if he had not heard her, 'and if you know anything about the Connors you'll think I'm going to steal all 'round me.'

'There's not much to lift around here, at least not anything a scrap like you could carry.'

He stood up then and looked down at her.

'It's late and I'm going to bed . . . Try and sleep.'

'And what then? What are you going to do with me?'

Bird stopped for a moment in the doorway, marvelling at

this voice full of life and urgency in a long-empty bedroom.

'I'm not going to do anything with you,' he said plainly. 'In the morning I'll get you home to your mother and father.'

And here the girl looked back at him, her wet hair sleek into her head and then in a fan on the pillow around her.

'My mother and my father,' she repeated, her voice meek and very quiet, the words pressing her down into the hard mattress, the big bed making her seem even smaller.

'Do not leave me here,' she told Bird suddenly. 'Do not.'

And he stopped his walk towards the door and turned again to face her. He glanced at the chair in the corner and then lifted it so that he could sit near her.

'What are you frightened of?' he asked. 'Is it your father? Because he won't get in here.'

'No . . . ' she said quietly and then she began to examine the edge of the sheet in a way that was childish. There was a long pause then as Midge tried to tie her thoughts up sensibly.

'It's so quiet here,' she whispered. 'I'm used to hearing our neighbours talking and in the morning you can even hear their alarm clocks ringing.'

Bird rubbed his eyes and looked closely at the face of his watch.

'It's after two in the morning,' he said finally, 'but I suppose I could run you home now . . . if you're feeling lonely.'

His eyes were beginning to close as he was speaking.

'Is that it?' he asked then, his voice without any interest or energy. 'You're lonely for your mother?'

And Midge, worn out now, was not capable of answering. She had never been inside a house so big. She had never been tolerated for so long by someone with money. For Midge this place without people was also a kind of heaven. Fuck lonely. Lonely was the empty plastic chair at the closed-up petrol station. Lonely was the flood of people leaving the Marian Hall after bingo, all walking as one out into the night air, never expecting to meet anyone, and there was Midge in the middle of the flood, walking against them – that was pure fucking lonely.

She was not ambitious. 'I only want to be treated like a person,' that was what she wanted to say to Bird Keegan.

She could not get over this man who had lifted her up towards the stars, taken her out of the wet as if she was worth something. To her, his arms were the boughs of a big tree, the free wind blowing through her and there was sunshine and leaves moving all around him. Her head had fallen gently into the plaid shirt that he was wearing, a shirt that was as soft to her as down and smelled of nothing. Not the 'cigarette-drink-sweat' sandwich that she had become used to from her father. It was only soap and through it she could feel the warmth of him in an orange haze all around her.

'I am not one bit lonely,' she answered finally and she turned over to sleep as he closed the door behind him. She lay awake then and knew that the next day he would take her back to the familiar dungeon where her father would wait until he was gone and then he'd give her the most awful hammering for telling someone. And she would not even have spoken about him. No. Not to anyone. But she would be given the hammering for being found, for not being invisible, for being noticed. Bird Keegan was silent, gentle, his eyes a still, pale blue – his forehead in furrows that she could have slipped into. His hands were like wide plates, the knuckles round as marbles. Fists, she guessed, were never made from those fingers.

And Bird walked the long landing away from her with his own bed calling out to him. He would fall face down and begin sleeping. The cow and her calf could die and the girl could rob him – the O'Neill boy could haunt him. He would not even get undressed or take his boots off. Bird would sleep and forget about everything.

61

10

The rain on the windows woke Midge. The room was still dark and she thought it was early morning. Her phone told her that it was almost 8am though and there were already four texts from her mother. And now the silence around her was frightening. To her, this house with its solid walls and slanted eaves was a castle. At home there was no distance between any of them and the walls were like paper. She had learned to put her fingers deep into her ears and roll over so she would not hear whatever words her father was saying. It didn't matter if he was a happy drunk or a sour one, she had given up on ever hearing anything good from him. And her mother, poor Bridget – a slop of a woman, a ball of wool unravelling, she was not a real person any more; she was like a shadow who allowed everything to walk through her. In Tostetti's she stood behind a small wooden hatch, her hands red and swollen from the detergent, the brown apron over her bloated stomach. Her hands were the only sign of life as they lifted the egg- and ketchup-stained plates and rinsed them. Now and then Mario asked her to wheel the white tub full of chips up as far as the fryer and she did this like a dray horse allowed out of a stable. Her appearance at these times was always a bit surprising. Once when Midge went in for some chips after school the other girls laughed at Bridget and said she was like a hobbit. And another time Bridget was heard to laugh from behind the counter, a deep thudding laugh, 'Huh huh huh,' and one of the customers said, 'What's that fat fuck laughing at?'

And Midge had sat very still and said nothing.

What could she say?

'That fat fuck is my mother.'

And when her schoolfriends laughed she stayed quiet then too and pretended to read the menu. Midge could not say anything to defend the woman who was a fat fuck and a hobbit and who was not supposed to be seen by people, a woman whose idea of a thrill was to roll the plastic trolley full of chips up as far as the fryer. No, Midge could not do much to help her now. But the hurt Midge felt on those days was like a scald that went through her, causing her skin to shrivel. It was not easy to hear people laughing at her mother.

Her phone was on the nightstand at Red Hill with one bar left on the battery.

'*Where are you???*' her mother had asked.

And

'*ARE YOU OK???*'

And

'*MIDGE???*'

And then –

'*Midge going out of my mind with worry.*'

And here in this strange, silent house Midge began to miss her and she punched in a quick reply – and her mother answered instantly.

'*Am fine Mam. Sorry – Will be home soon. Where is Charlie?*'

'*Thank God you're all right – don't know where he is.*'

Midge turned on the small pink lamp and looked around her. The bed was wide and there was a green canopy hanging over it. It was like a kind of tent and she was inside it and there were curtains on the windows with green and yellow flowers – and behind them, big wooden shutters which blocked any light from getting in. There was an armchair near a small fireplace and she could see that the bars on the electric heater were still lit and red. She stepped down onto a threadbare Persian rug and stood there looking. On the mantelpiece were an elegant blue jug, a black and white photograph of three children and a thick book by someone called George Eliot. This was how other people lived, she realized, they wrapped themselves up and built thick walls that would comfort and protect them. They had discovered – a long time ago – that true luxury was to escape other people.

There was a long mirror in the door of the wardrobe and here Midge saw herself framed suddenly. She was wearing a big pair of men's pyjamas and she could not remember ever getting into them. They had pink and white stripes and smelled like freshly washed cotton. There was a bandage across her forehead; small speckles of blood dry on it. Her knees too were stiff with cotton gauze which Bird Keegan must have cut and then wrapped around her. She sat on the bed again and tried to recall what had happened. She remembered Bird finding her and how she had not been afraid of him. She remembered his peculiar way of making light of things – and her nearly dying. She remembered that he was a brother of Margaret Keegan's and had pretended not to be.

Only last week Midge had run into her at the post office.

'Well, miss,' that was how her old teacher spoke to her.

And Margaret Keegan had changed since her retirement. Her face was no longer as smooth as a milk jug but looked like she had been left out in a storm, her skin all lined and twisted. The hands that had attended to Midge were never smooth though, that much she could remember, they were quick and rough and there had never been much kindness falling from them.

Bird himself had seemed worn out by everything. She only remembered small pictures of what had happened after he had carried her to this bedroom – the softness of the mattress under her, feeling herself sinking and wondering if she was finally dying. She had dreamed that Miss Keegan – with her sharp eyes and her mouth in a furious little line – came then and looked down over her. Midge had tried to get away and had made a sudden dash for the door and was lifted gently back onto the bed again. It was Bird who had laid her down then as if she was a newborn baby.

When Midge had turned to look at Margaret in the post office she had seen a sudden hot flush rising up from under her jumper. Miss Keegan was going through the change now and people said that could drive women crazy. One woman outside Tullyvin was said to have backed a tractor over her husband and then started laughing.

Midge lay back in bed again and let these thoughts circle her. She heard a door opening and closing somewhere in the distance and then a tractor starting and she listened carefully as the sound faded away from her. She was hungry and wondered if she could find the kitchen and make some breakfast for herself. She went to the window and unhooked the wooden shutters and was surprised to find that the sun was high enough now and glaring. She pulled a blanket around her shoulders and, opening the heavy bedroom door, she began walking.

11

It was just after nine on Sunday morning when the sergeant called to Tostetti's and asked for Bridget Connors. Bridget, who was tired from being on her feet, was cleaning up now with her coat on over her apron. She had worked through the night, feeling half crazy with worry for her daughter. But then shortly after eight Midge had sent her a text saying that she was fine. When she got home they would have chips and fried eggs for their breakfast as a kind of celebration. Bridget needed a drink more than anything but Midge had told her once not to drink before eating her breakfast.

Now isn't that a grand piece of advice to take from your own daughter? Bridget thought.

She was not capable of cooking but at least she could open up the parcels of newspaper and fill their kitchen with the warm smell of salt and vinegar.

'Bridget – I'm afraid I have some . . . troubling news for you.'

And here Bridget looked up at him and then continued mopping.

'I'm sorry to say that Charlie's car was found in the lake early this morning. I was just down there . . . with Father Conlon.'

And there was silence then apart from the swish of the mop beside her. In her clouded mind she was putting pieces of this tableau together.

'A Toyota?' she enquired casually.

'A Toyota, yes . . . and there were a few . . . well, you know yourself, cigarette butts and a few . . . bottles . . . floating about.'

Her silence, her calm reserve seemed to unnerve him then. He became awkward in his big high-vis jacket and began tapping his nails on the restaurant counter. Mario stopped what he was doing and turned to watch the scene unfolding.

'Was he a bit depressed, Bridget?' Sergeant Brennan ventured then.

'No more than any of us,' she answered.

She twisted the mop inside the bucket and the steam, filled with bleach, made her eyes water.

'Or maybe he had a drop taken . . . Rocky said he left the hotel with Midge yesterday afternoon at around four . . . Did he go home then or what did he do?'

'How would I know? When I was in here working.'

She turned away and went on with the cleaning. The information regarding her husband was still sinking in and as yet it made no sense to her.

'Was he drinking at the hotel yesterday afternoon?' he asked her.

'Yesterday, today and tomorrow,' Bridget answered, finally setting the mop down and turning to face him.

What was it this vulture wanted from her? Tears and a bit of fainting? she wondered. After the life she'd lived it took more than this news to shake her.

'Well,' he began again softly. 'There was no one in the car, it seems. It came up full of water . . . so it looks like he saved himself and went off somewhere.'

And here, Bridget's heart went sliding.

Not even this one thing, she told Charlie silently, could you do for me.

'We were concerned that he might have . . . well, you know.'

67

'Might have what?' Bridget was buttoning her coat around her, a wide beige article, shapeless and floating.

'Tried to do away with himself,' the sergeant said flatly.

She wanted to laugh at this expression. Instead she took two bags of chips from Mario and put them into her coat pockets. As she walked through the door she said goodbye to Mario and he nodded. She turned the sign so that it read 'Closed' and the sergeant followed her.

'You might let me know when you see him, Bridget. I'd appreciate a call . . . There's the car itself which is still at the lake, for one thing . . . so I'd like a word with him.'

'Oh, we'd all like a word with him, Sergeant,' Bridget answered without looking up at him.

Outside in the frosty air with the lights going out one by one in the restaurant behind her, Bridget turned then and faced him. She took a deep breath and tried to see off this giant eye that seemed to be following her. She felt something shift inside her then, a sudden bolt of anger sliding through her. When she got home she would have a few drinks to give her strength and she would finally stand up to him. She would wait for Charlie to stagger through the door and she would have the empty bottle – and it broken – ready in her hand for him.

'Of course he didn't kill himself,' she said, and her voice was dull with the disappointment. 'Charlie did not try to "top himself" or "do away with himself" . . . as you call it. The man I am married to . . . would not have been that useful or that intelligent . . . or that *kind* to me and my daughter.'

'Do you know where he is now?'

'He probably spent the night at Imelda Conroy's – he only comes home to me for breakfast.'

The bags of chips were hot in her coat pockets, their steam and vinegar making damp circles on the polyester.

'And where is Midge?' the sergeant asked. 'I'd like a word with her too – I'd like to know what happened yesterday between herself and her father.'

'I don't know where she is either.'

Bridget heard her own voice breaking through the cold morning air and Sergeant Brennan looked at her. There were no more questions from him and the truth was – on this Sunday morning in November – she did not know the whereabouts of her husband or even one of her five children.

'Can I give you a lift to Emmet Road?'

'No thanks, Sergeant – I need the fresh air.'

There was enough trouble in Bridget's world without being driven through the town in the squad car for everyone to see her.

12

Bird was sitting in the half-light of the kitchen when Midge eventually found him.

She had discovered a bathroom at the end of the landing, a strange place with a deep copper bath and tall narrow taps that were dripping. There was a swirl of green inside the porcelain sink, the same in the toilet – a high white throne with a wooden seat and flowers painted inside the bowl of it. She found a bar of rose-scented soap which pleased her. She loved soap, every kind, and had grown up without much of it. Without even thinking she dropped the dry bar into her pyjama pocket. A second door from this room led to some back stairs and a big high-ceilinged bedroom. She recognized this to be his, the bed unmade, shoes thrown and lying sideways, books in a stack on the floor, a round-faced alarm clock standing on them. Midge had stood in this doorway finding the sight of his things, a vest on the back of the chair, a wet towel on the bed, unnerving – and she backed out again. There was a watch on the dressing table and out of some old habit she considered taking it. She had not stolen anything for weeks but there it was and it seemed to be waiting. She lifted it up, felt the disc on the back made smooth by his wrist, and she remembered how it had felt to be lifted up from that field and she returned it. When she went back to the bathroom and used the other door she found herself on the landing again with the red

70

carpet and the three tall windows that looked out over the farm-yard. From here she could see the trees bending at the foot of the mountain and then the wind seemed to rise suddenly and hit the glass in gusts that could break them. The sky was blue and clear but she could already feel the cold of it. There would be white waves on the lake and still Mrs Doherty from the Glen would go out swimming because the doctor told her it would help her with the depression. The yard was a clean rectangle of cobblestones with a neat row of sheds surrounding it. A door opened then and she saw him, daylight presenting him to her again so that she knew now that he was real and not some fantasy. His red hat was pulled down over his ears and he looked like a clown in it. He was carrying two buckets of water – something farmers always seemed to be doing.

He looked up then and saw her at the window. He put one bucket down and the small dog appeared suddenly and went up on hind legs to drink from it. The sun was glaring and he shielded his eyes and watched her. Midge had a sudden impulse to hide then but instead she lifted her small hand to the glass and placed it there. It was not a wave as such but in her mind a kind of hello, to remind him that she was still in his house in case he had for-gotten. He was odd enough for anything – she had already heard that about him. He lifted his chin quickly in response and then picked up the bucket again and began walking to a shed close to the house. Midge followed the landing to the front stairs and went down, wondering if she might meet him now, and she realized that her heart was beating hard and hurting and that she was frightened of what he would say to her.

There was the square hallway from the previous night; the old rocking horse without a tail, a fireplace, the row of croquet mallets. A door opened into a dark sitting room that smelled damp. A second door opened into the kitchen and he was sitting at one end of the table now, waiting for her in his coat and wellingtons.

'Put this on you,' he said and he handed her a long green coat.

'Have you anything for your feet?' he asked then and they both looked down at them together. She had small feet. She knew that. People who were from good stock had big feet. He walked in wide strides into a hall near the back stairs and came back with a pair of small-looking wellingtons.

'There's probably a leak in these. But they'll do you.'

A cow in a nearby shed had just finished calving. She was lying flat with her neck stretched out and a bull calf had been pushed out behind her. Midge stood, thin-legged, in the doorway and watched in fascination.

Life, she thought. Life being made, life happening.

She was not in any way squeamish. Bird was rubbing slime from the calf and blowing into his wet ears to revive him. The blood made the straw stick together in clumps. The cow issued a low moan, saliva dripping, her tongue coming out sideways. And through the wide-open door Midge could see that the sky was still the bright surprising blue of a winter's morning. There were cypress trees waving at her. She had no watch and did not know what time it was now. While they were all sleeping, a world of things had happened.

'Get another bucket of water,' Bird said suddenly.

His voice was different from the night before – there was no deliberation, no silence – only panic and guilt caused by his own late sleeping. Midge found a bucket in the yard near a tap and came running with it. She wondered if she had found the right sort of bucket and if the water should be cold or hot. The water splashed down into it, a drum-beat sound against the metal. Bird met her in the yard and grabbed it from her hand. She ran after him, sliding in the boots, a small child again. He threw the bucket into the calf's face in a way that seemed merciless, and waited. The animal lifted his head then and shook

72

it, his ears doing a seesaw thing on either side of his head.

'Good,' Bird said – a different sort of man now again. 'He'll be all right . . . but we'll have to feed him. There's milk substitute in the scullery.'

Midge stood still and looked down at the cow and there was no sound from her at all now.

'What about the cow?' she asked quietly.

'The abattoir,' he answered.

Midge did not know yet that a small crane would come and pull that cow upwards by a hoof onto a flatbed truck. That it would be skinned, its skull left bare, every part of it used for something. Midge did not know what the knacker's yard was. She didn't know that in a short space of time the cow would be stiff and cold and the orphaned calf in a shed of its own.

'An abattoir,' she repeated in wonder, her eyes shining for the first time since they met. She thought it was one of those places for exploring the night sky, for watching the stars. Bird began to shuffle the calf out through the door.

'I bought a new bull last year and he's a disaster,' he told her.

'Why is the bull a disaster?'

'He's the wrong breed – the calves are too big for the heifers. Some dying before they're born and the ones that are born killing their mothers.'

Midge looked back at him steadily, thinking about everything he had just said.

'That sounds like hell on earth,' she told him. He glanced down at the cow who was no longer breathing, her eyes fixed and staring.

'That's exactly what it is,' he told him.

73

13

Bird washed his hands at the sink and watched Midge as she sat quietly at the kitchen table. It was nearly ten o'clock and they had still not eaten any breakfast. He saw now that her hair was red and not black – and that she was small and frail-looking. Truthfully, he had no understanding of her – no more than if she had landed in from another planet. She had seemed easier to manage when she was horizontal. Now that she was up and walking around he did not know what to do with her. She picked at the bandages that he had put on her knees and forehead and elbows. She was still wearing a pair of his pyjamas. Her own rags were in a small plastic bag hanging on the back door in case she went off without them. The idea of her leaving clothes in his house was also unsettling. She told him that she was hungry. Bird was still wearing his coat and hat in the kitchen and the keys to the jeep were in the pocket. He wanted to take her home and be finished with her.

'There's a phone in the hall,' he said to her. 'You should call your mother.'

'I sent her a text earlier,' she answered quickly. 'She's finished work and she knows I'm all right so there's no need for me to call her.'

Bird stood and looked at her, absorbing another detail of this small life outside of his. He was, in his own way, curious about her and her mother. There was no point in telling her to call her father. She would call him a 'bad bastard' again, the words triggered by any mention of him.

He made a pot of thick porridge and ladled it into two bowls for them. He did not know what else to give her. She pulled a loose strand of hair back behind her ear and stared down into it.

'What is it?' she asked.

'It's porridge.'

Bird's voice was flat when he answered and yet he could feel the slight movement of a smile on his lips. What sort of a woman was this, who didn't know what porridge was? His spoon floated over his bowl as he poured the milk from a jug. She would be used to seeing the carton on the table.

'Do you have any cornflakes?'

'What are cornflakes?'

She smiled at him then and ducked her head a bit as she began to use the tip of her spoon to take tiny scoops. He could see that she was hungry enough to eat anything. He looked at the clock and wanted to take her home. It occurred to him that Sean Weldon might stick his big head in the door as he was inclined to do on a Sunday morning, or worse, Olive or Margaret.

'What are you looking at?' he asked her then.

He was slicing up a loaf of hard brown bread and spreading butter on it. He could feel her eyes on him and he didn't like it.

'I was just wondering about you,' she said and here their eyes met briefly. Bird stirred the tea and poured a mug for her. He slid the milk jug across the table.

He folded his arms and drank his tea, finding the air between them a bit thick and awkward. He ate his bread and took slugs of tea and wanted to be finished with this breakfast.

'What's your real name?'

'Bird.'

'No, I mean what did your mam and dad call you at first?'

75

'They called me Bird.'

She was nibbling on the bread like a mouse and fidgeting about, looking around the kitchen, her eyes settling briefly on the ladles that hung over the range, the copper kettle and the assortment of mismatched chairs around the table.

'What's *your* real name?' he asked finally.

'Margaret.'

'Margaret is a good solid name.'

'I've always hated it – and Midge is not much better.'

Bird nodded his head slowly to this and glanced at the clock again, willing the girl to eat up so that his house could be as it always was, quiet and empty.

Midge was looking at his hair, her eyes hovering over it, studying the blond colour of it now that he had taken his hat off.

'Can I ask you a question?'

Bird gave a sigh and glanced at his watch.

'It's time for you to be getting on home now,' he said, although he said the words gently to her.

She asked for her clothes and went into the hallway to dress herself. When she came back he saw that she was in tatters, the tights like a spider's web around her legs, the buttons gone in the blouse and it half opened. The sight of her shocked Bird so that he stepped back a bit. He was reminded of her ordeal again but more startling was the glimpse of two plump breasts in a black bra which he had not before noticed. A black bra – somewhere inside his head of curls, these words were repeated. He went grabbing for some of his own clothes that were hanging near the range and the long green coat and he handed them to her.

'Here, you better take these,' he told her, 'and cover yourself up.'

The coat had been a good one once, made from heavy wool and lined in silk, but it was old and out of fashion and it went down to her feet.

'But it's a good coat.'

'It's an old one of Margaret's . . . take it,' and he pushed it into her hands, not wanting to see the state of her. In this house that was made for a man and his dog, her milk-white skin seemed to rattle the windows. He went outside and started the jeep. And Midge put on the coat and climbed up into the front seat beside him.

'You'll need to go into Tullyvin – we're on the far side of it.'

'Right so,' he said softly.

They moved together through the wet narrow roads with the jeep slowing on tighter bends. Heavy drops fell from the trees and made a rapping sound on the metal roof. Main Street was quiet, the blinds at Tostetti's closed as if everyone was still sleeping.

'That's where my mam works,' she told him and Bird noticed how a small stitch appeared between her eyebrows then. It was a strange thing for Bird to witness this girl who had her own mysterious reasons for talking to him.

'What was it you wanted to ask me?' he said suddenly but she looked at him blankly.

'In the kitchen . . . you wanted to ask me a question and I hurried you out.'

Bird himself did not know for sure why he was doing this. He had hurried her out because he wanted to get rid of her – but now that they were away from the house and the farm, he felt safer, less claustrophobic, and he had a sudden interest in hearing more from her.

'Oh,' Midge said softly and she seemed to relax suddenly, leaning her head back for a moment in her seat. 'I was going to ask you what age you are,' and here she gave a small, embarrassed laugh.

'I was looking at your hair,' she went on, 'and there's no grey in it at all – and thinking that your eyes looked like they are older than your face . . . like they belong to someone else.'

77

'Someone else?' Bird repeated and he frowned through the windscreen. 'Well, I have never been told that before,' he said and he could hear the amusement in his own voice.

'The eyes are mine,' he told her then, 'and I'll be thirty-one next week.'

Midge blushed then for no particular reason – and yet the very thought of the previous night and now this peculiar conversation in the jeep were both mortifying.

'Do you want to know what age I am?' she asked and her eyes were brighter and full of mischief.

'A man is not supposed to ask,' was his reply and he frowned again as he wondered where exactly this piece of banter had come from.

Midge continued watching him for a moment.

'I took a bar of soap from your bathroom. Stole it . . . you might say.'

Bird's eyebrows moved slightly and he glanced at his wing mirror. He could see an ambulance off in the distance, gathering speed as it left the town and joined the motorway – the fluorescent yellow, the blue of its lights, too sudden on this Sunday morning in November.

'I put the soap in my pocket,' Midge was saying, her voice sounding like it was on the brink of laughter. He wondered briefly if she had taken anything else and realized that he didn't care.

'You're welcome to it,' he told her.

'I'm twenty-one,' she said then and he took a deep breath and pretended not to hear her. 'Nearly twenty-two.'

The bell was ringing for second mass and one or two people were moving towards the church, looking cold and reluctant.

'Here,' she told him quickly. 'Stop anywhere here – that's my house – that one there.'

Bird parked close to a gate and didn't turn off the engine.

'Well, thanks,' Midge said but it was as if she had already gone somewhere.

He leaned over then and pushed the passenger door open for her.

'There you are now,' he said and he settled himself back into his own seat and looked through the window as he waited for her to get out.

Bird frowned into the glaring sunlight and pulled the visor down with a flap of his hand. He had never owned a pair of sunglasses in his life. He made an effort to direct his thoughts now to the day ahead – the new calf that needed a bottle, the call to the knacker's yard, the shed roof that needed to be fixed, his sisters who were coming up to him for Sunday lunch. And yet these thoughts ran away from him again like rain on glass, the wind pushing them off into different directions. Midge Connors looked like a sixteen-year-old. This odd thought suddenly presented itself. He had understood her to be a girl taking shelter in his house. A girl who was in trouble at every turn, a girl young enough to be at war with her father, and instead he had taken a woman in, a young woman, but a woman nonetheless. He swung the jeep around and returned to Red Hill and made every effort to forget about her.

II
The Kindness of Some People

14

There was war in the wind that Sunday – that was how Pat Noonan saw it. Blood falling with the rain – people broken, his own heart scattered. He was only off the plane from Medjugorje the day before when he heard about the O'Neill boy, and then the next day that an ambulance had rushed Bridget Connors into the hospital. She had been attacked in her own home on Sunday morning when half the town was at mass – and the news had flattened everyone. It silenced the people of Tullyvin and went to the bones of Pat Noonan. He was a man with a very soft heart anyway, which he had a habit of leaving open. More than anything now he wanted to see Olive Keegan. It was only Sunday – he had seen her yesterday but since then he had not been eating or sleeping. To everyone in Tullyvin he was the horse trainer, a small man with bow legs and a bad back from breaking the ponies belonging to spoilt children. His hands were warped from pulling the bridle. He had broken most of the bones in his body. But on that Sunday he would visit Olive Keegan even though she had not given any indication that she wanted to see him. His want, though, and he was full of it, was enough for the two of them.

What they had shared in Medjugorje was what you might call 'a passing thing' but they were both well into their forties and at this point in their lives, when good things came along, you at least made a snatch at them. He could not stop thinking about Olive and the warmth that she had given to him. He had worn khaki shorts when he was with her and brown leather sandals and they had walked the dry, narrow streets seeing each other's corns and pretending they were praying. And all they had wanted during that last day and night and morning was to be together. She had ignored him on the aeroplane then, cruel and not like her and yet all the more exciting. Three rows back from her seat in the plane he had devoted himself completely to her.

Pat left her to unpack her things and spend time with her sister and then got up and dressed himself and went to see her. He dressed carefully, taking a scalding bath and washing his bald head until it was shining. He shaved and brushed his nails and then his teeth until he was nearly spitting blood with the water. There was every chance that she would close the door on him. Women were changeable and could be very peculiar. It was, after all, a holiday romance – but his want for her had him lit up from the inside like a lantern. He considered driving but the idea frightened him. The sound of the car's engine and its wheels on her gravel could offend her. She might be sleeping. When he thought of her now, he remembered her round face, plump and full of good nature, and other things stayed with him – the softness of her arms when she put them around him, the strength in her legs from swimming which was 'her first love in life' – that was what she told him. And that night there were many secrets whispered between them. How he loved the horses and believed that they were sacred creatures and yet how at night when the world around him was quiet and the last of the ponies had been collected he would sit at his small kitchen table and by the light of a single lamp he would begin to write poetry.

'About what?' she had asked him.

'Things that move me,' he had told her.

He wrote about the morning light, the sound of hooves on the grass, and now – Olive Keegan. Here she had laughed and shaken the bed for the two of them. He loved her then and told her, his head buried in her bosom, and she had caressed him with such kindness.

'Sure I know, I know,' she told him and she shrugged then which suggested that they were two hopeless cases, their love doomed somehow and yet it was there to be enjoyed, every last second of it. She told him about her sister, Margaret, who she loved fiercely but felt sorry for because she had had her heart broken into 'smithereens' when she was a young one – so that there was, as she put it, 'no heart left at all' inside her. She told him about Bird, the only boy in the family and the youngest, who was moulded by their father and their mother to be a farmer.

'There was nothing as important as the farm to my parents . . . oh, the land, the land,' and she had whispered this out over the hum of a fan next to them.

'Bird is getting odd now,' that was what she told him, 'no good with people.' She said he was 'a fine man', but that he kept 'his good and gentle nature too well hidden . . . unlike you', and then she began laughing. And Pat had put his arms around her again and pulled her towards him so that they began to make love to each other. That was how it was, the love smoothing out the rough memories that were being stirred up between them.

He didn't bring the car but brought out his own hunter, Tomas, the chestnut, a beautiful animal, his noble head arching in the bridle, delighted to be taken out into the fields and down towards the lake again. To dispel his own nerves Pat kicked with his heels and released the bridle and they shot out over the hill and galloped along the crest of it and this was how Olive herself saw him from the kitchen window. Pat headed for the lane that led to the lodge. He would not use the short cut and take the horse through the orchard and jump the wall and perhaps ride into her clothesline. He would go right to the front door and be respectable. Of course, there was a chance she would do that thing that women were famous for. Full of admiration for him one minute and then like the Snow Queen herself answering the door to him. But Pat would go to the Keegan sisters' front door and lift the knocker. He would risk the rejection. He knew that, as far as many people in Tullyvin were concerned, Olive Keegan was a good few steps above him. But what he lacked in land and breeding, he made up for in pride and courage – that was what he told himself on the way there anyway. So she might close the door on him. She might freeze him in a way that would prevent him from ever feeling warm again. But this was still the Olive Keegan he had spent a day and a night with in Medjugorje and during that time no one else had existed for either of them. He had seen her bare toes, the creases behind her knees, her breasts, God be praised for them – he would risk rejection; she was worth every shard of it.

He took the horse down the long driveway that led first to Bird's house and then around the old sheds and coach houses to the second lane that circled the mountain and the lake and led to the lodge and the two sisters. And it was at this point that Pat smelled war in the wind. He glanced into Bird's front room and saw Margaret Keegan sitting bolt upright in a hardback chair facing the windows. There was a fire blazing in the hearth. The young brother had his arms folded and he was in an armchair beside her. There was tension in that room, enough to blow the glass out of the windows and cause the fire to roar up the chimney. From his place in the warm saddle Pat could sense it and he was only glad that Olive was not in there with them. He took the horse down through the yard then as he had often done before, saluting Sean who said, 'Not a bad day, Pat.' It was not unusual for him to exercise his horse on the long green flat in the upper field. The Keegans, being good neighbours, allowed this. He had seen both sisters almost every day since he was a boy and he had always had a soft spot for Olive. As a child he only knew that Margaret frightened him.

There was a light on in Olive's kitchen. The horse's hooves could be heard on the cobbles, a pretty sound and he hoped that she might like it. The horse continued moving until they were near the front door and Pat, more from habit than courage, swung down out of the saddle and stood beside it. He tied the horse to the fence and waited for a moment, feeling lost and suddenly in tremendous danger. What right did he have to be here? The sight of his own reflection in her windows was already a disgust to him and yet he wanted to see her, that was all, just so he would know he was awake and no longer dreaming. He saw the knocker, a cast-iron hand, creepy in its own way, the little knuckles turned for rapping, and then the door opened and Olive's face came around it.

'Come in, Pat,' she said simply and turned away, leaving the door open for him. She did not seem pleased or displeased to see him. She was like a woman who was bringing a man in to fit a new carpet. In the kitchen she stood near the counter with her back to him. He had never been in this kitchen before and could see now that the room was all about her – the floral tablecloth and the cream-painted chairs around it, the old dresser from Red Hill that she had painted a bright blue and then placed all that nice crockery inside it.

'Wasn't it awful about the O'Neill boy, Pat?' she said, clasping her hands together. 'And did you hear about that poor Bridget Connors? They're saying that her husband attacked her – and did you hear that it was *his* car that was pulled from our lake only this morning?'

'I did not,' he answered, his eyes looking into hers, unblinking, searching.

'Oh Pat,' she sighed suddenly. 'I'm just sitting here feeling awful upset about everything. That poor woman and what he went home and did to her – although he's denying everything of course. I didn't even want to go up to Bird's house for the Sunday dinner. I couldn't face sitting there with him and Margaret.'

And here Pat moved towards her now, feeling that the time was right for being friendly. And he gently held his arms out so that she could either look out over his head through the window or walk into them. She chose the latter and reminded him for a moment of a pony that was loose and confused and had spotted the stable door left conveniently open.

She seemed to melt in his arms, the faintest of sighs being squeezed out of her.

'And we should not be at this carry-on,' she said, her voice not completely serious, the words spoken into the wool of his jumper.

'And why not?' he asked into her hair.

She took a deep breath. 'Because, Pat Noonan . . . it is *ridiculous*. We are . . . being . . . a little ridiculous.'

'I don't think so. And if this is ridiculous then . . . I plan on staying ridiculous.'

'I told Margaret what happened.'

'Oh,' Pat answered and the idea of that gave him a feeling that his own skin might slide off him. 'What did she say?' he asked. 'Let me guess . . . wished us well . . . she was delighted.'

'She nearly had a conniption.'

They stood together in silence and then began laughing.

Pat kissed the top of her fair head, feeling the warmth from her forehead and her own sweet scent came back to him. She turned up her face and they began kissing.

'When will she be back?' asked Pat, his eyes narrowing a little and full of humour.

'Pat Noonan . . . you're a cheeky article.'

'How long do we have?' he asked again.

'I'd say a good two hours . . . three if she falls asleep at the fire.'

88

15

Bird had forgotten to buy the roast. He was pacing the kitchen and when he looked at the clock he saw that it was close to midday and too late for any kind of shopping. The big Tesco would be open but the meat was not good there. Margaret was on her way already, her quick strides breaking through the long grass of the upper field, small branches being crushed underneath her. She would be carrying a basket with peeled potatoes and a turnip, some gravy congealed in a blue enamel jug. If Olive was with her she would be holding an apple tart and some cooling custard, as thin as milk, the way they all liked it. As children their father and mother had created an event around Sunday lunch and the girls continued the tradition, always up at Bird's house at the same table they had shared with their parents. There were fish fingers in his freezer, which would have pleased him, but he did not want Margaret to discover this particular secret. He would tell her straight out that there was no meat for the dinner and that they would have to make do with potatoes and gravy. But what was a Sunday dinner without a roast, she would say, and she would not be able to stand it.

Sean Weldon appeared then with a cooked chicken. He had seen Bird pacing the kitchen with his hands red from rummaging in the freezer.

'Jaysus, Bird,' he announced in his low, deep voice. 'You can't give Margaret Keegan a fish finger.'

'I suppose not,' Bird said. He eyed the chicken and wanted to take it from him.

'How much for that cooked bird?' he asked.

'There's great value down at the filling station – and they have Scotch eggs as well.'

'I'll give you five euros for it.'

Sean looked at him and began laughing.

'Well, I'll do it to save you from your sister,' and he handed the bag to him.

Bird could feel the warmth of the chicken in his hands as he put it into the oven. He peeled a note from his wallet and when a bolt moved on the gate outside, the two men glanced at each other.

'She's here,' Sean whispered, hunching up his shoulders and pretending to be frightened.

'Like clockwork,' Bird answered.

Sean stood around the kitchen until Bird said, 'You better be going on now,' and the workman went off laughing.

Margaret came through the back door, her hand finding the hook for her coat and then stopping, as she smelled the chicken.

'I have a chicken in the oven,' Bird said.

'Did you not get a roast of beef?'

'They didn't have any.'

'They didn't have any? A butcher without a roast of beef . . . well, now, I've heard everything. Here,' she said, setting the basket down. 'Olive made an apple tart for you and some custard. She's not coming until later . . . she's too tired after all that flying.'

Bird sat down near the range and pretended to read the Sunday paper. Behind the pages and the smell of fresh print he closed his eyes, glad that Margaret seemed tired too and not in any mood for talking.

'Did Sean tell you about that poor woman who was rushed to the hospital this morning?' she asked suddenly.

'He didn't, no.'

'Bridget Connors. She lives on Emmet Road – I used to teach their daughter at school . . . She was as wild as a March hare.'

Upstairs the blankets were still tumbled in the guest room, the door swinging open as if a wind had swept through the house while he was sleeping. He had heard about the car in the lake from Sean and remembered the blue lights of the ambulance early that morning. And the mention of Midge now sent a strange nervousness through Bird, a feeling that was previously unknown to him. The phone would be ringing, Sean had told him that too, because the Guards would be down at the lake looking at the car again – and like all the locals Sean was fat with this new talk and gossip, enjoying taking the story apart and then putting a new version together, looking forward to the telling and re-telling over a pint of stout later.

And now Bird sat behind the paper, wishing he could close his eyes and sleep through all of it. He had helped the girl because he had had no choice but now there was a feeling of deep sand around him with his long body being pulled slowly into it.

Margaret and Bird sat facing each other across the broad oak table. She had set it carefully with the good silver and the plates with the pink willow pattern. They had a small glass of wine each and she didn't remark on the chicken. When Bird retrieved it from the oven it seemed orange in colour and quite tired-looking. She didn't say a word but covered it in gravy and ate it down with the mashed potatoes. Finally she began to talk and Bird, who had enjoyed this shared silence, sliced his chicken and poked it about with his fork.

'Olive decided to rest,' she announced. 'We were out in the boat earlier and she's tired . . . from the *rowing*.'

At this she looked over at Bird with one eyebrow raised and he returned her gaze, unsure of what was coming next.

'You will not believe what she got up to on the . . . *pilgrimage*.'

91

Bird chewed the chicken, willing it to moisten and go down his neck.

'This chicken is like a piece of cloth,' he answered and he registered her annoyance at this interruption.

'Did you not hear what I said?' she asked.

Margaret did not want to talk either but she felt this was something that needed to be out in the open and his lack of interest was not helping.

'She had a fling, I suppose you might call it,' and the words seemed to make a sour taste in Margaret's mouth. 'And you will not believe who with . . .'

'Pat Noonan,' Bird said flatly. He was scraping some potatoes onto his fork and didn't look up at her.

There was a long silence then as Margaret absorbed this.

'And how do you know that?'

'He's always liked her. He might as well get on with it.'

'What are you saying? You're talking through your hat, Bird.'

'Margaret – why do you think he's exercising that horse of his on that upper field?'

'Because he needs a long, flat stretch.'

Here Bird met her eyes finally and smiled.

'He has plenty of flat land himself.'

'So, do you think that's why he went on the pilgrimage?'

'Of course it was. Sure, he hasn't been in a church since his First Communion.'

And suddenly Bird wanted to laugh – something that had not happened in months. He looked across the table then and saw his sister's face. She was not disgusted any more. She was frightened, and he felt himself soften.

'She's not going to marry him, Margaret,' he said quietly.

'Of course she isn't.' She nearly shouted the words back at him.

You'll always have her, he wanted to say, knowing that

Margaret's fear of being left was prodding at the back of all of this. But he couldn't say it. That would be too much for the two of them. They had all grown up surrounded by fields and trees that were shaped by the wind. In his mind the land was not a place for people who felt things deeply – and anyone who feared being on their own had no business farming, no business going near it.

Bird opened a tin of peaches and cut two slices from a block of ice cream.

'Are you not going to slice up that apple tart Olive made?' Margaret asked him.

'I'm not in the mood for apple tart today.'

'Oh I see,' she answered, her face getting red again. 'You're in a tinned-peach sort of mood today, are you?'

'That's exactly it, Margaret – it's a tinned-peach kind of day.'

He placed the bowl in front of her and sat down and began eating. He had shared many moments like this with Margaret, where he sat down knowing she was annoyed with him and wondering if she was about to boil over.

'Have you had that new vet out yet?' Margaret asked casually then, the ice cream having a calming effect on her.

'I have. A useless eejit.'

She carved small spoons from her ice cream as she had always done, trying to make the most of it.

'I suppose you heard who his father is,' Bird asked.

Margaret let the ice cream sit on her tongue, feeling it melt. And here Bird wished he did not have to mention this. And yet it would be better if she heard it from him and not some busybody down in the post office.

'Tom Geoghan,' Bird said and he chopped at the peach with his spoon and then forced himself to look up at her.

'Tom Geoghan is his *father*,' Margaret said.

Her eyes were on the table and Bird knew that the very mention of his name was still enough to cause a hurt in her.

'It's a fact. Tom's moved back here and bought a practice in Glenview.'

'In Glenview,' she repeated.

'His wife died suddenly – apparently.'

Margaret looked up but didn't say anything.

'She was out dancing at her niece's hen party and suddenly put her hands on her head and said, "oh, my head, my head" and down she went – bump! A brain haemorrhage . . . died instantly.'

'And why do you think I would want to know about that?'

'I don't know. But it's unusual around here, I suppose . . . him moving back, you know . . . and on his own now again.'

'There's nothing unusual about him being on his own.'

'No – people are free to do as they choose.'

'Free indeed!' Margaret answered and she looked around the room as if she would find a prompt somewhere. 'Aren't those two fellows living together in that cottage . . . and they even went into the bakery and got a wedding cake . . . and had some special ideas about the icing and everything. Terri Maguire told me that they asked for two little men to be standing up on the top of it.'

'Two little men,' Bird repeated vaguely.

Margaret was flushed, her eyes bright, and Bird did not know now if she was on the verge of laughing or crying. But she was on the verge of something.

'This country is gone mad,' Bird offered. And in this way the man who had killed his sister's heart was dispatched from their table. He had needed her to know about Tom Geoghan being back – that was all. He did not want her to walk into him in the little shop with everyone else looking at her and still remembering how he had jilted her and watching for some sign of it on her face more than twenty years later.

'They're saying now that William O'Neill was unstable, that he was suffering from a kind of depression, that he was bipolar, God rest him,' Margaret said.

'That's the latest, is it? Depression, it seems, is to blame now for everything.'

'Half the country is depressed,' Margaret added.

They were at the sink together and she had turned on the tap so that hot water was splashing down on the dishes. Bird made some coffee and they went into the good sitting room to drink it. They sat at the fire and the warmth of the room and the silence that they shared was a kind of comfort to both of them.

The sound of hooves on the gravel woke Margaret – and Bird watched from the couch as she opened her eyes and then remembered which house she was in. She was a briar of a woman but he still wanted to protect her, some small splinter of brotherly affection still stuck in him. The fire was roaring. He had continued to stoke it after she had fallen asleep and in the late afternoon he realized that anyone looking through the window would see the room as very cosy. Margaret had slept deeply, her head falling backwards. In her hurry to get to his house on time for the dinner she had buttoned her cardigan incorrectly and it made her seem vulnerable. And now Pat Noonan was clip-clopping past Bird's house, close to the sitting-room window and looking down on them, fresh from a visit to Olive. It was getting dark in the late afternoon and the trees cut out against the twilight sky seemed cold and brutal.

'There he is now,' Margaret said in a slow and careful voice. 'The very man we were talking about . . . and where do you think he's been?'

'I would have thought that was obvious,' Bird answered, his voice dry and dusty.

He could see that she was steaming now, wide awake after her nap and glaring around her like an angry baby.

'And Miss Olive was not so tired after all, it seems.'

She got up from the armchair and whipped the curtains over the window.

'If you put a beggar on horseback they'll ride to hell,' she said into the folds of velvet, but Bird was not looking at her. He was staring into the fire with his arms folded across his green jumper. He was thinking about how they looked from the outside and how much warmer the room would have been if he was sitting here with someone other than his sister. How pleasant it would have been to enjoy the silence with a woman at his side, one who was warmer and still had some hope inside her. The O'Neill boy moved past him as he had been doing since Saturday, the image still too bright and clear and so he almost flinched in its shadow.

Bird stood, suddenly needing to be out of the house and away from Margaret. He went into the kitchen and pulled on his boots and hat and waited, wondering where he was going. In the briefest of moments he envied Olive and her fling with Pat Noonan. And yet how could he envy something so distant from him, so foreign as the idea of sharing his bed with another person? Outside, the night sky was cold and clear and he stood in the yard looking up at the new stars and the moon over him. He could see Margaret watching him from the kitchen window, pretending to be busy at the sink again. He considered checking on the new calf, the orphan, the hard, warm head already a form of company for him, but instead he went to the hay shed and sat on a bale and looked up at the stars again and tried to name them. Bird felt something fall away from him and he looked around and realized that in that moment his own life seemed lonely and empty. It was not a completely unfamiliar feeling – because 'being alone' was at the spine of every farm and farmer around him. And yet this was different because for the first time he had said the words to himself, he had acknowledged them. He could still feel the weight of William O'Neill in his arms and how, as he came down from the rope,

Bird had had no choice but to embrace him to prevent him from falling on the concrete. As bad as their situation was, Bird had wanted to save the O'Neills the unforgettable sound, the sight of their eldest boy sinking and folding.

He lay back on the bales of straw then and watched the stars grow brighter and then fade a little in front of him. He felt like a speck of dirt under them. He wondered if they were moving. Bird felt that he was a part of this world but that with each passing year he was becoming smaller and in danger of disappearing. The world was a peculiar place to him. Midge Connors had fought every day to protect her own life and that of her mother – and then there was William O'Neill, who had ended everything, a young and perfect boy who could not wait any longer for something good to happen.

16

When Pat Noonan went home Olive took a long hot bath and washed away all traces of him. They had been in the same class at school and apart from losing his hair and growing a bit taller he was in many ways the same boy to her. She was afraid of her sister Margaret though, and this in itself shamed her. The idea of Margaret finding them together was terrifying. And yet, she had needed him, his comfort was exactly what she had wanted, not the comfort of a sister or a brother or a parent but a man with wiry arms who loved her, a man who found wonder in the smooth hills of her body and could not get enough of her. And he was biddable too. She had climbed out of the bed, climbed over him in fact, the two of them laughing, and said something about tea and a bath and he had said his sweet good-byes to her. He understood when it was time to go and did not try to make any kind of plan for them. There was no mention of days or times and that suited her very well. It was the beginning of 'some kind of thing' and because they were not young and silly there was no need to make arrangements. Pat could find her at the lodge on any wet morning or down near the lake – the whole town knew that she swam every day regardless of the weather. And she could find him in the yard of his cottage, talking to a rich toff about a smart little pony for his second daughter.

Margaret had been good with horses but Olive was the

swimmer, her dimpled arms and legs often ringed in purple and blue from the cold but her muscles still strong from being in the water.

'Oh, but you feel great afterwards,' she told everyone.

She had found another lump, a small hillock of a thing under her left arm. A thing so insignificant that it was hard to believe it could make her sit down on the side of her bed and cry.

'My friend,' she had said out loud into the quiet of her bedroom. 'You've come back for another visit.'

The last blast of chemo had nearly killed her and she wanted to keep this latest discovery a secret. This was her plate of worry and she could do what she liked with it. It had been her reason for going to Medjugorje and in truth she didn't follow any religion. And yet she had been searching for a miracle and instead she had found Pat Noonan – and this would have to do, she told herself. She was asking for one thing and had been given another. That was the way it often happened. Olive felt more sorry for Margaret, even though she was healthy. Her sister was as stiff as a tree – and this business with the O'Neill boy had upset Bird and Olive could see it. There was something wild flying around inside his world and it was a great discomfort to him.

Before dinner at Bird's house Olive and Margaret had taken the boat out together. They had pushed it backwards, the wood scraping on the pebbles, and then Olive held it steady so her sister could step into it. Margaret had looked like an old woman when she did this, her feet and hands uncertain, her face full of fear at the idea of a twisted ankle or a bruised elbow. Olive pushed the boat and then as it began to float into the deeper water she swung herself expertly inside. This could be done in two simple movements and her grace always surprised Margaret.

'Good girl,' she told her and Olive smiled at her sister.

'The water makes everything easy.'

But Margaret was in no mood for talking. She sat facing into the wind and allowed her sister to row the boat for her. The lake was calm enough and they headed towards the small island.

Where do we begin? Olive wondered as she rowed, glad of the distraction. The sister with the broken heart or the sister with the cancer?

The last time Olive had seen Margaret cry was when she was eighteen and she had still not forgotten it. And there was something about Margaret crying then that was wild and frightening. Their father had come in from the yard with young Bird and they had all listened together, their heads to one side like spaniels.

'Her heart is broken,' their father said in a matter-of-fact way and he went into the scullery to scrape the dirt from his boots and to hang up his overcoat. And it was one of the few times Olive could remember him saying anything sentimental. After that she did not remember too much about what happened. She saw her sister flying down the lane on her bicycle with her hair floating behind her, the wind blowing some colour and life back into her.

'There now,' their father had said then, 'she'll be grand.' But Margaret was never grand. She was healthy. She was alive – but Margaret was never 'grand'.

In the boat Olive had stopped rowing and allowed it to drift gently as she looked up at the mountain. Margaret had her arms wrapped tightly around her knees, watching Red Hill as they moved past it. The lake was so calm that the boat stopped drifting and Olive leaned back and began rowing again. Closer to the island she let her hands hang loose over the water. She wanted to reach up under her jumper and feel for the lump and discover that it had disappeared on her.

'It's funny to look at the house from the island, isn't it?' Olive

100

said quietly. 'It's like looking back at life and seeing how small it is.'

'Like looking at the Earth from the moon, I imagine,' Margaret had answered.

Now Olive stood in the warmth of her kitchen looking out at the lake and the island, needing to visit her sister and her brother or they might begin to ask questions. She dressed and pulled on a waterproof coat and wellingtons and set off for the bigger house, walking. Her arms and legs, her spine, her neck were all pleasantly loose and relaxed from what had happened in her bed earlier that morning. The lake was rough again, like the sea, with the wind coming in over it. The trees on the island were moving. Two swimmers who were training for a triathlon thrashed their way out towards the yellow buoy, their heads rolling, their powerful pink arms rising and falling.

17

Midge was not ready for the emptiness of the house without her mother. It was almost a week since she had been dropped home by Bird Keegan and on the same morning her mother had been rushed to the hospital. Her father was staying at Imelda Conroy's house now and yet when Midge returned from the hospital every evening she could still see his shadow over everything. The ghost of Charlie was doing circles on the gaudy swirl pattern of the carpets, he was climbing the flowers on the wallpaper. To make matters worse, there was no electricity because no one had been putting money into the meter. The fridge was silent. There was no hum of life anywhere. The cat appeared then and made strange with her. She was starving and had pulled everything out of the bin in the kitchen. Midge cut open a tin of cat food and allowed her to climb up on the kitchen table. There was nothing to eat in the house except a soft tomato – and what was left in the milk carton had gone sour. She needed tea more than food, anything at all to warm her. She opened a drawer in the kitchen and lifted the cutlery tray to see if her mother had left any coins there. It was almost dark outside, the November light always seemed to run off on her. She felt a soup ladle with her hand, a can opener, a teaspoon that seemed to have a kind of sticky film over it. There was no money, just dirt and stale crumbs and the feeling that her life in general, the life that other people seemed to like and live well enough, was letting go of her. She was very still then, like a kind of spectre behind the kitchen window, barely breathing, aware of herself falling and disappearing

'Come back. Come back,' she told herself, this thin-looking girl with red hair.

Bridget had said a few words at the hospital and then closed her eyes on her. She had shut out the world and had a deep sleep and seemed very peaceful.

'I lost it.' That was the last thing she had told her daughter.

'Lost what, Mam?' Midge had asked her.

Earlier on the same day she had managed to tell Midge that she had 'gone for' Charlie – that was how she put it.

'For all the times he hit you, Midge, I gave every slap and every thump and every kick back to him.'

And now she was in the hospital and Charlie was sleeping down at Imelda's, saying that it was an awful pity that Bridget had come home drunk and fallen down those stairs again.

The nurses were kind to Midge – especially Destiny, who was from Uganda. She seemed to recognize the pain a daughter might feel when looking at her broken-up mother.

And Midge could ask her things – things that were too awful to ask anyone else.

'Do you think she can hear me, Destiny?'

'Well, it happens a lot, you know. People coming back and telling everyone what they could hear – and feel – when they were in a coma. Hold her hand. Talk to her. Let her know that you love her.'

'And do you think she will come back?'

'That part is up to her – but you can talk to her and tell her what you are feeling.'

But Midge could not do it. Instead she sat at the side of the bed and stared at this woman who had given birth to her, who had put her on earth and who could not be relied on for even a moment to protect her. Midge stretched her hand across the white hospital sheet but she couldn't touch her – and when she opened her mouth to speak, there was no sound, just an emptiness, an exposed dry place with nothing good coming from there.

'Honey, you need to eat something,' Destiny told her and she would stop at the door and watch her carefully before leaving for another day.

And finally Midge managed to pull three words together. She looked at the woman in the bed and said, 'Mam – I'm sorry.'

And there was a long list of things she felt sorry for – sorry for what Charlie had done to her and the fact that Midge herself had delayed at Bird Keegan's when she should have been at home waiting for her – sorry for not really knowing Bridget or even trying to understand her – sorry that down in the deepest part of her – through Midge's outer shell, past her muscles and away from her heart – she was sorry – most of all – for not really wanting her mother to get better, for needing to give up the kind of life that had to be lived around and around her, the jig of uncertainty, of never really knowing what to expect when she turned the key in the front door, of not knowing – as a tiny child or now as a grown person – what she was going to find there.

Down, down deep in that hot part – the part that would have Midge sent to hell if anyone guessed her thinking – she quietly willed her mother to slip away and leave her.

On better days – normal days – she weighed up the heartbreak of continuing this life with Bridget against the heartbreak of losing her – and she had some difficulty working out which heartbreak would be better, which one would kill her and which might finally release her.

She went back to the house on Emmet Road feeling wrung out, her energy taken from her once again by Bridget and the dead air of the hospital. And there were many small spikes of anger also – when she thought about her siblings and how they had escaped all manner of torture, and how her sister didn't come even after Midge had sent an email to her or help her to try and contact their brothers – and more anger like a mountain then when she looked back over her own short life, and saw Bridget as a kind of wayward child and Midge herself as the protector, as the mother.

Midge heard a noise then, a scraping sound outside the front door – and because she was so still and quiet, she observed this as something being put down, and then a small piece of stone or grit being trapped and then rolling under it. These were the slightest of sounds though, and then the more obvious one of the gate giving a creak and banging like an alarm so that she was suddenly waking up and running from the dark kitchen, through a kind of damp mist that seemed to have filled the house, down the hall and flinging the front door open and seeing then that there was no one there. Instead, down at her feet, someone had left a flat-looking apple tart on a chipped blue and white enamel plate.

'What?' Midge asked herself quietly.

She bent down and looked at it and when she went to pick it up she noticed a scattering of coarse sugar over it. She ran, licking her thumbs, to the gate to see the jeep turning – his head, the same shape and angles that had been somehow remembered, leaving her there. The jeep swung in a wide circle so that when it turned to face the way out of the estate, his window was next to her and he had no choice but to pull back into the footpath and let his window down.

'Hello there,' he said, his voice stern, formal.

'Hello,' she said back to him.

It was almost dark, the cold of night coming in dank and dripping, the amber street lights showing up a fog that in time would cover everything.

'My sister made the apple tart. She asked me to take it over to you . . . She heard you had some trouble.'

'*Margaret* did that? Miss Keegan?'

'No. Olive.'

Oh, thought Midge, the nicer one.

'Well, thanks . . . thank her for me.'

She remembered getting into the lake for swimming lessons as a child and how she had not even owned a swimsuit until Olive Keegan gave her one. She had even gone down into the cold water with her, and Midge was swimming by the end of that summer.

She had no idea what to say to Bird now but he was the only person with her on this dark street and she wanted to stop him from leaving.

'I'd invite you in . . .' she said – the words coming out awkwardly and without any real sincerity.

Here he cut in suddenly: 'How is your mother?'

'She's very sick,' Midge said and she could hear herself answering vaguely and then, remembering Destiny, she added 'bad', and here Bird's eyes were raised to meet hers suddenly. He had been leaning slightly out the window to talk to her, one elbow jutting, his eyes fixed on the halo of street light around her.

He looked at her now, and seemed more troubled than her somehow.

'I'm sorry to hear that,' he said.

There was an awful silence then and Midge considered thanking him again and like a normal person backing away, closing the old hanging gate behind her. But when she turned to look at the house, its dark windows, its blank dead eyes sent a chill through her.

'Can any of your family, your brothers or your sister, come and help you?'

'I don't have phone numbers for most of them. I sent an email to my sister – but she's expecting a baby and can't travel. But – if I know her – she wouldn't want to travel anyway.'

'Is that right?'

'None of them cared too much about Mam – they couldn't wait to get away from here . . .'

Bird nodded and gave a deep sigh as he looked up at the stars gathering above them.

'Where are you going now?' she asked him shyly and Bird paused for a moment, watching her carefully, seeming to listen to the secret hum of this odd conversation.

'Home,' he said simply.

She could hear him breathing. She was embarrassing herself but going back into the dark was worse than anything. Bird turned the engine off suddenly and dropped an arm so that it swung low outside the driver door and here he did a rat-a-tat-tat with his fingers.

'Actually I was thinking of getting something to eat . . . in the town. Are you hungry?'

And Midge was walking to the passenger side.

'Do you have a coat?' he asked. 'Did you close the door behind you?'

'I don't need one. It's fine,' she said and she was climbing in and strapping her seatbelt on. She looked straight ahead, willing him to start the engine – not once meeting his eyes, her small hands folded on her lap, waiting.

Take me away from here, she said inwardly. Take me, just take me away from here.

Bird put the jeep into gear and the engine rumbled down through the estate, the dashboard lit up with dials and clocks in this warm space that smelled of harvest time and animals. Midge could sense his discomfort, his unwillingness to share this space with her, and yet it was he who had suggested it. He would not have been her first choice of human beings to spend an evening with and she was certain that she was not his either. He was ten years older than her, not too much, she thought – but he had a

107

kind of ancient quality, a dryness, like someone who had lived this whole life before. He signalled left at the end of her road and drove down Main Street into traffic and people and all the things she already knew he hated.

The Dublin bus had just come in and people were piling off with holdalls and rucksacks, students home from university, Christmas shoppers back from the city.

Midge heard a sudden shuffling in the back. Twisting her head quickly, she saw a sheep looking back at her.

'Oh Jesus Christ,' she said in terror.

'Yeah,' Bird said in his matter-of-fact way. 'She was stuck in a hole. I had to put her in on my way here.'

'Is she hurt? The poor old thing.'

But Bird didn't answer. He had heard her but he just lifted his chin slightly in response, letting her know that as far as he was concerned, her question simply didn't matter.

'Tostetti's?' Bird suggested. He had forgotten that her mother worked there and she looked up at him in surprise. She had not suggested the Italian place because of her mother, knowing that her apron was still hanging behind a door in there.

'All right so,' she said and they parked and began walking up the wet street together. There was no one about now. The Dublin bus had disappeared and it all seemed strangely quiet to her. When she glanced back at Bird's jeep she saw the woolly head move, two glassy eyes looking back at her.

Tostetti's was busy. There was a dense hum about the place, something close to a frenzy. Katie, the waitress, was flying up and down the brown-tiled floor, a wide blue plate in each hand. Old man Tostetti, who rarely appeared, was at the grill working, a fine silk shirt tucked around his slender waist. Midge remembered her mother saying that he had looked like a movie star when he was younger. His eldest son, Mario, was standing back behind the coffee machine, his eyes in slits moving sideways as he watched her come in. Midge did not know any of them well, only that they were reasonable to her mother. They gave her a small bonus at Christmas. When she didn't show up for work they didn't come up to the estate looking for her. Elena, Mario's sister, watched Midge and Bird and then, turning to Mario and their father, spoke in a stream of Italian. Her words bounced back to Midge, who felt self-conscious and miserable. Katie pretended not to know her. She had been cruel to Bridget, had done her best to belittle her at every turn. She offered them the worst table in the restaurant, a one-sided effort so that when Midge slid in, Bird had to slide in next to her.

'We're not sitting here,' he spoke up to the waitress – the side-by-side arrangement hitting him suddenly. 'Like two kids in a classroom,' he added.

A part of Midge wanted to laugh when he said this but then through the small wooden hatch she saw a woman's hands working and they were red and fat-looking like her mother's. The hands were framed there, reaching for the dirty plates that Katie delivered, and Midge could not breathe at all then, this framed picture, the smell of grease, the rattling talk of the Italians, the whole thing piercing her. She saw her reflection in the mirror as she blindly followed Bird to a better table, one he had chosen without Katie offering, and she saw her own dark eyes looking back at her. There was a wedge of something, some kind of terrible hurt at the thought of her mother, stuck in her throat and it was trying to kill her.

Bird stepped back and allowed her to choose her preferred side of the booth. She could face the restaurant and the old man puffing up a blue cloud of pipe smoke and the arguing Italians. Elena was pitching a fit about something, eating the head of Mario who seemed impervious, his father drifting into the back room with a cigarette to get away from them.

'*Mania!*' Elena shouted at Mario. '*Mania, mania, mania!*'

Midge chose the street view. As low as she felt, she knew that looking out was always better than looking back in; at least that way there was a possibility of finding new air, of something different happening.

'I wonder what *man-ia* means?' she said very softly, not sure if she even wanted an answer.

She was aware that she had not looked at Bird since coming into Tostetti's, that she had drifted off to no-man's-land at the sudden realization that she would lose her mother, that this was what Destiny had been trying to tell her. The fear she felt was like ice running through her and she spoke to Bird only to prevent herself from going completely under.

'Crazy,' he said, and when she looked up he had put his finger to his temple and it was only then, at that precise moment, that she looked at him and he looked at her. His eyes, she saw, were still that pale grey-blue. She had seen the same colour in the sky when summer was over and the first chill of autumn was everywhere, and yet behind these eyes was another world and then another and another.

'So,' Midge continued in the same voice that was thin but it was the only thing she had to pull herself up with, 'Elena just said "Crazy crazy crazy" to Mario.'

Bird looked up from his red plastic menu and nodded slowly. He glanced around him, feeling comfortable in this kind of place, enjoying its shabbiness.

'I suppose she has her reasons,' he answered.

'My mother told me once about a man who came in here and ate everything on the menu. Everything. He started with a Large Mixed Grill and then a Special and then went through about four desserts – and then he paid for it all in coppers – and he had pyjamas on under his clothes.'

Her words came out in a sudden torrent and her eyes were bulging with tears. The tears were coming up from somewhere way down low inside her. She could see Bird watching her from across the Formica table, the image of his face wavy and distant. He seemed waterlogged but she could do nothing at all to help him. Midge took a breath inwards and made a dragging sound with it, a gate closing, the butt of it dragging on concrete.

'You better have something to eat,' Bird said.

Midge shook her head.

'I'll have tea. It's all I can stomach. I had something to eat at the hospital.'

She gave a great deep sniff then and she rubbed at her face roughly, pushing these tears back into her hair. When she looked down at the table he had slid a white cotton handkerchief across it towards her. She opened its folds, amazed by its strange purity, that he would have something like this in his pocket. He said nothing at all though and there was a great relief in this, the fact that he knew she was crying, his sudden intimate knowledge of her and that he just let her continue, said nothing, allowed her.

Katie appeared at their table, her small notebook and pen poised, a hip stuck out, one foot pointed, 'insolence in an apron' – that was what Bridget had called her.

'Yes please,' she announced.

Bird raised his eyebrows and smiled pleasantly at her.

'I'll have some chips,' he said. 'And two fat sausages.'

Midge swallowed and released moist air through her mouth; her nose had closed up on her.

'She'll have an egg and chips,' Bird said. 'And a glass of milk.'

Midge took slow deep breaths then and willed this sudden rolling wave of emotion to pass over her. If he got up and left she would have no one, only that tramp Katie who never had a decent word to say to her. With an effort Midge became quieter and busied herself with tying up her hair. It was a glistening red colour, not orange like her mother's, mostly amber with shafts of auburn running through it. She concentrated on raking it back

111

with her fingers, her hands bunching it into a fat ponytail which she twisted and flicked through a rubber band until it felt completely secure. Bird's eyes were turned sideways now, fixed on the salt cellar, the ketchup in its red squeezy bottle, congealed sauce in a hard red nub on the top of it. Midge took a single deep breath and with her face and neck clear of hair, her eyes visible, she looked straight at him. It was as if a great calm had come over her. She had managed to settle herself and not fall into pieces entirely. When he finally looked into her eyes, she felt that he had some small raft of respect for her. She hoped he would see some clearing in her eyes, a kind of honesty, a small bit of humour. At times when she looked at herself in the mirror she found the colour of her hair and her sea of freckles against the sudden white of her neck in some way alarming. She had the look of a small woodland creature about her, she thought, a baby animal newly hatched, or a goblin, not quite ready for life but hoping to live out in the world and one day conquer something.

'What are the doctors saying about your mother?'

'That she's very bad.'

He looked up sadly and waited for her to add something.

'I think she's probably worse than they're even telling me. She's lying there like she's in a deep sleep except there is no sign at all of her waking.'

Bird nodded at this, his eyebrows flickering slightly. His hands were resting on the table, one wide thumb tapping on the other. He had asked a question that had no real meaning and why, Midge wondered, would he not ask *what* had happened to her mother? Was it that it was old news around the town, people saying that her mother was in a coma and that it was all down to the mad father who had given her an awful beating? There was nothing worse for Midge than people not asking what actually happened, as if this tragedy was for her in some way expected, as if her mother lying in a coma was kind of normal.

But he would not ask her and so before another impossible silence fell down over them, Midge attempted some kind of chatter.

'Did you hear that Jackson's Alsatians got loose and pulled clothes off the Dalys' line, destroyed a blouse, chewed up Gertie's padded bra?'

'I didn't hear that.'

'Well, it happened – Ronnie McGrath's been giving me a lift to the hospital and he told me. The dogs took one wellie boot and it still hasn't turned up – Gertie had to go out and buy a new pair, so now she has three wellies . . . and what would anyone want with that?'

Their food arrived just as Midge felt like she was beginning to lose her mind completely. She had no interest in eating. The egg, which was deep fried, was repellent. Elena had steamed the milk and it was scalding. She lifted a single chip and forced herself to eat it. If Bird Keegan had not found her in his field, if he had not been forced into sheltering her, the story of her mother would not have made any impression on him. But he had driven her back to the chaos, he had returned her. She could see that Bird was involved now somehow, not in any way responsible and yet it occurred to her that he must have been thinking about her. She did not believe that Olive had made the apple tart for her either. Midge put another chip into her mouth and imagined him standing in a dimly lit barn, shaking out straw for lambs and having a brief wandering thought about her.

'Why did you come to my house?' she asked him and before he could answer, 'I mean I know you said Olive wanted you to bring something – but why? I mean why bother? Sure, you don't even know me.'

Bird was sawing at a sausage and blotting it into some ketchup. She could see that he was thinking about his answer. She felt it to be important, that what he said now could change the shape of everything.

'I heard what happened – and when.'

Here there was another long pause before he continued.

'I wondered if I should have brought you back to your house earlier on Sunday morning – if it might have made a difference. Then I thought maybe it was lucky that you were not there. And why did I call around tonight? To tell you the truth I'm not sure. To see if you were OK, I suppose. Margaret told me what happened . . . and to carry on and say nothing at all – or do nothing at all – seemed wrong.' Here he shook his head. 'I don't know why. I thought I should make an appearance.'

Midge was watching a yellow skin form on the top of her milk.

'There is nothing more disgusting to me than warm milk,' she told him and she could see his shoulders relax when he saw that she had stopped questioning him.

'If you have a glass of milk straight from the cow it's warm,' he told her, his own words in a bit of a rush now, 'although you'd want to be careful. It's not pasteurized . . . although there are a few headbangers who are going mad for raw milk. I wouldn't be in favour of it.'

Midge gave a sudden smile then. It surprised both of them. He was as foolish as she had been when she was rattling on about the wellies and the padded bra.

Bird signalled to Katie and Midge felt herself sink. He is going, she thought to herself. But he was asking for some tea – and wanted to know if they had any ice cream 'or a small cake' – and here Midge was again baffled by him. 'One of those French fancies,' he said, pointing to the glass dome that the Tostettis kept on the counter. In all her years of coming in here after school Midge had never seen anyone pick one. Now he picked two, a vibrant pink for her and the yellow for himself.

'What do you do all the time?' she asked him suddenly and he stared back at her in some confusion. 'I mean . . . I never see

114

you in the town. Do you go out? What do you do all the time?'

'The farm keeps me busy.'

'At night too?'

'Not every night – but during lambing, yes, at night too.'

'And when there's no lambing?'

Here he shrugged. 'I read a lot. I don't have a TV.'

'Do you have the internet? A computer?'

'I have an iPad,' he said.

'Are you on Facebook?'

Here he gave a low laugh and seemed to be genuinely amused.

'No. I am not on Facebook.'

'Do you have a girlfriend?'

Bird gave a deep sigh and allowed his head to roll back on his shoulders so that he was looking over her head and down into the long galley of the restaurant. He signalled for the bill and Midge knew she had crossed a line with him. She was tired herself from talking and the thoughts of going home were less frightening now.

Outside, the sheep had climbed into the driver's seat. She was standing up and seemed somehow relieved to see them coming.

'Our chauffeur is waiting,' Bird announced and Midge could not help but smile up at him. The light rain had stopped and the sky was cold-looking, the stars too sharp and near. Bird drove her back to her house with neither of them speaking.

'I hope your mam gets better,' he told her and she was disappointed in him. She did not know him at all but already she relied on him for a kind of honesty.

'She's not going to get better,' Midge said quietly. She was able to say this now and she did not feel like crying. That part was over. As a girl she had cried when her father beat her but that part was over too. Crying didn't help anything. What helped was keeping your head up so that you could breathe and if you could breathe

115

you could think – and then you could plan your way out of anything.

'I lost my own mother when I was six,' Bird said suddenly.

Midge didn't speak for a moment. She had no money to put in the meter for the electricity and the well behind the gear stick was full of loose change, in one- and two-euro coins mostly.

'Was it awful?' she asked and she tried to imagine his long stalking strides around the farm, the silence of him – and how even then no one would have known what on earth he was thinking, what he was feeling.

'I don't remember much. But yes, I suppose it was . . . awful,' he told her plainly.

Midge turned to look at him, his face in profile lit up from the street light.

The sheep shuffled in the back and let out a deep rumbling *baa*.

'Losing a mother is – how would I put it? – normal enough.' He spoke very slowly, faltering. 'Losing a mother when you're young . . . I mean as a child . . . is a bit different.'

Midge waited.

'It's an affliction,' he told her softly.

And Bird did not need to tell her anything else. Midge understood all of it and she herself was somewhere between a girl and a woman, still hovering between old and young. When he got out of the jeep to check on the sheep she scooped up two handfuls of coins and dropped them into her pockets. Her life was scattered around her but she had managed to eat and she would be able to turn on the lights and the heat that night at home. He waited for her to reach the door and as she lifted her hand he nodded once and drove away from her. He had lost his mother more than twenty years ago – that was the secret part of himself that he had given her – he was still in the shock of it. Now the possibility of her mother dying too had drawn something out of him, had

116

drawn his entire self, it seemed, out into the world again. Midge watched the red taillights of the jeep until they disappeared. She locked the door behind her and walked carefully down the pitch-black hallway and began loading his money into the meter.

18

It was close to December when Midge saw Bird again. He came into the Beacon and ordered a pint of Guinness and looked across the room at her. For everyone else she was like wallpaper but when he came in he nodded and allowed his eyes to settle on her. The people around him seemed to fade and drift. Bird had broken his usual routine and decided to go for a pint in Tullyvin. It was a cold night and he was wearing a red jumper and seemed swaddled in it. His beard had been trimmed to form a halo around his cheeks. Midge sang 'Danny Boy' and she could hear her own voice becoming sweeter. The very sight of him took her out of the mud that she had been swimming in.

She still went to the hospital in Portlaoise every day. Bridget had been there for three weeks now with tubes in her nose and throat and she was surrounded by several grey-coloured machines that beeped and pipped at her. Her mother was running on electricity – and Midge could not tell anyone what she felt there. She was Midge Connors after all and that made her lower than everyone, her heartbreak was not significant. The people in Tullyvin felt she had been preparing for this event for years – that she should have built up some kind of veneer – so that seeing her mother laid so low by her father would not really affect her. She should have run away like the rest of the Connors, they said. She should have run and saved herself from the two parents who were intent on killing each other.

But Midge still cared for her mother – she was born with a blind knot of love for her – and coming out of a poor house where the clothes and dishes were not washed did not make any difference. She had lied to Bird Keegan about her age. She was only just twenty and not twenty-one and still young enough to have a dab of hope on everything. She had never hoped that her father would stop drinking but she had hoped that her mother would get sense and finally leave him. She had hoped that one day they would go to a safe place together. And they would not go to England or anywhere close by in Europe. They would go to America, on the other side of the earth, a new world where people like them could start over.

But Midge still could not talk to her – more than anything she wanted to ask Bridget what was happening inside her and if she was going somewhere – if she was going to die or if she was going to rally and return as a different kind of mother.

'Miracles do happen,' she said to Destiny once – but Destiny, usually so full of hope and good humour, just stood still and looked at her.

'Your mama is very sick,' she told her.

A doctor came then and told her that her mother was fading, that in a matter of days she could be gone – and the words felt like hailstones raining down on her. Her secret thoughts – the idea of being free from this, from her – seemed to evaporate and Midge began to cry, loud wailing sobs that shocked even her and caused Destiny to put her warm arms around her.

'You need to understand,' the doctor said, 'that even if your mother lived, her quality of life would be very poor. She would need constant care . . . 24/7.'

'Yes,' answered Midge. 'But at least I would have her.'

And Bridget lived a bit longer, her chest rising and falling, her arms soft and warm when Midge finally put her hand there.

She continued to go to the hospital every day and got a lift from Ronnie McGrath who ran the taxi service in the town. And until that very day he was going in anyway and did not mind her, 'a wee slip of a thing' he called her, in the front seat of his Ford Mondeo. But then Ronnie dropped a radiator on his foot and broke it so he was off the road and Midge had no way at all of getting in to see her mother. The doctors still came and looked at Bridget and then glanced at the chair, which until now had always held the red-haired daughter.

Bird watched her from the bar and it was as if a map of the world had been presented to him. Motorways and mountain ranges and streams and cities and all manner of life were being laid out from there. He did not want to speak to her. He had just wanted to see her, to look at her from a distance and then sit with any feelings that might be stirred up in him. Perhaps the locals were right – he was a bit peculiar – and yet now he felt as if he was following some kind of light in front of him. He did not know where this light might take him. He did not even know yet if he would bother following it any further. For now he had managed to cause a hum in the hotel foyer because he had come out and was sitting at the polished bar surrounded by other people. Until now they did not even know that he liked a pint of Guinness. He ordered a second pint and thought about his father, a man who had wanted nothing more than to be out on the land, the nerves in his feet, his hands, his whole body connected to it, growing up from it like branches. And Bird himself had behaved like a mirror and until recently he had never once questioned it. When he thought about this he felt in some ways ashamed of himself now, given the world that was spread out all around him and knowing he had only taken the meanest slice of it. He watched the girl's hand adjust the microphone, a brave little hand that would probably be as soft as butter.

The men beside Bird began talking about Ronnie McGrath's

big toe then and how he had crushed it and had it in plaster. They laughed loudly at this, scratching their heads like chimpanzees and looking down from the high bar stools at their feet, which were swinging. And then the talk moved on to Midge Connors and who would take her to the hospital to see her mother.

'She's in a coma,' one of them said.

'She'll never be right, God bless her.'

'It's an awful thing to say,' someone else added very quietly, 'but she might be better off . . .'

This was followed by a silence then which everyone seemed to find awkward.

'And what about Midge?' a woman asked quietly. She was working behind the bar and trying not to look at the girl who was beginning to hand around her little basket. Midge sent it in the opposite direction to the bar and would not look at Bird when he put his hand into his pocket.

'Very few of us could go over to Portlaoise every day . . .' the woman went on. 'It's a fair drive and then to hang around and wait for her.'

'Well, maybe she could get a lift back with someone else.'

'I'd like to help her,' another man added, 'but I'm painting gates for the Wilsons all week.'

'Is that what you're at?

And so the conversation drifted and they followed it, these people who did not really want to help Bridget and Midge Connors.

Bird finished his pint and sat looking at his hands, which were folded on the bar. She passed him then, still the same wisp of a thing that he remembered except that she was wearing a green crochet beret now with a flower on the side of it. It followed the neat shape of a face that seemed as delicate as a teacup. He turned to her and she hesitated beside him for a moment. There was no point in him saying 'hello' to her. What use was 'hello' to either of them? He could remember feeling the small skulls of her knees when he had wrapped a bandage around them. There was also no point in the polite enquiry about her mother. The whole place knew that she was dying, that she was there and not there and of no use to a daughter who was brim-full of feelings for her. Bird looked into her eyes and then tried to find something useful to say, something that was not in any way false or pointless or an insult to her. He was a clumsy sort and felt his arms and legs grow longer, the broad wings of his shoulders reaching out towards her. His jeans were new ones Olive had bought him last Christmas and he felt as if he was wearing cardboard.

Midge made to move on, buttoning up her coat as she walked.

'What time do you need to be at the hospital?' Bird asked. His voice was steady, each word sent out clearly. It had taken a minute but he had uncovered what he felt might be the right thing to say to her.

Midge took what seemed like a deep breath, her nose and shoulders lifted by it. She reminded him of a small stoat he had seen once, stepping out into the lane on a bright summer morning, surprised to smell the freshness of the day and to see him there, a harmless bulk of a man, and the air dense between them.

'I try to be in there early,' she said quietly. 'The doctors do their rounds at around nine o'clock, sometimes earlier.'

They both waited for a moment, each one thinking about the possible implications of what she had said.

'And you need to talk to them,' Bird said and then nodded as if he understood everything.

'They're saying she doesn't have much longer – a few more days, maybe a week. I don't know . . .'

The men at the bar had grown quiet, he realized now, and the room was emptier without her music. The woman behind the bar

122

had appeared suddenly like a ghost near him and she became busy with work that was not really there for her.

Midge glanced around her but Bird did not. His mind remained clear and he was focused on doing something honest and right for her.

'I can have you there at nine,' he said and by now he had turned his body on the stool and was folding his arms as he faced her. He saw colour fill her cheeks then and the slightest smile cross her mouth. She stared back at him and did not say anything. It was as if she had been given a gift – something that was perhaps not meant for her.

'I'll have the milking done and I'll come and collect you. I'll be smelling of manure,' he added. Then as a further clarification, 'There won't be time for me to wash myself if I'm to get you there close to nine.'

'That's all right,' she answered.

She waited for a moment and then pushing her bag higher up on her shoulder she walked over the carpet and left the two doors swinging behind her.

Bird turned to the men then. 'What are you looking at?' he asked them.

'Good man, Bird,' one of them said. The voice high-pitched, insolent.

'She'd be waiting a long time for one of you to help her,' Bird answered and here he put his two hands on the counter and pushed himself away from it. He stepped into the Gents and waited a moment there. Now that he had made this arrangement with her, he felt strangely tired. He did not want to see her again – not so soon – her walking under the street lamps and then turning her head to look just once perhaps, to see him standing there looking back at her.

123

19

In the morning Midge did not wait out on the road for him and it was still dark when she saw the lights of the jeep coming towards her. She had washed at the kitchen sink and eaten a cold breakfast and waited then for his hand to knock on the door. She was ashamed of herself and the place that she came from – and yet, it would be better if he knew everything about her. She would be able to see her mother because of him and why he had offered her this was a mystery of sorts, but she would take it and ask no questions. She would allow herself to be steered through the narrow roads with the headlamps from his jeep stretching to the treetops. Tullyvin would be behind her. Her mother would still be sleeping at the hospital. Her skull was cracked, a line like the equator running around the world of it. But she would still be there. That was the thing about the machines that kept her breathing – her life was more certain than it had ever been before, her body was still warmed by her own red blood running through it – as long as the machines beeped and pipped she did not seem to be going anywhere.

Midge watched from the window as Bird climbed down from the driver's seat and walked to her door. She opened it before he knocked and together they witnessed what she referred to later as 'the usual circus' three doors down from her.

A man in pyjamas was holding a fork and standing out in his

garden – and across the street there was a woman with long hair screaming over the hedges at him.

And the man roared back that if she didn't shut the fuck up he'd fucking brain her.

Midge glided over this, the sound a kind of white noise around her. The door to her house closed with a rattle of glass and an echo and her courage was suddenly like a ghost running through her. She could not bear for him to see the inside of the house now. In the hallway she reached for a switch and the bright over-head light was quickly extinguished. There were old newspapers in a pile inside the door, the carpet worn thin, a cat with one ear stepping lightly over it. There was a meanness to everything, she knew that herself, the thin rail of the banister, the bend of the floorboards underfoot, the scuffed skirting boards. In the kitchen the bin was overflowing – the cat had got at it again – and there were dirty dishes in the sink, and on the floor her mother's old pink slippers.

On her way back down the hall she scooped up the cat and Bird stopped for a minute and looked at the creature in her arms, his face curling in a mixture of disgust and impatience.

'Leave that cat here,' he said.

'I'm afraid she'll run off – or someone will take her.'

'No one is going to steal an old cat. Leave it here.'

Midge did not argue. She loosened her embrace so that the cat made a high looping jump up and away from her. There were lights coming on in some of the other houses. Midge knew every person in the Emmet estate. These were people she had grown up with – decent types who had made her school lunch when she couldn't rely on her own mother. The man with the fork in his hand had gone inside now but the woman was still out in her garden watching his front door. Bird did not open the door for Midge. He left her to do this for herself and the cat slipped up onto a wall without any difficulty and sat, watching them from there.

He changed gears without speaking, waiting at the traffic lights even though there was no one else up at that hour of the morning. She wished for the lights to come on in the shop windows so that there might be other people out and about, besides them. But they were alone in the world on this winter morning and the idea of Christmas approaching made her heart feel hollow inside her.

'I'm deaf in this ear,' he told her suddenly, tapping the left side of his head with his finger. 'With you sitting on that side, it's very hard for me to make out what you're saying.'

'Oh,' Midge said softly and she turned to the window, knowing now that this small sound would never reach him.

He turned the radio on and they listened to the news and the weather and all the things in the outer world that were nothing to do with them. There were more cars on the main road and he leaned down slightly to change into another gear and then sat back in his seat and relaxed. Midge wanted to turn and look at him but she was afraid to in case he would also turn and then they would be looking straight at each other. The picture he had presented on her doorstep was an unusual one and would have had people talking. And yet on Emmet Road it was sometimes hard to know what exactly was normal and what was enough to spur the people who lived there into gossiping.

The early morning light was dull and rain came spattering on the windscreen. Bird waited for a long time before bothering with the wipers. She had heard that he was a man who was clever with money and she wondered now if he was trying to save on something. He leaned forward and tipped a switch finally and she saw then that he had only one wiper that was working. It was on her side and she sat there feeling guilty and not enjoying the clarity, wishing it was all the other way round, wishing that so many things were the opposite to the way they actually were. She was visiting her mother because the man driving her was being

126

charitable. She had seen the inside of his life and it was an empty enough picture. After the milking he had a kind of dead hour – when he would eat that porridge slop and look around the vast kitchen and probably wonder what to do with himself. She had heard that he was a hard worker but even the hardest workers must stop and think and feel the seconds tick slowly past, like a kind of syrup.

She saw a mule looking over a wall, noting its sleek back and long ugly head and it reminded her of Bird Keegan, the very idea of this making her cheeks warm up in case he could read the thoughts inside her. She would not turn her head and look at him. He smelled like manure as he had warned her. His boot on the clutch was thick with it. The hands on the wheel were massive. He could, if he wanted, kill a person with them. Her father had moved in with Imelda Conroy and for this she was thankful. It had been hard enough to get rid of him. He was a slippery bag of bones but he would not blow away easily like powder.

Bird signalled right and then slowed down at the barrier to the hospital car park. She saw his hand reach for a ticket and then saw how he pulled the jeep up into the drop-off spot in order to get her as close to the front doors as possible.

'There you are now,' he said and he turned to look at her. He was a strange-looking man, she decided then, not exactly ugly but not exactly good-looking either. His face seemed to be filled with angles and ridges, like a canyon. His eyes gave no clues as to what he might be thinking. He was not in any way nervous with her though. Lately she only had to walk into the supermarket for people to go skittering around the breakfast cereals and vegetables.

Now Midge wanted to ask if he might wait for her but could not stretch his generosity any further.

'I need to tell you something,' she said suddenly then and Bird turned to look at her.

'There are days when I go in . . .' and here she swallowed, 'and I hope she's not there any more.'

And here he nodded, his eyes looking straight into her, not flinching and not judging either.

'And other days when I think I might die without her.'

And here Bird seemed to think for a moment.

'I think you're doing your best for her,' he said finally.

'But is it normal to want . . .' and here she turned away, not able to look into his eyes any more. 'Is it normal to want – at times – to be free from your own mother?'

Midge put her hand on the door and opened it.

'What is normal?' Bird asked with a sigh then and he shrugged at her.

'Thanks for the lift,' she told him and he nodded without looking at her again, revving the engine now like a man who needed to be somewhere.

He did a circle of the car park and then drove to the exit barrier. He had made no plan with Midge, no arrangement to meet her later, and somewhere deep down he knew now that he could not leave her there. She would come out of the hospital later in the day – at what time? He had no idea. He did not know how long a girl might occupy a chair so that she could sit and stare at her dying mother. He did not know what room they were in or who else might be in there. He could imagine her coming back out through the automatic doors and stepping onto the wet tarmac in the early dark of a December afternoon and he worried for her. What news might she be carrying about her mother? She seemed too young for that kind of trouble, her shoulders brittle under the weight they had to bear. Bird did not like this new feeling of being somehow tied to her either but he was there now, and how would she get home with no one to take her?

He drove the jeep into the town, passing the secondary school

128

he had gone to himself every day, the bus filled with jeering teenagers. He had kept his distance from them too, sensing danger from the mist that seemed to hang over them. He had once watched a girl being kicked by one of the boys. Patricia Clarke, a plain, rough girl who was known for beating up girls younger than her. He was glad to be grown up now with a steering wheel in his hands, glad to be away from that particular island of life. The best years of his life, no – and they could not have been Midge's best years either.

He knew now that he was going to hang around for most of the day watching the light fade and simply wait for her. Sean was at the farm and it was a quiet sort of month. The bull was inside now, standing in the long shed behind a thick barrier, the ring wet in his nose and his eyes full of plans and schemes around what he might do when he got back out. At this time of the year the fields were empty and lonesome, lovely when a white frost coated them but mostly just lonely. He parked in a car park near a shopping centre and walked into it. There was a selection of wooden garden furniture for sale near the entrance and he stood for a moment and looked at it. A sign was attached to a swinging hammock asking people not to sit there.

Inside he was met with music and people and children and he walked through it absorbing the detail and the hum of the place. Who were all these people, he wondered, who came to walk around this form of hell every day? People who might like to sit on a swinging hammock in a car park in the middle of winter, he supposed. When he worked long days alone on his farm he had no idea that all of this was going on, that these people were out and about in shopping centres, that this – while he was using a short knife to snap the twine from a bale so that he could shake it loose for his cattle – this was their idea of living. He had no clue whatsoever. He found the noise of the place, the Christmas lights and the music, overwhelming.

He stepped into a small café and asked for a coffee and this was another trial for him. He was to collect a tray, the woman told him, and then a cup, and yes, of course, a saucer if he wanted one – or would he prefer a mug? Bird simply didn't know anything about it. He only wanted a drink of something and to hide in the shadows somewhere. He looked at his watch and wondered how he might wait all day for her. It would not be possible. And now the woman was guiding him to a machine where he would press a button to select what he wanted.

'A coffee?' she suggested.

'A coffee,' he repeated hopelessly.

He saw trays of mean little teapots but decided he would stand up to them. The hiss of the steam going into the little pot would have been welcome but he was stubborn now. The woman leaned in and pressed a green button so that a dark stream of black coffee filled the mug she had selected for him.

A mug for a mug, wasn't that what Olive said? If mugs were scarce you'd be two of them.

Now he understood her.

He eyed the cakes and watched in surprise as one of his hands reached for one. There were tongs for the job, fiddly things he wanted no part of, instead he gripped a pastry which had been baked in a twirl with raisins rolled into it and a splash of white icing for decoration. He had seen these on a plate at his sisters' house and he liked the look of them. And the woman watched all of this with considerable patience, frowning slightly at the large roll of notes he took from his pocket. He did not own a credit card and usually carried a few hundred in cash, which he rarely had any use for.

There was a corner table which he was watching and he made his way to it, stepping around a baby's pram and some wide-backed women, engaged in a heavy-looking conversation. Bird sank down into a corner seat where he was away from everything but could still watch the other people. He had not spilled a drop of coffee onto the saucer and this detail felt important to him. He took a sip and it was scalding. A black woman was sitting at a table reading a newspaper. She was wearing a bright yellow jumper and Bird thought in a sudden flash that he had never seen anything so dramatic and beautiful. He wondered how Midge was getting on and what he should do about her. From the moment he had watched her climb up into the jeep in the strange rose-coloured light of morning, he had felt as if he was surviving something.

A young mother came through the tables then, struggling with a baby and her bags of groceries. A bag fell, spilling out some apples and a rolling cabbage. 'Shit,' the woman said through her teeth and then dipped down with the baby balancing on her side. She came close to toppling and Bird instinctively rose and the woman, grimacing, confused, handed him the baby.

'Could you hold him?' she asked quietly and she was scrambling under chairs for her shopping.

Bird sat down and waited, the baby's weight warm on his knee. It was an unusual thing to be handed another human being. For the owner to ask, 'Could you hold him?' as if it was a horse who was being fresh instead of this neatly bundled, round-headed individual. The child was not more than two, cheeks like cushions, a raw energy for life radiating outwards from him. Bird held him carefully, his wide hands on his back and middle. The baby turned his head with a wobble to see him. Bird leaned back a bit, not wanting to frighten him. It was a boy for sure, he already had that sturdiness about him, his face forming angles that would not be called pretty.

'Ba,' the baby said and pointed to his mother.

'Ba,' Bird replied. He handed the child back into her arms carefully, immediately feeling that something had departed, that he had been deserted by someone.

He was getting up to leave when he saw the O'Neills moving

towards him. Joseph was carrying a tray and his wife, Susan, was walking slowly behind him. They were not looking at Bird at all. They were not looking at anyone. They were intent only on carrying the tray with two white cups and saucers on it and two of the mean teapots to a vacant table in the corner. Susan was limping. Bird could see that, and she moved with a heavy rolling walk that seemed painful. They glanced at him and he looked back and nodded, gathering up some change he had left on his table and hearing it fall with a jangle into his pocket.

'Bird,' Joseph said and he could sense that everything had changed between them. Previous encounters had been easier, the conversation plan laid out in front of them.

'Not a bad day, Bird,' Joe might say and Bird might nod and make some comment about the long-range forecast.

'The weather is too mild for this time of year. We'll pay for it later.'

But because he had been to their house on that particular Saturday and had seen the hammering that life had given them, there was no plan, no reason to discuss the weather, ever. They sat down in two small wooden chairs facing each other and Bird, who had been standing, sat down again in his own chair. He had no idea what he would say to them. He was awkward with people even when he knew them, even when he was related to them, but to sit down seemed right. His not leaving them, not pretending, seemed like the correct thing to do.

'You're out and about,' he said and they both nodded and they looked into each other's faces now.

Susan O'Neill, a big, heavy woman, looked as if she had been drained of her blood, her face like ashes in the grate on an early morning. Her hair was ragged and unkempt, her coat not buttoned. She was like a woman who wanted nothing but to be at home and yet could not stand being there either.

'Susan is getting her hip done,' Joseph said and here he placed one hand at his side to show Bird where the new hip would be and Susan shifted in her chair and looked at her hands folded in her lap. Neither of them seemed interested in the tea on the tray in front of them.

'We're early for her appointment,' Joseph went on and Bird nodded. He considered the day they were having and how in spite of what their son had done, their own lives could still demand some kind of living – tea would be poured, food eaten, hips replaced as if any of it actually mattered a bit to them.

'She's been waiting a year,' Joe went on, 'so I told her we'd go in . . . What would be the point in cancelling?'

A woman Bird had never seen before approached the table then. She was a small humped woman, round like a hedgehog, and she leaned down into Susan's face, her small dark eyes seeking out the other woman's as if she wanted to climb into them. She told her that she was sorry for her trouble, 'So sorry for your loss,' she added. And she turned to look at Bird as if he should also say something but Bird said nothing.

'You have an angel in heaven,' she told Susan and she patted her on the shoulder.

'I don't want him in heaven. I want him down here,' Susan answered.

It was the first time she had said anything. Joe poured a cup of tea for her and the tea ran down the spout of the cheap teapot and made a dirty puddle on the saucer and in his mind Bird was picking up the same teapot and smashing it on a wall. Didn't these people have enough trouble in their lives now without a pissing teapot? He felt anger fill his cheeks and he swallowed to dilute it.

The hedgehog woman moved on, at a loss and not sure if she should have said anything.

'We wanted to thank you,' Susan said quietly and Bird moved in his chair, eager now to leave them. He did not want to be thanked. He had been useless. He had fallen asleep in their kitchen.

'For . . . well, you know . . .' she continued. 'And for not talking.'

'Oh, it got out,' Joe interrupted, 'but not from you . . . We know that much about you, Bird.'

And Bird sat still and marvelled at the strange affection that these people seemed to have for him. There was a long silence then when Bird lifted his spoon and held it and the O'Neills took their tea in small sips that gave no comfort.

'We saw Olive up at the hospital,' Joe added.

'Oh . . . she must be in for a check-up.'

'That's it,' Joe replied. 'Routine . . . That's what she said.'

And Bird admired their ability to remain polite and to continue with any kind of conversation. If they had started throwing the dishes around and screaming, not one person would have blamed them.

'Olive is a very decent woman,' Susan said then and something in her voice made both men look at her and they saw that she was crying, suddenly folding in on herself and shaking gently. And Bird and Joseph were rendered helpless as if they did not know her, as if above all else they had needed her to keep herself together.

'The kindness of some people,' Susan O'Neill said from behind her bloated hands, her voice wet and gurgling. The death of her son had come on her suddenly, lifting her up, knocking her senseless.

Bird left them then, unable to bear any more of it, wishing he had not met them, confused by their need to speak to him. Outside the shopping centre he stopped near the garden furniture and stared at it again. He was aware that his fingers carried some kind of tack from the pastry he had eaten. Even the bolt of sugar felt peculiar inside him. This was the world outside his and it worried him. A man drank from a bottle on the steps of the bank with one shoe pulled off his foot, the black shoe left sitting there on the step beside him. The large naked foot was unnatural there in the cold and wet, and to Bird it was incredible. He walked on and wondered who the drinker was and how he came to be there and what would become of such a man.

Bird suddenly wanted to go home and lose himself in his house again, to think his usual calm thoughts as he went from one dark shed to another. It was a short drive back to the hospital but he had no wish to be there. And yet Olive was also sitting in a waiting room somewhere and Midge positioned near a window and he did not know which one was drawing him there. He only knew that he could not go home, that home as he had known it had changed somehow. He pulled a second ticket from the machine and watched the red and white barrier lift in front of him.

20

Olive was sitting in a row of other women and it pained him to see her there. She had a magazine open on her lap but she was staring at a small television that was high up in a corner. It was one of those shows where couples appeared on a couch and then argued as if there was no one at all watching them. Bird had seen one with her once when Margaret had gone out – which in itself was a wonder. She gave night classes to children who were repeating exams and they came from all parts of Ireland to listen to her – amazed by her ability to get numbers into their heads, enjoying her determination and the certainty that she was taking them somewhere.

'Bird,' Olive said, her face a mass of lines here, a run of different small expressions. He was out of place, taller than other men, still in his work clothes, the red hat sticking up from his jacket pocket.

'What are you doing here?' And by now she was smiling a little and he could see that apart from her initial confusion she was pleased to see him.

'I met Joe and Susan O'Neill and they told me you were here.'

'Ah, Joe and Susan,' Olive whispered as Bird sat down heavily in a seat opposite her. 'The poor things . . . and her in now to have her hip done . . . after everything that's happened to them.'

'And why are you in here?' Bird asked softly, aware of the other women, the television with the sound turned down.

Olive shrugged. 'A check-up,' she said and in that moment Bird saw into her and through her and around her. A cold river of worry ran over him but he didn't say anything for a moment. He kept looking at her until her eyes, which had taken off around the room, returned to him. Bird ran a hand back through his hair and then folded his arms and waited.

'Well, it's nice to have company,' Olive said finally.

She was different to how she had been on the day after her holiday. She was a person who was waiting and worried and weighed down by something.

'Where's Margaret?'

'Oh, don't talk to me about her . . . she has her knickers in such a knot that I wouldn't even let her come in with me.'

'And what's wrong with her?' Bird asked and then before Olive could answer, he steered her back into the pen again.

'What are you in here for?'

Olive took a deep breath as if bored suddenly by everything, bored by the couple who were screaming silently at each other on the television, bored by the woman whose elbow kept prodding her, bored by her brother, his sudden appearance an irritation now.

'I found a . . . *tiny* thing,' and she was leaning over and making a small pinching movement with her thumb and index finger. 'TINY,' she repeated and she swallowed suddenly and a gulp escaped from her and she pulled her lips in over her neat white teeth in a way that seemed painful. Bird watched and saw that her eyes were spiked with tears which she blinked away furiously, her hands squeezing the magazine into a tight roll of paper. She cleared her throat and gave her shoulders a shake, angry with herself, angry at Bird for seeing her, angry at the tiny thing she had found. She did not say when she found it or where. It didn't

137

matter anyway. Bird sat perfectly still. He did not know what to do with these women who seemed pleased enough to have him there and then kept crying on him. But Olive was not Susan O' Neill. Olive was his sister and a terrible sadness came in a flood over him then.

Not Olive, he said to himself. Not Olive Keegan. If ever a woman was meant to live it was Olive Keegan.

'They did a biopsy last week and called me in. When they call you in . . .'

She shook her head and Bird said nothing.

Olive turned and looked back at him suddenly.

'What are you doing in town?' she asked.

Bird's eyes were travelling around the waiting room as he answered.

'I brought that young Connors girl in to see her mother.'

Olive didn't speak for a moment.

'Midge?' she asked, leaning back in her chair as if she needed to have a different view of him. 'I taught Midge Connors how to swim – the poor scrap. I wanted to give her something.'

Bird said nothing.

'*You* brought Midge Connors in to see her mother,' she repeated.

'I did.'

'The whole place has gone mad,' she said.

She took a deep breath then and seemed to think for a minute. 'I remember Midge Connors very well, out swimming in her knickers because she had no swimsuit to put on her.'

Bird listened but didn't answer so Olive continued.

'Margaret is in a complete state because that long-nosed eejit Tom Geoghan is back and wants to meet her. If ever a man needed a swift kick up the arse, that one does . . . And now you're running some kind of taxi service for waifs and strays. And here am I . . .' She paused there. 'Waiting for news . . . Like a death sentence,' she said quietly. 'I don't know what happened when I was in Medjugorje but it's as if the whole place has gone to shit.'

'And you forgot to mention your own Pat Noonan,' Bird said and he had a slight smile on his face as he looked up at the television. 'Like Romeo and Juliet,' he continued, not looking at her.

'Ah, would you stop,' Olive said, laughing gently and shaking out her magazine as if to engage now in some serious reading.

She looked up quickly then with a question for him.

'And are you going to hang around here all day waiting for her?'

Bird did not answer.

'After this we'll both go and find out what's happening up there. Midge Connors could stay the whole night for all you know . . . Bird, you daft eejit.'

'Olive Keegan,' a voice called. The nurse was wearing blue and white, the kind of soft blue trousers and shoes that made everything about her silent. Olive swallowed and began to gather up her things. Bird stood too and lifted her bag for her.

'There's no need to come in with me, Bird,' she said suddenly and her voice was low and firm. He did not know what he would do or say to any doctor and yet he could not just leave her there. He placed a hand on her back and guided her forward, down a bright corridor in the same way she had taken him to school on his first day, showing him the route to his classroom.

The oncologist, Mr Greenwell, was of course a healthy, smiling man with a good-looking shirt and cufflinks, a kind of pure vitality springing from him.

'This is Bird, my brother,' Olive told him.

She sat down on the only chair and faced him and Bird leaned his behind on some kind of examining table near a curtain.

Mr Greenwell stood up and shook Bird's hand energetically.

'Ah, your brother the farmer,' he said with great enthusiasm and in that moment Bird wanted to hit him. He hated this man who was allowed to have such power over his sister.

'Well, Olive . . . I have the results of your biopsy here,' and his smooth clean hands began to turn the loose pages of a brown folder. 'And we've found something very small and benign, which . . .' and here he raised one of his Jesus hands as if to stop Olive from climbing over his desk to embrace him, 'is not too unusual given your history but we'll keep an eye on it and we might remove it if it gets any bigger or causes discomfort. But for now . . .'

'It's not *bad* news,' Olive answered very quietly.

'It *is* the better sort of news,' he said, smiling with his head bobbing at her. 'We'll keep an eye on your bloods of course but . . . I don't want to see you again for six months.'

'Thank God,' Olive said and she was nodding and looking down into her lap as if she was reading a prayer from there. Back in the waiting room there was no sign of tears and instead her face seemed radiant. She looked at Bird and smiled.

'I feel like celebrating.'

'And we should,' he answered. 'That Mr Greenwell seemed very optimistic.'

'God forgive me, Bird, but I can't stand him – he's like God sitting in there, passing sentence. And yet he's keeping me well . . . I should be more grateful.'

'You're a good girl, Olive,' Bird told her and she burst out laughing.

'I don't want to be good any more,' she answered, her eyes sparkling.

The door opened with its sighing sound and Pat Noonan stepped in, dressed in a suit and tie, his face open and smiling, his eyes fixed on Olive.

'Well, here's your chance now,' Bird said softly with a grin.

140

'He's taking me to lunch. He's been out in the car park waiting. I wouldn't let him come in with me . . . and now here he is anyway.'

'And where are you off to now?' Bird asked.

'We're going to have lunch in a posh restaurant in Dublin – I told him we would either celebrate or drown our sorrows.'

Bird smiled down at her and she laughed suddenly and threw her arms around him.

'I have my life, Bird . . . and I'm going to start living – tell Margaret not to wait up for me.'

21

Margaret had seen Tom Geoghan at the new twenty-four-hour Tesco. He was standing with a small wire basket over his arm, staring into the aubergines as if one of them might talk to him. She had some time to watch him, her eyes full of terror and yet completely fixed on him, her heart beating in every part of her body. She remembered the last time she had seen him, his hair as black as a rook, his young face ruddy and shining, how magnificent, how benevolent he had seemed as he allowed her to buy him a pint in a small brightly lit pub in Dublin and then walked down a wet street on his own – taking her heart with him. The images she carried from that wet evening in the city still haunted her, ghouls and spirits peeling away and away again but they would never leave her. There were still nights when she dreamed about him and would wake in the morning feeling the very same heartbreak all over again and with the same intensity and she would curse him and then herself for allowing a person, a boy really, to stay like a rent-free lodger inside her.

She stood quietly behind a special offer for muesli; bags of what looked like horse feed stacked high to protect her. A hot flush came then and almost knocked her, the heat feeling like a sudden scald from the kettle. Her hormones were like a red army marching through her and she cursed the menopause for punishing her body, empty vessel that it was – she had never had a child, had never even had sex with anyone – and yet she was still given the same punishment as every slut in the country. Her virginity at forty-nine was something she could not put words on. Even her own thoughts, the inner voice that reminded her, were embarrassing. Now her thermal underwear was soaked in sweat and stuck to her, her face, behind the breakfast cereals, like a chilli pepper.

'Margaret Keegan, how are you?' Frances Carney said loudly and from the corner of her eye she knew that Tom had heard her name and was looking across the aisle at her.

What does he see? she wondered. There had been a ball one summer and she remembered dancing out of the room and onto a balcony with him.

Here in the aisle of the big new Tesco, which she hated, was the actual reality. Margaret felt like she was under an avalanche of yesterday's mackerel. She could feel Tom watching her and she had no choice but to look back at him. There was an aubergine in his hands now, a second already in the basket.

'I don't know what's going to happen to this country,' Frances was saying. 'I turned around in the post office yesterday and . . .' here her voice dropped to a whisper, 'there wasn't a single white face in the queue behind me.'

'Really, Frances? I hadn't noticed.' Margaret began to move away from her.

'And isn't it awful what's going on in Dublin? The gays are out marching – they want to get married.'

'Isn't that their own business?'

'Well, you might not say that when they're running the country.'

'Well, maybe if they were we wouldn't be in the state we're in.'

'Well now, Margaret, that's a funny way to look at it . . .'

'I'll go on, Frances,' Margaret said suddenly. 'I'm in a bit of a hurry . . . I need to get home to Olive.'

'Ah, how is Olive?'

But Margaret was not able to stand another minute and she turned on her heel quickly.

Tom had changed more than she could have imagined. He was middle-aged now with all traces of boyishness washed away from him. He had become somehow shorter and thicker-looking like a small wide bottle. Gone was the sweet loping movement of youth and in its place was something very square and solid. He had seemed elegant before but had turned into a chess piece now, the castle maybe, or something you would stick in a gap to stop an animal from escaping. His neck and head in particular seemed to have thickened and the boyish face that had haunted her was just a flicker. His eyes, which she remembered as intelligent, had not changed much but seemed too close together – giving him the look of a stoat or a fox or some other narrow-faced creature. He was wearing a good wool coat and polished shoes, the basket on his arm holding the aubergine and a two-roll pack of toilet paper – the mark of a man who lived on his own now, someone who was vulnerable in this big bright place, whose late wife had done all of the shopping.

She could not bring herself to speak to him. She could not bear for their eyes to meet again and to hear his voice in case it would strike her as familiar. She could accept the pain of remembering but could not accept the risk of also 'feeling'. She was astonished now too by the reel she had been playing and replaying and had never once considered what the passing of the years might do to him, how a heartbreaking man could also be reduced by time to a squat, ordinary figure.

She saw herself then in a mirror as she went to buy some soap in the toiletries aisle.

Oh dear God, she thought.

A net of broken veins on her cheeks gave her a high red colour and her hair, which was a faded brown and full of grey rivers, did nothing to help her. Her curls and waves were dried out now, giving her the look of an old fern in need of watering. And below that, the narrow shoulders and trim waist were long gone and her clothes, well, she had not expected to meet anyone. She was wearing a pair of men's corduroy trousers and wellingtons, some kind of a Fair Isle cardigan which had not been given a thought – the whole ensemble a kind of a tragedy.

'Margaret,' a voice said and he was beside her and there was no place to hide, even though she wanted to pretend she had not heard him – pretend in fact that she was not Margaret Keegan but someone else, a woman who was happy in herself and not weak with the fear of having to turn around and face him.

'Margaret,' he said again and she turned.

'Tom,' she said, her voice coming out soft like a kitten, her breath all caught up inside her.

'How are you?' he asked and there it was. They could not really hide from history. He remembered what he had done and so did she. The tone he had chosen when addressing her gave all of that away – it was all kindness and embarrassment and with a genuine concern for her.

'I'm grand, thanks, Tom – and yourself?' she said and her voice was a little squeaky and he was smiling and telling her that he would recognize her anywhere. At least he did not lie and tell her that she hadn't changed as they both knew that age had come to them, that they had each taken the fair whack from it.

There was a pause then when neither of them said anything. And Margaret would describe this moment to Olive as 'only dreadful'. The grocery shelves seemed to bend and lean with embarrassment around them, the air feeling rigid with it and Margaret herself was beginning to feel very hot again.

'I was very sorry to hear about your wife,' she said finally, hardly believing her own decency.

'Thank you.' But he could not look at her now. His head was to one side and he was watching the toe of her welly.

'Margaret . . .' he began then and now she wanted to run away from him.

She looked down at her watch, a small-faced dial she had been given for her twenty-first birthday. Tom had bought her a watch too and she had thrown it away after he left, no longer able to bear the sight of it. She could still see the small thin straps flying as she pitched it into the slurry pit.

'I need to be going on home,' she told him. 'Olive is due back from the hospital and I want to see how she got on.'

'How *is* Olive?'

'She's doing well, thank God . . . She's just in for a check-up.'

'I have very fond memories of her . . . and you . . . and your father in your kitchen. And Bird, how is he?'

'Bird is Bird, the same as ever really.'

'Do you remember the time he chased the bat around the kitchen with the tennis racquet?'

And here Margaret's eyes met his and she wondered at him and this trip down memory lane that he was so interested in. He had no clue, this short square block of a man; he had no clue that he had ruined her. And she felt so foolish in herself and knew now that the pain and disappointment that she had felt over the years was largely of her own making. He had set the ball rolling but she had allowed it to travel on and on and on.

'Do you think we could meet for a coffee?' he asked. His eyes were empty with loneliness, his dire need to talk to someone making them seem hollow.

'What would we talk about, Tom?' Margaret wanted to ask, but even though she had every right to be cold towards him something stopped her.

'Ah, sure we'll see,' she said and the words were quiet and wandering.

She looked up the length of the supermarket, feeling as if she was flying away from him.

'Can I give you a call?' he asked. 'Or send you an email?'

'I suppose you could,' she answered vaguely.

'I've often thought about you, Margaret,' he began suddenly – but she was nodding and moving away from him. It had been hard seeing him again but not in the way she had imagined. It had not hurt at all because there had been so many years to buffer it. Time would not allow her to dredge up those same feelings – they had fallen down too deep a well for that. Margaret felt relief then, like a kind of sun that warmed her. Mostly, when she considered the years she had carried this man around with her, she just felt foolish.

Her grocery list had been forgotten. There were only one or two useless items in her basket. Listerine – what in God's name did she pick that up for? She would have to come back later. From now on she would shop at two in the morning when everyone else was sleeping.

22

Midge did not see Charlie when he looked in the window at her. It was not a proper window but more a small square of green glass in the door so that a nurse could look in at her patient. Bridget had surprised the world the night before by moving, her eyes, which were lost inside her bloated face, had given a sudden flutter. Now she was lying with her head to one side and her eyes were half open. Bridget seemed to look right at her daughter and Midge looked back into the strange dark cavern that was her mother. Then came some pressure from her mother's hand, the tremble and curl of a small fat finger, her wedding band embedded and disappearing into her. There was hope then and just as Midge was stepping onto the bright shaft of it, her father was looking at her through this window – her father who would come into this room now and surely kill her.

Midge held her mother's hand as if this could protect her and watched his face, the dark frightened eyes, the hook of a nose and the cheeks which were hollow. Lunch at the hospital had come and gone. The nurses were sneaking meals to Midge, bowls of soup and ham sandwiches – they all wanted to feed her. It was only two o'clock but already the light over the town was getting weaker, the grey sky of December close to the ground, the odd dash of rain hitting the window. Midge thought of Bird and wished without really knowing why that he was there with her.

The face at the window was changing, the eyes less afraid now. They were becoming wider and more curious, the narrow head turning slowly on its axis, first to look at his wife and from there his daughter and then another slow circle of the room, taking in Midge's rucksack on the floor beside her, an extra chair, a kind of leatherette recliner that a person might sleep in, a small wooden wardrobe for the patient's belongings, a range of machines and equipment he had never seen the like of before, a bedside locker, two plastic cups of water, the lunch tray with empty plates on it, a fruit bowl with some grapes and bananas hanging out of it – and then back to Bridget and finally Midge, stiff and white, a small wooden figure. He seemed to stop then, his eyes fixed on hers as if they might set fire to her. She had not seen him since he had pushed her from the car on that Saturday in November. He had settled in with Imelda Conroy. The same tramp who was pretending he was with her on the day he tried to kill poor Bridget.

Midge felt an opening inside her, down low in her stomach, her bowels heaving and breathing, a small seep of urine in her underwear. She was ashamed of herself, afraid that she was becoming a frightened child again. There was a red button on the other side of the bed but she could not reach for it. She was not able to move or to stop looking back at him. She swallowed, her throat dusty and catching, her legs seemed to have disappeared from under her – from her stomach down she felt nothing. She watched then as the door handle began to move very slowly and the door opened with a small wheezing sigh and he put one foot in. He did not open the door wide, just a crack, and then seemed to slide into the room, his foot and leg first and then, turning sideways, the rest of his rangy body was pulled in after him. She noticed then that he was slightly different. He had cut the ribbons of hair from the back of his head and now he looked close to middle age and as a result a bit less frightening. He had shaved too, his skin lean and sallow-looking where the stubble had always

149

been. His eyes were not bloodshot either and he didn't smell of booze or tobacco. He was wearing some kind of jumper she had not seen before with a childish zigzag pattern on it. The leather jacket had been left somewhere. He lifted a small plastic chair away from the wall and sat on the opposite side of the bed from her.

When Midge finally spoke to him her words were quiet and careful.

'What are you doing here?'

Charlie didn't say anything for a moment. He didn't look at her. Instead he was staring at Bridget lying in the bed as if he had been hypnotized by her.

'I *said* . . . what are you doing here?'

'Take it easy,' he told her and he was speaking in a whisper. When he looked across the bed he had expected to see a little face twisted and angry and instead saw one that was blank and unlined, every feeling and emotion buried deep there.

'Take it fucking easy,' he said again and this time his voice was a little louder.

'Now,' he said, and he sat back in the chair with his arms folded as if he had already spent enough time looking at her mother.

'I'm calling the Guards,' Midge said. 'And I'll tell them what you did to Mam.'

'Did to Mam? I did nothing at all to your mam . . . nothing at all.'

'Everyone knows what you did to her.'

'I did nothing and I have Imelda Conroy outside the door who'll swear to everything I'm saying.'

'Imelda Conroy,' Midge said flatly.

'Imelda is taking very good care of me.'

They both looked at Bridget as if she could sit up and explain everything to them.

'Look at her,' Charlie said quietly. 'Lying there like an old cow in the bed.'

Midge could think of nothing to say to him.

'I should have called the Guards myself,' he said then. 'And explained to them how she attacked me with a broken bottle.'

'They won't believe a word you say.'

'I know – and they won't believe a word you say either.'

Charlie and Midge sat on opposite sides of the bed, their words floating over Bridget.

'What good are you?' Midge asked and she was shaking her head and looking over at him. 'What good are you to this world? All you ever do is cause misery.'

'Misery, is that what you think?'

'I think you're a miserable bastard,' she told him.

'Ah, fuck off with yourself would you?'

Midge wished she had a weapon hidden under the mattress, not a gun or a knife but some kind of heavy truncheon that she could use to hit him. She did not want a bullet that would simply enter his body at speed and finish him. She wanted something that would break his skull and send his brains flying.

'Anyway,' he said, 'it's lucky for her that she started moving because I had a talk with the big man this morning and he was saying it was time to think about pulling the plug on her.'

'What big man?'

'That head doctor who's looking after her. I rang in and explained that I had been detained.'

Midge was amazed by him. '*Detained?*' she repeated.

'That's what I told him. It impressed him.'

'What's his name?'

'How the fuck would I know? He was smooth – sounded like a bollox . . . but you'd expect that from these fellas who are high up in hospitals.'

Midge had no idea what he was talking about.

151

'Anyway . . . poor old Bridget's ears must have been burning because she gave a kick and they rang back to tell me.'

Midge could not understand this new veneer he seemed to have grown and she wondered if being sober had taken some of the sourness out of him.

'What are you looking at?' he asked her and then, 'Jaysus, Midge, I'm starving. Would you hand me one of those bananas . . . or would you have a few quid that will take me on to tomorrow?'

And Midge stood up suddenly, feeling as if her body had been lit up with a bolt of lightning.

I will finish him, she told herself. I will, I will.

She picked up the bowl of fruit and flung it across the room at him.

'Fuck you and your fucking bananas,' she roared.

Charlie saw the bowl coming first – it took off ahead of its contents like a planet that was crashing – and he ducked, the bowl smashing at his feet and the bananas hitting him on the forehead, the sound dull and foolish.

'You're not my father,' Midge said. 'You're not. Mam told me.'

Charlie straightened himself up.

'What the fuck are you doing?' and he was holding the bananas now like an extra hand attached to him. 'Have you lost your fucking marbles? I only came in to see your mother and now you're throwing fucking bowls of fruit at me.'

And Midge was crying. 'Why can you not just go away and leave me and Mam alone? Go away, will you?' And now she was screaming. 'Go away from me.'

'You are under the illusion that I'm to blame for everything.'

Charlie's shoulders drooped and he put the bananas on the bedside locker. And then he was walking around the bed towards her.

Midge did not fully remember what happened next except that

she was being thrown onto the bed, her own feet in heavy Doc Martens, climbing and sliding over her mother. She became caught on a sheet and then fell face down on her and Bridget gave a strange wet gasp and a gurgling sound came up from her and then Midge was off the bed and onto her father, climbing his thin frame and feeling herself turn into an animal – that was what he had done to her. She clawed at his face, the loose skin being twisted and stirred around with her fingers, his eyes shut tight to protect himself, and he was trying to tear her off him when he fell, his feet going from under him on the polished floor.

'I hate you,' she told him and Midge cried these words into him – her mouth sending warm breath into his ears, her very lips touching them. Charlie rolled over and punched her face hard so that her head was sent rolling and she felt her tongue crush between her teeth, her mouth filling up with warm blood, and then he hit her again and her head went rolling the other way in a loose kind of rhythm and Midge stopped struggling, allowing it all to happen, giving up on trying, giving in to him.

'Go on and kill me so,' she told him.

And then it stopped, darkness came and her world was eclipsed by something.

Bird Keegan was lifting Charlie away from her and he was like a limp animal – so that Bird only needed to shake him. This was the sight the nurses and the security guards faced. Midge lying on the floor with a pool of blood coming from her nose and mouth, a single tooth sitting on the front of her jumper. Bird shaking Charlie away from him as if there was something sticky on his hands that he wanted to get rid of. Olive peeping from behind a door and Bridget staring at it all – and at that moment dying – without anyone knowing, her eyes empty and looking through everyone. Midge's nose was broken and she could only lie there and listen as Bird talked to the guards and waited then while the doctor examined her – and without really understanding why, she knew at that moment, the moment when he had made her father look like a rag or something even less significant, that she could love Bird Keegan – that she was already attached like a burr to him.

III
Hope's Hill

23

Three weeks later Margaret sat at her winged dressing table and put on some pink lipstick. She could not remember the last time she had done this and she had trouble locating her perfume and pearl earrings. The lipstick tasted of chewing gum and its fuchsia colour seemed old-fashioned. She had not examined her appearance for some time because she had had no reason to care about it. Now as she prised the tops off old make-up pots and tried to remember how to apply it, her hands were shaking and her eyes in the mirror were filled with worry.

Tom Geoghan had called and cornered her into meeting him – it was three days before Christmas and because her world was upside down with the Midge Connors business she had given in – and all day long she had felt as if there were ants running up and down the length of her.

The funeral of Bridget Connors had been a colourful affair with Connors and Carneys coming from every part of the country. Midge had endured a steady stream of locals offering their condolences until her poor hand was nearly wrung off her. The older sister appeared from England – a tall, austere-looking woman with auburn hair, not at all what Margaret had expected – and she was a teacher too, with a new baby and a few small red-haired children climbing all over her. There was one brother who had come from Manchester – a barrel-chested man with red hair

157

and a trampish wife whose skirt was not suitable for a funeral. Afterwards as they were filling in the grave – with the rain coming down in slants – Midge's legs had given way suddenly and when her brother caught her by the arm, her language was very colourful when she spoke to him. What on earth did the girl come out with and them burying their mother? Margaret tried now to remember. 'To get the F away from her,' or something of that nature.

It was a scene that Margaret and Olive wanted to put behind them for ever. She could still remember the white of Midge's skin against the wet clay, her hands falling flat into the earth and then holding on to it as if she was losing her grip there. A circle of starlings had come by then, sweeping past in a sudden cloud as if they might wipe this sad day away from everyone.

Most people agreed that it was 'a happy release' for Bridget Connors and sent long worried looks towards her youngest daughter. Charlie Connors had done the decent thing and stayed away, although someone said he was seen later in a drunken state at the Beacon.

Bird told Margaret and Olive later that the brother – Oliver was his name – and his wife had walked back to the house on Emmet Road then before Midge could stop them. Apparently she had walked in and found the brother's wife holding up one of her mother's old cardigans to see if it might be the right size for her.

'Midge walked in and there they were . . . going through everything.'

As Bird had repeated the story to his sisters his eyes were burning with disgust for these people. Margaret wanted to know how he knew all of this because it was only Midge that could tell him – which would mean that they were in some kind of communication with each other, and the idea of this was unsettling – but on that day after the funeral he was in no mood for being questioned and so she said nothing.

158

He had called in at the lodge again after the funeral and they were glad to have him there at the fire so the three of them could talk out the funeral together. She had noticed him watching Midge in the cemetery and yet he had not been able to do anything for her.

Or so Margaret had thought.

'Where is Midge now?' she had asked him as she put a fresh log on the fire.

'At the parochial house – Father Conlon's housekeeper is taking care of her.'

And then, a week later, a plan had been hatched to help her. As it turned out there was no one in the parish – and no Carneys or Connors either – who was willing to take her in, except for Bird, who in his own quiet way then foisted the girl onto Margaret and Olive.

'What would it look like to have a young girl sleeping under the same roof as a bachelor farmer?' Bird had asked them.

'Well then, you shouldn't have suggested it to Father Conlon,' Margaret had answered and she was spitting with pure temper. 'And why should we be the ones to step in? Why would we get involved with her?'

'Because, Margaret,' Olive had cut in very quietly, 'it would be an act of charity.'

'Exactly,' Bird had answered and he had the slightest smile on his face, which Margaret had found very annoying. The seed had been an easy one to sow and he had started where the ground was softest – with Olive.

Now the girl – with her nose still under a bandage – was sleeping in their guest room. She had arrived on 8 December, the Feast of the Immaculate Conception, and had been there for almost two weeks now. And as if that wasn't bad enough, her father, Charlie Connors, had starting calling their landline. He was being 'detained' and questioned by the Guards but so far they hadn't charged him with anything. She heard that they had already had to let him out once, for legal reasons, and then found a new reason to bring him back in – but as long as Imelda Conroy swore that he was with her on the Sunday morning when Bridget was attacked they couldn't pin anything on him. And only Margaret had the courage to deal with him now. Midge had troubles enough and Olive was too frightened.

'You again?' Margaret would bellow. 'Get on now or I'll call the Guards on you.'

'I just want to speak to my daughter.'

'She doesn't want to talk to you – and why would she? You're nothing but scum – and you should be ashamed of yourself after what you did to your wife and daughter.'

And with that Margaret would hang up the phone, a part of her enjoying this new vent for her temper, the knowledge that she could say anything she wanted to him, that she had a new receptacle for her anger.

There were footsteps on the landing now and Margaret called out to them.

'Midge Connors,' she said and the feet stopped moving. Margaret recognized the sound of those feet, quiet and stealthy like a little cat out hunting.

'Midge Connors,' she said again and her door began to open slowly.

The girl had improved a bit since her mother had been buried. She would not eat very much for them and she was quiet, but that was to be expected. Her eyes only brightened when Bird appeared, which was not that often, now that he had landed her on them.

And yet, it was right in its own way that this young broken woman should be there in this house, safe, between two sisters. She had her own attic room and there was hardly a peep out of her. Margaret knew that Midge was still frightened of her. As her teacher it had been her job to get things into her head and it had never occurred to Margaret to be kind to her.

'Yes?' Midge answered, her head coming around the door. She had not been inside Margaret's room before and did not want to be in there either.

'Come in, will you? I want your opinion.'

Midge looked at this wide-shouldered woman in a flowery dress and felt embarrassed. She stepped through the doorway slowly, looking around her as she walked. There was nowhere to sit and she felt awkward.

'Well, sit down,' Margaret said and she nodded towards the bed – and Midge perched herself on the end of the neat white cover.

'What do you think of this frock?' Margaret asked her and Midge felt her head spin with the idea of this, this woman who still frightened the life out of her, asking for her opinion.

Margaret, who was sitting on a chair at the dressing table, got up and moved into the middle of the floor so Midge could see her. She stood there with her big hands at her sides and waited and Midge had a tiny lurch of feeling and suddenly felt sorry for her. 'The frock', as she called it, was too small, tight on her waist and her stomach rose up a bit under the belt and made some of the flowers seem magnified, as if they were growing underwater. She was wearing shoes that looked uncomfortable.

'Well?' Margaret's voice was a little louder now with impatience.

'It's hard to see in here,' Midge said.

Margaret made a grab for the light switch and put on a searing bright bulb over her head.

She stood very still again and waited and Midge did not want to hurt her.

'Why are you all dressed up?' she asked.

Here Margaret gave a sigh, her shoulders limp suddenly. She walked awkwardly in the shoes to an armchair at the wall and sat down heavily in it.

161

'Because I'm an eejit,' she said and there was silence. Midge looked down at the floor and followed the path of the grain in the wood.

'I'm meeting that Tom Geoghan.'

'The solicitor?'

'Yes.'

'And what are you meeting him for? Is he your . . . boyfriend?'

Here Margaret gave a hard little laugh and began to shake her head.

'I don't know what he is. He asked me to meet him at the Mountain View Hotel for a drink.'

'That's where all the men who are having affairs go,' Midge offered.

'Really? Is that so?' and two red shots of colour appeared on Margaret's cheeks and Midge knew that she had made her angry. She had seen that sudden flush of colour before and she wondered if Margaret could still hit her.

'He's not having an affair because his wife is dead. He's a widower,' and here Margaret became quiet again suddenly. She caught sight of herself in the long mirror on the wardrobe door.

'I'm an eejit,' she said again. 'Dressing up for him.'

'Was he not nice to you?'

'No. He was not nice to me.'

'Then what are you meeting him for?'

'That's a very good question, Midge Connors.'

Margaret got up and went to the wardrobe and found a little handbag. She opened it and gave it a shake. There was nothing in it.

'Do you think people change?' Midge asked her. She was still sitting on the end of the bed, her fingers tracing patterns on the cover, lost in one of Bird's old jumpers, a pair of his jeans rolled up over her ankles.

162

Margaret stopped for a minute and seemed to think about it.

'I hope so,' she said finally and then she turned to Midge and said, 'Do you think I've changed . . . since I was your teacher?'

'Not that much.'

'Oh . . . well. At least you're honest.'

Midge gave a slight smile.

'And seeing as you're in an honest mood . . . are you going to tell me what you think of this rig-out?'

Again Margaret straightened up and offered herself.

You look like a man dressed up in a woman's clothes, Midge wanted to say but she was too frightened.

'You look better in trousers . . .' she said finally, 'and a hat.'

'Oh, I see . . . Well, maybe I should meet him with a bucket on my head,' Margaret answered.

Midge slipped out the door then, feeling that the air was becoming dangerous.

'Wait a minute, you,' Margaret said and Midge turned again to face her.

Margaret walked to the wardrobe and called her over.

'This is where the gun is kept,' she said calmly as if it was a perfectly normal item to have in the wardrobe, and there it was standing on its butt between shoes and boots and handbags, a wool jacket on either side of it.

'Have you ever used a gun before?'

And Midge stared back at her.

'I'm asking you a question,' Margaret snapped.

'Are you out of your head?' Midge said back to her. 'Where do you think I come from, the Wild fucking West?'

'Watch your language in this house, miss – and Emmet Road wouldn't be a million miles away from the Wild West.'

Margaret lifted the gun out and pointing it down to the floor showed her the safety catch.

'Both myself and Olive are out tonight . . . and if there's an intruder . . .'

'Where's Olive going?' Midge was suddenly worried.

'She's off to a wedding with that Pat Noonan . . . making a fool of herself but I can't talk to her. This is how you release the catch.'

Midge watched how Margaret's strong hands held the gun with confidence.

'Margaret – has my father been calling the landline here?'

'No, he hasn't,' she said very quickly and she hoped it wasn't too obvious that she was lying. 'Now you're not to be coming up here otherwise . . . but there have been break-ins and there are tinkers floating around looking for any excuse to rob a place like this.'

She put the gun back and closed the door of the wardrobe.

'Bird will visit me,' Midge said. She was insulted by the idea of her coming up to Margaret's room when she was out and wanted to annoy her now. She looked up into Margaret's face and stared at her.

'Will he now?'

'Yes, he will.'

'Don't be getting any ideas about Bird Keegan, miss.'

'What sort of ideas are you talking about?'

'Oh I don't know at all,' Margaret said sarcastically. 'He's a single man with a big farm of land and here comes Midge Connors like a little bee heading for the honey.'

A sheen of sweat had appeared on Margaret's top lip and she could feel that the armpits of her dress were already soaking.

'You think I have a notion of your brother?'

'I don't know what you have.'

'Imagine if I did marry him though . . . then there would be two Margaret Keegans – did you know that that was my real name? Same as yours . . . *Margaret*.'

164

Margaret turned her back on her and began to fasten a watch on her wrist. She wished she had never called out to her. The Connors were all trouble and she should have known better.

'Two Margaret Keegans,' Midge said again. 'The world would not be able for it.'

'You can get out now . . . thank you very much,' Margaret answered without turning.

She felt ridiculous in this dress with flowers all over it. At the sound of the door opening she turned quickly again and spoke to her.

'I remember you when you were a girl . . . and you're right, people don't change.'

'No,' Midge answered. 'And I remember you too. We all stay the same, no matter how hard we might try to please other people.'

24

Midge went downstairs and found Olive and Bird sitting at the kitchen table. There was no tea made and they were facing each other like two people having a meeting. His visits to the lodge had no rhythm, days would pass and there was no sight of him and then he would appear out of the blue, for breakfast, at eight o'clock in the morning. She felt weak from talking to Margaret. It was hard to put on a brave face when there were days when Midge felt terrified of the world around her. There was not a drop of kindness in the older sister, or if there was she had no reason to show it. And yet she had taken her in. Olive was all warmth and laughter and liked to put her arms around Midge and hug her. But it was Bird that Midge wanted to be near. The sound of his voice coming up from the kitchen, his step on the gravel, his long strides over a field on the other side of the lake, each of these things was a peculiar comfort at a time when the world seemed to have turned on her. They stopped talking when she came in and Bird looked up at her, his eyes meeting hers in a way that made them both look away again.

'Here she is now . . . and where were you all this time?' Olive wanted to know.

'Margaret asked to speak to me.'

'Oh,' Olive said and Bird lifted an eyebrow.

'That sounds dangerous,' he said.

'She wanted to show me what she's wearing tonight.'

The idea of this caused Bird and Olive to glance at each other in surprise.

'I see,' Olive said and she was turning the corners of her mouth down and Bird himself seemed to grimace.

'I don't know what to make of this thing with Tom Geoghan,' Olive said quietly.

'She has to sort it out for herself,' Bird answered but he was looking at Midge when he spoke – and Midge was looking back at him, her eyes fixed, unblinking. And then Olive was looking at first one and then the other. She got up quickly and pushed her chair into the table. She paused then as if she wasn't entirely sure where she was going.

'Here,' Bird said suddenly to Midge – and it was in his usual gruff manner. 'I've something to show you.'

He reached into his coat then and lifted out a small black kitten.

The kitten stood with its back in a curve and its tiny fingerprint paws held closely together. And Midge stared down at it – a good deal of the loss she was feeling, the hurt that she was holding on to, the whole idea of being so suddenly without a mother came at her then, hitting hard and without warning.

'Oh,' she gasped and her eyes filled with tears again – these tears that had a mind of their own since the funeral.

'She's lovely,' she said finally and the kitten began to step down the middle of the table in a way that was uncertain. No one moved to touch it. There was something untamed about it, as if a sudden movement would send it scattering in every direction, a wild bounce onto the dresser or up onto the curtain rail.

'It's a he,' Bird said and then very quietly, 'there are enough women in this house.'

And here Midge gave a sniff and then a laugh as she lifted the kitten carefully onto her lap and began to stroke him.

Olive had said nothing and then seemed to wake up again.

'Bird – Margaret will have a conniption if she sees that cat in the house.'

There was no answer as Bird's eyes watched the paleness of Midge's hand as it gently stroked the kitten.

'Margaret will have a fit, Bird,' Olive said again.

'Ah, let her have a fit. This is a visiting cat – I'll take it back to the mother in the morning.'

'I think we should call him Jack.'

'Jack,' Bird repeated and he nodded his head slightly with approval.

Olive issued a long sigh and shook her head. The stairs in the hall creaked and she suddenly looked at both of them.

'She's coming – and if I were you I'd be putting that kitten back into your pocket.'

Olive left them then and went into the hall, closing the door firmly behind her.

'Bird . . . Can I ask you something?'

He didn't answer but turned his eyes on Midge and waited for her question.

'Do you think I could go back to my own house and get some of my things . . . I'm worried about the cat – in case my father's not feeding her – and I might ask one of the neighbours if they could take her.'

'I'll take you over there tomorrow,' Bird said simply. He gave the table a gentle smack with his two hands and stood up.

'I know I can't stay here very long,' she said quietly. 'But I'm worried about the cat – I keep thinking about her.'

'Don't worry about the cat,' he told her and he turned to face her as he opened the back door.

'Olive and Margaret are both out tonight,' he said. 'You'll be on your own here.'

'I'll have Jack,' Midge answered.

168

'I could drop over for a few minutes later?'

'Great,' she answered.

He left then and Midge was not able to meet his eyes or to say a proper thank you. She could not fully understand what she felt for him. There was at times a sense of relief when he left her and yet the idea of him not coming back made the whole place seem bleak, like a plain and empty world without a lake or river or mountain.

It was getting dark when Bird took the narrow back road home from town, passing the forge with its bright red door in the shape of a horseshoe. He had been to the mart earlier and had seen the auctioneer knocked off his feet by a heifer. He had driven back through the streets, a mass of coloured lights and tinsel over everything. He had stopped to buy lamb chops and cornflakes and through all of it he had thought about Midge Connors. His feelings for her were clamped inside his chest now and he needed to find a release for them. He stopped the jeep at a lay-by and pulled in so he could step out and look at that view of the mountain.

The December light was its own quiet grey and it made everything seem deserted and lonely. He had time to admire the world around him though, to take in mouthfuls of the icy air and puff it back out again. He climbed onto the bonnet of the jeep and then up on the roof so he could stand high over the countryside. The air was clear and sharp with not a sound anywhere. The trees were black and bare with the night closing in around them. A tractor with its lights on began to move slowly through the O'Neills' back lane and out into the fields again. Joe O'Neill was feeding his sheep, shaking out loose hay for them into a big round feeder. From where Bird stood at a distance, he could see Joe lift a bag and throw feed into a trough. Bird stared, his eyes following a straight line across the two fields that divided them. The other man had a broken heart inside him. He was lit up when he crossed through the beams of the tractor headlights. He could do nothing about the heart he had, so he continued working. That was what farmers did – regardless of the death taking place inside him, the cattle needed to be fed and he would do that, it was not as if his leg or his arm was broken.

It was the coldest December on record and for the first time Bird could remember, the entire lake was frozen over. He would have Christmas Day at his house this year. He would put up a tree if she wanted it and there would be plenty of good food, heat everywhere. Afterwards he might ask her to stay on with him and they would have a chance to be on their own at the fire. Her parents, wasters that they were, had done something good in producing her. As the cold air filled his chest, he could feel the taut wires inside him unfurling. The girl herself was pulling the fear out of him.

25

Margaret parked at a distance from the hotel to avoid the traffic from the wedding. Susan Cox had got married that morning and had booked the whole of the Mountain View for the reception. There were already two children by two different fathers and now she had found a third mug to marry her. Margaret had not been invited but she had been to mass earlier and could not avoid stepping under the white rose and ivy garland. The children were ring bearers, Olive told her, and afterwards they had walked down the aisle scattering petals ahead of their mother.

'You can cover anything up with a few flowers,' Margaret had answered.

Olive had stopped off at their house to change her shoes so she could dance at the reception – and Pat Noonan had waited in his car with the engine running.

The idea of Olive going out with Pat – for everyone to see – made the collar on Margaret's dress feel too hot and tight for her. She had not bothered to change it. She had looked at herself in the long mirror again and thought about what Midge had said to her – that people couldn't change for anyone. She had wondered if Tom was still as charming as she remembered, and she sprayed on a little perfume and then batted her wrists together. She was going out with a man. She was going out somewhere. The idea was exciting and yet also sickening to her. She had not told Olive much about it – because if she had, Olive would see that when it came to men, Margaret was a bigger fool than her.

The wedding was at 'the messy stage' as she called it, with not a person sober. The priest was long gone and the children were twirling on the dance floor, mad with exhaustion. The bride was ignoring them and shaking about on the dance floor in her dress, the train dirty from being trampled on, her hair still ironed onto her head with hairspray.

Margaret regretted agreeing to meet him at the hotel. She had forgotten about the wedding and didn't want to call him back to discuss it any further. He would be in the small bar at the back, he had said, reserved for residents. The owner knew him and would always find a place for him in there. The tiled hallway was lit with two chandeliers and there was a fire blazing inside the door. A Christmas tree stood near a sideboard, surrounded by what Margaret presumed were 'fake' presents.

'Deirdre,' someone shouted in a voice climbing upwards with hysteria. 'Deirdre . . . you're here. We thought you went into the bog on the way from Offaly.'

The woman, who was drunk, took Margaret by her two hands and began to pull her towards the ballroom and the dancing.

'She's here. She's here,' she was shouting at the people inside – a mixture of men without jackets and ties slopping pints at the bar, women throwing their heads back and cackling, and children wearing the big hats that belonged to their mothers.

'I am not Deirdre,' Margaret said and she shook her hands so that the woman had to release them. She felt very hot then and the last thing she wanted was to be touched by anyone. She glanced around and saw a door that had been opened to let some air in and in her mind she was running and making her escape from this awful place and the idea of seeing Tom Geoghan.

172

'Sorry about that, Miss Keegan,' the bride said and she was walking towards her and laughing gently.

Margaret remembered teaching her and she had been as thick as a brick so it was as well she had found someone to marry her.

'Will you come and have a drink or a sausage roll . . . or something?' she asked and Margaret could feel her own nostrils flaring with awkwardness. A man came up behind her and put his two hands on her waist then.

'I have my hands full here,' he announced.

'It's great to see you out enjoying yourself, Margaret,' someone shouted from the dance floor.

'Stop it, will you,' she said quietly.

When she looked up, Olive and Pat were standing beside her.

'Are you all right?' Olive asked and her face was full of concern for her sister. 'I didn't know you were coming here . . . They were giving out free champagne before the meal and they lost the run of themselves completely.'

'I'm meeting Tom Geoghan . . . . and don't even ask me for a reason because I honestly don't have one.'

'In the back bar?' Olive asked quietly.

'Oh yes, that's where you'll find us . . . . although I'll probably be gone after five minutes.'

Margaret walked to the door and out down the hallway until she was somewhere quieter. She knew that Tom was sitting behind the door waiting for her and she could not bear the idea of it. She went to the bathroom and washed her hands and face in cold water. She put a mint on her tongue then and applied more pink lipstick.

She saw tears in her eyes as she looked in the mirror and she tried to swallow the lump in her throat, which was painful.

The lipstick was for a younger woman but she had only ever known one colour. She had nothing else to put on except that and the perfume and this flowery dress that suddenly seemed like a pair of curtains wrapped tightly around her.

'Get a grip, Margaret,' she told herself over the noise of the hand dryer.

She would open the door to the small quiet bar and through the low ochre lighting she would see him turn on a high stool to face her. He would smile the way he had always done and everything would feel strange and yet very familiar.

She rummaged in her handbag then without really knowing what she was looking for. She was finding it hard to leave the bathroom. Two drunken girls came in and squeezed into a cubicle together.

'Me first,' one of them gasped. 'I'm bursting.'

Margaret rolled her eyes at her own reflection in the mirror. People seemed to have lost all sense of decorum.

Deep down she believed that Tom Geoghan was only meeting her because his wife had died and he was lonely. And she was meeting him because in all the years since he had left her, she had never met anyone else who had made her as happy.

She left the bathroom and did not pause at the low door to the back bar. She took no pleasure in leaving him there but walked quickly down the long tiled hallway, where a Labrador looked up at her from the fire. She stopped for a minute and put her hand on his head.

'I'm a fool and I'm a coward,' she told the dog and he lifted his head a little higher as if he was questioning her.

'Margaret,' a voice said and she straightened up before walking quickly for the door and out onto the gravel, where the frost was glistening and the sudden cold of the night hit her.

'Margaret . . . wait.'

She turned and faced him and he stood in the doorway looking bewildered, an overcoat on his arm.

'No, Tom,' she said quietly.

'I was waiting in the small bar – and then I thought maybe you thought it was the big bar I meant . . . but there's a wedding going on there. Were you not able to find me?'

Margaret lowered her chin and looked down at the frosted pebbles.

'I didn't look for you,' she told him. 'I wasn't able.'

'Come in and have a hot whiskey.'

'I don't think I should.'

'You're cold,' he told her and then he was crossing the gravel and draping his coat over her shoulders. She felt ridiculous and yet warmer and surprised by the feeling of a man wanting to take some care of her.

She checked herself again though and began to hand the coat back to him.

'I can't, Tom,' she told him. 'Too much has happened. It feels strange. It feels . . .' and here she paused, 'frightening,' she said, her voice barely a whisper – and she glanced around at the hotel and at the dancers through the windows. 'I'm forty-nine years old, Tom . . . almost fifty . . . and you're fifty-four. We're both too old for game-playing and being here feels like opening up a sore.'

Tom stood close to her then.

'I only wanted to say two things to you, Margaret – so let me say them.'

'There's no need to say anything . . . and I better be getting home.'

'The first . . . is that I did love you but because I was going abroad to university I didn't see how we could have continued. And the second thing is that I'm sorry. I'm sorry, Margaret . . . Do you hear me?'

Margaret looked back at him.

'I'm sorry, Maggie – I'm sorry I hurt you,' and he reached out and pulled his coat tightly around her.

'Now,' he said firmly. 'Was that so frightening?'

Margaret relaxed a little and then straightened up again.

175

'Tom, I'm going to go home . . . maybe another time.'

'Ah, Margaret, you're out now. Let's just get in somewhere warm and have a chat about it . . . Is there any harm in that?'

'I suppose not,' she said, giving in to the cold and to him. 'Maybe we should go inside before we get frostbite.'

'Or we could go to the blue pub up in the glen and get away from all these people.'

And as Margaret crossed the gravel to his car with him she wondered how she could be in this situation, how after all these years she was warm inside a coat that belonged to Tom Geoghan.

In the ballroom Pat Noonan held Olive tight to him on the dance floor.

'Poor Margaret,' she said into his shoulder and yet at this moment in time as she swayed to the music, the warmth and smell of Pat all around her, she did not really care about anything.

'What lemon fell into her bucket of milk to make her so sour?' he asked.

'The same lemon that's in the back bar waiting for her.'

'Well, maybe meeting him will . . . *release* her.'

And Olive smiled happily into the tweed of his jacket, smelling his pipe and the faintest whiff of the horses and realizing that she was beginning to love this small bald man who seemed so full of wisdom. She held him a little tighter and rested her head on his shoulder and she felt his chin and then his lips as he kissed her and she didn't care a bit what anyone thought about herself and Pat Noonan.

Bird stood still when a car appeared on the road, its lights picking up the frost on the hedgerow. The people inside, 'a couple' he thought at first, were Tom Geoghan and his sister. Time stood still then, the family he knew, the girls he had grown older with, had all been picked up and thrown backwards. He had already

176

seen this very picture, his sister Margaret, rosy-cheeked on a cold evening in December, in love with a boy and inwardly planning her wedding, her whole imagined life with him. The trees had not changed since then or the fields or the mountain or the lake, only the young people had moved on and away – and yet they seemed to be moving backwards again. He had already seen these faces through a windscreen. It was the briefest of moments but in it they were both smiling. Margaret looked happy, which in itself was a strange phenomenon. By midnight the road would be glassy with frost and a part of him wanted to shout after Tom – to tell him to slow down a bit and to be careful with his sister, more careful than he had been previously. But they were all fully grown now and surely this time around they could take better care of each other.

He stood high on his jeep and saw that Joe O'Neill had gone back to his yard, leaving a dark field behind him. Only Bird remained looking at the same fields that had always surrounded him, not fully sure – in that brief moment when he had seen Margaret smiling – if he was a man or a boy again. He stepped down onto the bonnet and turned the jeep for Red Hill and the lodge where he knew Midge was waiting for him.

'Was that Bird?' Tom Geoghan asked a minute later. 'On the roof of his jeep?'

'It was, for sure,' Margaret answered.

And they were quiet for a moment.

'Probably trying to count the cattle?' Tom suggested.

'I hope not . . . they've been in the shed since November.'

'Oh . . .' and he was quiet then before adding, 'a strange place to be standing.'

Strange? Margaret thought to herself. He doesn't know the half of it.

26

Midge turned off the lights in the kitchen and sat in the dark so that a person coming to the house would not see her. To this person – a bald-headed man, thin-faced like a greyhound – she would be a coat hanging on a hook or a piece of furniture or a dark shadow in the grey of a moonlit kitchen. She left the radio on for company and listened to a lady scientist talking about a lunar eclipse which was going to happen in April. And Bird had already discussed this with her. He was planning to take the boat out onto the lake and wait for the moon which would look, he told her, as if someone had bitten into it. During the previous weeks Bird Keegan had asked her questions and listened to her and this she realized was 'conversation' and what she said did not provoke any kind of sneering from him. He treated her as a person, as his equal, and because of this – there was no other reason as simple or as powerful – she already felt bound to him.

Margaret frightened her and Olive was as soft as putty and yet in their own way they too had prevented any further harm coming to her. But on this night in December when Margaret had driven away in a kind of fury to meet Tom Geoghan, the phone had begun ringing and at first Midge had not answered it. When it rang again, however, she had no choice but to lift it and she was relieved to hear the soft voice of Sergeant Brennan, a quiet man for a Guard and someone who did not like any kind of confrontation.

'Midge . . . it's Sergeant Brennan,' he began and in the tone of his voice she heard an apology because he had somehow failed her.

'I'm sorry to say that we had to release your father again this morning.'

'You haven't charged him yet?' she said, her voice high and thin like something that was on the point of shattering.

'Ah Midge,' he sighed and she could picture his fat hand making the receiver appear tiny, his head lowered as he spoke to her. 'His alibi is sound,' he said slowly. 'We don't have anything completely concrete to go on.'

'He killed my mother,' Midge whispered.

'The post-mortem results show that your mother died from organ failure.' Here there was a pause.

'But he hit her with something – wasn't it his fist that landed her in the hospital?'

'He has an alibi,' the sergeant said patiently. 'We've held him for as long as we can *legally* without charging him with some-thing. And we've pulled him in again for being drunk and disorderly. We've kept tabs on him for weeks, Midge – and we're running out of options.'

'He's been beating my mother for as long as I can remember.'

'There is a history of domestic violence, yes . . . but it's very difficult to prove that he killed her – and actually because there was no one else there that Sunday morning we can't even prove that he hit her. In fact it looks as if he didn't. The bruises to her head were caused by her falling, by the look of things, and—'

'Fell because he pushed her,' Midge said.

'Possible – but difficult to *prove*, Midge.'

'And what about manslaughter . . . Aren't his fingerprints on everything?'

'We found no weapon, Midge, and his fingerprints are there because he lived in the house . . . We can't prove anything, that's

179

the problem – no witness, no evidence at the scene – *and* he has a solid enough alibi.'

'You think anything Imelda Conroy says is solid?'

'Well, she's prepared to swear in a court of law. She says he went to her house on the Saturday night – after his car went into the lake – and then stayed with her all day Sunday.'

'So what are you saying to me?'

'We have no reason for locking him up. We've questioned him twice now but he's back at your house. I saw him there myself this morning.'

'And do you know he's been calling here?'

'I didn't know that – but I can't prevent him from making phone calls. And once he's back at home – the best we can do for now is keep a close eye on him.'

To this Midge said nothing.

'But I wanted to let you know, Midge. I didn't want you going into the town and well, you know, meeting him at a corner.'

'So it's all right now for a man to hit a woman, is it? The dogs in the streets know it was him that killed her.'

'Well – we have Bird as a witness to what happened at the hospital . . . and that's a start – but at this moment in time we can't lock him up because of what we *think* he might have done to your mother. We simply don't have the right ammunition. Now if you want to press charges yourself from here . . . that's a different story.'

And now Midge was silent again, wanting the phone call to end before she cursed at him.

'You're quite safe at the Keegans',' Sergeant Brennan went on. 'Don't be afraid now. I'll call Bird and Margaret in the morning . . . Are they at home now? I might just have a quick word with them . . .'

But Midge was gone, putting the phone down on the table. She did not want to hang up on him but needed more than

180

anything to stop hearing these words from him. She went upstairs then and lifted the gun from Margaret's wardrobe and after she had turned off the lights in the house she sat at a table in the dark waiting for Bird to come and find her.

The lake was almost frozen when Bird looked down from Hope's Hill. For his whole life this water had been a kind of axis for him. He knew its whims and currents and how it changed colour with the seasons, most often reflecting the grey of the sky but also the red of the trees in autumn and the dark shadows from the mountain. Now the trees were pure white around him, the grass brittle under his feet. It was too cold for snow, the sky clean and bright, the sharpness of the air could make a person dizzy. He blew on his hands, feeling the warmth of his lips against them, the tip of his nose, freezing. He was not wearing his gloves – until this winter he had not needed them. He could not remember a frost as severe. The lake had never frozen like this. The duck pond, yes, and it was fine and safe for children to go skating. Bird and his sisters had lost a small dog through the ice once. The idea of it alone – the dog's fate as these children imagined it – traumatized all three of them.

Tonight was different to anything Bird had ever seen though and it almost frightened him. He considered the fate of William O'Neill again, that face in the barn whose visits were now less frequent. Nothing had been the same since that morning. The fields around him were strange and ghostly, the moonlight casting long grey shadows over everything. The silence as he stood at the top of the hill was heavy and overbearing. There were no cars on the road, only that fool Tom Geoghan and if he let any harm come to Margaret he would kill him.

Bird said these words to himself, knowing well that Tom was a responsible individual and that he himself would never kill or even hit anyone. He crossed the first field, following the curve of the lake, feeling the stiff wind coming in off it, and then slowly climbed a second. His breathing was harder now, the cold taking some of his energy from him. He saw then that there was no light on in the lodge, which was very unusual. He knew that Olive was at the wedding and he had already seen Margaret, but Midge was supposed to be there waiting for him. This plan had taken some courage on his part and he realized now that the entire contents of his afternoon had been shaped by this, that he had been looking forward to it, foolishly perhaps, that just the idea of sitting in the warm lodge with Midge Connors had had him floating.

He worried then that she had run off on them, that she was still as wild as a hare and needed to travel. And yet she had talked about this often, how safe she felt when she was with his sisters, how lovely their house was, how much she felt she owed them, him in particular – and at that point he had always shushed her.

What could have happened to her? Could she be in bed? he wondered. Hardly, she was like a cat when it came to sleeping – staying up half the night and then sleeping late in the morning.

Midge would think nothing of curling up on a cushion and sleeping during the day if the mood took her and he would sit there with Olive, amused and watching. At night she came to life though and it was always late when they had these conversations, words that finally seemed to melt the fences between them.

Bird quickened his step and his boots rattled the gravel as he reached the back door and lifted the latch. He knew by the feel of the house that there was no one in it. He called her name, trying to ignore the panic that made his voice slightly different. He followed the short hallway off the new kitchen and climbed the narrow stairs to her attic bedroom and found the door open. When he turned on the light he saw her things scattered about – jeans borrowed from him hanging on the back of a chair, a pair of Mickey Mouse pyjamas in a ball on the floor. His face softened slightly then because he knew she had not run away from them.

'Midge,' he called again.

'I'm here,' her voice came back to him. 'Here,' she said again, like a person who had fallen into a well somewhere.

Bird followed the sound, irritated now by whatever game she was playing. He found her in the smaller sitting room beside a dying fire, the room already cold, the gun laid out on the couch beside her.

'What in the name of God are you doing?' he asked and as he spoke he was crossing the room and reaching for the gun and taking it from her. He ignored her for a moment and snapped the safety catch, checking the barrels and finding that they were empty. She had not even tried to load it. His anger evaporated as quickly as it had risen and down these dark empty barrels he saw her innocence, her fear, and he wanted to comfort her.

'What are you doing sitting here in the dark . . . and how did you get this gun?' he asked.

He watched her face as he spoke and saw that it was different to the one he had grown used to. Midge's eyes were hard and frightened and when she began to speak she was glancing left and right and seemed suspicious of everything. In her mind, it seemed the floorboards might give way, the chair could collapse under her, and even he – Bird – was a person now who could in some way injure her.

'Margaret and Olive are gone out and I'm here on my own and I started to think about one thing and another.'

'And where did you get this?' Bird was sitting in an armchair holding the gun. 'It's an awful cold night,' he added then for no particular reason.

'Margaret showed me where the gun is kept – and how to use it.'

'Did she now? Well, at least she had the good sense not to show you how to load it.'

183

'She did show me . . . but I forgot to do it.'

Here Bird pulled his red cap off and gave a short laugh.

'Thank God for that,' he said and he shook his head.

Midge was at the window now.

'Is the lake still frozen?' she asked.

'It is.'

'Will we go out and look at it?'

'Are you mad in the head? It's like the North Pole out there.'

And Midge turned and looked at him.

'I feel safer outside,' she answered.

She could not explain that in her mind, the dull moonlight and the cold, the icy water, were things that might act as a buffer between her and her father.

'He can find me here,' she said very quietly. 'He knows where I am.'

'Who?'

'My father . . . He's out again and back at the house . . . They can't put anything on him.'

Bird nodded slowly, understanding everything.

'You're safe here,' he told her and his voice was slow and deliberate.

'But tonight . . . here on my own . . .'

'I know . . . but I'll make sure there's always someone with you.'

'I don't want any harm to come to Margaret and Olive either.'

'They're big girls,' he answered and here his eyes met hers and he began laughing and she smiled back at him.

'I've never seen the lake frozen before . . .' she said, still smiling.

There was a pause then and Bird gave a long sigh and looked into the fire. There were some well-dried-out logs and turf in a neat basket on one side and with a few dry twigs he could have it roaring up the chimney in no time.

184

'You better put on a warm coat . . . and do you have a good pair of boots?' he asked and Midge was gone, scampering down to the back hall ahead of him – her fear, because of him, forgotten.

Bird sat for a moment and a small wave of worry passed through him. Here he was in a warm room where they would soon be joined by Margaret and probably Olive – who would make tea and toast for everyone. And yet he was walking away from it so that he could take this girl out over the white fields to show her frozen water. He wondered what was happening to him, what wind of fate was lifting him and would not release him. But for now he could think of no other place to be than out at the lake, naming stars, and perhaps putting his arm around her.

Midge walked quickly beside him as if the lake had some pull on her. They crossed the front lawn from the lodge together and then down the long wooden steps that led to the water. The moon was still high over them and as they came to the bottom of the steps the lake showed a long trench of moonlight on its surface, like a smooth path that could be followed. She stood at the very edge and then, with Bird watching her, she put one foot onto the ice and then the other. She leaned over, looking at her feet and seeing the smooth round stones on the bottom. This was the side where no one ever swam except Olive because she knew the water. People talked about a sudden drop, a series of uneven shelves that could surprise a swimmer, some parts extending almost to the middle of the lake or running in a thin line to the furthest island and one that dropped half way into the deepest water. Bird remembered Olive as a child skipping from one shelf to another. Now he looked at Midge and wondered what she was thinking, what she saw when she looked down at her feet which were able to stand on water. The ice was very solid at the edges where the water was shallow and it was thick enough further out too, but even from where he was standing Bird could see the waves in the middle where the ice had not yet formed and probably wouldn't either.

'They say drowning is one of the easiest ways to go,' Midge said and she was still on the ice but her hands were in her pockets and she was looking out towards the islands and the deeper water now as if that was her future.

Bird did not reply but a thin vein of fear ran through him. The girl was in a peculiar mood and he was worried about her. He felt like grabbing her and pulling her back but something stopped him. He did not want to show his own sudden panic, the terror he felt of losing her.

They did not speak for a moment and Bird heard an owl whistling. God's creatures, he thought. Out on the coldest of nights, a sweep of wings then as the owl descended to a mouse in a field, already dead and frozen.

'Don't be getting any ideas, Midge,' Bird said suddenly, his voice loud – and the quick knot in his throat almost choking him. He could not understand these people with the carpet of life spread around them in every possible direction – and all they could talk about was doing away with themselves. Midge was just standing there – like a fairy on the ice – and the thoughts of William O'Neill and then Midge herself, the idea of losing her for ever, were almost enough to make Bird hunker down on the frozen ground and cry like a child – such was the sudden devastation he was feeling.

When had life become worthless? he wondered. A kind of burnt-out forest where people looked around and saw nothing anywhere for them.

'Bird,' Midge said and she was turning slowly to look at him. 'I want to go out further. I want to go out over the ice and see if it will hold me and if it does it's a sign and if it doesn't it's a sign. You'll let me do that, Bird, won't you?'

And before he could answer and as his hand reached

automatically to make a snatch for her she was gone, her feet slipping this way and that, her hands stretched out as if they could lift her up into the air over the water. The ice held and she seemed to hover over it and Bird opened his mouth but he could not speak and could not breathe and could not call out to her. He wanted more than anything to say her name but it was not his to say somehow. Midge was on her way to another place and it was her choice because even though he wanted to prevent this from happening it was as if a spell had been cast over him.

But now he was moving and shouting at her.

'Midge!' And his voice was cracking. 'Midge,' he roared at her. 'There's a drop. Stop, Midge. The ice won't hold you. Stop, Midge. Come back. For God's sake, Midge. Come back. Come back.'

And Midge turned slowly on the ice, her face a small white circle in the distance, her warm breath in white puffs around her. The ice gave a crack close by and she did not move an inch but stood still and waited for the sign she had wished for.

Bird stepped onto the ice himself and in a few long strides was close to her, his anger warm and visible. The ice shifted around her feet and he reached for her, his hand like a tight claw around her forearm and he spun then, his boots sliding, and he began to drag her, the ice cracking and shifting all around them. Midge and Bird began to race the ice – their boots jumping from one moving piece to another, the water beginning to slop up at them and they raced this shattering until they were close enough to the edge and then up to their knees in water. The ice remained solid near the shore and they stepped up onto it, over the round stones again, and held each other.

'I got my sign,' she told him, her voice happy, breathless.

'Fuck your sign,' he said into her ear. He was trembling.

'I'm sorry, Bird,' she said and she was shaking with the cold and the fright the lake had given her. He was still holding her arm too tightly and she imagined the row of small dark bruises that she would find in the morning from his fingers. She had seen it before from the times her father had lashed out and grabbed her – and now Bird was a different kind of person who had used his strength to save her.

She lowered her arm and his hand came down with it, still not able to release her. And then as she stepped forward, he quickly gathered her in his arms and pulled her to him. They were both shaking with cold and the wind off the lake was strong now and clouds were forming.

'It's going to snow,' Bird said. 'I should drop back to the lodge and see if Margaret got home safely.' But Midge had pressed her face into his chest and did not answer. There was a small V shape near his neck where his shirt was open and she pressed her lips on it, feeling his skin for the first time as she kissed him there. Bird stood very still, his eyes watering with the cold, his arms locked around her, not wanting to release her and feeling her warmth on his torso, her lips and breath bringing heat to his chest and his neck – little Midge Connors warming the long, thin length of him. He lowered his head and kissed her.

27

The next morning Bird sat at his kitchen table, his head bowed low. He could hear doors opening and closing as she continued to touch each part of this house, which lately had been known only to him. His hands were red and raw-looking from being washed in the icy lake water. After kissing her at the lake he had taken three lambs from a dying sheep and then gone down on his knees at the shore and broken some ice with a rock and forced his already cold hands under. He used a smooth stone as a kind of pumice, to scrub his palms and his fingers. He had sat back on his hunkers for a moment then and looked around him. The sheep had become confused in the snow, sixteen of them in total, all slipping into a ditch and then forgotten. Earlier on, before the wedding, he had gathered up the flock and taken them into the shed and had not missed the others. He blamed himself and now he had ten pet lambs that needed minding.

Midge had waited for him all night at his house and then made his tea hot, strong and without sugar. His bones were beginning to ache inside him, his hands so numb that he could not feel if the mug was burning him.

There was no sign now of the loneliness that he had felt before he met her. The feeling he'd had – of being without anyone at all – had been changed for ever by this small person. Midge was filling the corners of his life now, replacing everything. She found the sausages he had bought the day before and some eggs and made a breakfast that was passable – the winter tomatoes were as hard as stones but that was nothing to do with her. They ate in silence and now and then they would glance at each other and see something that they had not previously noticed. For him it was the pale skin on her neck, like skin that had been hidden from the sun, from all natural light, and he wanted to look away, finding it altogether too private. He saw the gold of a chain hanging around it and a small crucifix swinging. She seemed to have the body of a girl underneath her clothes.

And for Midge it was his hands and how they reached forward for the bread, the knuckles high and round, the fingers long. For her it was the frown that crept over his face then as he ate it. For her it was the silence that they now made together. Behind him the morning sun was beginning to pierce the window, an orange light coming in over the snow and making everything around her familiar.

'I bought cornflakes,' he told her suddenly and she smiled at him.

He showed her where the hot press was and how to turn on the immersion. She was worried about using up the hot water for a bath – and he said nothing.

The size of her . . . wouldn't she wash herself in a teacup, he thought to himself.

After that he took her into a small room off the dining room.

'This,' he said, 'is where the gun is kept,' and she turned her face up to him, waiting for some kind of explanation.

'The Keegans are very fond of their guns,' she said quietly.

He felt embarrassed then and tired. He realized that a good deal of extra energy was required when there was someone else in his house, someone who needed a bit of minding.

'The gun is for crows . . . or a fox – if it's cleaning out the henhouse, and even if it isn't.'

190

'Have you ever shot a person?' Midge asked and he turned his head quickly to look at her.

'What sort of a question are you asking me? Have I ever shot a person?'

'Or killed a person,' Midge clarified.

'No, I have not shot a person . . . *or* killed a person.'

She had stepped on a wire somewhere down inside him and she could feel that he was finding her exhausting.

'I only mean one of the tinkers . . . you know . . . coming around trying to sell you a roll of carpet . . . sniffing around all your new farm machinery. A few pellets up his backside to send him hopping.'

'No, Midge,' and he seemed baffled by her. 'I have never shot a tinker . . . or sent him hopping.'

'I was just wondering,' she answered and she felt like laughing. Because she was in need of sleep, a part of her was tipping like a seesaw towards hysteria.

'We could go to your house later and get your things . . . check on that old cat. She could maybe stay here with you,' Bird said. 'If you like,' he added carefully.

'All right,' she said, smiling.

Despite the size of the house the bedroom he brought her to was the one just off the long low-ceilinged dining room and kitchen. She remembered the small wooden shutter in the wall and how it backed onto the low calving shed in the yard. Bird slept there when he knew he would need to get up in the middle of the night and the shutter was for keeping a close eye on the animal.

'I have a cow ready to calve,' he told her and Midge came and stood beside him and then on her toes looked into the shed from this bedroom and could smell warm dung and feed then. The cow was getting up and lying down and flicking her tail with the pain she was feeling.

'I'll check on her in an hour,' he said.

The bed was pushed into the wall to make space for a small chest of drawers and a chair where they both put their clothes. Bird left the room so that she could undress and it was then under the cold sheets, which felt heavy and well washed, that Midge suddenly missed the shambles that she had come from. Her own home was warm and filled with noise and now she would try to sleep with only the sound of a man breathing next to her. A man she hardly knew really, a man who had depths that were hidden from everyone. She lay there waiting and prayed to her angel guardian that Bird Keegan was not some kind of sex maniac. He came back a minute later and he was in his underwear, a pair of perfectly white cotton shorts and a T-shirt. And his eyes were sliding at her sideways.

More than anything he needed to sleep and he lay flat and released a long sigh that seemed to come from every muscle in his body, and Midge, although she too was exhausted, could not help but turn to face him. And she could not resist putting her hands on him then. She placed them around his eyes, framing them, and then on his beard, her face burrowing into it. She was not afraid any more. There was no one to harm her. She was safe with him.

And in the silence of Red Hill with a foot of snow on everything – she went to bed with Bird Keegan, finding a man who was both awkward and tender. He would not hurt or force her and with a full sun joining the previous night's moon over the house which she would call home, she gave herself to him willingly, and when he turned over then and slept like death she turned away too, hearing the cow next door give a low moan, and feeling the heat from Bird's back as it grew flat against her.

192

28

When Midge woke it was late morning and he was gone, the blanket rolling back like a wave from her. She lay still and looked at the solid walls around her, feeling a kind of calm, like she had arrived somewhere different. She had found someone who seemed to care for her. Bridget had cared but she was not capable of giving. She was a woman who seemed emptied out by everything that had happened to her. The room was cold and when she got up she saw that Bird had left the small hatch window into the shed open. When she stood on tiptoe she could see him in there, rubbing down the new yellow calf, born while they were sleeping.

Bird glanced up then.

'You're up,' he told her. The new mother sniffed the calf, her large head floating in some kind of confusion as if she was not sure what this creature was, this bolt of new life that had come out of her.

'A fine bull calf,' Bird said and he was up from his knees with his hands on his hips looking down proudly at him. 'Did it all by herself,' he said and with that he gave the cow's flank a gentle slap and moved to lift a bucket of water towards her. And Midge smiled as she went to get dressed. This new arrival, the newness of life, seemed to put an extra shine on everything. Her mobile phone rang then and it was Olive.

'Well, there you are now – and myself and Margaret here going out of our minds with worry.'

'Oh, I'm fine,' Midge said vaguely.

'And where are you?'

There was a pause then and Midge knew that Margaret was in the background, her eyes in two dark, narrow squints as she badgered Olive to get more information. She thought for a moment and decided that lying would not help anything, that her life was complicated enough without adding a second layer of false information.

'I'm up at Bird's,' she said simply.

'Oh grand,' Olive said. 'Well, thank God for that.' And Midge could hear her turning away and saying, 'She's up at Bird's,' to Margaret.

'Right so. Well, I'll leave some lunch here in the oven for you if you're hungry. I have a meeting to go to and Margaret is giving a class to the slow learners.'

Margaret seemed to take the phone from Olive then.

'Your kitten is here.'

Midge could not say anything.

'I gave him some milk and he's now curled up in one of Olive's slippers.'

She sounded as if she was on the brink of laughter.

'Thanks, Margaret. I'll be back later.'

'And your lunch is in the oven. Olive did a nice roast chicken.'

Midge realized that it had not occurred to either of them that she had spent the night in Bird's house, that she had slept in the same warm bed as him – that it was, in their minds, simply unthinkable.

In the kitchen she made tea for herself and willed Bird to return to her. The longer he stayed outside, the more she believed he wanted to distance himself again from her.

194

She found the green coat then and a pair of boots and opened the door to release these worries out into the frosted air. It was almost noon and there was no thaw anywhere. Icicles hung from the corrugated roof of the hay shed, the water barrels had been frozen – she could see a great triangle of ice that Bird had broken so he could fill a bucket from them. The cattle in the long shed were eating silage, their breath coming out in puffs. There was no wind to shake up the air and the smell of the stuff was almost overwhelming.

She heard the tractor and could see Bird lifting silage on a grape and flinging it into a trough for the cattle. He glanced up at her and continued working and in that moment she felt her life drain out of her. She went into the smaller shed and sat on a hay bale waiting. She could see a mother cat in a box in the corner, a kind of makeshift nest that Bird had made for her. The kittens were on the move, mewing and tumbling from the box, stagger-ing about, playing. She wondered at Bird and how he showed such kindness to these dumb creatures and how he had looked up from his work and seemed then to look through her. It was snowing again, small flecks coming down in circles. She could see them through the open shed door.

'A bad sign,' Bird had said. 'The bigger flakes melt quicker.' Midge knew what she was seeing now was the first sign of a blizzard. She stepped out into the yard and found that the tractor was gone, driven back into its own shed for shelter. The engine had been cut and so it was silent and then he was coming around the corner towards her wearing a hood, his hands in work gloves, a scarf around his face so that only his eyes were showing. He said something but she could not hear it clearly enough and instead stood without moving and stared back at him. She pushed her hands down deep into her pockets and tried to smile at him. The snow was falling faster now and sticking to everything. She was close to tears when she felt his arms around her. He pulled her slight frame into the vastness of his where she imagined ships' masts and scaffolding, a kindness that was in its own way industrial. His chin, the cushion of his beard, rested on her head for a moment and covered her. She felt a gloved hand placed on the back of her head as a kind of shelter.

'Midge,' he said quietly. 'Don't be worrying.'

She looked up at him and could not help smiling.

'Do you hear me?' he asked and without waiting for an answer, 'You're all right,' he told her and she nodded and smiled again, laughed even, understanding everything he said completely and believing him.

They drove through the snow to Tullyvin, the swirl of flakes making Midge feel dizzy. There were no other cars on the road but Bird drove with confidence, the jeep holding its own and not skidding.

'Snow makes everything so quiet,' Midge said.

'It does,' he answered, 'and it's a lot of work for farmers. The main thing is to keep the water to the tanks flowing . . . The cattle go crazy without a drink of water.'

'It's lovely though,' Midge said quietly.

'It is,' he agreed and he smiled over at her. 'If it stops, maybe we could walk down to the lake later.'

She turned her head and smiled out through the window. 'In years to come,' she said very softly, 'I think I will remember driving through snow with Bird Keegan.'

'You're a romantic,' he told her firmly.

He changed gears and slowed down as they went through the town.

'Not really,' she said. 'At least not until very recently.'

Bird stopped the jeep outside her house.

'How recently?'

'Since yesterday.'

196

He gave a slight smile and lifted his eyebrows.

'Midge,' he said quietly. 'I need you to be honest with me.'

He stopped then and seemed to think.

'If you think there is something in this . . .' and here he stopped again, his fingers fanned on the steering wheel, 'this . . .' he repeated, except now he was waving his hand between them. 'Us,' he managed finally although he said the word so quietly she could hardly hear him. 'Then good . . . *or* . . . if it's . . . I don't know how exactly to put this . . . if it's just a place to go, somewhere to "be" . . . after everything that has happened to you – that's all right too. If you want to stop now – that's also fine.' And here he really struggled, the weight of his own feelings almost breaking him. 'I need to say these things out to you. I don't want you to feel in any way *beholden* – no, that's not the right word either . . . I don't want you to feel cornered because of the help the Keegans have given you.'

'Shush, Bird, will you,' Midge said softly, her face feeling warmer.

There was silence in the jeep. The snow was falling thick and fast, the parked cars like small white hills around them.

'I understand what you're saying, Bird – but I feel sure enough about what I'm doing . . . but what is it *you* want? That is something you haven't told me.'

'It's hard to say for sure.' As usual he answered her with honesty.

'Well then – at this moment in time – what is it that you hope for?' Midge took a deep breath, worn thin by the conversation, exhausted again – and frightened, never realizing until now that there was a kind of power in plain talking.

'I hope . . .' Bird said, and he paused before turning to see if she was still looking over at him, 'that you might stay with me.'

*

197

They went inside and found Charlie slouched down low in an armchair watching the television. Only his eyes moved when they came into the kitchen, first landing on Midge like a stamp and then rolling higher as they travelled over Bird, climbing the height of him.

'What is it you want?' he asked. He was sober and there were no empty bottles near him.

'I came to collect some of my things – and I thought I'd bring the cat . . .'

Her father lifted his head, his chin swinging upwards as a form of agreement.

'You're welcome to her,' he said. 'She's full of bloody kittens.'

Bird waited in the kitchen as Midge went upstairs. He stood leaning against the fridge in the flickering half-light of the television. He could hear Midge opening a drawer and then coming down the stairs again. She had a Tesco carrier bag and the cat held awkwardly under one arm.

'Let's go,' she said quietly.

Charlie turned his head then, his eyes settling on Bird for a moment.

'I believe you're Bird Keegan,' he said and he stood up and extended a thin hand towards him.

Bird looked at the hand.

'We've already met,' he said, not taking his own hands from his coat pockets. 'I was the one who threw you across the room at the hospital.'

Charlie looked back at him and didn't say anything. A thin smile covered his face. He was pale and hopeless-looking.

'Big man looking down,' he said. 'I can't say I'm pleased to meet you.'

And Bird and Midge turned away together. They shared the same feeling of escape, of leaving something, stepping out into the white snow light with a new version of life ahead of them.

29

In Roche's shop Bird's nod was almost imperceptible. The shop was busy with the January sale but they were still approached by a big-breasted shop assistant, her perfume clearing a path in front of her. The woman looked at them with sympathy and then she put a fat-fingered hand on Midge's back and took her away from him. He did not know for certain yet if he was shopping with a woman or a girl. He only knew that Midge had arrived into his home with nothing and that it was his responsibility to provide for her.

'Do we have to buy the clothes here?' Midge had whispered as they stepped through the sliding glass doors. 'Could we not go up to Dublin and get some . . . cool gear?'

'Cool gear?' he had repeated and he could not help laughing at her.

'When we have a thaw and the roads are clear again, we'll head to the city,' he told her, 'and we'll come back like a pair of hipsters.'

Bird found a chair and watched the two women disappear through the white foam of underwear. There was a whole area dedicated to bras and knickers and he had never seen so many of them before. To him they were like foreign seashells, molluscs collected from the coral reef, shells falling through his big hands as he tried to put names on them. He had not known until then that Midge was badly dressed. But he noticed her runners now, the rag of a raincoat, how her little skirt hung on her.

'Dress her, for God's sake,' he wanted to say to the woman. 'Cover her up, make her look like someone cares for her.'

When Midge came back she was wearing a plaid skirt and a cardigan with a pale lemon-coloured blouse underneath it.

'Well?' she asked him. He could not tell if she was serious or joking.

'There are plenty of clothes like that at home in my mother's wardrobe,' he told her. 'God rest her,' he added, as if for further clarification.

'Something younger . . . more modern?' the sales assistant asked. 'Well, you should have said so,' and the last part was murmured because she was not fully sure if she had the courage to talk back to him.

Bird took a deep breath and crossed his legs.

'Get on with it,' he wanted to shout at them. This was a kind of torture for him, pure torture under fluorescent lights and now with other people watching.

Eventually Midge came back again wearing a red jumper and a pair of beige corduroy jeans. The boots were suede, little flat ones with laces.

'Grand,' he said, not really looking.

In the end he paid for three pairs of jeans and two pairs of wool trousers, three jumpers, a new wool coat, a bag of air which was the underwear he guessed, a little hat, some blouses and two dresses. Before leaving he opened an account at the shop for her and he said he would get her a credit card. The next time she could come shopping on her own. He already knew that a second shopping trip was more than he could bear.

Outside the shop the morning light was dazzling. They had come into Tullyvin early so they would have no trouble parking.

'Will we go for a coffee?' Bird asked. 'There's that little place

200

around the corner,' and Midge's smile warmed him. He would do everything he could to make life normal for her. He would parcel up his own bad memories and hide them with hers.

'Coffee and two of those Danish pastries,' he added and she laughed up at him.

Over coffee they would decide what kind of car he might buy for her. Something small and red, he thought. She was an easy person to bring happiness to and he was enjoying buying nice things for her. Bird and Midge would sit down in a restaurant now as if this was an ordinary event for them – as if they were having breakfast together like two normal people.

30

Midge lay on her side under a blanket and he cradled her. The fire in the sitting room was warm on their faces and even the coarse wool on her skin was strangely comforting. She had been living with Bird for three weeks and they had begun by ringing in a new year together. It had been a cold January but she was not aware of the weather. Instead she found herself thinking about the farm cat in the box with her band of kittens, how at ease in each other's company they were, how content they had all seemed together.

'Bird, before me . . . was there anyone special, anyone that you cared for?'

And as soon as her question was out it seemed dangerous, as if something might be broken.

'Before you . . . ?' he began.

Midge already knew that Bird was shy, that he was modest with his heart and his body. And yet she could feel the draw between them, that as the many small dykes and walls began to come down, they could not help but touch and kiss each other and make love, over and over. The freedom they felt as Midge began to live at Red Hill seemed in itself extraordinary – that two people could stay away from the rest of the world and be in the precious company of each other, without diversion, without interruption from anyone.

Bird spoke slowly as he often did then, the organization of his thoughts and feelings always evident – and she could feel his breath through her hair, warming her.

'Before you, Midge? No, not really,' he said. 'No one of note.'

'But someone?'

'Ah, I've met some girls over the years . . . you know. I used to go to the rugby club in Aughrim and I'd drive a girl home now and then, go to the cinema with them a few times.'

'And what happened?'

'Not much.'

'So is this a kind of . . . *first* . . . for you?'

She could feel the vibration of his chest against her back as he laughed at her.

'First? First what, Midge? I'm thirty-one.'

Midge said nothing for a moment.

'Say what you're trying to say, Midge,' he told her.

And Midge turned to face him, her hands planted into the hair on his chest, his bare knees touching hers, his eyes bright and dazzling with humour and feeling for her.

'I love you, Bird – I think I do anyway.'

The words seemed to float out of her. She had not planned to say them and yet now, in this warm pocket with him, she found she meant them. He did not say anything or repeat them back to her and she didn't mind it. Bird was a person who never said anything unless it was necessary and right in that particular moment.

'Midge,' he said after a long pause. 'Have you ever thought about having children? I mean . . . is that something you think you might want in the future?'

And with this she moved to the end of the couch taking the blanket with her, so that Bird had to grab at a corner and try to cover himself and he was laughing at her.

'Easy, easy.'

'Children . . . no,' she said quietly.

203

'What do you mean – no?'

The air changed and the fire seemed to die away in the grate next to them.

'I just mean it's not something I've ever really thought about – I'm twenty-one.'

'I see.'

There was another long silence then, one which they both tried to see through, a kind of mist that made them lost and unable to find each other.

'But you would want to be a mother at some point?'

'It's not something that ever really occurred to me.'

'Well, do you think it might "occur" to you in the future?'

'Is that very important to you, Bird?'

'Yes. It is.'

And here Midge envied his certainty, his ability to say what it was that he wanted without worrying about breaking something between them.

'I inherited this place from my father and it's been in the family for four generations – so it's always been important – it's been a given almost – that I will pass it on to someone who will care about it – and that means someone *born* into it.'

'I see.' Midge was vague, as if she had lost him. In her mind they were both floating away from each other and she found this frightening.

'I know it's early days,' Bird said, 'but it's better to know now – don't you think? I mean . . . you need to be honest with me.'

'If it happened, Bird – I mean if there was to be a baby – I think I would be OK with that.'

And Bird smiled at her. He frowned and smiled at the same time, which she knew by now meant he was not at all annoyed but that he was not entirely sure of her either.

Midge did not need him to say that he loved her. She felt that they had already moved on from that, that they had stayed on the green velvet couch and had travelled a considerable distance together.

Spring came late in January – a scattering of snowdrops appearing under the beech trees and followed overnight by the mustard and purple of the crocus. This sudden burst of colour broke through the sodden moss and made anything at all seem possible. Rain still hung in the bare branches and the wind had a chill to it. Midge watched the lake from every window. She learned to cook simple things and was not bothered by the rabbits Bird shot and brought home to her. And once there was a pike from the lake, not caught, but shot by Sean Weldon.

'Delicious,' Bird said and they laughed as they picked lead shot from their mouths and heard it clink on their plates in front of them. Happiness, like a mist, came down over Red Hill during that time. Pat Noonan and Olive went on another holiday together, a cruise this time with no religious element. They emailed photos back to Margaret and Bird – Olive standing boldly in a one-piece swimsuit, with Pat sitting on the sand in front of her, her hands resting on his sun-browned head, his face lit up with love for her. Margaret continued to meet Tom Geoghan and they went to 'the blue pub' in the glen and also saw a movie together once a week. And Midge and Bird retreated to an unknown place where large fires were lit every night and talks were had and afterwards they made love – and if they were parted for any length of time, they each missed the other greatly.

Sean went to the pub in the evening and after one pint too many announced loudly and for all to hear, 'The Keegans of Red Hill are in love. All three of them.'

IV
The Violence of Living

31

Bird Keegan went out to thin turnips on the day he got married. His neighbours, most of whom were not invited, gathered on the high ridge near McEnroe's quarry and saw everything. They watched as he walked away from the house with his head bowed, leaving Midge Connors to talk to the well-wishers. The O'Neills came and there were some relations from Galway. Olive and Pat Noonan arrived too although they didn't stay long – they were flying out to Lourdes the following morning. And Margaret was there, of course, although what contribution she made on the day was not known to anyone.

And Bird left them all to it, slamming the back door after him and looking up into the stark new light of springtime. It was March 2014 and the cut of the east wind was typical, the trees moving in it and the clouds crossing the sky in lines and ridges.

'This is what it means to be married,' the neighbours said. 'This is what happens when Bird Keegan gives his heart.' But he was not capable of being idle or of making small talk. Bird wanted to be on his own, to be kneeling in the ridges of clay as if marriage had not made a dent in him.

The couple had picked a small church well outside the parish, paying fifty euros to a priest who didn't know them – and Midge wore a pale suit, the same colour as a biscuit. Bird came in a raincoat because it was the only coat he owned that did not have cow dung on it.

'He was like bloody Columbo,' one of his neighbours said to the cocked ears in the pub.

There was no mass at all, just a few vows and then silence and a few more words when the priest felt that God had married them. The top button of Bird's shirt was undone and even though he had washed himself that morning, the clay was still deep in the crevices of his knuckles. There was only one photograph taken of the couple outside the church – both grimacing because the sun came out suddenly and seemed to bleach everything. They had asked a few people back to Red Hill for tea and sandwiches and then Bird had gone out to the turnips and left them. The guests had stood around chewing on flat white bread and ham with the tea slopping out into their saucers, not quite sure what to do with themselves. They had looked around the walls and remarked on old paintings and plates that were of no real interest. And Olive carried tea to Margaret, who sat deep in a butler's chair talking to Tom Geoghan.

Midge said the goodbyes for her new husband and worked out where all the Delft went. When everyone had gone, she could find nothing at all to do in the house so she decided to join Bird in the field, the wide-open sky inviting her to escape to him. She opened the back door and stood for a minute with the wind pushing against her and reaching her skin through the thin material of her suit which she didn't think to change. She knew nothing in the world about farming but understood that she was joined to Bird by something that was unbreakable. She walked out into the lower field smelling the wet earth like fish and blood around her. She did not know what to expect from this new life she had committed herself to. The house on Emmet Road was clear and empty in her mind even though she knew that her father still lived there. She had not seen him in months but it didn't matter now. Bird had married her and in doing this had built a solid wall around her.

Bird's face was down near the clay, his long torso folded over, his hands working in a steady rhythm, and the small turnip plants that were already plucked lay in a long row to the side like corpses. His legs were in a tent shape and he turned his head awkwardly to see her. The sun was at her back so he could see only her slight figure and her hands and feet. At heart they were both romantic people but after the locals – and Margaret – had had their say, the idea of celebrating their union had died a kind of death in them.

'You are going to marry *Midge Connors*?' Margaret said to Bird under the new recessed lights of her kitchen – and Midge standing there beside him.

'We'll be there,' Olive said firmly. 'Myself and Pat – and we'll be throwing the confetti.'

And that was why they had 'a cod of a wedding', and went out in their good clothes to work. What they had was a pact, Bird thought – and it was more solid than a vow or a promise – it was something that was taller and more majestic than a white gown and a pretty garland of flowers over the door of the church.

Midge had cut her hair shorter before the wedding and it suited her and when she saw the long red strands falling to the ground around her she hoped it was the last of her old life that she was casting away from her. Her large eyes often seemed furtive, as if she had something to hide or some secret she was ashamed of, and Bird thought all of these thoughts as he looked at her in the church and he loved her regardless. When she lost that furtive look, which was really born out of embarrassment about her teeth which had been cleaned to a shine before the wedding – then a person might notice that her eyes were dark brown and good-looking with a strong glint of intelligence. Until now she had never had a man turn his head to look at her. She had grown used

211

to being in many ways invisible, so when her new husband turned his head awkwardly over the turnips, his eyes squinting into the sun, and smiled at her, she was glad and thought nothing of going down on her knees, the beige skirt sinking into the dirt and her hands finding the sudden wet cold of it.

The people around Tullyvin were spending a great deal of time talking about Bird Keegan. He was popular enough in his own way but they were often annoyed by his lack of interest in them, and now he had married Midge Connors and her out of a cottage – a real sty of a place with wrecks of cars scattered around it and clothes drying on the boxwood hedges.

'He wants a servant,' someone said.

'He wants an heir,' someone else added.

They could find nothing in particular to dislike about Bird except that he was not interested in them and they resented him for it. His only interest, in fact the only point to life in general for him, as far as they could see, was work. They concluded that from a distance he was a grand-looking man, well mannered enough when you met him, but that inside there was a map instead of a heart.

Bird and Midge worked together in the turnip drills until dark, turning earth and vaguely aware that there was a handful of people still watching them from the ridge. They could easily ignore them though, and concentrate on more slim green plants cast to one side, more earth showing between the seedlings.

Darkness came slowly, the sky becoming a heavy blue and then close to black. Midge was cold but didn't want to go inside yet. She was fully in the rhythm of her husband's work, the darkness falling over them in a sheet, only faintly aware that her empty stomach was making her light-headed. Finally, Bird hunkered back and looked up at the sky and the air was silent around them. There was no sound of traffic. The stars had come out without them knowing. There was no one left standing on the ridge watching.

Bird stood up and stretched his back, his head tired-looking and hanging. He seemed to think for a long time and a rush of memories went through him. Snow, grey in the night, yet bright in a way that was unnatural, black branches wet as they whipped at a boy chasing his sisters. It seemed a world away, like it had never happened. A lone seagull flew over them, heading east towards the coast in a way that was very determined.

'We'll leave it at that,' he said to his new wife. And she was aware that it was the first time that he had spoken to her since they had taken their vows in the church. But what he said was inclusive, they were already working together – and even though the work was menial, she felt that she was his equal and that he was fully aware of her there with him, that they were working together, there was a space beside him for her.

Her wedding suit was destroyed. There was dirt up to the waist of her skirt, muck up to her elbows.

'You may as well put that behind the range,' he said.

'I'll soak it in the bath. It'll be all right.'

He stretched his arms up and then out. He placed his hands on his hips and looked around him.

'It's cold enough for snow,' he said, and then as if suddenly aware of her he took off his gilet and put it over her shoulders.

They continued for another minute with the work, the earth becoming too cold in their hands then and less compliant.

'Midge . . .' he said then and his voice was quiet and strangely innocent, 'have you thought any more about children?'

'No,' she told him truthfully. She had seen what childbirth had done to her mother and the idea of having some herself was still terrifying.

'Well . . . we'll probably have some,' Bird said and he was smiling. Then he was quiet for a moment.

213

'If we have a girl,' he went on, 'how would you feel about calling her Margaret? It was my mother's name – and your name too, of course, and it would be nice to continue it – unless you'd prefer something else, or some other version of it . . . and I'd want her to go to a good school, away from here, and to see that there's a world outside this place – where people are not talking about the Keegans.'

'What about Margo?' Midge suggested.

'Margo,' Bird said quietly, 'that has a nice musical sound to it.'

Here he waited as if Midge should say something but she too was silent. It was then that she realized her entire life was mapped out for her, that from now on there would not be any surprises, and yet despite this loss of freedom she could also see that she was a vital part of this plan and above all else *wanted* – needed by someone. For that reason, when he spoke to her like this, she felt a wave of power move to her from him and she felt bigger and more important. She had a sudden urge to tell him that she did not like the name Margaret, in fact she hated it – and that the idea of having a baby was utterly repellent – but she was too afraid to say that. She did not know why she was afraid – he did not frighten her one bit – it was that she did not want to break this spell that he was weaving.

'No matter what happens,' Midge said then and she would not look at him, 'you're never to hit me . . . I'll take on anything else that you ask – but there's to be no hitting.'

Bird looked down into the small round face, turned up to him now, her eyes firmly on his, waiting patiently, even though both of them found this talk uncomfortable.

'There's no beating in this house,' he said quietly, part of him insulted and another part sorry for her that she had to ask for this. 'And you must always be honest with me.'

'I don't tell lies,' Midge answered and they stood for a moment in the field looking at each other.

The church and the priest had meant nothing at all to them really – but here, in the dark clay under the stars, their vows were exchanged and it was here that Midge Connors became Mrs Bird Keegan.

'You have nothing to worry about,' he said suddenly and he cast his hand around him.

'All this . . . these fields – and there are a lot of them – the lake and the mountain belong to both of us – and if anything happens to me, you, as my wife, will inherit everything.'

And Midge stood still and looked around her, her face softening into a full smile and in the distance she could almost hear her poor mother laughing.

Bird looked at her steadily, the light in his eyes fading a little. Tiny feathers of snow began falling and they stood side by side and surveyed their land that stretched out around them.

'The gawkers are gone,' she said pleasantly as they began to move over the field then, his gilet snug around her. She was aware that her voice was high and childish, that it came out strangely in the twilight, like a bird in the dark blue branches.

Bird glanced up at the sky and she remained silent. He placed a hand flat on her back between her shoulder blades and she felt her spine relax into it. The snow was still falling in light, floating flakes. There were no lights left on in their house but they could both see it like a low round cave in the distance. He began walking towards it and she followed.

32

It was June when Bird saw Midge step out of the bath and he knew that she was pregnant. He had come in late from the yard stinking of manure and had gone straight upstairs to the bathroom. He had grown used to seeing the signs of new life in the cows and ewes but with this small doll of a woman everything was different. After three short months her legs were more shapely – although the lack of good food as a child still showed where her legs were attached to her hips, the mechanical joints plain to see as they prevented this small structure from collapsing. But between her small round stomach and the dark flash of hair, there was a low mound as if fresh earth had been dug up and something new buried there. This place had been disturbed and filled, leaving the white skin smooth again but higher.

The baby would come, as was the natural order of things – and yet now when he saw her, wet and innocent-looking, standing and reaching for a towel and then catching sight of him covered in muck, watching, Bird was overwhelmed by her. She seemed to have a new power, a raw strength coming up from her narrow body. Her eyes were bright and full of life looking back at him. He knew what he wanted from her but could not understand the urgency. He put his two hands on her shoulders and leaning in, kissed her mouth until he heard her give a small gasp, a tight little sigh pushed up from her ribs, her lungs compressed behind them.

He wanted to make love to her there in the bathroom as she stood shivering in her damp towel while he began peeling his clothes off and leaving them in a heap beside him. He paused for a minute, catching sight of his own head in the mirror, his bare back covered in rough bristles, his shoulders white, and she pulled him to her – this time lifting one of her legs so that he could enter her quickly. He was not able to help himself or control it – but he was very gentle with her as always. He made love to her down on the bare boards then, with the wet towel in rolls under them, the rugs smelling of dust and age. He was free of his parents and his sisters and the farm here, free of everything. Whatever he had, belonged to her. She owned the farm and she owned him. He lay on her for the briefest moment, before he lifted himself up and off her again.

This first sight of their child, hidden there, had affected him deeply. He began filling the bath again and she sat up, pulling her knees into her chest, and watched him. He sat on the edge of the bath and listened to the water splashing. The evenings were long again. It was still bright after dinner. Like all farmers he faced this season with apprehension – the sowing had been late and he was still in the middle of lambing. Everything was running behind, the rain having delayed him. He gave a sudden laugh then and slid down into the hot water and when he glanced up at her she was smiling.

'It might be time to see the doctor,' he told her quietly.

'Not yet,' and she seemed distant and not overly happy, 'I want to make sure it's definite.'

Midge did not know what was supposed to happen between a husband and a wife when the wife was expecting. She had seen her own mother curse the same early signs and only the other day when she was walking around the lake to the lodge she had felt the baby moving. Was this something a woman told her husband? Or was it something private to keep hidden? It was as if she had swallowed a feather and then felt it land in her stomach. She had felt the child sweeping around her insides, a tiny limb or the dot of a hand touching her belly.

'I felt the baby move,' she said suddenly and she sounded perplexed by this.

And Bird, whose curls became longer in the water, turned and smiled at her.

'That,' he said, 'is very definite.'

And for Midge in that moment the idea of a living, breathing creature depending on her for life was terrifying.

The room was cooler now and the steam had drained out the small window which she had left open.

He reached for the soap and began lathering up and covering himself with soapy water.

'They're forecasting a very dry summer,' he told her. 'We'll be washing ourselves in the lake.'

'I wouldn't mind that,' she told him and she came and sat on the bath so that she could talk to him.

Bird looked up at her and could see no beginning or end to the love he felt for her. He had not been alive before her. The idea unsettled him and he lifted great handfuls of hot water from the bath and began splashing his face with them. When he looked up she was gone, taking his dirty clothes with her. He had no appetite for his dinner and later he lay down beside her and listened to her sleeping. He could not close his eyes, his thoughts about his unborn child keeping them bright and open and staring. And so he lay awake for much of the night watching the moon give way to the first bleak light of morning. He slept late then and woke to find his right arm cold from being outside the covers and warm on the other side from being around her.

218

33

Midge walked the long boreen to Julia Watkins. She left the red car at Red Hill knowing that it would be a giveaway. What she was doing was secret and no one could know about it. She had prayed that the baby would fall out of her but it was – as she herself had been – determined, only not as lucky. The heat of the early summer sun made sweat come out on her forehead. It was quiet and she could smell jasmine from the hedges. She stopped and ate a few blackberries and stared at the bad lumpy land around her.

'Child,' she said out loud and she put her hand on her stomach, 'there is nothing here at all for you.'

She had been to see Doctor Coffey and he had said that she was 'as healthy as a trout' and that the baby was moving.

'All is well,' he announced and Bird, who was standing at a slight distance, smiled at her.

Then the doctor had watched her carefully and afterwards said to Bird, 'Keep an eye on her.' He had seen plenty of women in the early stages of pregnancy and this one had no real joy in her. The idea of a baby had softened Bird and he was doing everything he could to please her.

This is the thing he's been waiting for, Midge thought. The baby will come and I'll end up worn out like my mother.

Now the sun was heating the stones on the lane around her.

She wished she had brought a drink of water. Two fields away she could see a broken-down ruin of something, a small church by the look of it. Heaped stones and archways were everywhere – country people were always looking for places to pray in. Before the pregnancy Bird had been different. He had always been generous but also watchful and at times a bit cold towards her but now she could feel a change in him, as if he was warm inside and had some kind of new respect, no, *awe*, for her. He didn't ask what she was doing when he was out working. If she stayed in bed watching TV, he said it was good for her. He was ordering things on the internet to surprise her – a pram, a cradle, a high chair, small sheets and blankets. He talked about turning his old bedroom at the top of the kitchen stairs into a nursery but said he would like the baby to be in their bedroom at the start so they could watch her. He said he was well used to being woken up to care for newborns. He joked, which wasn't like him either, and Midge took all of this in and was amazed by the dreadful secret thoughts that she was hiding.

This was not her first time on the boreen to Julia Watkins. She had been there twice already with her mother, a peculiar mission to bring a young girl on, and they went in two different kinds of weather. On one day it rained and Midge could remember the sound of it on the thick leaves of the trees and how she and her mother stayed dry when they walked underneath them. It was a summer rain and they were in short sleeves. Her mother had stopped and sat on the grass verge because she was feeling sick and weak with the heat – the same kind of creeping sickness Midge herself was now feeling. On another day in a different year, it had snowed, the sky thick with dirty clouds, which began to release small white flecks into the air. And Midge had watched them stay briefly in her mother's hair and she had held her hand and she had loved her. She was the baby that her mother had held on to. The others – the older sister and the three boys – did not matter.

Midge was frightened on the boreen now – in the dark of night it would have been easier. Here in the dense heat of a summer afternoon, with the hedges thick with blossoms and berries, there was a peculiar silence. Not the night sounds that she was familiar with, the rustling in the shucks, the short bark of a fox, these things were better than this silence and heat – when everything should have been innocent and sweet and sleeping.

No cars passed her on the road as the farmers were making hay – and the mothers and children were at the lake baking, coming home with hot red backs and feeling pleased with themselves. Julia had welcomed Bridget and her daughter before, opening the door and standing back to let them step in as if she already knew them. There had been no real conversation that Midge remembered, just her mother sitting at a small round table in a dark room where there was a smell of turf and a fire smoking and everywhere she looked there was clutter. There were tall stacks of newspapers reaching the ceiling and saucepans, ladles, colanders filling a corner, which was used as a kind of kitchen. A grey cat was sitting high on the back of a sofa.

'She's a hoarder,' Bridget told Midge on the way home.

And Midge thought she had said, 'She's a whore,' and had believed her.

There in the dark room, Midge remembered a small tumbled bed in the corner and Julia lying down there in the mess of it all and sleeping. She remembered envying her the peace of this place, this dump where she was not bothered by anyone and could have her house just the way she liked it.

Julia had called Bridget 'daughter' even though she was no relation to the Connors.

'Well, daughter,' she had said. 'Hard times have come to us again,' and to this Bridget nodded slowly, keeping her eyes lowered. Julia stood then and went to place a hand on her mother's stomach and she lifted her head and seemed to listen

221

and during all of this Midge remembered feeling happy because with each passing second the tension seemed to be draining from her mother and her face was becoming smoother as the lines of worry released her. Julia put the same hand on Bridget's face and smiled sadly at her with a shake of her head and she disappeared out the back door and when she returned she gave Bridget a small brown bag and then they left her.

Midge did not remember what happened after that. She had a vague image of her mother taking to the bed and how she was left to mind the youngest boy. There was no money for the doctor, Charlie had said, and then he would open the bedroom door and look in at Bridget. Bridget, who was crying and sweating and then finally sleeping, and sleeping for a time that seemed to last for ever. And afterwards she seemed happy enough but still not able to mind her children.

Julia Watkins was sitting on a chair in the shade of a tree near her house. She was wearing a wide-brimmed straw hat and her hair was still long underneath it and, as Midge remembered, the colour of rusted metal. Her hands were lying idle on her lap, and her feet were bare, a long skirt coming down to her shins. She had seen Midge on the lane and had felt her coming closer. She had seen many young girls walk the lane on their own at all hours and she hated to see them coming and yet this, she believed, was her calling. These pregnant girls needed someone to help them. The ones that came were lost and had no money to go to England. And even if the boy offered to pay – for some girls the sin of it was still too heavy. What Julia offered was something different, some-thing spiritual and it did not work for everyone. It worked for mothers who were really not ready or not able – it was that simple. And yet there was nothing simple about it. It was the taking of a life and Julia knew this too, so when she saw Midge Keegan coming and her a married woman with no shortage of money she was surprised and had no welcome for her.

'Mrs Keegan,' she said and as she spoke she leaned forward in her chair, putting her elbows down on parted knees in a way that was mannish.

Midge did not speak for a while. She was tired now and thirsty. She thought about Bird out in the fields, his shirt stripped off and hanging on the trailer, checking the hay bales before he wrapped them.

It gave him great pleasure, he had told her only the evening before, to see a field clean of grass and the rows of bales like small houses, a miniature city, and the whole farm smelling of warm grass and summer.

Warm grass and summer. Midge allowed these words to float inside her head now as she bent her legs and sat down on the ground beside Julia.

'Could I have a drink of water?' she asked.

'There's a barrel at the corner,' Julia said but she did not get up to bring it to her. She looked steadily at Midge. 'You're not welcome here,' she said.

'I need your help.'

'I have no help to give you.'

Midge felt confused then and she looked up at Julia and wondered why she was closed to her.

'You helped my mother.'

'You are not your mother.'

'Not yet, but I will be.'

Julia had struck a small nerve in Midge that seemed to be under her heart or very near it. She gave a sigh and put her head down into her hands. Julia got up and carried a ladle of water back to her.

'What ails you, child?' she asked and now there was a small bit of kindness in her voice when she spoke to her. 'You're a healthy young woman, there is no reason for you not to have this baby.'

223

'I can't have it.'

'Why not? And you a married woman now.'

'I don't want to bring a baby into the world.'

'And what does Bird Keegan have to say?'

'He doesn't know I'm here. He wants the baby more than me.'

'Bird is a good man – and he'll make a good father.'

Midge took a deep breath and tried another direction.

'But you helped my mother – I remember it.'

'You don't remember everything.'

'I remember her being here and then being sick at home – and then no baby.'

'Your mother needed the help. You're stronger.'

'But what if I'm not stronger? What if I'm useless and I ruin this baby – and the baby ruins me? I don't want to end up like my mother.'

Julia looked back at her and waited for a moment. A thrush hopped over the grass beside them.

'There's rain coming,' Julia told her.

And Midge remained silent.

'I saw her before you were born and I refused her,' Julia said quietly.

Here Midge sat still and looked at her. There were tears in her eyes and she wanted to lie down on the grass and curl into a ball and let the woodlice and beetles crawl over her.

'She wanted help when she was expecting you and I said no to her.'

Midge lay down and brought her knees to her chest. She curled her arms under her head and used them as a pillow.

'There are times when it's not right and on that occasion it felt that you were meant to be here.'

'You should have given her what she wanted,' Midge said quietly.

'Now don't be getting foolish on me, girl,' Julia answered and she gave a deep sigh and let her head roll back so that she was looking up through the sycamore branches.

'I will do it myself,' Midge whispered and her eyes were staring into the roots of the tree. 'I will do for the two of us,' she said. 'Me and the baby.'

Julia watched Midge, who had closed her eyes and seemed to be sleeping. She heaved herself out of the chair and walked heavily across the grass and around to the back of her house. When she came back she had a small brown paper bag, which she handed to her.

'Mix a spoonful with a mug of boiling water and drink one every hour.'

'What is it?' Midge asked, sitting up now, her face flushed and her eyes bright as if she had a fever.

'Herbs,' Julia answered flatly, 'and it's important that you talk to the child. Tell her – because it *is* a girl – that you love her.'

'Thank you,' Midge said.

'There's no need for thanks – because I am not helping you. I'm doing what I always do. I hand over the bag and what happens next is up to you.'

Midge took the paper bag and got up from the grass.

'Eat pineapples,' Julia said then. 'They can help to move things along. It's the acid in them.'

'Thanks,' Midge said very quietly.

'Don't thank me. In a few years from now . . . you'll wish you never came near me. That I can promise you.'

The boreen stretched away in the distance and Julia watched her.

'There's a short cut back to your house I can show you. It will take you back around behind the lodge and no one will see you.'

'Bird is in that lower field saving the hay.'

'Then give him a wave and a smile and keep on walking,' Julia

225

said. 'It is not every girl that would do a thing like this to a man who loves her.'

'And how do you know he loves me?'

'I've known Bird Keegan since he was a boy . . . He's deaf in one ear, isn't he?'

'He went diving into the lake and it popped.'

'His father hit him with a paling post,' Julia said flatly. 'But he didn't tell you that, did he?'

She stood up then and pointed out the route home to Midge.

'I don't want to see you here again,' Julia said quietly and with this she turned and disappeared into her cave of a house.

Midge was surprised to find Bird in the kitchen with Sean. They were eating slices of bread and butter and Bird had boiled a saucepan of eggs which they were tapping on the side of the table and peeling. There was a small hill of salt on a plate between them. The farmer's wife was supposed to come with the food basket to them. To come inside in dry weather at this time of year was a kind of failure, an embarrassment. Midge was expected to appear over the hill with the basket full of tea and sandwiches and maybe a few slices of fruitcake. Bird looked up when he saw her, seeing her T-shirt wet with perspiration, her hair damp at her neck and forehead. He glanced quickly at the brown paper bag she was carrying. He continued eating and Sean reached for an egg and then he shook some more salt on the plate beside him and rolled the egg in it. Midge felt as if she had stepped into some kind of painting. *Farmers at Harvest Time*, she would call it. She went to the sink and got a tall glass of water.

'Where were you?' Bird asked casually and she knew then that he was watching. That in spite of the baling, he had come inside for his tea so he could keep an eye on her.

'I went for a walk,' she told him.

226

'Ha,' Sean said quietly for no apparent reason. Then, 'A grand day for it.'

'Did you go to the lake?' Bird asked and his voice was light, friendly.

'No, it was too crowded. I couldn't bear all those screeching children.'

'Your own house will be full of screeching soon enough,' Sean said and he slugged the tea noisily from his mug. They were both dark from working in the sun, Bird's hair bleached blond because of it, his arms brown and strong-looking.

Midge came to the table and poured herself a mug of tea and sat with them.

'I was thinking of going over to the lodge to see Margaret.'

'You better ring first – she might be out . . . *socializing*,' Bird answered.'

Here Sean looked over at Midge and started laughing.

'Isn't she having a swinging time these days with Tom Geoghan?' he added.

'What have you in the bag?' Bird asked casually. He had folded a large piece of bread over and was biting into it. She had put the paper bag down on the table beside her without thinking. She did not want to lie to him – that was their agreement and she would keep to it.

'Leaves,' she said.

'Oh,' he said, his eyes round as he looked at a knot in the wood of the table.

He pushed his plate away and stood up and stretched himself.

'I have to run into town and get some oil for the bailer. Do you need anything?'

Midge drank from her cup and then, looking straight into his eyes, said, 'A pineapple.'

'Be gob,' Sean said as if it was the moon she had asked for.

'A pineapple?' Bird repeated.

'A few of them.'

'My missus loved a jar of olives when she was expecting,' Sean said helpfully.

'You didn't call your daughter Olive?' Bird asked and when Midge looked up he was smiling. Here was more of his new happiness and she felt strangely betrayed by him. The idea of becoming a father had turned on some kind of lamp inside him. Before now she had had a clearer understanding of him. She had understood his coldness towards her at times and had only to step away from it. She was familiar with his serious face and his eyes which always looked directly at her even when he was saying something that he found difficult.

'We called our first daughter Róisín,' Sean said slowly. 'The little rose – even though she turned out to be a bit of a tulip.'

Here all three of them started laughing.

Bird had put a straw hat on the back of his head and was leaving. He whistled some light tune and jingled coins in his jeans pocket. And Midge was left sitting with Sean, who looked steadily at her now that her husband had left them.

'You'd want to eat something . . .' and he pushed the bread board towards her.

'Have something,' he said again, nodding. 'It's a fierce long walk down that lane to Julia Watkins.'

And Midge took a slice of bread and it sat on her plate unbuttered. They sat then for the briefest of moments, their eyes meeting, resting on the thoughts and secrets they were now keeping.

34

Margaret took her rosary beads in her hands and lay back on her pillows to wait for Midge Connors. She had no time for her brother's wife but she could not refuse her completely. It was after nine when Midge had called to say that she had some news for her and Olive – and wasn't it obvious already? The girl was glowing from head to toe and the dogs in the streets knew that she was pregnant. And now she was bursting to tell them and 'No,' she said, it could not 'wait until morning'. Margaret could not help feeling some happiness for her though, and the idea of the farm being filled with children. Her own life was changing too, just at a time when she thought change was no longer possible.

She found it hard to believe that she and Tom Geoghan were meeting regularly – that they talked easily now and enjoyed each other's company. After a quiet drink in the Glen they would step out over the smooth stones to his car, calling goodnight to the owner. And Tom would take her hand or place a warm protective arm around her shoulders. They would often stand for a minute and look up at the stars – the Plough with its points and angles, Orion and Taurus just above them. Close enough, Margaret thought in her newfound happiness, for her to reach up and take them. And all the time as she stood there with Tom, admiring the sky, the dark shape of the night mountains, the lights of Tullyvin in a scattering below them, she could feel how his arm stayed around her and realized with sudden joy that they were side by side again, marvelling at nature, at everything.

Tom had not tried to kiss her and she knew that he wouldn't because he was waiting for her to give a signal. They had gone around this circle before and now they were older and things could be slower. The kissing would come later. The kissing and the caressing would follow a fair few drives through the country-side and hours and hours of talking. As she left the blue pub in the dark there was no space left inside yet for wanting anything more from him. She had been set free, released from years of anger – and realized that the joy she was feeling now filled all of her.

Tonight she had come home earlier than usual because they were planning a day trip to Brittas Bay the following morning. She had waited in the kitchen for Midge and then, feeling tired, she had pulled on her nightie and climbed into bed, hoping that Midge would wait until tomorrow.

Lying in bed she closed her eyes and remembered undressing and peeling away her underclothes a moment earlier. She was still a woman after all and her life, she realized, was running freely inside her. Even if a part of her needed the hours of conver-sation before allowing a man to touch her, her body was ready, her body, which only a few weeks earlier had seemed so stiff and cold, was running on a stretch of hot sand miles ahead of her.

She took a deep breath and wished her sister was at home so she could talk to her.

'What is the point in being angry with Tom?' Margaret might ask her. 'Life is short enough without winding it up tighter and tighter with feelings that are like a poison.'

She heard the back door closing softly.

Olive, she thought to herself and she was smiling. Or Midge, but she hoped it was her sister.

230

Olive would sit on the end of the bed and wait to hear all about Tom Geoghan but Margaret would tell her nothing. It was still too personal and awkward for her. Instead she would just say that it was late and that she was tired – but Olive would know from the very air in the room, from the new warmth coming off her sister, that Margaret was happier.

Margaret could see now that she had spent her life like a pickle inside a jar of salt water. Now she had a new heart and it was open. Margaret Keegan was not dead. Long live Margaret Keegan!

The door to her bedroom opened very slowly. It did not creak at all, the hinges had been oiled recently by Sean Weldon – and then someone, a person backlit from the small lamp on the landing, appeared and stood there looking in at her.

'Olive?' she called out but there was no answer.

Midge? she wondered – but no, it was too tall a person to be Midge Connors.

The shape of the head and shoulders was somehow manly.

'Is that you, Bird?' she asked in some confusion – and then whoever it was stepped into the mostly dark room and she heard the door moving quietly behind him.

The lights from the tractor lit up the field and Midge watched it from the kitchen window. She had seen Margaret's car going down to the lodge and she knew that Olive was out at a parish social. From her window she could see the lake and there was a boat out there and it wasn't moving. The water was calm and quiet now, the families gone home and already sleeping. The world was a peaceful place and she had almost caused a kind of wreckage. She wondered about taking a baby's life and if such a deed would create a kind of echo – a star falling or even just a leaf floating to the ground to mark its passing. She had made the tea as Julia had told her. It was dark brown and smelled of the earth,

231

red and wet and familiar. She had let the steam rise up to her face and the smell seemed to take her somewhere. She had closed her eyes and tried to think good thoughts about the baby. The door to the kitchen had opened suddenly then and Bird had appeared carrying four pineapples and looking younger than she had ever seen him.

'Is four enough?' he asked and he was smiling down at her.

'I thought you were out in the field . . .'

'That's Sean . . . the trailer has a slow puncture and I had to take it up to the yard to fix it.'

Midge crossed the floor quickly to put her arms around him then, an impulsive gesture that could still make him awkward and shy but he softened and hugged her close to him, and she could smell grass and sun from him and there were hayseeds gathered in his beard and hair.

'I love you, Bird,' she whispered and the words were surprising even to her and Bird himself stood back and looked down into her face as if puzzled because no one had ever said this to him before. And they held on to each other, her stomach against his, her heart beating, their foreheads touching -- everything she had inside her was safe between them. She felt slightly dizzy then and went and sat on the floor near the range, her arms around her knees, her head resting near her elbows.

The sun was going down red and dragging the blue of the June sky with it and Bird could see the picture of his own life around him. He was standing in the warmth of his own house with a wife who loved him, the hay was coming in without a drop of rain on it and at that moment he had never been as happy. There was a child to look forward to and he realized that the night he found Midge was in itself a blessing.

'I'm going over to the lodge to tell your sisters about the baby,' she said. 'I called Margaret and asked if I could come over.'

'I'm not sure if Olive is at home this evening,' Bird said and this was, of course, a kind of warning. 'I think she plays bridge on a Thursday.'

'It's Margaret I want to see . . . I'm hoping the news might make her warm to me.'

And Bird listened to her words and tried to imagine Margaret's reaction. It was possible now that even she would be happy for them. A strange charm had been cast over Tullyvin and he could trace it back to the dark night he found Midge in his field – and to the sight of William O'Neill hanging – and since then accidents were happening a bit too freely. Bridget Connors was dead. Charlie Connors had been in and out of the Garda Station. Tullyvin seemed to be in the eye of a miniature storm with no sign of it lifting.

He had an image then of Margaret sitting up in the car beside Tom Geoghan, which was by now a regular occurrence – and she was almost unrecognizable because of a kind of light that was shining from her.

Dear God but women are very complicated, he thought to himself. That a woman as intelligent and as capable as Margaret could change like a flicker of light – and all because of that old badger sitting there beside her.

Until now Bird had not felt the influence of other people. And here on the floor of his own kitchen was a person, curled like a cat on the rag rug and waiting for him to say something to her, happy with everything he seemed to do, her every look and word a kind of praise for him. He could feel it now – she actually loved him.

'It's still bright enough to walk over,' Midge said and he nodded.

'If it's dark when you're coming back, call me and I'll drive over.'

He stood for a moment and watched her.

'I'll walk you as far as the lane . . . I have to get some of those sheep in from the paddock anyway.'

He pretended to be gruff with her but outside the door he took her hand and opened every gate so that she would not have to climb over. And when they reached the back gate to the lodge he kissed her, smoothing her hair back from her face so he could see all of her. Midge watched him walk away from her then, his shoulders, the length of his legs, the swinging strides which were so familiar to her. He moved through the halo of light thrown out from the kitchen and into the shadow and it was there she left him. She knew that he was going out to work with a light heart and the comfort of a girl at home who loved him. She knew then that Bird would never want anything different – and now she would keep the baby safe for him. It was impossible for her to hurt him, to carry out any kind of secret plan and then have it sit silently, for ever, between them.

35

Charlie Connors stepped quietly into Margaret's room and pushed the door behind him. He had seen this woman around the town and when he spoke to her on the phone, she insulted him. 'Scum', that was what she called him – and now she was sitting up in bed in a flannel nightie that did nothing to improve her. The state of the woman – her eyes wide in her head with fear and her hair standing up like barbed wire.

'Now, Miss Keegan,' he began in a sort of whisper, 'don't be making any noise or thinking of doing anything foolish,' and he paused for a moment and looked around the room, lit only by the soft pink light on the landing. He saw the odd shapes of the frilly lampshades and the floral wallpaper, the old-fashioned heavy furniture, the bed four feet off the ground and her lying up on it like Queen Victoria.

Margaret's mouth had remained open during this short speech, her breathing tight, a hot funnel of panic rising up inside her. No man had ever been over the threshold of her bedroom before, even Sean Weldon had used his oil can from outside the door. Her mouth was very dry and her lips tight and hurting. Her arms were down by her sides, neat and rigid, outside the eiderdown. She became aware of herself then and sat up straight in the bed – and swung her legs out from under the covers. Her nightdress had curled up around her thighs and she had a distant memory of removing her tights and underwear earlier.

'And where did you come from?' she demanded loudly. 'And what are you doing inside this house?' and her voice was rising further. 'And inside my bedroom?' she shouted.

When her feet touched the floor, her nightie caught on the mattress and Charlie noted the round bowls of her knees, the purple veins on her ankles, the thick calves which were covered in hair. Here was a woman who was – as far as she was concerned – in every way superior, the kind of woman who treated a decent man like an animal. The higher part of her legs was very white and soft-looking and in seeing that secret place, he considered the idea of putting his hands on her.

'Now hold on,' he said back to her. 'Hold on a minute, missus. I am only here to see my daughter – I'm wondering if she might loan me some money . . . or perhaps your good self, my lady, now that we are all – *related.*'

Margaret stood facing him, straightening her nightie, her bare feet flattened on the carpet and the pink light shining from behind him. She could not see his face clearly and his voice was still new to her. She did not want to step closer to examine him either. The sight of her own bare feet caused her to lose confidence suddenly and she was frightened of him.

'Your daughter does not live here and you should be locked up. Get on with you or I'll be on the phone to Sergeant Brennan,' she added.

'Now, ma'am,' he said and his voice was slurring. 'There is no need to be insulting . . . and you've been very insulting on the phone as well . . . but I'm only here to see my daughter.'

She could smell the whiskey on his breath when she tried to step past him.

'I'm calling the Guards,' she told him.

And here he stepped into her path and put up his two hands on her shoulders.

'There's no need for that, missus . . . you won't let me talk to Midge on the phone and now you are being very unsociable. Will you hand me that bag there of yours? And you can drop your little watch and ring into it . . . Is there more cash in the house? There's no point pretending . . . because I'll find it. I'm in no hurry now that I know it's just the two of us.'

'Midge will be here in a minute and she's bringing my brother with her,' she said quietly.

'I told you to hand me your bag, Miss Keegan.'

'Olive,' Margaret called and she could hear the fear in her own voice, rising.

'Olive,' she called again and of course there was no answer. It occurred to her then that Olive might not come home at all, that it was just her, Margaret, and this tramp, that she was entirely on her own with him.

'Get back into bed like a good girl and we'll pretend that this never happened and you won't tell anyone – because if you do . . . I'll come back and do for you and your fat sister.'

'Don't speak to me about my sister! You're not fit to lick her boots,' Margaret said to him, her voice slow and even. 'You're an animal, that's what you are.'

'Give me whatever money you have in that bag,' he told her again and she had no choice but to hand it over to him. He came and stood by the bed and looked at her. She was the kind of woman who was used to looking down on a decent man – and there was a solution for women like that, if she pushed him.

'I happen to know that your fat sister is at Pat Noonan's house – they're up there in the bed together . . . Do you ride much yourself? Margaret, that's your name, isn't it? Margaret . . . I'd say that old Tom Geoghan is delighted with you . . . And what about Midge? She's up there at the big house now with your brother – making little Keegans.'

237

Margaret lay flat in her bed, her body sinking down into the mattress, and prayed for him to leave her.

'Midge is on her way over and she'll have Bird with her,' she said again and her voice had a new strength in it.

'Is that right? Well then, I'll take a seat downstairs and I'll wait for her. Sure, it'll be a great old surprise, we'll have a little party – us Connors love a get-together. And I don't think Bird will be there because I saw him out on the hill in his jeep trying to corral those sheep and they were running in every direction . . . It would be unusual for a farmer to abandon his flock and go visiting his sister.'

'You're nothing but filth,' she told him. 'You're filth and I'm not a bit afraid of you.'

Charlie had turned for the door but what she said seemed to affect him.

'Now, Margaret, don't be calling me that – I told you to shut your trap or I'll have to shut it for you.'

'We all know what you did to your poor wife and you should be locked up for it. Hanging is too good for you. You're filth and you're scum and the whole town knows it.'

She made a small sound when he put his hands on her. He found the softest spots under her jaw, the smooth tube of her neck which he began to squeeze tightly. The sound she made was the glug-glug sound of water being poured from a long-necked bottle. The Guards had made his life a misery, weeks of questions and a few awful beatings – all thanks to this one's brother.

She struggled for breath and it pleased him.

'Am I filthy now?' he asked her quietly.

This woman of great learning and education who was so superior had been reduced to something much smaller. He got on top of her then, pushing the covers back behind him. His face was filled with wonder, one hand big enough to keep the squeeze on

238

her neck so that her head would soon be as purple as a turkey's. With the other hand, he put a finger to his lips.

'Shhhhh like a good girl,' he told her and her eyes bulged up at him. 'Shhh,' he said again. 'Now are you going to be a good girl for me?'

And Margaret, whose eyes had grown into huge lakes underneath him, could not say yes to him. He released his hold slightly and felt her head give the slightest nod and he grinned down at her. He folded his legs under him and sat for a moment with his full weight on her. She was gasping now, trying to catch her breath, and there were tears running down her cheeks.

'Please,' was what she was saying to him now. 'Please . . . oh please . . . oh please . . . I beg you.'

So he was not filth after all. He could feel the warmth of her body moving into his thighs and he found himself watching her neck again, fascinated by the whiteness of it, the red blotches left by his hands like a map of different countries. In his mind he was opening up her nightdress and seeing her breasts, soft now with age and hanging sideways, nipples big like coat buttons, but that was not the kind of business he had intended. He wanted to see Midge now and remind her that he was as good as his word – that he had come back for her just as he had promised.

Margaret's breath had become deeper and slower but her body was beginning to shake underneath him.

'Get off me . . . you dirty . . . dirty bastard,' she whispered at him.

There's no talking to some women, he thought to himself.

Margaret screamed only once as his hands and fingers found the soft damp parts of her. And then to silence her crying he turned her face down into the pillows and she became limp then, with no fight at all left in her. He was taking her hair in a fistful, using his knee to part her legs – the whole town knew she was still a virgin, he thought . . . he was doing her a favour, she should be thanking him – and there she was crying, the great Margaret Keegan wetting the bed like a child. He pushed his fingers hard inside her and heard a cry from deep in the pillows. That was all he needed to do. He had found the one thing that would break her. She had been reduced to nothing.

A small amount of light was still coming through the door and as her eyes became used to the dark Margaret watched as he opened it wider and the room was flooded with light from the landing.

That was just a shape and not a person at all, Margaret told herself, tears running down her cheeks to her jawbones. She turned on her side slowly and pulled her legs towards her.

'Move one inch out of this room and I'll knock the head off you,' Charlie told her.

And with that he slipped quietly out and closed the door behind him.

36

L ater Midge would say that she was drawn to the lodge, a force
pulling her faster than she was capable of walking. It was as
if all of the earth's gravity was located there and she was tumbling
headlong. The dizziness she had felt in the kitchen returned and
a light rain fell on the lane, the wind suddenly cool against her.
The cows took shelter with their calves under the trees, their
heads hanging low in a way that seemed hopeless. The bailer had
stopped because of the rain and when Bird's jeep moved slowly
out over the fields Midge waved to him. This was something that
happened regularly between them – Midge waving to Bird from
an upstairs window as he stood on Hope's Hill counting the
cattle. He would lift his stick to salute her, the connection
renewed again and again between them. Once she had waved
from the lodge – and from the far side of the lake, close to Red
Hill, he had seen her. She could have sworn that she could see
him smiling at her over the water.

She was happy on her way to the lodge, knowing now that
Margaret must have softened slightly towards her. Why else
would she let her call at this late hour? In time Midge would have
liked to think of her as an older sister or as a kind of stepmother
but she was not too hopeful. She had tossed Julia's dark tea up
into the sky outside the scullery. She had heard it fall, making a
scattering of dark spots on leaves and gravel and concrete. For

241

now Bird himself was making a whole new life for her. She was someone. He had saved her. She watched as he parked the jeep in a far-off field and how the cows began to run towards him, their own young momentarily forgotten.

Charlie sat on a chair inside the back door and waited for her. The lights were turned off and the house was silent around him. Margaret had not moved from her room and the only sound was a clock ticking somewhere.

'Midge, Midge, Midge,' he whispered as if it was a little cat he was calling.

He closed his eyes and released the images of her one by one from his brain. Midge as a baby in her nappy. Midge as a schoolgirl. Midge as a pain in the backside, always running to her mother and telling tales on him. Midge telling Bridget – his wife – to leave him. Midge finding money and giving it to the youngest boy so he could move away and his father would never see him again. Charlie had hated Midge from the minute he laid eyes on her. She had been born with a caul, which he had found revolting. Until recently it had been kept in a drawer in the bedroom. Only the other day he had come across it – the shape of the little head still left in it – and he had squeezed it in his hand until it broke into light flakes as fragile as eggshells. It was a great pity he had not done that to her head when she was a baby. He had also discovered that Bridget had been saving every penny she earned from the Italians. There were bank statements in the same drawer with only her name on them. Cute old Bridget. Over the years she had put away a tidy sum and she had made a will – she was smarter that he had ever given her credit for. And in this will she was very specific about the money going to Midge and not to her husband. And that did not seem fair to Charlie Connors, who had, in his opinion, fed and raised that daughter and she was not a good girl either.

What sort of girl runs to the Guards about her own flesh and blood? Calls him a murderer, tries to bring all manner of bad luck and misfortune down on him?

He heard feet on the gravel then and saw her faint shape pass under the light at the door. Her hand was reaching for the doorknob and he could see it turning.

He smiled and said quietly to himself, 'She's here.'

Midge herself did not remember what happened at the lodge. The smooth brass of the doorknob in her hand made no impression, although she did recall the small pilot light on the new oven making the kitchen seem homely. She had carried the memory of Bird down the lane with her, her head filled with ideas of him and their life together. She was glad that Julia Watkins had made it difficult for her, glad that both Julia and Bird believed that she could deliver this child into the world safely and go on to be a decent sort of mother.

Charlie came at her quickly – she remembered something dark and vast – a kind of cloak, she said later, swooping towards her. Then a light flashed on and there was Margaret framed in a doorway, her hair on end, her eyes red from crying, spots of blood falling from somewhere – and Olive then with Pat Noonan near the window and Charlie giving a small sudden cry like a girl, like the coward that he was, and bolting through the still-open door, his feet skating in the gravel, his thin legs going everywhere. As Midge looked at him and saw the sudden flash of his eyes, which had no love at all for her, her whole life and all the life she was carrying seemed to heave inside her. An earthquake formed under her skin and began building, building until she was curled up in a ball with all the faces in the world looking at her. There was blood then, and it was in a pool all around her and where was it coming from? For once, for the only time she could remember, Charlie had not even laid a finger on her. But she believed that his shadow alone, that strange shroud that had come at her, had somehow gone through her. She had not been ready to fight him and he had injured her, hurt the baby, frightened the baby and driven her away – and Midge rolled herself up tighter and tighter so that no one, not Olive nor Margaret who were all comfort and tears, using tea towels, anything they could find really, to try to plug up this wave of blood that was coming from her. The baby, oh God in heaven, the little baby was up and running away from her own mother and who would blame her? And Midge formed a kind of shell again, a barricade to protect herself and the person inside her but her daughter was determined to get away – she was gone, it seemed, from the moment Midge realized how much she loved her, how much she needed her.

37

Bird came in from the field with Sean Weldon shadowing him. He had noticed that Sean was quieter than usual, as if he was distracted by something. He did not press him for any conversation, enjoying the silence himself, the peace and quiet of night that surrounded them. They followed the lights from the kitchen windows, their tired feet catching in the stubble and no words were spoken between them. Later Bird would remember this walk in the dark and realize that as long as you knew a person, and he had known Sean Weldon his whole life, you could never be sure what another person was thinking or the mistakes that they were capable of making. Bird himself was thinking about Midge and looking forward to seeing her curled in a chair or already in bed, sleeping. Instead he found Pat Noonan at the back door waiting in the light of his car's headlights and telling him to go to the lodge immediately.

'What is it?' Bird asked. 'Is it Midge? Has something happened? Is she all right?'

'She will be,' was Pat's answer. 'But she needs you with her. There was a—' and here Pat grimaced slightly and gave the slightest shake of his head. 'There was a kind of incident . . . with her father, and your sister too . . . He got into the house. He got at them.'

It was as if a rain of stones came down on the three men then.

'He got into the house. He got at them.'

Bird repeated these words and he stepped forward as if he needed to see Pat more clearly. He felt a hand on his arm and it was Sean's, the weight of it, its rough warmth on his own in no way familiar. They had worked side by side as boys and men and had never once touched each other. Their hands were always occupied with lifting and scraping and digging. They had nothing in common except work and the silence of the farm was like a friend to both of them. Now Sean had placed his hand on Bird's arm because he thought he was going to swing a box at Pat Noonan. What he had said was unthinkable and in the briefest of moments Bird had wanted to drive the words back into him. Pat did not move or flinch but Sean had guessed what Bird was thinking.

'I'll stay here and lock up,' Sean said. 'You go on to the lodge with Pat and see to the women.'

The moon was full again. 'Full but not blue,' that was how Sean had heard Bird explain this phenomenon to Midge. 'There is no such thing as a blue moon,' he said. 'It's just a full moon twice in the month and it doesn't happen often.' All this for a girl who, in Sean's view, was not deserving of Bird's kindness or education. He turned off the lights in the kitchen and locked the door behind him. This house which he knew as well as his own and yet he would never venture upstairs or even open a press door in the kitchen. He cycled home and did not meet a single car. He passed the lodge, which had a light on in every window with people moving over and back behind them. It looked like a kind of chaos and Sean could only imagine what was happening. He met Doctor Hughes, the locum, coming at speed then and knew where he was going. Sean could not bear to think of it and so looked up towards the mountain and the moon and away from the pain and awfulness that people were forever causing.

246

Bird carried Midge to a bed in the attic. She had been there before and now the bed was freshly made with white sheets stretched tightly over it. She clung to him and when he tried to lay her down flat he had some trouble prising her fingers from his collar. From the other side of the bed Margaret took her small hand and held it, and this caused a kind of peace to cover Midge so that she closed her eyes and began to sleep deeply.

'She'll be fine,' Doctor Hughes said and there was a sadness in his voice, knowing that he could not do anything to help them. These two people, this man and woman who had lost something, a new life that could not be saved and which would always register as a loss to them. She would need to come into the hospital later in the week, he told them.

'For a routine procedure . . . following these things.'

'These things.'

Bird repeated the words quietly and as she slept he lay down gently on the bed next to her, so that when she finally woke she would not have to reach for him. And Margaret hovered in a pink dressing gown, her face pale and her hands pushing Olive gently away from her.

'I'm all right,' she said vaguely without looking at her sister. 'He took my bag and my watch. He didn't kill me.' She seemed more worried about Midge and spent the rest of the night washing out the cloths and mopping the floor and tiptoeing up the narrow attic stairs to listen at the door for any words that were spoken between them.

In the morning Bird built a fire at a safe distance from the barns of new hay. He checked the direction of the wind, his face tilting upwards so that his beard shifted a little in it. The dog came and danced around him, thinking it was a game that they were playing.

'Go away, fool,' Bird said as he dragged more branches into the

247

circle and shook diesel over them. The liquid landed in splashes on the wood and he didn't hesitate before tossing a lit match onto it. The flames rose up quickly with a crackle of burning wood left behind them. And he stepped back and left it. He turned his back and saw Sean watching from the doorway of a shed.

Always damn watching, with his mouth open, Bird thought.

He returned from the jeep carrying the once-white sheets, a blanket, a nightdress all streaked in dried blood, a peculiar clay colour. He threw them onto the fire and then, reaching for a pitchfork, pushed them deeper into the blaze and watched as a thick funnel of smoke began to come up from them. The smoke was dense and stinking at first and his eyes became red and raw from it. The fire worked on slowly and then gained pace so that more of the branches caught and the flames crackled.

When it was safe to leave it Bird went and sat at the end of the shed, his world burning up around him, and while he knew the loss of the baby was something they could both recover from he could not bear the idea that he had not protected her, that he had promised he would keep her safe and in that, which was all that she needed, he had failed her. He put his head into his hands and with the fire burning out behind him and spots of rain beginning to drum on the roof over him, Bird cried, knowing that no one could hear him. A hen cackled and appeared mysteriously from behind a bale where she had been laying and keeping her eggs a secret. She cackled on in pride and from instinct – unaware that the farmer crying on the bale had seen everything. And Bird thought about the animals and all their foolishness and how compared to people they were easier, their tragedies so much smaller and more manage-able. People, as far as he could see, especially women, were far too easily broken. The rain pounded on the galvanized roof, the sound in itself a comfort. The last time, a few days ago now, that he had come here, it was to ruminate on the idea of a son or a daughter and the things that he would show them.

He heard Sean opening the wooden door behind him then.

He should know better, Bird thought, than to come near me.

'The fire's going out and the blanket is only half burned . . . Do you want me to throw on a drop more diesel?'

Bird did not turn around but just shook his head slowly.

'Is the wee girl all right?' Sean asked then and with that Bird stood up, his long legs suddenly strong again underneath him.

'She's grand,' Bird said quietly. He made to walk past Sean and for the second time he felt his hand on his arm.

He stopped and the two men looked at each other.

'It is a painful thing,' Sean said slowly and close up Bird was aware of the dark liquid of the other man's eyes, the rings of dirt on his neck, his face unshaven.

'Yes,' Bird said and he walked to the door and away from him.

'But I've heard that the girls who go to Julia do well enough after . . . What I mean to say is,' and here Sean stopped and found that he was shaking. He had never spoken to Bird so directly before or in such an intimate manner. 'I believe she manages it all very gently for them.'

And Bird stopped at the open door, the yard full of smoke now from the half-burned blanket – and carefully placed the pieces of what Sean had just said together.

'What?' he whispered and he turned but Sean was gone, heading out through a crack in the bales, sending the dishonest hen, the sly one, because there was always one, running and flapping away ahead of him. Later Bird would find a nest full of eggs. He would count twenty-five of them, all of them rotten and her the fool wasting her time sitting on them.

By the end of June it seemed that summer was over. Wind and slanted rain marked the lake and made white waves on the water. The islands became black caves from a distance and the swimming lessons were cancelled for the first time Olive could

249

remember. Bird had confronted Midge, finding her pale and still in bed, but he was not able to contain his own anger, the shock pushing all sympathy out of him.

'You went to Julia Watkins,' he told her, 'and on the same day you told me you loved me. I remember the paper bag. I remember you there in the kitchen. Sean saw you, Midge – and if he hadn't I'd be none the wiser. And why, Midge? Why did you do it?' and then he had cried, frightening her for the first time since she had met him – something inside him giving way too quickly, his shoulders slack, the whole length of his body seeming too heavy.

'Why, Midge?' he asked her again. 'Why did you have to?'

And she had sat up stiff in the bed and faced him and all of his anger.

'I went but I didn't drink the tea she gave me. I made the tea but I didn't drink it, Bird, and you have to believe me.'

'But how can I believe you?'

'Because it's the truth – and I'm telling it to you.'

And here a kind of plank was placed between them and everything they had, their love, their union, was suddenly walking on it, slow and unsteady.

'You have to believe me, Bird,' she said again.

'How can I, Midge? You went to Julia Watkins – and then you lost the baby.'

'I didn't lose the baby – the baby was lost because she wanted to be.'

And to this Bird said nothing, his insides feeling weak and empty, the world around him, the slanted roof of the lodge attic where she still slept because they were afraid to disturb her – the wind batting at the windows, the clouds moving over a pale sun – all seemed unreal to him.

'You have to believe me, Bird,' Midge whispered again and she was out of her bed now and crossing the floor towards him. But he could not look at her and when she tried to put her hand on his arm, he lifted it away as if it had no business there, as if it might injure him. And he had left her standing in the attic alone then, retreating into a place of silent agony where he went over all that had happened and everything she had said – and he did not believe a single word she had ever told him.

38

'Come on,' Margaret said, 'let's climb the mountain together.' It was July and Midge was still pale but it seemed like the right kind of day to take her. The sky was low but there was no wind, which would make the climb easier. They reached the first resting spot and saw a white fog rolling past them. A fire the previous summer had scorched the ground and the gorse was still dead and blackened. Bird had watched them briefly from the doorway of a shed, his sister striding out in her usual determined manner – and Midge floating behind her. The small dog had wanted to go with them – his loyalty ever changing – and Bird had allowed it. And all of this had passed without a word being exchanged between the man and the woman, the brother and his sister.

The women did not talk at all then. Margaret led, the dog weaving in and out between them, and they crossed the flat green spaces that began to slope upwards, smooth moss and grass shorn by sheep giving way to gravel. At the second rest stop Midge sat on a flat rock and looked around her. She had never known Margaret to invite her anywhere. She was not feeling completely well in herself yet and did not want the ham sandwich that her sister-in-law offered her. Margaret produced a flask then and poured her a cup of scalding tea and waited while Midge drank it. There was only one cup between them. The fog was thinning and they could see the lake now, the full circle of it, far away below them.

'And over there the sea,' Margaret pointed.

She flicked a crust of bread to the dog and splashed the last of her tea out into the gorse bushes. She reached for her walking pole and they began the last of their climb together.

'It's like the road to Calvary,' Margaret said suddenly. 'But we'll go right to the top, it's a great feeling to climb a mountain.'

Closer to the top, the stones became a blur, each one a different shade of grey or sand or fawn, and the women tried to find the smooth solid ones to place their feet on. They crept on their knees through narrow crevices and when Midge lost her footing Margaret turned and stretched out a hand for her. In a moment they would slip sideways through a narrow passage – Midge had heard about it before – and then, on the other side, they would find the flat square space that was the top of the mountain. She took the other woman's hand, surprised at its softness and then its sudden strength as Margaret hauled her upwards so that she was next to her.

'There you are,' Margaret told her and then she was turning again and moving on ahead of her.

At the top they sat side by side, deep in the fog now and not able to see anything except the immediate rocks around them. There was no view, nothing at all to see, except the jagged edge and each other. Someone had left an empty Fanta bottle and some orange peel behind them.

The dog darted from one side to the other, light on his feet and never in any danger.

'People have jumped,' Margaret told her suddenly.

She had produced a bag of boiled sweets and was offering them to Midge.

'From that side there,' and she made a wiping motion with her hand to indicate the place. She took a sweet herself then and lodged it in her jaw, sucking contentedly.

'I've considered it myself,' she added calmly. 'Almost every day since June.'

Midge took a deep breath and wrapped her coat around her.

Summer was gone again and the mountain had its own season.

'And what has stopped you?' she asked quietly.

'I'm not sure – but I climb back down again, knowing that I can't let life beat me, that there is a sun waiting for me, that there is water and trees and people.'

Midge pulled her knees up and hugged them to her.

'Shouldn't we begin to climb back down now?' she asked.

'Not yet,' Margaret answered.

A patch of fog thinned suddenly and a broad beam of sunlight filled a corner of the valley. There were fields divided by hedges, the purple of the heather, the lake, the sea in the distance.

'Midge, do you remember anything at all of what happened . . . that night with . . . your father?' Margaret asked and suddenly she seemed to give way to something, feelings like a boulder coming free inside her. She seemed to cough and then tears flowed, her shoulders shaking with the rush of them, her back hunched, her nose running. She clapped two childish hands over her eyes then to prevent Midge from seeing.

And Midge sat watching her, her mouth slightly open, her brows creased from the pain she was witnessing. This was not a woman numbed from a punch or a kick but a person who was destroyed by some kind of hurricane, her insides in tatters from something she might never rise up from.

'I only have a vague idea. Bird has talked to me but he doesn't give me any details,' Midge said quietly.

Margaret stared at her hanky as if she had no notion what to do with it.

'What did he do to you?' Midge asked, her voice low and frightened.

254

'He tried . . .' and here she took a deep breath, 'to ruin me.'

When Margaret spoke now she was looking off into the distance.

'But he didn't. I'm still here and not ruined by anything. 'Do you see how my little watch is gone?' she asked suddenly then and she gave a little smile and tugged at her sleeve to show Midge a wrist as white and soft as a three-year-old's.

'It's gone,' she said simply. 'He ran out the door with it – and we've looked all over the yard and can't find it anywhere,' and she was frowning down into the sea of pebbles around them, a sea of grey and blue, and the mist rolling over the mountain so that, to anyone watching, they were two women appearing and then disappearing again.

'He took the watch off my wrist and then he tried to strangle me – that is what he did, Midge Connors.'

'And did he do anything else, Margaret?'

And instead of answering Margaret climbed the granite slope and then stood near the edge of it. She seemed lighter in herself now that she had shared part of her secret.

'I thought he was going to kill me . . . but I'm alive. Look!' she said suddenly and she spread out her hands as if she was flying.

Midge was finding it hard to breathe, the wind rising cold around them.

'Bird knows?'

'Of course he knows. And didn't they arrest your father finally? Yes, Midge, Bird knows everything.'

And Midge already knew this about him. Bird was a man made of rivers and mountains, each one deeper or higher than the last one. He was a person of many different shades and colours.

'And now I'm thinking of travelling,' Margaret said. 'I still have my life so I might as well have some kind of adventure. He tried to ruin me, Midge, and I think I should try and have a life now to spite him . . . I think now that perhaps that is the point of it.'

'Bird and Olive would miss you.'

And at the mention of his name Midge's face clouded over.

'You've had a falling out,' Margaret said and she returned to her cold seat beside her.

And when Midge stayed quiet, she added, 'You and Bird.'

'Yes.'

'He opened himself to you – and you hurt him.'

'I didn't – at least I didn't mean to,' Midge answered. 'It's because of the baby. He thinks I didn't want it.'

'And did you? Want it?'

'Not at first – but I changed my mind – then I wanted it more than anything.'

Neither woman spoke for a moment.

'And now he doesn't believe you.'

'No. Now there's a distance . . . a coldness between us.'

'He'll come round surely,' Margaret said and she poked Midge gently with her elbow.

'I don't think so. I'm not sure things can ever be right again between us.'

Margaret and Midge faced the valley below them, and the lake. The water was lit up by the sun now, like a far-off spoon that was shining. They sat side by side then and shared some more tea from the flask, the same cup passed over and back between them.

'So where are you thinking of going?' Midge asked finally, the silence of the mountain more than she could bear.

'I wanted to go to America since I was a teenager – but then I thought myself and Tom would get married and settle here. Do you know I have a Green Card? I got it in a lottery but I never used it.'

'Are you really going to leave Tullyvin?' Midge asked, the idea suddenly unsettling her.

'Tullyvin? Midge, I'm going to leave Ireland.'

256

'And what about Olive? I don't think you really mean it.'

'The fact is I do. Olive is very happy with Pat – and leaving Tullyvin would not be enough for me – that would be like a week-end in Bundoran and I've had enough of them. No, I want to have an adventure. Leaving Tullyvin would make no difference to me – I want to leave everything.'

And Midge stared back at her, her eyes wide and bright as she tried to imagine this new Margaret alive in America.

'You're really going to go,' Midge said quietly. 'What about you and Tom?'

'Tom?' Margaret repeated and she turned to look out at the view around them. 'I feel like I've woken up from something.'

'But I always heard he was the one that left you heartbroken,' Midge said very quietly. 'And still he came back for you – and now you're leaving.'

'I know. Funny, isn't it?' Margaret said but no part of her was laughing. 'I wanted him back for years and then when it happened . . . well, it wasn't really the same – I found that I didn't want to be a second thought for anyone.'

'There are some women that would jump at him.'

'Oh, I know – but I'm finished jumping, Midge. I'm fifty years old and I'm not jumping for anyone.'

'Do you worry that you might be lonely?'

'No, Midge, I don't . . . because I think everyone is lonely.'

The women got up then and began to walk slowly back down the mountain.

'Do you think you can fix things with Bird?' Margaret asked.

And Midge could not look at her. Instead she shook her head and looked away so that Margaret could not see what she was feeling.

'Well, it might be possible for you to make a fresh start some-where else too – if that's what you want . . . if you think there's nothing here for you?'

257

And Midge turned and listened to her.

'I have a past pupil living on the West Coast – in Oregon. Sonia Reilly is her name, now a real knucklehead if ever there was one, but I could ask her if she could help you out . . . Would you work as an au pair or something? Is that the kind of work you would be able for? To tell you the truth I've no idea what else there would be in America for you.'

'I'd take anything,' Midge replied flatly. 'Anything so long as it's in a place where people know nothing about me.'

'Well, news of you has not yet reached America, I can assure you.'

Midge's mobile rang when they reached the bottom of the mountain. There had been no signal until then and Sergeant Brennan had been trying to reach her.

'I have news, Midge,' he told her, his voice level although barely containing the satisfaction he was clearly feeling,

'Imelda Conroy came down to the station last night. She's made a new statement about your father's whereabouts the night your mother was attacked. He was at Emmet Road.'

He paused then and waited for his words to sink in.

'Midge,' he said quietly, 'we have him.'

And on the way back to the lodge Margaret walked slowly as if she had aged on the mountain and Midge, who had been weak, marched ahead now, somehow rejuvenated, a new sense of freedom, a kind of strength ringing out from her.

39

Midge found him down near the water. Bird was standing on the smooth round stones with his hands pushed deep into his pockets. His eyes were trained on the islands, their dark shadows out over the lake, a lilac sky behind them. It was early morning, warm and calm again and there were fish making pockmarks on the water. He did not turn even though she willed him to. Even now she would have cast off her plan to go to America; this plan, hatched carefully with Margaret, could still fall into little pieces with just the right kind of look from him. But he would not turn. Midge could do nothing but stand next to him and see how his chest rose and fell from his own breathing and marvel at the time when she had touched him freely.

'Bird,' she said finally and she felt him stiffen slightly.

I'm like a thorn in him, Midge thought. He wants nothing to do with me.

She had hoped, of course, but there was no point really. Even now she would have given anything in her world for him to turn and put his arms around her.

'I'm thinking of going to America,' she said.

Bird turned then and she felt the air change between them and this was a season she could not read, a place she had not yet visited. His face relaxed and his eyes seemed to soften but he was not reaching for her, he was nodding, he was agreeing and clearing a smooth path for her to travel on.

'Margaret is taking you with her?'

'Yes, if I want to go – she can get me a job with a family in Oregon.'

'And what is Margaret going to do?'

'She wants to go travelling.'

'Travelling,' Bird repeated quietly and then almost to himself, 'the whole world wants to go travelling.'

And Midge wanted to say. 'But *I* don't want to go, Bird – here is the world I've been looking for and it's just a few miles from my own door. Here are the mountains and the canyons, the adventures, the freedom – after this, nowhere else is worth seeing.'

But she said nothing because he was not open to her now. It was as if she had never known him.

'And how long are you going to stay there?'

'Margaret says a few months, maybe six – it depends on how things go, I suppose.'

'And then you're coming back . . . to Tullyvin?'

And here Midge wanted to say, 'If you'll have me,' but she had been through enough and she was too frightened of another rejection. They had both built this new wall between them. He was letting her go because of the baby – and because of the parts of her brain, her thinking, that he would never gain access to. Her reasons for going were simple but even stronger. She was leaving because he had not believed her.

'I'll see how it goes,' she answered quietly.

'Well, take care of yourself,' he said and he looked down at his boots on the stones and her feet opposite them. She heard him swallow and then turn his head again, his eyes just grazing hers before they turned to rest once more on the water. An early fishing boat was out, its silent gliding a kind of comfort. Midge was glad of it, glad that there was someone in the world to witness this heart and its breaking.

'Goodbye, Bird,' she said finally and she placed a hand lightly on his. He turned then and as she closed her eyes, waiting for him to withdraw again, she felt his other hand, a knuckle it seemed, brush the delicate spot under her eye and then a thumb touch her cheek and he was gone, his boots rattling the rocks of the shoreline as he released her.

Late in September the countryside began to lose its lush fever and with it the vibrancy of its flowers and leaves, the hum of bees and clicking of insects. The children still swam at the lake but did so now in a way that was wistful. School loomed like a prison sentence and they thought there would never be another summer. Margaret went to America and took Midge with her for what she described to anyone who asked as a long-overdue holiday. She said her goodbyes to Tom Geoghan and did not ask him to wait for her.

'There might be something else out there for me,' she said to Olive. 'Something I've been missing, something better.'

And the days ended earlier, a chill coming in the open windows over supper. Everything seemed quieter then, as if the world was waiting. The first leaves fell from the beech trees nearest the lake and floated on its surface. The water became cold again and no one wanted to swim in it. Not even Olive – who had taken to the water every day of her adult life as a kind of meditation. But she could not do it without her sister. She realized that, like so many other things in her life, she had done it because she knew that Margaret was behind a window, watching. Margaret was her witness – the person who would tell her she was a fool to swim in the rain but would always have hot tea and a towel waiting for her. Margaret who had organized Midge's passport and had arranged a job for her with a decent family in Oregon.

261

'How quickly life can change' was all that Pat Noonan said when Margaret told them she was leaving. The idea alone caused a shock to come down on Olive, lighting up the room in its white flash so that she could not move at all and was frozen on a path between old and new, between denial and acceptance. And after Margaret and Midge left for the airport, Olive stayed in her chair, her hands flat on the wood of the table as if to prevent it from rising up to the ceiling and taking everything with it. The tea and cake that had always been so pleasant, the light-hearted talk with Pat, all of this was suddenly repellent. And when Pat finally rose to place two worn hands on her shoulders she flinched slightly, her sudden grief making him a stranger to her. At that moment there was no one in the world she wanted other than her sister. Later she walked around the house looking out of each window and seeing a different season from each of them.

Bird retreated further, spending his days with the gun, shooting jackdaws from the chimneys from inside the horsebox – until one day when Sean Weldon spoke to him, he realized he could not hear him. Bird entered a world which was, at times, completely silent. The gates opened noiselessly, the telephone was no longer ringing and the iron bed stopped creaking. Here his world felt as if it was lined with velvet, silent, distant – and he was once again disconnected from everything and everyone. And almost a year to the date he had found her in his field, he woke to find the bed empty and could no longer imagine the warmth from the nights she had spent beside him.

V
The Sound of Other Voices

Portland, Oregon,
September 2016

40

It was late when the Ellerys found Hagg Lake. They had cleaned up after the party and left the lush green of their garden under sprinklers, crossing the singing bridge to head south through Aloha and Cornelius and later the dried-up Tualatin and Scoggins valleys. Midge saw high red barns that must have been hot and airless and a green and yellow combine working in a cloud of dust. A farmer on the radio said that it had been a hard year for him, the driest he could remember. His cattle had begun to eat the leaves out of the trees, they were so desperate. Outside Cornelius where the farms were bigger the combines worked in rows, covering hundreds of acres together and making the whole thing look like a blizzard.

'Well, here we are,' Michael said. The air conditioning was running high, burning up the petrol and making a sound like the ocean. The older children, Billy and Nora, were sleeping in the back, leaning to one side as if they were melting. The youngest, Joseph, was asleep in his booster, his blond head falling forward.

'Here we are,' Annie repeated quietly.

Midge was thinking about the farmer on the radio. She imagined being under the shade of those trees with the hot cattle stretching for leaves and their wide necks pulsing. She had sheltered under a tree with Bird Keegan once, and here on the other side of the world the memory of it still returned to her – that sudden dash of rain in summer and how the weight of the drops, their speed and intensity, had made them laugh and run, giving them a kind of energy. Here the heat was taking the life out of her. Even now after two years, these people, this country, still seemed unreal to her.

Annie turned to look at Joseph and then, getting up on her knees, leaned in and pushed his head back into his seat like a footballer blocking a tackle. She sat back down then and said, 'I suppose we should let them sleep a bit . . . they were up so late.'

Midge remembered five-year-old Joe at the party. He was running around, his bare feet wet from the grass – and Billy, out on the front porch talking to one of their neighbours. Billy was just fourteen but over the summer he had taken on the long lean look of an adult. Only the week before he had come home with the news – an atom bomb of sorts – that he had a girlfriend.

The Ellerys had renovated the attic space for Midge and she slept under the eaves in a wide bed surrounded by green-and-white sprigged wallpaper. It was a nice room but there were nights, even now, when she closed her eyes and imagined she was back at the lodge and that Olive and Margaret were downstairs in the kitchen. She knew that Ireland was eight hours ahead of Oregon so that when Bird was getting ready to begin his day, she was thinking about sleeping. She would look off towards the yellow of the evening and wonder if he might briefly think of her as he watched the sun rising. At times Annie would knock on the door and invite her downstairs to watch a movie, but most nights Midge preferred to stay on her own. She preferred to lie on her bed with the windows open, listening to the night-time sounds of Portland.

At Hagg Lake the Ellery kids began to stir themselves in the back seat.

'Where are we?' asked Joseph.

'At the place you've been begging to go to for about a hundred years,' Billy answered drily.

'At Hagg Lake?' Joseph shrieked.

'The very same,' replied Michael. 'Although heaven knows why you wanted to come here so badly.'

The Ellerys tripped over dry brush and followed a steep dirt path down to the water. Midge carried Joe – and Michael took the blanket and two deck chairs. Annie took the picnic of iced water and sandwiches. Halfway down Nora took Billy's hand and when she slipped he saved her from falling. Then they took Joseph from Midge and the children walked in a line with her, all of them laughing and holding on to each other.

People were beginning to leave, others staying on in deck chairs, allowing their belongings to stretch out all around them. They had been there for so long that they seemed to have some claim to the shoreline. These were fat people with rusty-red hair who were having giant steaks off their barbecues and drinking beer in the sun and cat-calling if one of them went into the water.

'Oh dear,' Annie said very quietly and she began to smooth out their blanket.

Midge took Joe's hand and they watched a speedboat swirl in circles and saw how the lake curled too perfectly around the valley and under the dark points of the evergreens. The red sand was like porridge under their feet but Joseph wanted to swim immediately.

'Come on!' he shouted and he took his father's hand and tried to drag him.

Joe's forehead still bore the scabs from a recent fall and he had fallen hard, scattering himself and soaking the path with tears and curses.

'JESUS CHRIST!' were the first words out of his mouth.

Midge knew that he had learned that from her and Annie had

taken her aside for a quiet talk about what language was appropriate and inappropriate around Joseph. It was then that Midge first saw a kind of strength in Annie, a fierce determination when it came to protecting her children.

'You can't protect them from everything,' Michael often told her and his wife would only smile to show him that she did not agree with him.

And here on this red-dirt shoreline with the dead heat sitting on everything, Midge watched Annie as she organized her family. Beside these other people the Ellerys seemed invincible, as if nothing bad could ever happen to them.

Michael covered his head in sunblock and lifted Joseph in his arms. He was followed by Billy and Nora, who stepped into the warm lake gingerly but uncomplaining. Midge perched herself on a rock to watch and made it clear that she had no intention of swimming. She was wearing a floppy black hat and slathered in the Factor 50 that Annie had given her.

From the rock she could see a woman watching Annie with interest. She had red hair and was spread out in a deck chair with her white thighs flopping open. She held a cigarette in one hand and in the other a beer bottle. Her kids were scampering around her in bare feet, covered in red mud, looking at her with hungry faces. She told them to 'go play', her face dull and without any interest in them. And Midge felt herself turn hot and then cold suddenly. There was no doubting the likeness – it was like coming face to face with her own mother.

'What age are your kids?' the woman asked Annie suddenly.

And Annie told her that Billy was fourteen, Nora twelve and that Joseph, her youngest, was five the previous week.

'I have a five-year-old too. Does he want to play with him?' She swigged from her beer bottle.

'And a six- and a seven-year-old . . . somewhere roundabout.' She gave a short, crusty laugh, and made a circle in the air

268

with the bottle, as if her children might be flying around her.

'I guess they keep us busy,' Annie said politely and she called Michael and the children for their picnic.

Midge left her rock then and joined the Ellerys on the blanket. The speedboat was silent now and as the sun went lower, a calm seemed to descend over everything.

'I'm bored,' Joe said, his mouth full of turkey sandwich. 'Can we go back in the water?'

'You need to eat your lunch, Joe,' Michael answered, 'and then you can swim again if you want to.'

'This lake is awful,' Nora said very quietly.

'It's not actually a lake at all – it's a man-made *reservoir*,' Billy said.

'Can we go climbing?' Joe asked, his eyes following the steep line of the red-dirt cliff behind them.

'No,' Billy and Nora answered.

'Didn't I read somewhere that there was some weird story about this place?' Midge asked Michael quietly and he looked out over the lake as he tried to remember.

'Oh yeah,' he whispered. 'Someone drowned. A girl, I think – and then there was some bullshit about bad luck or something.'

The woman with red hair was watching them again and when she caught Annie's eye she called over, 'Nice day for a picnic!'

And Annie smiled her small, tight smile and looked over at Michael.

'OK,' she said very softly. 'We've been here for . . . forty-five minutes? That's *almost* an hour – I say we give it another ten and then pack up and head back to Portland.'

'But you said I could have one more swim,' Joseph wailed.

'All right, all right . . . let's tidy up – and then you can roll around in the mud again if you want to,' Michael said.

Billy and Nora helped Midge to pack up and then Annie took the older children and the tote bag to the car park.

'Five minutes, Joe,' she called.

'But that's not long at all,' he cried. 'Five minutes is not long enough for anything.'

'Don't forget our blanket,' she said to Midge over her shoulder and then she was gone, disappearing over the red cliff with the two older children.

'You leaving already?' the woman with red hair asked and she seemed annoyed with them.

The lake was calm and empty now and in a sudden move to escape her Midge trotted down to the lake and dived into the water. It was murky and warm – and then the ground changed from mud to cold pebbles – and then nothing. She felt herself fall, taken by surprise, and the water grew very cold and clear around her. A part of her wanted to reach out and touch the red-haired woman and another part wanted to run away from her. And she could see how uncomfortable Annie was too – and how she did not want these people, this place, to touch any of her children.

Midge let herself fall downwards and could not believe that after ten, fifteen, twenty feet she had still not landed. She paddled with her hands and feet, coming up with a gasp, loving this clear icy water.

Far away on the shore, Michael was standing holding Joe's hand and they were both watching her. They were not concerned – she was a strong enough swimmer, taught years ago by Olive Keegan – but they seemed surprised by this new distance she had created between them.

Midge swam in a wide circle, closer to the evergreens. The sun had gone behind them, leaving the lake in a cool shadow. Every lake seemed to have its own sad story – and this one was no different. She stopped swimming then and turned around and she was surprised to see how far away the shore was. She could hardly see Michael and Joseph now. She had not been swimming for very long and yet it was as if something had pulled her away

270

from the shoreline. Through watery eyes she saw how the red-haired woman jumped up suddenly then, the beach chair staying attached to her and her broad feet planting themselves on the sand. She threw the chair aside and she was shouting over at Michael and then Michael was taking Joe to the hard mudbank away from the shore to sit him there. Midge had planned to swim towards them and then to lie back and float, watching the sky from the water – but now she couldn't do that. And then Michael was plunging into the lake with the woman close behind him.

Midge was momentarily torn between swimming to the shore, to Joe, so small sitting there, or to the adults bursting their way through the water and over the soft red mud to the cool of the pebbles and to the sudden drop beneath them.

'There's a drop, Michael,' she called out suddenly.

Her voice was raspy and wet from the cold of the water, her Irish accent still peculiar as it echoed around the tree-lined valley. Michael fell first and then the woman, her red hair lifting upwards in a sudden umbrella on the surface of the water and then Midge knew what had happened, knew immediately that the woman's older boys were missing, that they had strayed past the hidden shelf, perhaps following Midge out to where she was swimming. She took a deep breath and swam steadily towards Joseph. She could not bear the sight of him sitting there, growing pale with worry, his face full of questions. He would not move from his spot because he had been told not to – but the idea of him becoming frightened and seeing both of his parents and Midge leave him was not right either, so Midge swam to where her instincts took her.

Michael found one of the boys on the floor of the lake and pulled him upwards. He lifted the body up through the water, the eyes still open, the arms and legs moving, bubbles coming from the nose. Midge stood on the shore with Joe in her arms, wrapped in a dry towel somehow, and then Annie appeared – without Billy

271

and Nora – and stood on the shore next to her. She cried out when she saw what was happening, called for more help, shouting and pointing, her usually calm face becoming white and petrified-looking. Men left their barbecues and made a human chain out into the water. Michael passed the first boy into the arms of a strong man, a brute of a fellow, and went under again, duck-diving, and found the mother, still breathing – and then after many dives down and much searching, he found the last boy, who was the eldest.

'None of them can swim,' the fire officer told Annie and Midge later. 'They just look at the weather forecast, pack a truck full of beer and come out to Hagg Lake . . . Anyone from the area knows about the drop, knows how dangerous it is.'

And he was looking sadly out over the water and he sounded angry and disappointed in everyone.

Down near the water Joe was repeating the same question over and over.

'What happened, Daddy? What happened?'

'Nothing at all,' Michael said finally and Midge remained quiet and sad, staring into the lake, her skin grey and cold-looking. She would never have allowed Joseph out of her sight in a place like this – or anywhere. She remembered the red-haired woman clearly. How she had plunged blindly into the water, the fact that she couldn't swim forgotten in the panic over her lost children. The woman had no sense, no clue at all and it was at that moment, as Midge watched her, that she had seemed to merge again with Bridget Connors. And Midge knew that there was no escape, that she could never be free from the woman who had given life to her.

Later she heard someone say that her name was Tanya Olsen. She looked like a slovenly type but whatever she was, she had not deserved this. Midge could not even think about the two younger ginger-haired boys surrounded by strangers now.

272

Someone was asking about the father.

'There is no father,' someone else had whispered.

And it was Midge who said very quietly, 'Everyone has a father.'

Her chest was filled with a feeling of great sadness then, for the boys, for the mother, for the father who didn't even know what had happened – for Michael, for Joseph, safe but frightened, for the eldest boy, who was still unconscious in the ambulance.

'I've never liked lakes,' Midge said as if no one was listening. 'They have too many secrets.'

They drove back to Portland without speaking, relieved that the older children were not aware of what had actually happened – and because Joseph was quiet and looking out the window, there was the hope that he had simply forgotten.

'Can we go back to Hagg Lake again?' he wanted to know.

And Annie had said quickly, 'No, sweetie . . . we're thinking about taking you guys on a longer trip next time.'

'Like where?' Nora asked immediately and Midge could feel the story snowballing.

'I don't know . . .' Annie's voice was quieter now as if she was daydreaming. 'Maybe Canada. It's not so far to drive there from Portland . . . Vancouver maybe.'

'When are we going?' Billy asked.

But neither of his parents answered.

Instead Michael turned the car into the driveway and it was then that Joseph asked his real question. The images from the lake had stayed in his head, twisting and turning, so that by the time the car engine was silenced, he had pulled all of his thoughts and questions together into one perfectly structured sentence.

'The second boy that came out of the water. He was dead, right?'

There was a beat of silence as both parents wondered how to negotiate this.

'Right, Daddy?' Joe asked again.

'We don't know yet,' Annie suggested.

'But he *might* die . . . right, Daddy?'

He looked over at his nanny but Midge was silent. She herself did not know how to help this child understand the inevitability of death and still live on and not be frightened by it. Annie did not know what to say either. Hagg Lake would stay with Joseph and she had not been able to prevent this.

'He *could* die . . . right, Daddy?' Joseph persisted.

Billy and Nora were wide awake now too and listening. And Michael finally answered.

'Right,' he said.

41

Midge walked through the quiet house opening every window. She could hear the car doors slamming and voices behind her but at that moment she needed air and to be separate from the Ellerys and their children. She crossed the back deck and followed the stone steps down under the clematis and she could feel a faint mist on her arms from the sprinklers. The evening air was still dense and warm, the grass pure white in places. It didn't matter that Michael watered it every day, by September the lawns were dead all over Portland.

A seaplane landed in silence then and barges, heavy with logs, still moved on the Willamette River. Midge understood now that the evergreens and the river belonged to each other, that the water and the trees formed a kind of foundation here, a constant backdrop to everything.

America was not at all what she had expected. On that first night with Margaret, Portland had seemed small with just a few people wandering around it. She was ashamed of her ignorance now – but she had expected yellow taxis and skyscrapers.

'It's not New York,' Margaret had told her quietly. 'That's on the other side. This is the West Coast, where things are a bit more laid-back and friendly.'

And Midge could still remember seeing this house lit up at night and hearing crickets for the first time ever – and how Annie had opened a bedroom door to show her the tumbled bodies of her sleeping children. Over time Midge would learn that porridge was called oatmeal, that scones were called biscuits, that what she called biscuits were actually cookies, that Joe's buggy was known as a stroller, that the garden was the yard – and nothing at all to do with farming.

Now she gathered up some toys from the grass and a book that had been forgotten. She dismantled a fort she had built earlier with Joseph from pillows and blankets. Traffic moved slowly on the highway, a stream of black and silver heading into the city for early dinner. On a certain kind of night, when it was too hot for sleeping, she and Annie would get the kids into the car in their pyjamas and go to Ruby Jewel for ice cream. Outside the rush of school runs and the squabbles over music lessons and homework, she looked at this family now and marvelled at them, treasured them. There was real happiness in the Ellery house and yet she was on the outside of it. She could never belong to them. She wondered about Margaret then and what she was doing. The last she had heard she had been on holiday in July in Gearhart – which was not that far from them – and she had already travelled all over America. She had returned to the Ellerys once in a hire car, which even Midge could see she had no clue about driving.

'I just need to remember to stay on the right,' Margaret had announced and she had come inside and asked for a glass of cold water. Later Midge heard that she had almost caused an accident on the freeway.

'I stopped at an orange light,' she told them. 'In Ireland the light is orange before it's red.'

'So you stopped in the middle of the *freeway*?' Annie asked.

'It wasn't pleasant,' Margaret answered quickly. 'And passing a school bus is not a good idea either.'

Now through the porch door Midge could hear Annie running a bath for Joseph and in a moment she would come looking for

276

her to help with supper. Billy was watering the plants on the deck because his father had asked him. Nora was walking through the kitchen, carrying a glass of iced water. Midge saw her long braid of hair swing on her back and she wanted to stretch out and catch her.

She stepped out into the yard to gather herself, to get calm, to try to shake off Hagg Lake and the red-haired woman. Tanya Olsen was the image of her mother – and she worried now that more and more of these women with red hair would begin to appear everywhere. It was not just her red hair but the soft outline of her face – and most of all, the trouble she was in – her *shame* – because she could not care for her own children.

Midge sat down on the steps of the deck and looked out over the yard. The snapdragons and zinnias made great clumps of colour and the birdbaths were overflowing from the sprinklers. A second crop of raspberries was beginning to ripen.

What happened at the lake had frightened her. It was as if a small crack, a fault line of sorts, had suddenly opened inside her. Dull clay had been turned over, revealing a plot so that everyone could see who was buried there. And deep inside was Lough Rinn and Tullyvin – her mother, her father – and Bird Keegan. Even now in this strange place, with its peculiar weather and its overly friendly people, she could not forget them. And she had not even tried to forget Bird – she had really only separated herself from him. Midge had lifted herself from his side and then travelled over oceans and continents, knowing all the time that he was with her. She had left because he had not believed her. But they were still married. In the beginning, every day, she had wondered if he might come and find her.

Two raccoons appeared with their round faces turned towards her. They were the picture of insolence with their tails high and in a curl, their eyes inquisitive, uncaring. Midge felt a cold wad of fear settle on her breastbone and there was something immediately depressing about them. She sat very still and then moved down the wooden steps very slowly. Billy had gone inside and left her with the yellow watering can, fallen over and empty, in its own way dramatic. She could hear the phone ringing and she guessed that he had gone to answer it.

'Scat!' she shouted and the raccoons did not scat. They just stopped walking and looked at her.

'*Fuck off!*' she shouted again and the tranquillity of the summer evening was broken.

She took a deep breath. It was still too hot down on the lawn – it seemed to hold on to the heat, keeping it there in a warm bowl for her. She hated this weather and could not wait for the first rain in October. She wanted to see grey clouds again, to feel the stiff wind cross Portland's bridges and then barrel through its corridors.

'Midge?' A quiet voice spoke to her from somewhere.

And coming around the corner from the front of the house was Annie in denim shorts, who at first glance seemed just a little older than Nora.

'Yes?'

'Do you want to give Joseph his bath and I'll start supper?'

And Midge stood on the grass and looked straight up at her without speaking.

'Midge,' she said again. 'Who were you shouting at?'

'Raccoons. I told them to fuck off . . . but so far they're not listening.'

And she looked at Annie and Annie began to laugh so that Midge remembered that she liked her.

'Sorry, I completely forgot about helping with supper.'

'That's OK . . . Everyone's relaxing inside. It's almost too hot to eat anything.'

And here Midge paused, frowning.

'That's what I thought,' she said absent-mindedly, and she

278

looked into Annie's eyes wishing the other woman could see what was happening inside her.

But Annie said, 'I'm thinking burgers for supper – I'll get the grill going . . . if you could get Joe into the bathroom.'

'Annie?'

'Yes?'

'That woman at the lake? Tanya? Do you think we should check in on her? I don't know . . . See how she is or something. See if her son is OK? I just feel . . . I don't know . . .' and here Midge shrugged, not sure herself what it was that she was suggesting, 'that maybe I should call on her.'

Annie frowned a little and looked out over the raspberry bushes. She nodded slowly then.

'Sure. That's a good idea. Maybe take Joseph with you. She has a five-year-old, doesn't she? Just call on her and see if there's anything we could do for her.'

'The raccoons are still on the deck,' Midge said then but she was feeling happier.

'Fuck them,' Annie said very quietly.

And Midge walked ahead of her through the screen doors and began calling Joseph. She would try to shut off these new thoughts about Tullyvin and her mother. Tonight her main task would be to bathe Joe and to give this family some dinner. The Ellerys were not difficult people. The children didn't fight and Michael and Annie had respect for each other. This, Midge now realized, was a normal family. Or as Michael liked to say, 'Ladies and gentlemen, the Ellerys: liberal, secular, more handsome than good-looking, two brave adults and three brave children.'

42

On her day off Midge went to a former mechanic shop behind a green roll-up shutter in NE Portland. The studio, which belonged to Todd Meyers, was under the Fremont Bridge and she helped him to make soap there which he sold at the local farmers' market. When she told Todd that she was still married, his reaction was to shrug and smile at her. And he continued to give her a place to go that did not involve the Ellerys. The scent of soap and his physical warmth, his recent interest in sharing his bed with her, all helped to stave off her recurring homesickness. Behind a vast floor-to-ceiling window they worked together then and watched the endless streams of traffic as the cars moved from the highway to the soft line and occasional snow on the Cascade Mountains. Every day Todd lived his life like this, seeing through the ant run of daily irritations to the thing that was always more beautiful in the distance.

The studio was too hot in summer – Todd could not afford air conditioning. When they opened the windows for air they had to shout at each other to be heard, and for two people who were naturally soft-spoken this was a kind of agony compared to a little stale air and sweating. Instead the studio was dotted with fans picked up in second-hand shops, some antique and charming, others like the one next to the bed, a giant piece of grey humming plastic.

On Monday, when Midge opened the front door, the long muslin curtains were lifted higher and she guessed the window in the little corner bathroom was open. From the slow steady hiss of water, she knew that Todd was in the shower. The breeze created by the door and the window together was so refreshing that she stood there, just breathing, and feeling the air move around her. Midge waited there, thinking about her long bike ride from the Ellerys', how she had begun at their gate and then sailed swiftly down towards the bridges and the river.

'Yaaaaahoooooooo,' she had whispered. She did not want to draw attention to herself, ever.

The giant curtains lifted and billowed and she closed the front door with some reluctance.

'Hey, girl,' Todd shouted.

He was walking from the bathroom in bare feet, the long sallow form of his torso broken by the blue towel at his waist. His short dark hair was still wet and sleek from the shower.

'Hi,' she answered and she was still thinking about the family who lived high up looking down over Portland.

'HOT!' he announced. 'We might need to jump in the river.'

'Yeah, we took the kids to Hagg Lake on Saturday.'

'Yeeeee-haw!' Todd answered and together, without speaking, they were both seeing the boom boxes and the gazebos.

'There was an accident. Michael saved someone.'

'Seriously?'

'Yeah. One boy was taken to hospital. His mother was hysterical.'

'That's intense.'

'I've asked Annie if it's OK for me and Joseph to go see her.'

He placed a hand gently on her hip and kissed her.

'You're a good girl, Midge Connors.'

'That's the first time I've been told that.'

And now they were both laughing.

'Nora liked the rosemary soap, by the way, and Joseph wanted to know why there were green bits in it.'

'Did you tell him to taste it?'

And Midge laughed again.

'They're actually very nice kids, nice people.'

'Nice?'

'You know – *nice*.'

'They sound horrible.'

Todd sank down into the brown leather chesterfield, his one valuable piece of furniture, a gift from his father. He pulled a wooden chair closer with his toe and then lifted his feet up so they could rest on it.

'Well,' Midge said with some kind of apology, 'the Ellerys are quite rich, I think.'

Todd ran a hand back through his hair and pulled her down to sit next to him.

'Their house is all wood and glass and concrete and their garden – I mean yard – is perfect.'

'Are yards supposed to be perfect?'

Midge thought for a moment and then leaned back into the couch so that their heads were touching.

'That's what I mean . . . it's tidy but really natural-looking and Annie's got all these rows of beans and raspberries and there's clematis and rhododendrons – and a lot of trees . . . ancient, most of them.'

She could smell soap from Todd when he put his arm around her.

'They have a second house in Yachats, right on the beach.'

'But will they buy my soap?' he asked in a whisper and Midge laughed because only the day before he had tried selling some to the postman.

'I think they're probably OK for soap. I said goodnight to Joe before I came over and he smelled so good after his bath – now there's a scent you should try and copy.'

'Really?'

'Yes – I wonder what we could call it.'

'"Freshly Scrubbed Boy"?' Todd suggested.

'I would just call it "Joseph", I think.'

When they made love he turned her onto her stomach to kiss the small black cat that lived on her lower back under the T-shirt. This quiet girl with pale skin had picked a black cat tattoo with green eyes and a curling tail to show what was in her heart and it was her secret. That was what tattoos were for, she said – and there would be no hearts and arrows for Midge Connors. He had asked about her husband but she would not tell him anything and he had not pressed her. She would not even tell him his name, as if the name itself, said out in the open, could cause some hurt in her.

Afterwards they worked late, seeing the light fade and the sky turn pale blue and then pink and silver. The lights from the trucks and cars lit up the Fremont Bridge and when they began to thin out after midnight Todd opened up the windows. And this was how they slept, in the freshest of air, to be woken early by the first rumble of a truck near sun-up. Todd was determined to make a business out of handcrafted soap and to avoid obvious scents like 'Rose City' or 'Coffee Vanilla'. Before they slept they tried to catch the scent of a wild-flower field in Oregon and, at Midge's suggestion, 'October Rain't ', after all the burning dryness of summer. She went to sleep thinking about the Ellerys and Annie, who was frightened of the coons and pretended not to be – as a mother she was brave enough to fight anyone or anything that might harm one of her children. Midge drifted into a deep sleep, her arms around her lover's shoulders, the image of Annie Ellery, fading and returning, fading and returning, the smallness of her out there on her own with the raccoons in the garden.

43

On Tuesday Billy came to Midge and stood under the kitchen archway to speak to her about 'his girlfriend'. He chose a time when he knew that Joseph was on a play date and Midge was on her own making dinner.

A girlfriend, Midge thought, unable to say anything back yet but allowing the words to whip around the inside of her head, a slight frown line forming between her eyes, a headache beginning somewhere. He spoke very quietly because the subject embarrassed him and also because his voice was breaking. This was his own way of communicating though – he was always quiet and gentle – and Midge loved him for his kindness and his consideration, his interest in her as a real living person. She wondered briefly then what this girl had done to deserve him.

And yet she was the reason he had come to her, carrying his feelings on a plate, and offering this new development up for what it was, something massive and untamed, and then she heard 'Beaverton' and the movie theatre and knew that he was sharing this information not because he trusted her but because of, as he put it quietly himself, *logistics*.

Oh, Midge thought, he needs me to drive him.

She took all of this in and said that she would have to check with his mother. She nodded and said, 'Hmmm,' or something like that and washed the lettuce very briskly, all the time watching the driveway for a sign of the car and Michael. She remembered then that he had cycled to work and had a late meeting at the university.

Hurry up, Michael, she thought and she had no idea why this conversation was causing such tension.

And yet this was Billy's young heart – *unsupervised* – Billy's heart walking down some lonely pine trail – and at fourteen it would be a pointless one at that . . . because really what else could it be? How else could it turn out for these boys? For little Billy, medium Billy, big Billy, voice-squeaking Billy . . . his heart expanding and then shrinking back from some possible hurt. But it was *his* choice – and while he needed to share this with her, a deeper, less responsible Midge would have enjoyed her evening more if he had kept it to himself.

'So how did you two meet?' Annie asked later over dinner. She had heard that there was a girlfriend and now that she had recovered from this news she wanted to know more about her.

Billy had been concentrating on eating his lasagne and Midge watched carefully for a deep flush to bleed into his cheeks.

'At Frisbee,' he said casually.

'I didn't know girls were in Frisbee.'

'It's more interesting with girls . . . . they show different skill sets.'

Billy's cheeks were their usual mix of peach and olive and Midge could see that he was much calmer than his parents.

'What's her name?' Annie asked then.

'May – with a Y,' Billy said and Midge smiled at him then, at this name that implied hope after a long winter in Portland.

And during this exchange both Nora and Joseph stayed quiet. There was some silent understanding that what was happening between Billy and their parents was in another world above them. Annie's forehead remained in a frown though, the muscles twisting the skin over her eyes into slants and circles. She was always frowning, even when she was laughing – as if laughing hurt a little.

After dinner, when Midge was putting Joseph to bed, Billy retreated to his bedroom and Nora disappeared with her latest obsession, *Flowers in the Attic.*

'It's not that I mind about the date,' Annie was saying. 'It's that we'll have to visit with the *damn* parents . . . We need to do the right thing. You know, meet the parents of the girl our son is dating.'

'Oh, the things we do for our children,' Michael murmured as he turned the dishwasher on. They did not know that Nora was under her quilt crying or that Midge had already kissed Joseph goodnight for them. This was their eldest child's moment. Billy was like a cat that had brought home an unwelcome gift to its owners, a bird that was still warm after bashing itself on a window or a limp mouse with its tail hanging.

The Sunday date discommoded a whole troop of people in the end but not one of them was low enough to say it. The parents met for coffee first and Billy and May sat close to each other, their self-importance and embarrassment bringing a fresh bloom of youth to them. It was much later when Midge heard Annie say, 'There is no place in that man's fat Republican head for a family like us because he is and always will be . . . an opinionated ASSHOLE.'

'I know, I know,' Michael said quietly. 'But it's not like Billy's going to marry her.'

And he looped an arm around his wife's lovely waist and together with Midge they looked out over the girder bridges of Portland, at a fierce white sun that was disappearing, at a whole season whose colours were already fading.

And then there was Joseph.

The phone was ringing when Midge and the boys came inside

from throwing Frisbee. Nora was stretched out on the sofa reading and Joseph, who was tired, curled up quietly beside her. Billy had just received a text from May and as a result the Frisbee was abandoned and he went straight to his room, slamming the door behind him.

On the phone was Judy Marsh – Joseph's pre-school teacher at the local co-operative. Annie had wanted to be part of her child's education and would somehow, miraculously, work and also fit in her morning helping out in the classroom. As it happened it was usually Midge who took her morning at the pre-school.

'Miss Midge,' Judy said. 'I'm looking for Miss Annie or Mr Michael.'

Her voice, in this cheerful singsong tone, indicated that something catastrophic was coming.

'They're both at work, Judy . . . Is there anything I can help you with or pass on to them?'

'Well . . . Joseph introduced some new vocabulary into our classroom today,' and there was a long pause then, like a black river, and Midge was expected to navigate her way through it.

'OK,' Midge said and she was beginning to smile as she walked around the kitchen with the phone, her eyes scanning the scalloping over the sink which the Ellerys were both keen to be rid of. There was a scorch mark on the Formica counter top, a bruise on its old-world charm and Michael could not decide if this was something to repair or a piece of precious history. Joseph had been using the drawer handles as a ladder again.

'Cocksucker,' Judy said brightly.

'Oh.'

Neither woman spoke for a moment. These short pauses were, Midge realized later, the actual punishment for raising foulmouthed children.

'And . . . motherfucker.'

Here Midge began to cough violently, choking on her own laughter as it happened.

'OK,' she said then, her voice quite bright. 'That must be from the night he climbed into their bed when they were watching *The Wire*.'

In her heart she was wishing that Annie was there – Annie with her steady voice, her clarity of thought, her earnest grey eyes, her ability to manage Judy Marsh expertly. But some other part of Midge was telling the story to Todd, sitting around the fire in winter, rosy with wine, their faces and bodies creased with laughter, the mock shock and horror of it. The five-year-old who said 'cocksucker' at pre-school. What a great story. But, no . . . they were not there yet. She was still hearing the story from Judy Marsh, his teacher.

Her cell beeped with a text from Annie. They had agreed that she would text in the evenings and that Midge would update her on everything then.

'*Everything OK?*'

And Midge began texting back with Joe's teacher there waiting.

'Mm . . . I'm just jotting all of this down, Judy . . . and I'll pass it on to Annie and ask her to call you.'

'Thank you, Miss Midge. I would like to speak to her as soon as possible.'

She sent a text to Annie then that had nothing to do with Teacher Judy.

'*The Arnetts have invited you over for Thanksgiving.*'

Midge could remember sitting with them at the Arnett table last year, behind a hill of turkey, giving thanks for nothing at all and wondering when the talk would turn to guns or sport or politics, three things she knew the Ellerys hated.

'*I say we hide out in the basement . . . with some pop tarts and the toaster.*'

288

'What should I tell them?'

'Say we can't do it . . . we're going to Vancouver. Anything else?'

'Judy Marsh wants you to call her.'

'Did she say why?'

And here Midge paused for a moment, seeing Annie in her grey wool suit and heels, her hair well cut, her work and her children, her whole life balancing neatly.

'Joe said cocksucker at school.'

And somewhere in downtown Portland Midge knew that Annie had become slightly limp in a low-lit restaurant and that her colleagues were seeing two red spots hit her cheeks as her ice cream sat there melting.

44

Tanya Olsen lived on Cedar Row on the east side, off Hawthorne. The house was small, painted grey and covered in shingles that were curled up and rotting. On a hot afternoon early in October Midge picked Joseph up from pre-school and then, each giving the other courage, they went there together.

'Where are we?' Joseph asked from the back seat.

They were parked opposite the house and in the dead hour between three and four there seemed to be no traffic, no sound, no sign of life anywhere. There was a soft grey cat sleeping on the front porch and on one side what Midge would describe to Annie later as 'an incredible amount of junk' – a broken-down sofa with chairs, a picnic table, plastic bags, a bicycle – all piled on top of it. And then a small wooden boat, white, flung on top of everything.

'Midge, is that a boat up there?'

And she gave a little smile and nodded. 'Yes . . . that is a boat up there.'

'But why is it up there? On top of all that other stuff.'

'Maybe they had nowhere else to put it,' she said.

She knew how it would look to Tanya Olsen, this 'do-gooder' in her white shorts and navy T-shirt holding this perfect little boy by the hand, thinking they could help her. Midge could imagine what a pain in Tanya Olsen's arse this was – and yet, since Hagg

Lake she had felt pulled back to her. There was nothing she could do to help her. She knew that too. She was, in fact, useless. But to stay away, to get on with her life as if nothing at all had happened, seemed unforgivable to her.

The steps to the porch were sticky – the creosote melting in the heat – but they tiptoed up and knocked on the screen door, Midge's heart beating and Joseph not speaking. Through the door she could see a red couch and an orange swivel chair near the big front window. There were white fairy lights strung around all the windows and an electric guitar up on the wall, an acoustic one on a stand underneath it. A door further in opened and she heard heavy feet walking, feet that had moved from the bedroom, moved by a person who was in every way reluctant.

'Mrs Olsen. Tanya? I'm Midge Connors.'

The woman looked like she had been sleeping. Her hair was loose around her shoulders and Annie could see that as well as being red it was also bleached blonde in parts. She was wearing a similar black top and shorts to the ones she had worn at the lake in September.

'Yeah?' she answered. Her voice sounded ragged, uninterested.

'We were at the lake . . . that Saturday,' Midge prompted.

'Where those kids nearly died,' Joseph announced.

'Stop it, Joe.' Midge twisted towards him quickly.

'Right,' Tanya said as if everything they said had no meaning for her. It was more like they were delivering a package, something that she hadn't ordered, something that was meant for her neighbour.

Midge placed a hand on the screen door gently and smiled.

'Would it be OK if we came in for a minute?'

'Sure.'

And here Tanya went and flopped onto the couch, with one hand stretching back to fish out a cigarette from a pack behind her. The lighter made a metallic grinding sound and the flame flared up. She took a long inhale and then exhaled blue smoke out into the shafts of sunlight and when she did this, she pushed her lower jaw out.

Midge went and sat on the orange chair and then Joe spotted a toy car and went for it.

'Joseph, you need to ask before . . .'

'He's all right,' Tanya said, her eyes never leaving a spot on the floor.

Midge took a deep breath and swallowed.

'Tanya, I just wanted to call in and say hi . . . I just wondered if there is anything I can do for you.'

'Hmm-mm,' Tanya replied.

She seemed to have heard this song a few times before. She got up and walked back into the kitchen and opened the refrigerator.

'Beer?' she called.

'No, thank you.'

The sound the bottle cap made when it twirled on the floor caused Joseph to glance up and then he walked towards the kitchen.

He stood there looking up at Tanya, who took a long drink from the bottle and frowned down at him.

'You're supposed to put stuff like that in the trash,' he told her.

'Ha,' Tanya replied and she went and sat back down on the couch, her legs falling open, the beer bottle resting down near her crotch. The hand that held it had many different rings that looked like they wouldn't come off too easily.

'Joseph . . .' Midge said very quietly but she used a tone reserved for other people's houses and he glanced at her and went back to playing with the car.

'He's five, right?'

'That's right.' Midge's voice was too enthusiastic, there was too much relief as she felt herself move off the iceberg.

292

'Would he like a play date with my kid . . . the younger boy?' Tanya asked.

And Midge smiled and leaned over in her chair, her elbows resting on her knees.

She was buying herself a few seconds.

'Well, I would have to check with his mother, Annie,' she said and she licked her lips and wondered what to do next.

There was a long pause and Tanya looked at her. She looked at Midge for so long without speaking that Midge felt herself begin to shrivel.

'Midge? Is that your name? My youngest boy is missing his big brother who is still at the hospital. The middle boy is all right. He's at school and he has his friends. The younger boy is . . .'

She dragged from her cigarette and wiped her forehead with a soft pink hand. She dragged it over her face and down her cheek and then sat resting her jaw in it.

'The youngest boy is lost,' she said, her voice empty and with no emotion in it.

Midge nodded sadly at her.

'How is the older boy getting on?' she asked.

Tanya made her lips into a small trumpet shape and blew smoke out through them.

'It's not a picnic,' she answered. 'He's just lying there . . . and he needs help with his breathing.'

'What's your youngest boy called?' Midge asked quietly.

'Nathan. Nate.'

'Is he at pre-school?

'I don't have money to send him to pre-school. He's with a neighbour down the street . . . in fact I better go pick him up.'

'OK . . . well . . . we better be going ourselves . . . we just wanted . . .'

'No . . . you wait here,' Tanya said. 'I'll go get him and then the boys can say hi to each other . . . right?'

'OK, right,' Midge said.

Joseph had turned around and was listening to this.

When the woman left he looked up at Midge.

'Why did she leave us here?' he asked.

'Good question,' Midge murmured. 'She's gone to collect her little boy . . . He's called Nate and Nate needs a friend . . . Do you think you can do that? And maybe play with him a little bit.'

'Okaaaay,' Joseph said, his voice full of worry, his small back already bending under the responsibility.

Midge walked down towards the kitchen and looked at the dishes piled high in the sink. She had just finished drying the plates when the front door opened and the cat floated in.

'Get out of the house,' a small boy shouted. Nate appeared suddenly and then Joe too jumped up and began to dance around the cat, shouting, 'Get out, get out, get out.' The other boy, who was smaller than Joe, stood and watched and then gave a sudden short laugh. He had the same colour hair as his mother, and the neck of his T-shirt had a dark ring of dirt on it. He was wearing a pair of sweats and his feet were bare.

'Nate, Joe. Joe, Nate,' Tanya said, pushing past them and heading towards the refrigerator.

'I cleaned up a bit for you,' Midge said, her voice apologetic.

'Oh, right.' Tanya's voice floated across the room. She did not know what Midge was talking about. She was not aware that she had left any dishes in the sink. The cap fell from another beer onto the floor where the cat watched it spin and fall flat, and the wheel inside the lighter gave another little grind as a cigarette was lit.

'So, Joe?' Tanya called from the couch. 'You want to come here for a play date with Nate?'

'OK,' Joseph said very quietly.

'Well, maybe Nate could come to the Ellerys' house . . . I mean it would be a change of scenery for him.'

Inside Midge was panicking at the idea of ever leaving Joseph in this house with them.

Tanya watched her carefully when she said this, a slight smile, a sour one, curling on her face.

'I guess you're a kind of big shot,' she said very quietly. 'You and those other people that came swanking around Hagg Lake that Saturday.'

'I'm not a big shot,' Midge said, her eyes searching the other woman's for some kind of light, wanting Tanya Olsen to recognize something in her. 'I'm just the nanny,' she said then, her hands open on her knees, her face slack and sad-looking.

'*Nanny*? You hear that, Nate? Little Joe here has a nanny.'

When it was time to leave Tanya stayed on the couch. She preferred to say her goodbyes without having to get up.

'I suppose you're wondering why I haven't said thanks.'

'Thanks?' Midge asked, confused.

'You know . . . to that bald guy who pulled my kids out of the water.'

'No, not at all . . . there's no need to say anything at all to him.'

'Good. I'm not exactly feeling thankful for much these days.'

'I can understand that.'

'You see . . . I've as good as lost my eldest child,' she said suddenly and she turned her head up so that Midge could see it, so that Midge could see what was happening inside her.

'I have two left but I can only think about the one at the hospital. The eldest is always the most important. That one is the star. That's the child that makes you a mother . . . that one. And the others that follow, they make you . . . oh yeah, they make you a mother too – but they also make you a nurse and a cop and a servant. Do you know what I mean . . . what it is that I'm saying?' Tanya asked.

And Midge felt her shoulders grow slack and she thought about her own mother and about Bird and about the baby they had lost. She thought about Billy, whose eyes were full of honesty and intelligence, and she could not imagine a world without him in it, at least not a life that his mother would be capable of living. If anything happened to Billy, Annie would also stay on a couch and drink beer and smoke cigarettes and forget to wash.

'Yes,' she said. 'I understand what you're saying.'

Midge took Joseph's hand in hers and walked down the steps. The sun was lower and she could hear the rumble of the first school bus bringing the children back to their mothers.

'Why did we go see that lady?' Joseph wanted to know.

Midge stood for a moment by the car and looked down at him. How much could a woman love a small boy? she wondered. There was no limit to it.

'She reminded me of someone.'

'Of who?'

'My mother.'

'That was your *mother*?' Joseph asked in wonder.

'No,' Midge said very firmly. 'But she reminded me of her.'

Joseph was quiet in the back then and Midge was not capable of speaking. The Olsens had taken everything from her, even though she had not been aware of it. She drove over the Willamette bridge, the radio playing to make her feel normal. She was spent, empty and still not clear what it was that Tanya had taken from her, not clear what she herself had been giving.

45

The Ellerys left Vancouver and headed for the mud-cultured landscape of British Columbia. It was November and soft clouds came low and seemed to surround them. There had been sun earlier in the day, enough for them to drive through Stanley Park and see the mermaid. They watched as a seagull came and stood on the statue's head and Midge took a picture. It was still fall there somehow, the leaves clinging. Across the water smoke stacks puffed under a girder. Next to that two mounds of sulphur, bright yellow in the grey light, out of place, incandescent. They stood and stared at the yellow, each with the same question but too tired to ask it. A seaplane glided in over the water and Midge squinted up at it. Nora and Billy yawned hugely. They were bored, pale-faced, sleepy. The vacation had made the kids tired and fractious, only Midge enjoyed the rain and the cold, only she could embrace it.

The sun was weak and it was getting colder. Michael turned the Volvo around and they left the park, detouring into South Granville to look at the houses. Here, the wealth was numbing, vast concrete blocks with swimming pools and turrets, three Range Rovers at the doors, everything half hidden behind huge evergreen hedges.

'Hideous,' Annie said. Her voice was low, a bit hoarse, as if she needed to spare it.

After three days in Canada, she was looking forward to seeing their house again in Portland.

'How about I drive for a while?' she asked Michael.

'Let's wait till we're out of Canada.'

'But wouldn't you like a break?'

'No, I'm fine. I like driving . . . Really.'

Nora gave a long exaggerated sigh to this, slid down into her seat and closed her eyes on all of them. Outside, the rush of the rain and wind on the windscreen was soothing. Midge had seen Nora's relationship with Annie change recently. She had watched the girl grow and at times distance herself from her mother. She had seen all of this happening, knowing that there must be whole days now when Annie yearned for her daughter's embrace, the long, slender arms around her neck, the warmth of her skin near her – and she had been careful, wise, Midge thought, not to ask for this. The love Midge herself felt now for these children was more than she could manage. On an average day there was a tidal wave of it. It was a tall order at times to be responsible for things that were both strange and beautiful. In her mind was the image of Nora at Salt and Straw and how she had sauntered in with her friends for an ice cream in the soft light of a summer evening. Midge remembered Nora's long brown legs in white shorts – and how foolish she had felt, herself and Todd, and how silly their waves. A sweep of colour had risen in Nora's cheeks when she saw her nanny out on her own date night and waving a little wooden paddle at her.

They crossed the border into Washington State, handing over their passports to the guard and taking off their sunglasses for the inspection. Midge could see the dark uniform leaning in to see Annie sitting next to Michael. She could make out the glint of handcuffs, the dull outline of a baton on his belt, and she sat quietly allowing this form to look into her face also. And in that brief moment she and Michael and Annie were completely united, frightened for no reason, as nervous as if they had a bag of weed in their suitcase. The guard stared intently at them and then looked into the back seat, casting his eyes over Midge and the three children before waving them on again.

They passed the loneliest of places then, faded red barns built bravely into the wilderness, rained-out houses lost to subsidence. Rain pelted the road and the other cars moved through the mist and disappeared behind it. They all turned off at various junctions, reached their destinations and abandoned the Ellerys. Annie and the children were sleeping and the rain made the world seem very empty. It washed everything else away and left no kind of company.

'And all this because the Arnetts invited us for Thanksgiving,' Michael said.

And at that moment the Arnetts were to blame for everything, the gnawing cold of Vancouver, the seagull with no respect for anything, those ugly mounds of yellow, the 'check engine' light on the dashboard of the Volvo.

They stopped at the Coffee Pot, a roadhouse built with logs, and they went inside for a snack and the use of the bathrooms. There was an elk head hanging over the door, another one over the alcove that led to the kitchen. There was a silent pool table, a TV blaring, rows of empty tables looking out over the water.

Outside Michael spoke loudly as if he was addressing a room full of students.

'I know the guy is a Republican but it was hardly a reason to flee the country.'

He was looking over at Annie standing with her shoulders hunched and trying to bait her. But her hands were deep into her coat pockets, her narrow back turned slightly.

'Are you and Mom fighting?' Nora asked.

'No,' Michael answered tersely.

299

'Yes, you are,' Joseph whispered very quietly.

The rain began to fall steadily again and they all climbed back into the Volvo. Midge wanted Michael to drive away from the awfulness of the rain, into more awfulness as it happened – and rain that came now in violent dashes against the windows.

'Why do you always insist on driving?' Annie wanted to know suddenly. 'Why?' she asked.

Michael handed the keys to her and she reached for the door handle but he was out in the rain before her. She climbed over into the driver's side, adjusted the mirror and the seat, sliding it forward, suddenly wide awake and alert again.

Portland was a relief when it finally appeared. The weather had been horrible for driving, the whole trip, the idea of it, misguided. The stag leaped on the neon sign and it seemed to be Christmas. Home, Midge thought. She wondered when the city had seeped into her blood and her bones. She heard a solid click as Annie released her seatbelt. She had a bad habit of doing this close to home, feeling 'stifled by the harness', she said, 'claustrophobic'. They would see the house soon. A second click of the seatbelt then, as Annie clearly thought better of it.

In the back Billy gave a deep sigh, thoroughly fed up with his siblings, his parents. Midge knew that he was planning on running from the car to their porch, the rain splashing through his T-shirt, soaking him. He could only think of his girlfriend now and he would find the key which always hung on the side of the window box and once inside he would call her.

'I'm too hot,' Joseph whispered to Nora. And she turned to face him. 'I feel sick. I want to take my seatbelt off . . . Nora.'

And Nora looked up ahead and knew that they were just minutes from their gate. She put her fingers to her lips and eased the button down so that the belt released in silence. Then she took his hand and kissed it.

'Nearly home, buddy,' she whispered and Midge leaned over and fastened his seatbelt again.

'Ah, Midge,' Joe wailed, 'why did you have to do that?'

Midge took his hand and relaxed back into her headrest. She did not see the truck pull out into the rain in front of them or how the second trailer swung quickly to the left turning this juggernaut around so that it suddenly faced them. The headlights were blinding. Annie herself gave a loud ragged gasp and watched as the truck's headlights flew closer, closer, closer and then the same headlights were – how was it possible? – coming right through their window. The Volvo turned over on the road first and Annie could only grip the wheel tightly as Midge screamed, felt Joe's hand suddenly pulled from hers, the car roll sideways then into the soft rustle of bushes and then fall, how far? Down and down and finally landing, shuddering, shattered but back on its wheels again. Then Midge could see nothing. She could not speak or move except to pat the back seat with one hand and discover that Billy was there but underneath something. She lay in her seat and could feel the night rain falling in on them. In a moment she heard Nora's cry, a high shriek that tore her. And Midge was not able to move her legs or to open her door. Michael opened his eyes and looked back at her. She could see that part of the car, the metal part that attached the roof to the hood, was on him and it was making his breathing difficult. Annie was beginning to move against the airbag and call out to each of her children.

Nora put her head back and began to wail, a long wild sound coming from deep down in her windpipe . . . 'MOM–DAD-MOM-DAD-MOM!'

And Midge could feel a warm river of something running down her back and legs. Her hair was wet from it, the sunroof was gone, Joseph had flown through it. She could lift her hand up – the one that had been holding his – and see that it was empty. She prayed that, from the scrub bushes, Joseph would not hear his mother calling for him, the sound of her crying, the sound of other voices, shouting.

More than anything Midge wanted to comfort Joseph, to draw him up into her arms and muffle his sobbing, but she could not move to find him. She needed to believe that he had felt no pain at all, nothing, that when he sucked air into his lungs and strung his thoughts on a final brain string together, he remembered his mommy and daddy and Midge – all three of them embracing him. Midge lay in the dark and waited for someone to find them. She thought about Lough Rinn, the house where her husband still lived and in that moment she could not remember his name – only that she loved him.

46

Midge got up and walked past the doctor who had explained everything. She was limping on a bruised foot, using a knee that had been 'knocked out' and should have been raised, rested. The doctor, who seemed in some way familiar to her, had been sitting on a stool at her bedside, giving the kind of news that came like a sudden fire, burning everything in sight.

The idea that Michael was lying in a white grave down the corridor came to her in a silent skull-splitting moment and she understood everything the doctor said. She got the 'dead but not dead' component. She had been there before with her own mother. The doctor said that he was not optimistic about Michael's chances. Even if he survived, even if he regained consciousness, which was unlikely, there would be no recognizable part of him left.

And what good is that? Midge had wanted to know but she had asked this question inwardly, knowing there were no good answers left.

She did not speak to this doctor with his great dark pools of eyes. Instead Midge quickly washed over what she heard about Michael, even the part when the doctor told her that he 'looked perfect, not a scratch' but that his spinal cord had endured a terrible impact.

Midge was already moving, upwards, slowly, barely able to

carry the weight of everything else that the doctor had told her.

There were two nurses in pink scrubs hovering, checking machines, pretending to check them really, but ready to catch her when she fell under the weight of the real news, which was that Billy was alive and currently having a few thousand pieces of glass removed from the skin on his face and even with plastic surgery he would not look the same, because the face which was just finding its way in the world would now be sewn and stitched in a range of different places.

'But the same boy underneath?' Midge had astonished herself by asking.

'Right, absolutely,' the doctor answered.

Nora and Annie, the angels that they were, had risen above the chaos and were sedated, unmarked, unharmed except for a few scratches and a fractured arm. Nora had broken the pinky on her left hand, which in later life might prevent her from 'playing the guitar?' the doctor suggested and then looked down at the crumpled white coat on his lap, surprised by his own sudden foolishness. Where did music, a guitar of all things, belong in a conversation such as this? And yet each person needed their own diagnosis – even those less seriously injured needed a spot. He had been working all night – she could see this – to save their lives and he had failed them. And Midge realized that her life was no longer just the beat of her own heart but that it was these children and their father and mother – and the doctors were wasting their time because Michael was all but gone before the ambulance even got to the scene of the crash, and—

'The youngest child, the five-year-old . . . Joseph?' Midge heard herself ask.

'I'm so sorry,' he told her.

And she hated him and these final words of his, which were as lifeless as stones.

*

304

Midge watched then as Annie became Michael and herself com-
bined. She knew she was on a tightrope and did not know how
long she would last on it without him. Annie's glasses had
vanished and she told Midge that she needed to find her second
pair, despite the chaos – she simply needed her glasses now
because there were forms to complete and sign. These glasses
were necessary – in the same way that she would need to eat soon,
to feed her thick-skinned body – because her life and the lives of
her two remaining children literally depended on it. Michael was
the most composed, 'the luckiest', as it happened. Somewhere in
the distance were the hills of Willamette Cemetery and that was
where they would be taking him. Michael had escaped a kind of
torture.

But – Midge could see now that Annie would survive all of it.
That there was no choice because of these children. And this
moment of clarity came early and almost knocked her unconscious.
As much as Annie loved Joseph and Michael, the broken, living
children were what mattered. Midge's thoughts slipped away from
her for a moment and she and Nora and Annie all slept briefly
and then woke again only to find each other and be reminded of
everything that had happened.

Midge lay on the high narrow bed then with her arms around
Nora – Nora who was crying into her torn shirt, crying as if she
might drown in it, and Midge was praying that she would exhaust
herself and fall into a healing sleep and give her some peace and
some time to think about everything. But the crash kept coming
back to her, the empty seat, Joseph flying, her knowing somewhere that there was a hand that had dropped down to the
seatbelt on his booster and with a deep click had released it – and
Midge had been bored with the journey and wanting to round
the corner and see the house and be back in it – but she had
reached in and buckled the belt again . . . securely? And then, the

burning white light, the noise that seemed to roar through them, the screaming and the awful silence that followed everything. Nora's hand in plaster lay heavy on Midge's chest. This was how their life might be now, a mother, the nanny and her two children, their hearts like dead weights around her and Midge trying her best to keep the family from drowning.

VI
The Final Blue

Gearhart, Oregon, July 2016

47

Margaret went to the beach again, staying longer on her second day. The sun had gone when she finally got up from the sand and a chill had fallen over everything. Even then the beach was not lonely – there were other people dotted in this wide constellation, stars connected by the space they shared and never touching. Without the sun the sand turned grey though and the sky became a curious amber colour. Lights came on in the beach-front houses and the sea continued moving. She found the walk back to the village easier. It was cooler and she felt refreshed, better, the holiday already working for her. She paused on Main Street again where the same bench was vacant. The scene had not changed at all. It was still deserted. In time she would realize that all the action took place before breakfast in Gearhart, that it all happened in the queue for freshly baked croissants at the bakery. When she returned to the house it was dusk and there was a white-haired man standing behind his picket fence, watching her.

'We should meet,' he said over his gate, his voice not brimming with enthusiasm. He spoke loudly and with an air of resignation and he was not entirely welcome in the softness of the evening. Margaret felt awkward about asking him inside the house she had not yet unpacked in. Still, he crossed the sandy street without looking, not caring about the traffic, certain by now that there

309

would not be any. His head was large, his face tanned and lined like a walnut.

Someone was running an outdoor shower. There was steam billowing over a wooden fence towards him. Margaret offered him a chair in the middle of the small lawn where the grass had already turned yellow. A fire had been lit at one time and they sat down together and honoured this circle of black sticks and ashes. She remembered something about watering the plants for the owner and presumed that this would include the awful child's shoe that held the geranium. Another thought regarding the litter tray surfaced and she allowed this to float away from her.

'Eric,' he told her. 'Eric Schumann.'

'Margaret,' she answered. 'Margaret Keegan.'

'Where are you from, Margaret? You don't sound like an Oregonian.'

He offered her his hand then and its palm was soft, the fingers unusually strong as they clasped hers, forcing them together. There was something about this hand in hers, this contact that might – she worried – wreck her evening. She had spent her first two days at the beach and was still sensitive to her new surroundings. She wanted to be on her own now, needing this time to begin to feel at home in them. She had planned to open all the small doors in the kitchen, see where the coffee cups went and what sort of glasses were next to them. She had already placed a sleek bottle of Pinot Grigio in the fridge and was not inclined to share it with him. She didn't care at all if this was petty or selfish. There had to be some small compensation for being a single woman. Margaret had planned to drink a tall glass of water from the tap and stand at the sink looking through the window and allowing her mind to wander.

The bus from Portland had taken more than four hours and she was still tired from the journey. When she went back there her savings would be gone and she would have to find a way to bring in some money. Her friend Sally would help but she did not want to burden her. She missed Bird and Olive a little – but she was not ready to go back to Ireland. She had not been homesick for a single moment. Olive kept in touch by email, telling her shyly the previous year that she was moving in with Pat Noonan. They were engaged now and Margaret had written back asking why Olive and Pat would not live in the lodge together. She knew that Olive wanted to stay there and Margaret gave them her blessing.

Besides, when she thought of Tullyvin she was not sure now if she could ever return there. She would sell the last of her rings, her watch, her necklaces to stay on in Portland. She would pack groceries at Whole Foods so that she could eat and pay her way and stay with Sally, but none of this really mattered. Why would it? After all that had happened in her world, what was there that could finally harm her?

'I'm from Ireland but living in Portland now,' she told Eric Schumann.

'Ah . . . I see.'

She sensed some regret from him then. He had wanted to call out over the gate and be done with it, knowing that once they had introduced themselves their relationship could be reduced to little waves as they went in different directions – him to the grocery store, her to the dunes and the beach. But because she had not answered by calling out her name, 'Margaret!' over the street and then hearing it echo, brush off the roofs and trees, he had had to come over and now he was in a chair and it was more than either of them wanted.

'So you're renting the Gilberts' place,' he told her.

'Yes. Do you know them . . . the Gilberts?'

'Oh, sure . . . we've been coming down here for years. Now I've retired we live down here. My wife's gone to the meeting about the farmers' market . . . or a barn dance or something, you can catch her another time. Edith, that's her name, Edith and Eric Schumann.'

'Where is the farmers' market?'

'I've no idea. I hate going there. A lot of assholes in straw hats trying to sell me their own cat-piss beer.'

'And kale crisps for eight dollars,' Margaret added. 'Blueberries the size of a child's head.'

He looked at her then, his face creasing into a smile because he could not help it.

'That too,' he said.

'What did you do before you retired?' asked Margaret.

'I was . . .' and here he stopped, the pause lengthening and his eyes closing slightly as if he was trying to see his life, his former career, in the trees, caught in the black branches.

'The fawn,' he said quietly.

'Ah . . . He's back,' Margaret answered.

They sat still then, as quiet as children.

And Eric, she could feel it now, was in a state of complete happiness that changed the air around him.

'How delightful,' he whispered. 'Isn't he?'

The sun had disappeared behind the trees, long shadows coming down over everything. The fawn stepped over the lawn, his nose dipping as he quietly inspected his surroundings, not completely interested, his departure back through the woods imminent. He slipped away again and took the last of the day with him.

The air had chilled slightly and Margaret rubbed her arms and smiled at him.

'I've been watching him from our place,' Eric told her. 'I've been wanting to get a little closer.'

'Well, come over any time you like.'

'How long are you staying?'

'Oh, just a week.'

'Ah . . . that's a pity. A week is nothing.'

Margaret smiled at this and let her head relax back on the lawn chair. The arrival of the fawn had dissolved any tension between them.

'I used to be a surgeon,' he told her briskly. 'That was what you asked me? Yes, and then we had our little visitor.'

'Oh, I see.'

'When you asked me what I'd done for a living . . . I couldn't remember. There's a chance I won't remember your name tomorrow . . . or even later this evening. Margaret . . . Margaret,' he repeated, his voice soberly willing the name to stick somewhere inside him.

'What kind of surgeon?'

'Brain,' he answered.

The crickets began and Margaret wished that she had offered him something but it was too late now, the offer of a glass of wine at this stage would be awkward for both of them. Still—

'Would you like some tea? – I was thinking of making some.'

'I have Alzheimer's,' he told her suddenly. 'Early onset – although I'm seventy-three, so not that early maybe.'

Margaret took a deep breath and closed her hands, one fan of fingers comforting the other. She was not sure what to say now but this did not seem to matter to him.

'For days and days I remember everything. On days like that I could open a person's head and fix them. Deft and sure. Not a worry. And then . . . boom . . . I go to the grocery store and it's not that I can't remember what I've gone there for . . . it's that I can't remember what the white stuff in the bottles is called.'

Eric looked right at her then, his eyes dark and full of life under a thick shock of white hair. Until now he had been devoid of humour. Now when she looked at him she realized there was hope for him too, hope everywhere.

'What *is* it called?' she asked him.

He gave a low deep laugh that caused his shoulders to shake slightly.

'Orange juice,' he shouted and she smiled at him through the dark.

Eric heaved himself out of the chair. He extended his hand again, warmer now.

'Margaret,' he said. 'It's been a pleasure talking to you . . . welcome to Gearhart.'

He laughed again then and said 'milk' quietly as if to himself and looking at her, 'Margaret,' as if he was planting the name on her forehead.

She got up with him. There was a light on in her little kitchen. The house was snug now and warm-looking.

'You know about the cats,' he said as he released the latch on the white gate.

'Oh, sure.'

'Are you a cat person?'

'No.'

'Dogs?'

'No.'

Eric looked up at the stars which were appearing in a sky that was not yet dark enough to show them. He leaned back very slightly and reminded her of someone.

'People?'

'God, no,' Margaret answered.

And he was gone, one hand over his head briefly in a wave to her. She waited until he was inside and saw a light going on and him moving through his own kitchen. Strange, she thought, how we people want to live in separate compartments. She turned then, not wanting to see any more of him and the secret world he lived in. The cats had settled down in the sitting area. They looked up briefly when she came in as if she had no earthly right to be there.

Earlier in the day, she had seen Eric's wife, Edith. She was younger than her husband and trying very hard to hold on to him. She was slim and blonde, not much more than fifty. She was very thin though and she brought to mind a grasshopper, all structure and angles, no real warmth anywhere. Margaret could see that she would hold the parts of Eric's brain like bits of wool as the wind tried to take them. She had waved to Margaret from her kitchen window, her hand flat as if she was pushing the air away from her. And Margaret could sense her loneliness, her fear at the changes taking place around her. She did not regret leaving Tom Geoghan but there were still days even now when he could create a soft well inside her. She had finally got what she wanted and it hadn't been enough for her. Tom had come back but she had not wanted that faded version of him and her together. Now the worst had already happened. They had both left each other. She wanted to tell Edith this but she did not know her well enough. She wanted to explain to her that there would be a time when she would not be afraid of anything any more.

48

The dance at Wilson's barn took place on Wednesday night and Margaret had no concerns about being on her own there. She had an easier way with people now – she said less – and it seemed to draw them to her. She would enter the party smiling, a fine silk shawl in fuchsia pink draped around her shoulders, and she would sit on a bale of straw with some punch and watch the dancing.

At home she put on sandals and wondered if there would be a walk across a field at dusk, blades of grass, their seeds catching between her toes, to remind her of her girlhood. This was the part she would enjoy most, of course. She wore white linen trousers and a loose blue shirt over them. In the mirror she saw a face that had been in the sun, her eyes bluer, it seemed, than before.

She began to walk down the street, the air fresh and cool around her. She had a feeling of excitement behind her breast-bone – a kind of joy that was, she thought, quite irrational. She was going to a dance where she would just sit and watch other people. Then she met Eric at the corner and he was bewildered, a different kind of person from the one she had met on her second evening.

'I can't find my house, Margaret,' he told her and his fear had almost derailed him. He was panicking and yet he remembered her, knew her name, treating her now like a beloved sister.

'There it is,' she told him and she began to turn him slowly and two people, women in shorts and white sneakers, stopped and watched this strange scene unfolding.

'Look,' Margaret told him and she was leading him firmly by the hand and he had his other large hand up to his face covering his crying and his fear, the shame of it already stinging him.

'Is Edith at home?' she asked.

He stood at his gate and took a long full breath, filling his lungs and then casting it back out again.

'She's at the barn dance,' he answered slowly. 'She's on the committee.'

'Would you like me to go and get her?'

'No . . . there's no need. I'm OK.'

'When it's dark it can be hard to read the street signs,' she told him.

Eric looked right at her then.

'I've been coming here for twenty-two years, Margaret.'

'Will I come in and make some tea for you?'

'No need,' he said, his voice brisk now, dismissive – and he was already turning and heading towards his door.

'Panic averted,' he said but his voice was still thin from crying and his shame around this made him want, more than anything, to get away from her. She saw it then and wished she hadn't, the damp circle on the front of his chinos, moving to the legs, the cotton sticking slightly to him. She released him and realized that to leave him alone to wait for Edith would be her greatest kindness.

There were small Chinese lanterns around the barn and extending from one side to join a long rectangular marquee. She stopped in the middle of the lane and decided to cross a field of corn to get there. The stalks were high but she could hear a couple laughing from somewhere within them. Under the moon, which on this night was a silver crescent, a charm, minuscule, she

317

looked ahead to the dance and heard the music beginning and wanted to run for fear of missing the excitement. She had not even been invited and had no friend with her but that made it all the more appealing – the fact that she could go and then leave when she liked without being attached to any of these people. Someone had set up an antiques stall near the tent and she stopped and looked at enamel jugs, a lawn mower, some gold watches and earrings. She bought nothing. She looked like she had money to spend, that was the best thing about the silk shawl. The dance was a kind of beacon in the distance. There were people gathered in small groups outside, the light from the tent creating silhouettes, their voices moving out across the evening quiet like birdsong – and Margaret felt great happiness. There was something ahead of her after all. A young man offered her a cup of fruit punch at the door.

'Does it have any alcohol in it?' she asked.

'Yes, ma'am – but this one doesn't.'

The shawl slipped from one shoulder and unfurled behind her.

'I'll have that one,' she whispered.

'I'm sorry, ma'am . . . this one? This one has the rum in it.'

'Yes . . . that one.'

He was young and awkward with her, his Adam's apple sliding up and down, his newly grown cheekbones giving him the look of a modern painting, something by Braque or Picasso.

She found a bench to sit on and sipped her drink and felt the rum relax her. She drank it slowly, knowing already that she could not finish it, the hard liquor already too much of a jolt for her.

This made her laugh suddenly.

Am I drunk? she wondered aloud and the people sitting at the end of the table looked up at her.

'Hi there,' they said.

She did not want to talk to them. The women were what she

would describe as very American, which was unfair, but as far as she could see they were horse-faced women, long in the jaw with teeth that were white and terrifying.

'A beautiful evening,' she told them.

'Wonderful,' one of them called out to her.

A man asked her to dance then. He was much younger than her, a hardy type in a cowboy hat and she could feel the strength in his hand when he laid it gently on her round shoulder.

'I have bad knees,' she told him cheerfully, not caring if this made her sound like his mother.

'Don't worry, I'll take care of you,' and he winched her up from the bench and out she went onto the sawdust floor and they did a kind of slow waltz that seemed to be known to everyone, everywhere.

'You're a pretty lady,' he told her.

He was of no interest except to remind her that she was still a woman and to turn her in slow smooth circles on the floor.

'How long are you staying in Gearhart?'

'Just a week.'

'And then?'

'Back to Portland – and after that, Canada, I think. Maybe home . . . Ireland.'

'Are you *Irish*?'

'People from Ireland usually are.'

'It's very pretty and green there,' he told her.

'It's very wet and green,' she answered and this made him laugh.

'Your first time in Gearhart?'

'My friend sent me here for a holiday.'

'Sweet.'

'Actually I think she's trying to get rid of me.'

Everything she said was droll and this man was in the mood

319

for laughing. To the outside world they looked like they were having a fine time together.

She saw Edith and Eric walk in then and they stood back shyly, waiting for someone to approach them. They both saw Margaret at the same time and seemed puzzled by her presence and how she could be out on the floor dancing with a man so much younger, her pashmina in a wave behind her.

For a moment Margaret felt exotic, a woman of mystery. She thanked her partner and moved over the floor to Eric and Edith.

'Our son Will is coming to visit tomorrow,' Edith told her proudly.

'I hope you'll get to meet him,' Eric added. He had distanced himself now from everything that had happened earlier.

Margaret left the tent then, the sounds of people, the music, the lights fading away behind her. Eric was wearing fresh pants, red, the colour of cranberries. There were stars overhead, the air crisp and clean around her. She could not hear the sea. It seemed to have dried up everywhere. The field was silent when she followed the long smooth ridges between the corn. At the house, the two cats were waiting. She had forgotten to put them inside during the day and she had returned from the beach to find them hot and brimming with resentment. They had found the cool shadows at the baseboard of the house but they were angry and unforgiving. Now they took up residence in her bedroom, one on the loft ladder, one on her pillow. She allowed this, fed them, gave them catnip as a treat, which drove them crazy. She was aware that she was giving them mixed signals. Now they were outside in the dark again, on the back lawn grass, dancing, playing with each other like a love-struck couple. There was a new wildness in the air. Their eyes sparked at her from the hedge. When she turned to open the door they ran at each other, both flying into the air, patting paws and then twisting as they fell, their ears back, hissing.

'You're gone stone mad,' she told them.

Edith had left raspberries on the back steps. They had called for her – only to discover that she had made her own way, had been brave enough to go alone, had abandoned Eric like a wet parcel. She took the cats inside and shut them in England. After three days she had begun talking to them.

'The first sign of crazy,' Eric had told her, 'and I should know.'

Later they all fell asleep on her bed together, their purring making a sound like the ocean moving somewhere near and then far away from her.

49

Margaret saw him cross the street, her heart noting the smooth loose walk of a young man coming towards her. Will was twenty. Edith had already told her.

'Our son,' she had said – and then, taking a deep breath, 'it's complicated. He's going through something. Over the past couple of years he's become a kind of stranger. Do you think that people change?' she had asked Margaret then. And Margaret remembered having a similar conversation one cold night with Midge Connors.

They were sitting with Eric on the small lawn the day after the barn dance sipping iced tea, hoping for a visit from the fawn.

Years before, Margaret would have answered, 'No, I don't,' but she had become more aware of people's feelings, of their ability to inflict hurt on each other.

'I think their behaviour can change,' she had said quietly and Edith and Eric had both nodded gently, not hopeless about their son, but not hopeful either.

Now Will came with his hands in his pockets, a full head of dark curly hair. There was something intense and vital about it, this hair with its own unruly nature.

'I'm turning into a weird old biddy,' Margaret said to herself suddenly, and yet, as she saw it, this was not in any way sexual – it was a feeling of being connected to this boy's vitality, like getting an electric charge from him. His youth was smooth and hard like an apple. It amazed her now, how each and every person had to accept the loss of that. Her own face in the mirror was at times the face of a stranger. Worse, there were times when she had almost flinched at her own reflection, certain that it was the ghost of her mother or even her father. She had never minded gaining weight. Her father had been skin and bone and a few extra pounds prevented any real likeness from developing.

'Ma'am?' the boy Will asked.

The screen door placed a veil over his features but he was beautiful. There was no doubt about that – but then she had been beautiful too, she just hadn't known it. But he was like a kind of sand-fairy – and she, particularly in the red and yellow swimsuit, more like a beach ball. She had just come up from the dunes and could only imagine the vision she presented to him. A bathing suit was acceptable on the beach – but here, with her flesh bulging out from it like a kind of hot lava, her back glowing with some accidental sunburn, if he made a citizen's arrest she wouldn't blame him.

'Mom said you have a problem with your window . . . You want me to look at it for you?' he asked.

No, Margaret thought, I want you to look at my big backside in this swimsuit.

'Just a moment,' she called over her shoulder, a glass slipping from her hands and breaking in the sink.

'Shit,' she said quietly. She would have to replace it and for a split second she felt as if she was unravelling. She had sat with Edith for an hour on the lawn after breakfast and mentioned that her bedroom window wouldn't open – and now here was this young man ready to fix it for her. A part of her delighted in Edith's memory for detail and another part wanted to kill her.

Margaret crossed the kitchen and stepped into the bathroom, where she found a robe on the door and pulled its waffle cotton fabric around her body. She caught sight of herself in the mirror then and was slightly taken aback by the pleasant change that had taken place in her. Her face was tanned and her eyes clear, her hair, brushed cleanly off her forehead, a mixture of white and silver.

'I'm still alive,' she said and she returned to the kitchen where Will was waiting. He was sitting on the wooden stoop looking out over the grass, aware that his mother was watching from her kitchen window. When Margaret saw his shoulder blades pulling forward as he reached for a blade of grass she felt a slight nervousness, a fear that she could not understand, from being around him.

'Hi,' she said, extending a hand, hers cool, his warm, the two connecting and then releasing quickly.

'Come in. I'll show you the window and you can see if you can do anything with it, although I've tried everything. Your mother . . . you're very kind to come over.'

'It's no trouble, ma'am.'

'Margaret,' she told him.

She showed him into her neat feminine room and watched how he stepped around the bed to the window and tried to push it upwards.

'Nope,' he said quietly. He stood on a chair and looked at the frame.

'Painted,' he said. 'You have a knife of some sort?'

'Yes, of course . . . although I'm a little worried about what the owner will say if we force it.'

'Hang on, I'll go get my pocketknife.'

And with that he was gone, leaving a faint scent behind him, soap and seawater, a hint of fabric conditioner, lavender. That was Edith and she was all around him. That's why they don't get along, Margaret thought. The woman is suffocating him.

While he was gone she managed to splash her face and pull on a sundress. It was blue with small white leaves printed on it. Pretty enough, she thought, and she put in her silver and pearl earrings and then wondered what exactly she was doing. She had planned to spend the whole day in her swimsuit. She was going to eat oranges and read women's magazines and all the back issues of *House Beautiful* and not wash until bedtime and even then she might not have bothered.

Will did not come inside but went straight to the outside of the window and Margaret watched, standing well back, and he turned once and said hi to her. He did not look twice or seem to notice that she was in a dress instead of a robe or that she was wearing her earrings, and this was a relief to her. It was enough that one of them was being ridiculous. He stabbed his pocket-knife into the paint and began to drag it sideways.

'Hmmm,' Margaret said, her tone doubtful.

'It's not your problem,' Will said suddenly. 'It's the dumb-ass painter . . . and the lady who thinks you can sleep in a bedroom without a window.'

'Mrs Gilbert,' Margaret said. 'Do you know her?'

'Yeah. She's a pain in the ass. Real uptight about everything.'

Margaret laughed quietly.

'Would you like a drink of something?'

He glanced back at her for a moment.

'Iced tea? Water? I have a bottle of wine in the refrigerator.'

'Any beer?'

'No . . . I'm afraid not. I'm not a big beer drinker.'

The window shot up with a push.

'Great!' Margaret announced.

'Will I leave it open?'

'Oh yes, please do. Well, thank you, Will. It's been so hot at night . . . I haven't been able to sleep.'

'Me neither . . . must be something in the air.'

*

She was finishing supper at the small table in the kitchen when he returned with two bottles of beer. Will folded himself into a soft white chair in the living room and rolled a joint as Margaret washed her dishes in the kitchen. Across the street his mother was doing the same thing and Margaret felt as if she was protecting him, hiding the boy behind her skirts so no one could hurt him. They opened the windows and Margaret accepted the weed when he offered it to her. The first time she had smoked pot with Sally she had been depressed for three days, the whole world feeling like a fresh weight, the steering wheel of the car difficult to turn, the shopping trolley at the store running away from her. And yet, here was this boy, all the perfect elements of him sitting next to her, in a way that was trusting. Tomorrow he would be one day older and so would she. Next week she would be somewhere else and so would he. The transient nature of seaside dwellers always made her feel lonely – as if loveliness was something that a person could not hold on to, as if life was always slipping away, moving.

A soft bell jingled in the distance and Will looked up quickly.

'That's your gate,' he said quietly, and quick and soft like one of the cats he jumped through the bedroom door and out the window, leaving Margaret sitting on the seagrass carpet looking at his sneakers.

Through the screen door she saw Edith. Edith who was knocking lightly and being sorry and embarrassed about it.

'Come on in,' Margaret called, the weed already making her too heavy to get up from the floor. The walls of the house seemed to be moving towards her. There were seashells behind frames, pictures of babies long since grown up, lace doilies like snow-flakes scattered here and there.

Edith's arms seemed very long and slender in a sleeveless white linen blouse, her shorts neat khaki, to the knee.

Dressed like an army of annoying women all over America, Margaret thought. At least her arse is not the size of Oregon.

'I'm sorry to bother you, Margaret,' Edith said and then she paused. The smell of pot was like a muslin curtain that had become wrapped and knotted around everything. She could not help but give a little wave of her hand as if to clear the air immediately around her.

'It's for medicinal purposes,' Margaret said very quietly and she nodded her head sadly at the other woman.

'Oh dear,' Edith answered, one thin hand resting on a hip that was as narrow as a dado rail. And then she didn't know what to say so Margaret helped her.

'It helps with the pain,' she added and she had a sudden urge to start laughing.

'I'm looking for Will,' Edith said suddenly. 'I thought I saw him come in here.'

It was only now that Margaret began to see the kind of pain that Edith was in and she got up from the floor with some difficulty – and Edith, who was beginning to cry softly, held out her hand to hoist her upwards.

'My husband is missing,' she said. 'He went out for a walk without telling me . . . I didn't even hear the door close behind him. I was in the laundry room and the dryer was running. I need to find Will and we need to go look for him.'

And Margaret, cursing the fog she was in, saw Edith's problem but was not able to feel anything. She was watching the other woman from a distance and now felt like laughing.

'Don't worry,' she said.

'But is Will here?'

'No, he is not.'

'But aren't those his shoes?'

'No – those are mine.'

Edith looked back at her in astonishment.

'I'll find him and send him back to you,' Margaret offered but Edith was gone, pushing Margaret gently away from her.

'Stoners,' she said loudly and the screen door slammed behind her.

'You need to call the police,' Margaret called after her – and then she put her hand over her mouth and started to laugh helplessly.

When she leaned out the bedroom window she found Will sitting on the grass, his back to the white gable. The moon was high and full, casting a silver glow on the grass around him. He stood up and she saw that he was also laughing.

'Did I tell you about the time they tried to cut down a tree on this street?' he began.

'Your father has gone missing – you need to help your mother find him.'

'Oh shit,' Will said softly but he was very fluid and relaxed about it. She could see his bare feet on the grass, the turn-ups on his jeans. She remembered his toenails, white and smooth, that his hands would be something young women would notice. His thick hair would also drive them crazy, his eyes – green, she thought – could cast a spell over anyone.

He reached up to the window then.

'Romeo, Romeo,' she said and they began to laugh again.

In the back of her head was a small clockwork train going around and around and it reminded her that Edith had gone down the street in the dark crying because her husband might have fallen into a hole somewhere.

Will reached up, his hands strong on both sides of her head, his thumbs under her jawbones. The hands were manly enough though and full of confidence – as young as he was, he saw what he wanted and took it. He put his lips on hers and moving one hand under her chin kissed her and in this moment, every nerve in his still-young body, every vein and fibre, seemed to be present and focused entirely on Margaret Keegan. And Margaret allowed herself to be kissed like this and did not rebuke him or hurry over the moment. In time she would recount the story of the young man in bare feet under her bedroom window.

'No,' she said finally but he was gone running silently to the kitchen door and finding her there in the bedroom waiting. The pot was thinning out and she could feel a headache forming like a crown that was too small for her.

'Margaret,' he said but the light was too bright for them.

'We need to help your mother . . . your father . . .'

'I know he's lost . . . but he's not *really* lost . . . it's happened before. He'll be at the beach, that's where he always goes. He's like a crab, must return to the water. I'll go get him in a few minutes.'

'Will, you better hurry. Your mother is almost hysterical.'

'I heard you laughing,' he said then and he smiled widely at her and then they both began to laugh quietly.

'This is shameful,' Margaret said.

Will stepped towards her.

'No, no, no,' she said quietly.

'Why not?' he asked and he reminded her quite suddenly of a child asking for more ice cream.

'No, Will, no . . . I am not permitted to kiss a person like you.'

'What do you mean *not permitted*?'

'What I mean is I'm not Mrs Robinson in black lace lingerie and you're not Benjamin.'

'Mrs who?' he asked.

'Oh well . . . there now, you're even younger than I thought.'

'Or maybe you're older than I thought.'

'Oh, the cruelty of youth,' she said cheerfully but because she was older she did not care enough to be injured by him.

'Can I ask you a question?'

'Go ahead,' she answered and she was yawning.

'As kisses go . . . how would you compare it to other men's kisses?'

'That's a ridiculous question. Now, are you capable of driving?'

Will drove in bare feet and she sat silently beside him. She hoped that they wouldn't see Edith, that they would make it to the beach and look for Eric, that there on the sand they could continue this small adventure together.

50

The beach at night was strange and lonesome. Eric was standing near the water, his clothes scattered around him, the moonlight illuminating his shoulders, the long thread of his back, his legs frail and bowed underneath him. He had wrapped his arms around himself for some form of comfort. Will said he wasn't lost – but there on the black beach of Gearhart close to midnight, he was gone from everything.

Will crossed the sand, running, his hair blowing behind him. He was not running to protect his father. He was not at all worried about him. In the car park he had said in a voice bored now with everything, 'There he is. Told ya.'

And then he was off and running over the sand because the beach in the dark gave him a sudden feeling of freedom. He is running, Margaret thought, because he is a child. He is running because he wants to feel the wind in his face, the rush of the waves near him, and because, out there, no one can catch or confine him.

He dropped a hand here and there to pick up some of his father's clothing, the long red pants quickly slung over his shoulder.

Then Margaret followed, moving slowly, her gait relaxed and floating. High on the sand dune where the wind was fierce and cold, only Edith was rigid, watching this tableau that did not seem to belong to her.

'No,' Eric said. 'No,' and he sounded petulant and childish. He smacked at Will's hands as he draped a now-damp shirt around him. The wind tried to take it and for a moment the father and son tussled, their roles reversed completely.

'You can't go swimming,' Will said firmly.

'I want to swim.'

'You can't. It's dangerous.'

'I want to go in the water,' Eric roared and the bellow of that over the wind and the waves made Margaret feel for him.

'Let him go in,' she told Will. 'Let him. Leave him be . . . It's what he wants.'

Edith was next to them then, patting at Eric's arms, trying to put his clothes on, his limp buttocks still hanging out and she was doing her level best to hide them.

'Are you crazy?' she asked Margaret. 'Let him go in the water . . . why? So he can drown himself? Why would you say such a thing?'

And every tiny spear of anger she had held back from her ailing husband she directed now at Margaret, and Margaret could feel herself bristling.

'Because it's what he wants.'

No one spoke for a moment and Eric's eyes continued to look out over the water as if he was watching something, trying to find a precious item lost in there.

'He wants to go swimming,' Margaret said. 'I'll take him in. I grew up on a lake. I've been swimming my whole life. I'll keep him from drowning.'

And there on the beach she removed her blue and white sundress and it joined Eric's underwear on the sand near the water. She continued to speak as she undressed, saying, 'At this point in our lives, Edith, you give a person what they want. In a while he may not be able to tell you. In a while he will not want anything – from you or anyone.'

332

Her back was still hot from the sun on the same beach earlier. She was fearless though, uncaring, standing in large white pants and a bra like a warrior.

She-ra! she thought to herself. She had forgotten all about Will and his mother, her entire being was focused on taking this man down to the water. She took his hand then, amazed at its softness, feeling his bones weak in hers, wondering if this poor hand could break in the current.

'Come on, Eric,' she said quietly and then she stopped for a moment, dropped his hand and, unhooking her bra, released her breasts to the night air, her shoulders relaxing, her skin dancing in this newfound and unexpected freedom.

In her peripheral vision, Edith was like a ghost now and grabbing at her own hair like a mad woman. Will was sitting down, his arms around his knees, watching.

And afterwards Edith wrapped Eric in a towel and bundled him into her car with a hot coffee. She did not offer a towel to Margaret or even speak to her. Will went ahead to his car and turned on the heating and she followed.

'So now,' she said, 'I've finally frightened you.'

'No,' he said and he was shaking his head slowly.

He turned the dial on the radio and drove the car slowly towards Chinook Lane.

'I'm leaving early in the morning,' Margaret told him as he parked. 'I've had a wonderful week – and I'll remember you – and your father and mother.'

But he was not listening. He was still the silent boy back on the sand watching the older people.

'Tonight,' he said finally, 'you were kind of *magnificent*.' He shook his head slowly. 'Seeing you with my dad out there in the water . . . Man, that was really something.'

And on the bus back to Portland Margaret was reminded of night swimming in Gearhart. How they had run together and

333

then felt that first touch of the water, the insistent swirl of the waves filling them with a terror and a delight that was instant. She and Eric had shrieked together and then there was great laughter. They had gone in up to their waists and then folded onto their knees so that they were submerged, cold and wet all over. He had had no desire to go any further but was happy to stay with her in the shallow water.

And Eric had stretched out on his back, allowing the waves to wash over him.

'Look at the stars,' he had told her.

The sea was black then and churning around them, the night sky magical and the earth turning with them, everything becoming new again, over and over and over.

VII
Dear Bird

51

The letter came in autumn when the air was becoming thin and the trees around the lake were changing colour. Margaret and Midge had been gone for over two years now and Bird knew that this flash of orange and red would be short-lived. It would take just one wild night to strip the trees bare and send him headlong into another winter. It was still warm enough for swimming, although once the children returned to school the lake was usually empty. Only Olive walked down her wooden steps to the shore in any kind of weather. There were mornings when he would see her from one of his fields, a light drizzle of warm rain on her shoulders and a red towel hanging on a tree near the shore. Her routines were a comfort to him. He missed Margaret more than she did now, which was peculiar. There were things he wanted to say to another person but it could not be Olive. The sadness he had felt when Midge left was too much to leave with anyone. Olive would respond to his loss with great emotion and her concern for him would be overwhelming, the whole thing bogging down in a swamp of directionless feeling. He needed Margaret with her dry anger, her unromantic nature, her ability to see things as they were. So what he felt, therefore, stayed inside him like a secret clamp around his chest, a cage to prevent his heart from expanding.

Bird tried to take comfort in his surroundings and from nature, ever changing and yet also familiar. He liked to walk on the grass without boots or socks and this reassured him – the sight of his own feet, so physical and alive, moving through the grass and holding him up regardless of everything that had happened. Even the wind-shaped trees without leaves had their own grace and beauty and could console him. In the evenings he watched the light fade over the lake and how the mountain seemed to change its shape and colours with each passing season. The dog got old and died on him. Midge's cat had crossed the fields to the O'Neills and then stayed there. There were a few kittens of dubious lineage hanging around the barn. He got a new dog, who was young and foolish and had a habit of dragging things up from the yard – a sweeping brush, empty flower pots, anything – and leaving them at his feet as offerings.

Bird saw how the highest peak of Maggie's Mountain was like a girl's lips slightly open as if waiting to be kissed by someone – a giant – who was perhaps never coming. Whenever he felt his own sadness closing in on him he concentrated on bringing his attention into the present, and nature in all her strength and constancy carried him.

I suppose I'm being 'mindful', he thought vaguely to himself. He had read about it on the internet and was doing it now – by accident. And there were people who made money from teaching others how to master it. The internet was a stream of endless rubbish – he could find himself watching a video of a small kitten trying to climb out of a box and be transfixed until he suddenly became aware of what he was doing.

Bird allowed his depression to live alongside him, but not in him – and because of this he did not go under completely.

The country is full of men who are not talking to anyone, he thought, and he was no better than any of them. He himself would have preferred if the feelings and thoughts that he had could have words wrapped around them, words to carry them off and away from him. As it was, his body felt drained and worn – and he was stuck – more or less where Midge had first found him. A part of him still could not understand that she had gone and had not returned to him – how she had actually done this and how he had allowed it to happen.

How could one person do that to another? he wondered, when he had always thought that love would have prevented any kind of parting. She did not want to be of 'any further trouble', that was what she had said to him. And yet on the day she left he had heard her crying in the dark of the kitchen in a way that showed a kind of devastation.

Now he watched Olive as she walked slowly out into the water, her hands skimming the surface as she passed through it. She was thinner than before and wearing a yellow cap that reminded him of a lemon. Her shoulders were tanned and strong-looking. She stood still for a moment and looked out at the islands. The sun would occasionally fall on one of them, making it seem precious, sacred – the lake and the other island left in shadow. Olive seemed to take flight then, a single glide and a noisy plunge out into the deeper water. He never worried about her swimming alone – it was the one thing she could do better than anyone. She moved in a graceful breaststroke first and then turned over onto her back, her arms becoming like propellers in their slow, steady turning. Her pace quickened and she held her head very straight with her feet kicking in a rhythm. She would turn around and swim back when she was ready.

Women were good at talking, Bird knew that, there was nothing they could not say to each other. But for the men, here in this place full of light and shadows and wide empty spaces, feelings were clamped inside them. And when there was no release, these thoughts and worries could become a cancer or a depression that could overwhelm the strongest of men. William O'Neill still haunted him in November and with it came the reminder that he himself must not succumb to the dark of winter. For Bird, the lake and its water must be hope. The trees – life. The grass – blood. These were the thoughts that broke down the pain of the loss he was feeling. He returned to nature. The grass under his feet. There it was. Always. He could not rely on people.

52

The first wind turbine had come during the night, the roads closed off and some people from the town watching. Frances Murphy was there, 'chief objector', as Pat Noonan called her, looking out over her ditch like a cow and even the new priest came – and him after falling out with everyone. There was a truck to carry each of the turbine's blades and another to take the smooth silver belly and Bird himself was mesmerized by its vast structure, its man-made beauty.

'Shame on you, Bird Keegan,' someone shouted and he stood his ground staring back at that person, the words flung like mud into his face and he did not care a bit about them, the words or the person.

He had lost Midge – worse than that, she had left him – and he himself had allowed it to happen, and so instead he acquired a giant made from white metal and silver to stand in one of his fields, and as the trucks carrying it rolled in over his land and down around the lake he was reminded of Gulliver.

In the beginning, just after she left, Bird had pretended that Midge was still with him. In his mind he had taken her to see a film and they had had lunch once at a hotel in Dublin and as usual the whole town was talking about them. At that time he could not sleep for thinking about her and wondering if she was all right or if anything bad had happened to her. After her father

341

had run from the lodge, it was Bird who had held her because she would not allow another person near her, no one else could feel how brittle her limbs were and how they became molten as he put his arms around her. There was blood everywhere. Her blood covered him and he didn't care about it. He felt its warmth through his clothes and still he held and held her.

The whirr from the wind turbine could not be heard from his bedroom but when he woke he could see its blades moving and felt less in need of company. It was a stake in the ground and it told the locals that he didn't care about them. And he got twenty thousand a year to insult them. They had all opposed it. They were opposed to anything different. Sometimes he imagined that Midge still lived in her old house in the hollow and there were days when he would make a point of driving past it. It too had died on him, no loss – the windows all broken, the net curtains billowing out through them. It was in its own way a kind of monument to her. She had slept in there and survived a kind of war before she met him.

And as Bird saw it now, Midge was entitled to go where she wanted. Given how she had been treated by her own people, she was allowed to have her freedom if she needed it. He had not wanted to force Midge to stay with him *or* to try to find her. She was his wife, but she was free to build a nest anywhere.

But – if she returned to him he would take her to see the turbine. She was the only person who would appreciate its wonder. Olive and Pat Noonan were talking about getting married and Margaret had stayed away and would not be home again until next summer. The last he heard she was planning on visiting every state in America. Tom Geoghan had found a new woman, a young one – and they were living together. Margaret, it seemed, had been right not to bother too much about him.

At night when sleep evaded Bird – as it often did – he lay in his bed and tried to imagine where Midge was and what she was doing. When he tired of that, he turned his thoughts to Margaret and imagined her, staff in hand, crossing mountains alone, like a pilgrim. In the deepest part of the night when it was tipping towards dawn he would wonder if Midge ever thought about him. He imagined them walking over the bare fields together, the winter sky of late afternoon turning purple ahead of them. They would walk closer to the turbine until Midge felt that she was becoming smaller and smaller and that the turbine was growing in front of her. Now the noise would be overwhelming and Midge would feel it down in her stomach and behind her chest bone.

'I think it's lovely,' she would tell him. The light becoming very sharp then and the air cold because the first hard frost was coming.

'Could you live here again?' Bird would ask her suddenly.

'I could live anywhere,' she would answer.

Bird and Midge would stand side by side looking out over the water, the world feeling empty around them, the turbine making a sound that was not like any other. Bird had heard that they killed seagulls and sometimes collapsed in a storm, the blades flying off into the air around them. One man down in Kerry had had to move house, the noise from it 'driving him off his head', he said, the vibrations down in his chest 'giving him heart trouble'.

53

The letter came then with its American stamp and a strange wave of inked post-marking, the paper light and flimsy and, as it happened, deadly.

He did not open it immediately but took it from inside the front door and looked at it carefully. He had seen her sign her name once before. She was not a person who had a great need for writing. There were shopping lists – which he still kept in a drawer – that she had compiled at the kitchen table. And he had sat opposite her feeling great tenderness as she copied out recipes and wrote words like 'coriander' and 'cumin', which were all new to her. She had wanted to be his wife then. She had wanted to be with him. This was the simplest and bleakest of his memories. Now she had written his name from a table somewhere in America – the sun warming her arms, the light streaming in any number of windows. There were big yellow school buses in America. Tall buildings. The people were fat there. And in between these vague ideas that he had was *her* – alive and remembering, casting a line out to him from somewhere.

Dear Bird

His legs were soft under him and he sat down, his hands flattening out the creases in the paper so that every word would be clear and not a single one missed by him. And afterwards he took a deep breath and lay back in his usual chair, allowing his legs to fall open. There was no heat from the range. He had not lit it since before the summer. The quick sliding thought that she might still want him after all this time – that she too, like him, had not forgotten – had been a kind of elevation. He felt almost sickened by his own sense of longing. He realized that for a person like him, time did not heal anything. It only hid the hurt away so that it could rise up again and surprise him.

Dear Bird

He had felt his life tumble from him.

Olive came to visit and found him in the kitchen garden. He had reclaimed a plot of land and turned it into clean drills of kale which he sold at the new Saturday food market.

'The whole world is mad for kale,' Olive told him cheerfully.

She was sitting on the low stone wall and patting the new dog as she spoke to him.

'This fool is after bringing me a paintbrush,' she said, her hands on either side of it as she tried to take it from between the collie's jaws.

Bird did not answer although he was aware that she was speaking to him. He could feel her watching and could sense that she was worried about him.

'You haven't been down to the lodge in a long time.'

Bird placed a foot on the spade and felt it slide into the damp earth in a way that was satisfying.

'I'm thinking of going organic,' he answered.

And Olive said nothing. She got up then and moved towards him. She put her face around the spade and spoke loudly.

'What's wrong with you, Bird?'

'Nothing – no more than usual.'

'Something has happened to you.'

'And what makes you think that?'

345

'You're like the weather,' she told him, returning to the wall again and sitting. 'There's no need for you to say anything. The air just changes around you . . . and besides . . .'

Bird leaned the spade on the red door of the shed and came and sat beside her.

'Besides what?'

'Sean says you got a letter.'

'It's a wonder he didn't read it before me.'

'He said you've not said a word since you got it.'

Neither one spoke for a minute. The autumn sun came out suddenly and it was hot there in the small sheltered garden. Bird pulled off his cap and ran his hand back through his hair and let out a sigh.

'It was from Midge.'

'Ah,' Olive said very quietly. 'And how is she getting on?'

Bird did not seem to hear her question.

'She wants a divorce.'

'A divorce,' Olive repeated quietly.

The word had no place in this garden. It was as if a sudden crop of weeds – dandelions in all their ugly glory – had suddenly grown up around them.

'And what else did she say?'

'She asked after you . . . she didn't mention Margaret.'

'Margaret's in California at the moment . . . says the heat is crucifying – she's doing a little detour before going back to Portland.'

'Do you think she'll ever come home?'

'I'm not sure – but now that you mention it, I got an email from her this morning and she's asking if the two of us would go over and visit her in Portland.'

'To Portland, *Oregon*?' Bird sounded astonished.

'And sure, why not? What else are the two of us doing that's so important? Look at us now, sitting on a wall talking.'

'Oregon is about three times the size of Ireland,' Bird said for no particular reason.

'Isn't it funny that both Midge and Margaret ended up in the same place – and the great size of America?' And here Olive was looking at him slyly.

'Midge mentioned that it rains a lot in Oregon.'

'Well, great, we'll be quite at home there by the sound of it.'

And Bird leaned back on the warmed bricks of the wall behind him. He closed his eyes and allowed the sun to bake him. He knew that winter was only around the corner and the idea of that was like a blow to him.

'And what else did Midge say?' Olive asked quietly.

'That she's not coming back.' The words created a gap, an opening somewhere in his chest.

'This family she is working for . . . she seems happy enough with them. She says they need her.'

'And you're not surprised, are you?' And now Olive spoke very gently to him.

And when Bird didn't answer, her words continued slowly and carefully.

'The girl is trying to start a new life for herself.'

'I don't blame her,' he answered.

'I'm not sure she was ever quite ready for what it was that you were offering.'

'She was ready . . . I was the fool who wasn't.'

And Bird's feelings swelled suddenly in his chest, big and round like a beehive and as painful. He felt that he might cry and he wished with all his heart that his sister would leave him. She was talking nonsense now and she was of no use to him. He got up and began to walk down the lane that led to the lake – with Olive sitting on the wall watching. He walked quickly to get away from her. On the shore he stripped off everything he was wearing and then, standing for a moment, took a deep breath and

347

ran out over the stones without feeling them. He dived into the dark of the water and here his head ached from the sudden cold and his arms became tired and heavy. But he kept swimming, stroke after stroke until his entire body was numb and he could not feel anything.

When Bird looked ahead into his own life now, he could see only the letter and with it a sudden and complete loss of hope written into the paper.

He tried to remember what, until now, had saved him.

Wasn't it the land itself, and all of nature?

No. It was the notion that she might somehow return to him. There were no trees growing in the lake, no grass with roots in its sandy bottom. The water swirled green and brown around him and he suddenly understood everything. He understood these men who left their cars near the river with the keys still in the ignition. He understood what had happened to William O'Neill and how he, Bird Keegan, was no different to any of them. These men were not failures. They had each accepted something – and what followed was a beautiful and natural surrender. Bird had taken a meandering route and now he too had found the door he had been passing.

It was not a shameful thing at all . . . or cowardly. Why had that thought ever occurred to him? A plan carried out carefully and with thought given to other people required great courage – and the reward was simple.

When Bird was ready, when he had tied up the loose ends of his life and left things in a way that was tidy, he too would step through the door and have that final freedom.

348

54

Bird was reluctant to leave the farm – and it was Olive who persuaded him. 'The size of you,' she said loudly in his kitchen. 'And you've never been on an aeroplane.' And he had sat silently watching her lips move, hearing the hum of her voice but only some of the words taking. He could read the conversation on the lines of light in her very blue eyes, full sentences lifting from her hands and the shapes they were making. The foolish dog whined at him and Sean came in and banged the door. The loss of some sounds did not bother him. There were times when he felt a great relief in the limited conversation.

'I believe she's smoking pot,' Olive told him. 'And she's in Washington State at the moment, where it's legal. Margaret Keegan is as high as a kite,' she announced in the quiet of his house where the lights should have been turned on to fend off the dark of an autumn evening. Bird could lip-read the words and there was no doubt about what she was saying – except in its absurdity.

'Margaret is getting high,' she said again.

And he could not help but laugh at her then, their eyes meeting, his face softening into a smile finally.

'Ah, you're back,' she said lightly. 'You have not been here at all since that letter came from America.'

Bird had no idea until then how much she had been caring for him. He did not know that whenever he sank into these dark pools Olive had been there with him.

She took a deep breath that almost lifted her entire body.

'We need to get away from here,' she said suddenly. 'Pat will be at the lodge and Sean can keep an eye on things at Red Hill. There is no real work to be done in November.

'We should visit Margaret,' she went on. 'Wouldn't it be great to just get on a plane and go and see her?'

And Bird dropped his head so that his eyes could not see and therefore read another word from her.

'I would like to see her,' he said finally.

'There you are now – that's more like it.'

'I don't mean Margaret – although I would, of course, like to see my sister.'

'Oh,' Olive said and he could see the perfect quick circle of her lips as she turned to him.

'You mean Midge, Bird?'

She came then and pulled a chair towards the range so that she could sit down near him.

'What good will that do, Bird?' she asked, her voice gentle and full of kindness.

'I don't know,' he answered simply. 'I'd just like to see her. It is an unfinished thing between us – we've been married for all this time, neither one seeking out the other – and it left me with the feeling, the idea, that she might some day come back to me.'

Olive sat upright on her chair, her hands flat in her lap, the extent of his pain, this sudden confession, creating a kind of shimmer between them.

'But Bird . . . it's more than two years since she left here.'

Olive looked at him steadily and waited for him to say something.

'Would you think about sending her an email – or a text – and not just arrive at her door, maybe?'

'A text, God no.'

For Bird a text was like putting a cowardly little toe in the water. If Midge was who he believed her to be – a girl better than any other – then at the very least she deserved a properly worded letter.

'I wouldn't want you to get knocked back,' Olive said quietly.

'Knocked back?' And here Bird put a hand flat on his forehead and gave a short dry laugh. Could the whole world not see that Midge had killed him already, that every bone had been made soft in him? He was like that poor man whose wife had run over him with the tractor.

'Do you remember Mattie McGrath?' he asked Olive suddenly.

'Oh God, I do,' Olive said. 'His wife took a turn one day and went for him in the tractor.'

Bird nodded.

'He survived it,' she added. 'And forgave her – apparently.'

Olive paused then for a moment, her eyes floating over the kitchen furniture.

'Two years,' she said quietly, not sure if he would hear her.

'Oh, I know,' he said quickly. 'But I'd like to see her and at least say a decent goodbye – you know, there was not an ounce of badness in her.'

And Bird stretched out his legs and put his hands behind his head, his body like a long, thin shadow across the kitchen.

Olive had already filled in the forms for the passport and he only needed to sign them. They drove into town then for the photographs. And this, to Bird's horror, involved going into the bright new pharmacy that sold teddy bears and gifts wrapped in cellophane as well as medicine.

'They're giving out antidepressants like Smarties in here,' Olive said as they stepped through the swinging glass doors. 'Half the town is on them. And . . . would you blame them?' she continued.

People no longer looked at him when he came to town. It was already full of people who had moved down from Dublin. Now he was made to stand in front of a white screen and a young girl with high painted eyebrows and red lips stood laughing behind a camera.

'How's Bird?' the pharmacist himself called out from behind the counter. Recently he had tried to sell him a hearing aid for several hundred euros.

'There is no point in trying to sell me a hearing aid,' Bird had explained patiently. 'There is nothing to be done. I am completely deaf in one ear already. I might as well be wearing an earring.'

Now he didn't answer, using his deafness as an excuse. Instead he concentrated on standing very still and looking into the single eye of the camera. Olive sat nearby in a chair, her legs crossed, her toe bobbing, delighted about getting him this far already.

'Bird,' she said suddenly. 'Take off your hat, will you?' and she gestured at him, taking a kind of hat from her own round head to help him.

This was why the girl who was wearing the mask of make-up was laughing at him. Here he was, surrounded by smells that were meeting and crashing together – perfume, make-up, the new cotton of facecloths, baby shampoo, medicine, pills popped from bubbles of plastic. Since losing his hearing, or a good deal of it, his sense of smell had sharpened and at times it overpowered him – and he felt weak now from this new assault on his nostrils. But no one was looking at him. The town's seams had split from all these new people. There were burglaries every other week. He slept with the gun in the bed beside him.

'Are you heading off somewhere nice?' the girl with the eyebrows asked him.

He wondered what she had thought about as she had painted herself at the mirror that morning. What had been her intention? It was more Judy Garland than Amy Winehouse but she wouldn't know Judy Garland. People thought he was out of touch but he wasn't really. He read all the papers. He had the internet set up in his kitchen. He knew all about poor Amy Winehouse too and what had happened to her. At night he found dating websites which he clicked away from quickly. The mouse became warm under his hand with all his hurrying away from things. And he found women, strange big-breasted phantoms doing extraordinary things. And he found Washington State and Oregon and knew all about it and what it had to offer. He thought it would not be too difficult to find a person, to perhaps find a picture of Midge or even the people she worked for – but he resisted it. And then on an evening late in summer when the light faded quickly and there was the first smell of winter, he did type her name in with one steady index finger, 'Midge Connors', and then all the other Midge Connors of this world faced him. Women twice her age in wedding gowns and graduation caps. There was even a man in America by that name. In Ireland she had left no trace of herself anywhere. She had simply disappeared from him. And then her letter came and she was with the same family. She signed the letter 'M'. That, thought Bird, was all that was left of her. A single letter. As those two long years had passed, she had become smaller and smaller as if she was being slowly erased from him.

'Time heals all wounds,' Olive had promised him. The same white lie that was promised to everyone.

And as usual he had not answered but became busy with some aspect of animal husbandry. He did not want time to heal him. He did not want to forget about her either. Even the hurt and the loss were better than forgetting completely. He was going to America to remember and to say a decent goodbye to her. She would be oblivious to the other plan that he was hatching. He was going to do away with himself. There it was, he had said the words and the door was open for him too, finally. He could see no other way around things. Reaching this conclusion had come as a great relief to him.

When the time came he would pick a cold morning with the frost dense and white over everything. The new dog would have been left over at the lodge the night before, the back door opened and the dog pushed into the warm dark of the kitchen. He cared about the dog and knew that Olive would let no harm come to it. He would take the gun then and walk through the frosted grass to the white copse and then deep in the heart of it – to the old icehouse which had not been used in twenty years, full of leaves now, its doorway stuffed with briars and fallen branches. And here he would make a bed of leaves, a kind of crypt for himself. He would lie down on the damp floor with the gun, his legs straight and neat, the fungal scent like a blanket, the earthworms and woodlice shifting around him.

Bird would not display the usual carelessness – where one person's misery became another person's haunting. In the icehouse where no one ever went he was sure the gun would not be heard and that he would not be found by anyone. Yes, it would be hard on Olive, the disappearance of her brother, this part he could not help. But she was not alone. Margaret would come home and Olive was loved by Pat Noonan, who had become a kind of hero. How wrong Margaret had been about that one. Pat was a prince among men. Without him to care for Olive, Bird could not have carried out his plan. And without the letter from Midge he would have gone on hoping for something impossible. The sadness he felt when Midge left him and then left him again through that letter was something he could not express to anyone. She had been the finest thing that had ever happened to him. He had never been happier than when he was with her.

*

'Take your hat off,' Olive said very loudly in the pharmacy and she made a grab for it – and the girl at the camera was convulsed now with laughter.

'Hold still,' she said, 'and try not to blink.'

She was shaking with the same laughter as she took the first picture.

'Janette, you're lucky that camera is on a tripod,' the pharmacist said sternly.

He was looking worried. He knew Bird of old and did not want to offend him.

Click.

'Lovely,' the girl said but her laughter was still controlling her. Click. Click.

'You look like a vampire,' Bird said quietly and there was a beat of silence. Olive stood up looking confused and the girl shook her head quickly as if trying to pull herself from a dream.

'Thanks very much!' she said, her affront showing, her face a sudden flush of red and the pharmacist frowned and stepped through the white door that protected him.

The photos arrived quickly in a small white folder and Bird looked at them carefully although he did not know what he was expecting. There was the pale blue of his eyes, his feral hair and beard, his skin weathered, the lines around his eyes and forehead. Olive glanced at them too and then marched him up to the barber.

'A bit of a tidy-up all round?' the barber suggested.

'The full works,' Olive answered.

'No,' Bird said suddenly and he walked out again, tossing the barber's satin cloak away from him.

55

Fall was over in Portland and the hard light of winter was everywhere. Annie and Midge took the children to the house in Yachats because they could think of nothing else to do with them. Before leaving Portland, Billy had taken the summer screens down from the windows – a job done previously by his father – and Midge had lowered the wooden blinds, leaving the house in semi-darkness. The drive had seemed interminable then and they were all broken. Midge was still on crutches and they walked slowly over the wet concrete towards the summer house as if there were pieces falling from all of them. Rain was running in veins on the windows, the sea in the distance grey and churning. Billy was silent – there were whole days when he would not speak to anyone. His face carried the scars, most of which would fade to nothing, but his eyes were unblinking and staring, a doorway to the pain he was feeling.

'A boy of fourteen needs his father,' a neighbour had murmured sadly.

'Then I will have to be a father and a mother to him,' Annie had answered sharply. She had become rigid with loss, her whole focus on surviving.

Billy had asked if he could bring May to Yachats and then waited, his eyes counting the knots in the wood of the kitchen table, wondering how this request would be taken.

'Yes, of course we can take her,' Annie had answered. She could not refuse him anything.

And Midge's arms had a separate floating agenda which she could not share with anyone. Even when she was sitting still her arms were always on the point of reaching for someone. Out of habit, she was stretching for the smallest child, the child who had still needed to be lifted by her, the one who came and climbed onto her knee for no particular reason except to be close to her. Their need for touch and warmth was mutual, a kind of secret thing between them. Todd had left a small brown bag on the porch for her. It was a new kind of soap he was working on, white and smelling of fresh air and pure cotton. He had called the soap 'Joseph'.

There was a part of Midge – the one she was trying to push behind her – a part that was as weak and as thin as a pool of clear water, that wanted a whole avalanche of sadness to come down on her. And if she did that she would cast a line back to Tullyvin and then Bird too and begin to yearn for him. But when she looked at Billy and Nora, their young lives just beginning, she refused this wandering and remembering. She had watched the burial of her own mother – and now a small child and his father – and she would never fully recover. She had known this fact instantly, from the moment she had released Joseph's small hand – Midge knew that these were all the black rocks that she would have to live with for ever.

Nora blamed herself. She had owned up to Midge about unfastening the seatbelt and Midge had held her tighter and had assured her that she herself had fastened it again. But in the weeks and months that would follow, the weight of this act of unfastening a seatbelt would make Nora older, the innocence and wonder at all of life suddenly punched out of her.

'*I* was driving,' Annie had whispered fiercely to her sobbing daughter. 'It was not your fault at all. It was mine . . . *entirely*.' She did not tell her that they had ended badly, that before the crash she had been fighting with Michael.

On their last day at Yachats Billy came to Midge in the kitchen. His grief was normally private but there was something important that he wanted to tell her.

'This house is too empty,' he said. 'We're not like a family. I keep wondering where Dad and Joseph are.'

And Midge, who was sitting at the table in her bathrobe, her red hair wet and combed, slipped a slender arm around him and pulled him onto the bench beside her.

'You're still a family,' she told him.

'But what if you go back to Ireland?'

'I won't leave you,' Midge answered.

When the children were asleep finally, Midge and Annie built a large fire and pulled two armchairs up beside it. Midge needed to rest her leg and they didn't talk much – except now and then, in between sips of tea and wine, Annie would offer something up to Midge that seemed at that moment, in that shared space, of vital importance.

'I'm glad I told Mike that I loved him.'

And Midge nodded sadly. These were the right words to sink into a man as he lay dying and she imagined that they had travelled into him, through his ears and into his brain, his muscles and sinews, his veins, warming every part of him, closing the door softly on his world, taking him away then.

They could not speak of Joseph. It was impossible for either of them.

When Annie dozed in her chair finally, Midge travelled back to Red Hill in her mind and to its magical people. If anyone asked her when she was happiest, it was there and it was with them. She did not regret the letter though, knowing that if Bird had ever wanted her back he was capable of crossing the world to find her. She did not regret asking for the divorce either, two years was long enough. It was only fair to give him his freedom.

Midge and Bird had parted without any expression of love between them and she wondered now if that was in fact the real truth of them. For now she would carry him with her. Red Hill. The lake, the mountain and Bird Keegan.

56

On the aeroplane Bird sat next to the window and looked at the clouds below them. It seemed strange to him that this was not more exciting, that sitting high up over the world as he knew it and actually flying seemed quite natural. They changed in London and ate tasteless food at the airport. Olive had arranged a rental car in Portland and she had a map and detailed instructions from Margaret.

'OK,' she began, 'we're looking for Airport Way to I-205 . . . South.'

And Bird was sitting in the driver's seat, adjusting mirrors and producing a pair of new sunglasses from a black case.

'Would you look at Mr Cool,' Olive whispered.

This he ignored and poked the key into the ignition and turned it.

'Then after that,' she went on, 'we turn right onto I-205 South and then . . . according to Margaret we follow this until we see the I-84 exit.'

Bird was not able to hear all of what she was saying. Even though she was talking into his good ear, it was like a foreign language to him.

'What direction are we headed?' he asked.

'East. Hawthorne Boulevard. Isn't that a nice name, Bird? It reminds me of home.'

Bird knew that she was missing Pat Noonan already. And she was suddenly tired, her eyes closing.

'Maybe we should get some breakfast,' she murmured and the map was folded on her lap because she trusted him, even here, to know where he was going.

'Right,' he said and he checked his watch. It was early morning and they were joining a stream of cars heading to offices in the city. He looked for the sun.

'East,' he said and he began driving with his sister sleeping next to him.

In the distance he saw Mount Hood and it seemed to stand like a beacon in front of him. It was sunlit and covered in snow, vast and majestic.

As soon as he saw the Village Inn he pulled in for breakfast. There were orange seats arranged in circles that reminded him of pumpkins. The sky was grey and it was raining. The waitress poured coffee into thick white mugs and carried over two tall glasses of water. They looked at their menus and were slightly baffled by everything. Bird smiled at Olive and told her he was going to have some of those famous American pancakes. He was surprised then because he was suddenly enjoying himself. The coffee was watery but the pancakes arrived in a stack with little pots of cream and maple syrup parked next to them.

'This is not bacon,' Olive told him. 'It's ham.'

The waitress watched them carefully.

'Do you have butter?' Bird asked.

'Right there, honey,' and she was pointing to the tub of fluffed-up cream next to the syrup.

Bird waited for her to leave and then sampled it.

'They know nothing about butter, that's one thing I'll say about them.'

'Oh, Margaret says the very same. Although she's gone all healthy now . . . organic everything. In her last email—'

And here Olive paused to take a drink of her coffee.

'She was talking about harvesting rainwater.'

Bird gave a laugh to this.

'She was joking. It was a joke,' he told her.

The pancakes were not like anything he had ever tasted. They were good in their own way and yet had an unreal quality, like something synthetic.

The waitress came back with several more plates which she arranged on the table and Olive and Bird stared up at her.

'Home fries, toast, hash browns – these are your sides.'

'Our sides . . .' Olive said and Bird thanked the waitress.

'Look at that fella over there,' he said to Olive.

'Shhh,' she told him.

'He's as fat as a snail.'

'Will you stop!' And then looking at the food on their own small table. 'Did you order these?'

'I did not.'

'Well, what are we going to do with them?'

'They're our sides – *honey*,' he said, and he was laughing.

'We'll all be as fat as snails,' she answered and then a sudden fit of hysterical giggling overtook her.

Bird ate what he could and then waited as Olive used 'the restroom'. He had heard about that before. He had seen the tour buses stop in Tullyvin and watched the Americans clambering off in rainwear and big white 'sneakers' to relieve themselves at the Beacon.

'An amiable lot,' that was what Rocky, the manager, called them, 'and good for leaving a tip . . . unlike the locals.'

When Olive returned he was asleep on the banquette, his head thrown back, his mouth open.

'Would you look at him?' she said to the waitress and she handed over her Visa card to pay the bill. She needed Bird to wake up and help her leave a tip that was appropriate. And at this

362

Bird sat up suddenly, pulling his head forward and waiting a moment to get his bearings. He had no idea where he was, what this place was for or what he was doing. He sat blinking around him in confusion.

'Bird, we're in America,' Olive whispered and she slid onto the orange seat next to him. He nodded, the information slow to take inside him. And Olive took his hand and pretended to haul him upwards. Watching him as he woke, she had never seen her brother look so vulnerable.

Bird was not out of place in Oregon. He did not stand out – like a signpost – as he did in Tullyvin. His height and sharp angles found spots to soften in. The weather was cool with intense showers – and sudden slants of wet sun. As he drove through these new streets, there were rainbows all around him. Bird and Olive crossed the singing bridge without knowing it. They found its hum oddly comforting, but like so many things it was unusual and they added this to all that Margaret must explain to them. They were being pulled towards her now, the older sister who knew everything. Bird was already at ease with driving on the right and with the automatic gears. He pushed on the accelerator and they flew over the Willamette River. Margaret seemed exotic to them now. They had not seen her for two years and so she was like the steel bridges and the red-nosed trucks and the people running, running, running – it was all new to them, the newness of this place making them like children.

'Why are so many people out running?' Bird asked. 'Is there a dog after them?'

'They're all keep-fit mad here, Margaret told me.'

To this Bird said nothing but continued to stare at these slim figures in tights and caps, running in a way that was determined.

Rain spattered the windscreen.

'And it's not warm,' he added.

'In some ways it's like being back in Ireland,' Olive said and she sounded a little disappointed.

They found the street where Margaret lived and she was sitting on the porch waiting for them. Her hair was completely grey but she was tanned and bright-looking and she was heavier – they could tell as soon as she stood up and let her purple shawl fall away from her.

'She's been eating those pancakes,' Bird said quietly.

'Shush, will you,' Olive snapped at him.

But Bird was still enjoying himself. He could not get over the freedom that he felt from leaving his farm for the first time, the liberation making him giddy.

'You made it,' Margaret called out to them. She was wearing moccasins and opening her arms, which in itself was awkward. The Keegans were never a family for hugging. Olive, who would take a hug from anyone, lurched forward and then Bird allowed himself to be enclosed in his sister's cardigan, her hair touching his, his arms suddenly remembering the strength in her. She was still the Margaret he knew, only a softer version.

'I've made tea,' she told them. 'Have you had your breakfast?'

But Olive was standing on the porch looking around her. She was taking in the row of wooden houses opposite, the garden ornaments, a carved wooden horse standing among the flowers, a child's high chair left out on the street, wind chimes jingling around them. A man passed and waved at her and she waved back to him.

'Oh, this is lovely,' she told Margaret, who was watching her and smiling.

'It's home for me,' she answered.

'And what happened to Wyoming . . . and California?'

'Oh, I decided to stay in Portland and live with my friend Sally.'

'Well, now let me have a look at you . . . You look so fine, Margaret, so well.'

'I'm *grand*,' Margaret said and Olive laughed when she heard this expression.

Bird was sitting in a rocking chair and looking at the stop sign at the end of the street.

'What is that?' he asked.

'Someone knitted a hat for the sign,' Margaret answered, a certain dryness to her voice bringing them all back to the Red Hill kitchen. 'They do that sort of thing around here,' she said, and she was carrying a tray of tea and biscuits out to them.

'That and rain harvesting,' Bird said.

'Oh, that's no laughing matter . . . I'll give you a tour of the garden later, Sally has her own tank for collecting the rainwater.'

'And what about the pot?' Olive asked suddenly.

'What about – *the what*?'

'The pot? Didn't you tell me you were smoking a bit of gangy?'

'Will you shut up, Olive.'

Here Margaret put the teapot down firmly on the table and looked steadily at her sister. She had not changed all that much and Bird and Olive seemed to bring the worst out in her. He winked at Olive and lifted his cup and saucer.

'And have you bought a house, Margaret?' Olive asked shyly.

'God no, this is Sally's. I rent a room from her.'

'Well, you still have the lodge of course,' Olive said. 'Myself and Pat are building a new place after we're married.'

'Oh, stay in the lodge, will you? I won't be in any hurry coming back.'

Margaret smiled and nodded over at their brother.

'Bird is feeling the jet lag,' she said.

And they looked at him for a moment, his eyes closed and his breath becoming slower as he fell into a solid kind of sleep.

'He looks very well. He'll fit in here. The beard and the flannel shirt. He was made for Portland.'

'Now we just have to get him to smoke some pot,' Olive added and Margaret put her head back and laughed.

'Will you shush about the pot?' she whispered, sitting back in her chair and smiling at her sister. 'I like to have a little smoke now and then. It relaxes me.'

'Oh, I can't wait to try it,' Olive said.

'I'm not sure it's a good idea in your case,' and the two sisters began laughing. 'You're relaxed enough,' Margaret told her.

They sat without speaking for a minute.

'I've made up beds for you. Sally is delighted with all this company . . . and the houses are so big here. You should get some sleep and then I'll wake you for lunch. You'll be fit for nothing if you don't get a little sleep after all that flying.'

'And what about Midge Connors?' Olive asked.

She had been trying to find a way to introduce the subject and then, enjoying herself with this new relaxed Margaret, it had come out too suddenly.

'What about her?'

'Well, did you get my email about her letter? Do you still have an address for her?'

'I do, of course,' Margaret said, looking out over the street.

'Well, I think Bird might like to see her,' Olive whispered. 'If you could help him to find her.'

'Portland is not that big a place, you know.'

'You mean you know where she is?'

'Of course I do. But I've no idea why Bird wants to see her. For God's sake, Olive, it's ancient history if you ask me.'

'I know but I think it would give him . . .'

'I know . . . *closure.*'

And Bird, who had fallen into the deepest sleep, heard Midge's name like a rock dropped into dark water. He tried to open his

366

eyes so he could see these two women who were always one step ahead of him. The sisters went into the house then, the worn planks on the porch creaking under them, and Bird opened his eyes, not sure if he had been awake or dreaming. The idea of seeing Midge was a blow to his heart – he was afraid of it – and yet another part of him, which owned the same heart, was holding it up high and singing. He worried about seeing her and yet he was really enjoying being in America. He could not sleep then but stretched his long legs out and rested his head back on the chair, looking up to the sky, the clouds moving, the jaybirds flapping in the trees over him.

That night they had supper together at a round table. Sally bustled in from the farmers' market with food and poured a glass of wine for everyone. She couldn't stay because she had a meeting at the Rotary but she was keen to meet them.

'To the Keegans of Red Hill,' she announced, raising her glass, and Olive looked at Margaret and started laughing.

'I've heard so much about you from Margaret,' Sally said. 'Red Hill is like a kind of Irish fairy tale.'

'It's a fairy tale all right,' Olive said and she took a gulp from her glass.

When Sally left, the Keegans enjoyed a roast of beef together and it was only after their apple pie dessert that they seemed to relax again into each other's company.

'So when is this wedding, Olive?' Margaret asked. Her younger sister was wearing the emerald that Pat had given her.

'Ah, there's no rush,' Olive answered. 'But you better make sure you come home for it.'

'I will of course,' answered Margaret. 'I wouldn't miss it.'

She was rosy-cheeked from wine and looking more relaxed than Olive had ever seen her.

'And how was the harvest, Bird?'

'Dry enough – the yield was high . . .'

'And did you send the grain to Quinn's as usual?'

'Half to Quinn's and the rest to O'Rourke's.'

'Do you remember the time we were all helping Daddy with the grain?' Olive cut in suddenly – and the smell of warm, newly harvested corn seemed to fill the room around them. Bird and Margaret remembered playing in the small mountains of it, the grains filling their socks and going up the sleeves of their jumpers.

'And Margaret thought she got a grain of barley in her ear,' Bird said and he looked over at his older sister, grinning.

'Oh God,' Margaret said, shaking her head. 'Daddy nearly had a fit over that.'

'It didn't take much,' Olive said and they all laughed quietly then to stave off the small beat of sadness that prodded them.

'He should have had *your* ear checked out,' Olive said. 'Not yours, Margaret – that was a false alarm – but poor Bird's, after that time you went off the high diving board at the lake. Do you remember, Margaret? And Bird couldn't hear in his left ear then?'

And Margaret lifted her eyebrows and said, 'Hmm,' and looked at Bird, who looked back at her.

'That wasn't how Bird went deaf,' she said.

But Bird shook his head at her.

'What do you mean?' Olive asked.

'Ancient history,' Bird answered.

The Keegans were sitting down together for the first time in two years and, as Bird saw it, Olive did not need to know about the day his father had swung the paling post at him.

'What was it you did to annoy him, Bird?' Margaret asked.

And Bird gave a short laugh before answering.

'We were fencing and I dropped the box of nails in a puddle.'

'And what did Daddy do?' Olive asked, her voice full of girlish curiosity now.

'Ah, nothing at all . . . but I saw a few stars, I can tell you.'

Bird and Margaret looked at each other. Then Olive, to release some kind of tension, topped up their glasses and began opening a second bottle.

'It doesn't matter now,' Bird said quietly. 'It's part of who I am – and a person doesn't need to hear everything.'

'Come on now,' Olive told them. 'Let's have a toast.'

'To Olive and Pat?' Margaret suggested.

'To the Keegans of Red Hill,' Olive answered and Bird, who did not hear what she said, took a sip from his wine and said nothing.

Later that evening Bird left his sisters and took a bus into the city. He had seen enough of Margaret to know that she was well in herself, that she had conquered something. And Olive was delighted to be with her. She glowed a little on the front porch, a blanket around her shoulders, savouring every minute with her sister, and it was only then that Bird realized how very much Olive had missed her. He was reminded of the companionable air in their sitting room at the lodge and knew that as usual they did not really need him – and he, feeling restless, wanted to be away from them. He climbed onto a bus and was not embarrassed by his dealings with the driver or by his fumbling with the weak curled-up bills in his wallet. And the driver smiled and didn't seem to care a bit about him either. Bird had the feeling that there was a space for every kind of oddity here. The bus followed a snake of cars, crossing a bridge and onto a street busy with shops and restaurants. It was wet and dark but Bird climbed off and headed straight for an ice cream parlour. The girls behind the counter asked him to sample a goat's cheese and vermouth concoction and he did it. He stood in the blazing white light and let the tiny spoon rest on his tongue, tasting cheese and ice cream together. And the other kids behind the counter – these girls with

369

big glasses and grins, clownish in their friendliness, young men in beards, their earlobes stretched out with studs the size of saucers – willed him to try it, telling him it was 'awesome'. In another shop he was persuaded to buy a denim cap, enjoying the company of another bearded man who said it was 'made for him'. He tried on suede boots and bought them. Bird, who had always been careful with his money, felt it unravel pleasantly from him. He sat on a small ledge outside a bookshop and ate a second waffle cone. He had gone for the more reliable salted caramel flavour in the end and the kids behind the counter were not at all disappointed in him. They had shown great empathy, explaining that that was everyone's favourite in the end.

He put his purchases down beside him on the street and, with one hand pressed to the warmth of his forehead, he allowed his mind to travel to a place he had been avoiding. What was it Margaret had said about Midge? 'She has a new life now,' as if she was preparing him for something. And here he was, running away from his sisters in case, out of their own love for him, they forced him into a kind of armour so that he would present the same brick wall to Midge again. He was ashamed of the new burst of life he had felt uncurl inside him since coming to Portland. He felt raised up by the place, by the very air, and yet deep down there were dark cinders of worry. She might not care at all any more. He knew he should tell himself this now and be prepared – and yet this hope that he felt was like a shaft of light running the length of him. He would prefer to suffer the disappointment than to lose it.

'And how are things going at home?' Margaret had enquired.

'I have no idea,' he had answered. He had not called Sean once since the plane landed – and he avoided any news that Olive had from talking to Pat Noonan. Now he looked out over the wet street, enjoying the flash of the neon signs and the friendly sounds of these people who seemed to know him from somewhere.

'Who knew?' he whispered. 'Who knew that all this was here?'

57

Bird had trouble finding a place to park. The house was high up over the city and the streets became narrow when they curled around the hills and rocks and pine trees. He walked until he found the post box with the house number printed on it and returned then to the car to steel himself. He opened out the plain brown envelope again and flattened the creases. He had written her a letter and, as was right and proper between a man and a woman, only they would know the contents. He had always planned on leaving her something when he died. 'Oh, not the house,' he told Olive and Margaret, 'but some bit of land . . . so that she would always have somewhere to go.'

And they had looked at each other without speaking. Whichever acre he decided to give her was perhaps the final knot in the twine that seemed to bind them. Their only brother remained a mystery to them.

'But will he be any happier after he sees her?' Olive had asked Margaret in secret.

'Probably not,' her sister said flatly. 'He might feel some relief – but happy? No. I don't think so. I'd be keeping a very close eye on him when you get back to Tullyvin.'

And Olive was quiet, trying to imagine what Bird was thinking.

'He's from another place,' she said softly, 'and sometimes I think Midge ruined him.'

'Bird will always be Bird,' was Margaret's answer. 'And you can't blame Midge Connors for everything.'

The house was quiet in the late afternoon, the November sun pale and at times sudden. Bird observed how the weather was changeable here and felt quite comfortable with its vagaries. The sun was more intense than at home and the rain more persistent. It could hammer on the roof for a whole night without stopping. He liked to lie in bed and listen to it. He carried the envelope in his hand and walked the short smooth path down to this big house that had a new Volvo parked outside it. The wood surround on the porch was painted green and there were two wicker chairs with cushions and there she was – finally – asleep in one of them. He had guessed that he would find her at home at this hour, knowing that the children would be coming from school and that she would be waiting for them.

He had already seen the school buses on his way there and had taken note of Margaret's warning.

'Whatever you do, don't go passing any of them. That's practically a hanging offence over here.'

So he had waited behind them patiently, seeing children with tanned legs and oversized school bags being greeted by their mothers, the earth so vast and yet the intensity of this love the same the world over.

'Life is temporary,' that was what a wise and peaceful Margaret had told him.

Midge was sleeping under a light blanket with her feet stretched out on the small wicker table. Her hair was the red he remembered, longer now and falling in a deep curl over one shoulder. He saw then that one of her knees was in a cast and that a crutch was leaning on the chair next to her. He knew those feet too, those toes, those ankles. There was a purple and yellow blotch on the side of her head where she must have banged it hard on something. Even now he recognized the curve of her bones, the shade of skin stretched over them. He could not get over these injuries though and wondered how this girl could not seem to mind herself. He wanted to reach out and touch her but he was overcome by shyness suddenly.

He held the envelope out to her and did not know how – or why – he would wake her. Midge was the same and yet she was also very different. He could see that there was a new refinement about her. Her skin was smooth and her clothes were decent, a silk shawl in a vibrant blue pulled around her shoulders. Her face was still very lightly tanned and her hands, which had not changed at all, were wrapped into each other on her chest as if it was a small bird that she was holding. And he did not want to wake her now at all because she would get a fright when she saw him. He hadn't realized until now the effect this visit might have on her.

Leaves came down in a sudden flurry – a reminder of the season – and she stirred herself, her eyes opening briefly and then closing again. There were dark swirls under them as if she had not been sleeping.

Bird moved very quietly and placed the envelope on the table next to her feet and then retreated.

He had planned on talking to her but he realized now that it was impossible.

There had been too much time, too many seasons, too many other people lined up between them. He walked back to the gate and considered the icehouse and the dog being pushed gently into Olive's kitchen.

Another school bus climbed the hill and released two older children – and with them came a new palette of colour and all of life seemed to swell suddenly when they passed him. They were young, this good-looking boy – and a girl, who was a graceful thing. They glanced at Bird and then looked at each other.

'Hi,' the boy said.

'Hi,' Bird answered and there was a slight raising of eyebrows between the brother and sister as they continued walking. He saw Midge stir herself and smile up at them. Bird waited at the top of the low hill looking down on her. A sudden gust of wind made the trees bend and move around him. The clouds were stretched and dashed, the sky a blur of pale shades and colours. The rain when it came was strangely comforting.

'Ha,' Bird said out into the air. Perhaps he would stay on in Portland and climb Mount Hood with his sisters. He turned his back on the house and faced the mountain and if she saw his shape she would recognize him – the fair head, the angular shoulders, his wide strides and his loose way of walking. The late sun was still on her face and beginning to dip behind the laurel hedge again. To her he would look dark, lit up from behind, offering only a black outline. He turned for the last time and saw that she was getting up from the wicker chair with some difficulty. She held one small foot up and leaned down to pick up the crutch that had fallen. She righted herself and then, before turning for the house and the open front door, she saw the letter on the low table and sat down again. Without thinking and perhaps out of habit, he lifted his hand to salute her and waited to see if her own small hand would hesitate briefly and then wave back to him.

'Bird!' she might say, 'Bird!' her voice confused and urgent.

What would she say to him? he wondered. Would she be pleased by what he had given her?

For now it was safe in his imagination.

'Thank you, Bird Keegan . . . you are all kindness.'

'And you – Midge Connors . . . are all trouble.'

'It is not the first time you have saved me.'

'Perhaps it is that we save each other.'

Bird waited for a moment and then turned towards the mountain again. He faced the wind that was full of rain now, and a future unknown to him.

Acknowledgements

In writing this book, I have been helped by many generous and inspiring people. My sincere thanks to Emer O'Beirne and Claire Kerr – godmothers and so much more – for reading the earlier work and encouraging me to keep going. Thank you, Juliet Prendergast, my great friend who is often the first to read the earliest pages. Thanks also to Grace Addington in Portland, Oregon, for sharing her unique sensibility with me. I feel very lucky to have Bella Bosworth as my editor. She has been tenacious and clear-sighted from the start. Thanks to Eoin McHugh at Doubleday Ireland and to my agent Faith O'Grady. I read the first chapter at the Birr Vintage and Arts week in 2014 and I am grateful to Martina Needham for inviting me to share the stage with the brilliant Donal Ryan whose support has meant a lot to me. My mother, Eleanor, believes that you should 'always finish what you start'. So here it is, Mum, finally. And as always, so much love and gratitude to my two menschen Steve and Arthur; life would be a blank page if not for you.

Alison Jameson grew up on a farm in the Irish midlands, a secluded and beautiful place that continues to inspire her work. She is the bestselling author of *This Man and Me*, which was nominated for the IMPAC Literary Award, and *Under My Skin*. Her third novel, *Little Beauty*, was published by Doubleday Ireland in 2013. An English and History graduate of University College Dublin, she worked in advertising for many years before becoming an author. Home is Dublin where she lives with her husband and son.

Little Beauty

Alison Jameson

Laura Quinn has lived on the same remote yet beautiful island off the West Coast of Ireland since she was born, and leaving it behind seems the only way for her life to really begin.

A year later, Laura is back, and this time she is not alone; the company of her new baby, Matthew, is all she needs. But the consequences of her return are astonishing, and soon Laura has courageous decisions to make – decisions that could last a lifetime and break her heart forever.

Stylish and captivating, *Little Beauty* tells a powerful story of love, motherhood and one woman's courage to survive.

'A starkly beautiful and haunting work'
DONAL RYAN

'Finely crafted and featuring a brilliantly complicated heroine, Jameson's heartbreaking novel is a moving story about social mores and the power of parental love'
IRISH TIMES

'Original characters and flinty dialogue . . . [a] darkly stylish tale of human behaviour'
SUNDAY TIMES